Failing the Trapeze

Failing the Trapeze

Susan V. Meyers

Winner 2013 Nilsen Prize for a First Novel

Southeast Missouri State University Press | 2014

Failing the Trapeze by Susan V. Meyers

Copyright 2014 Susan V. Meyers

Softcover: $15.00
ISBN: 978-0-9903530-1-0

First published in 2014 by
Southeast Missouri State University Press
One University Plaza, MS 2650
Cape Girardeau, MO 63701
www6.semo.edu/universitypress

Disclaimer: *Failing the Trapeze* is a work of fiction. The characters, events, and dialogue herein are fictional and are not intended to represent, refer to, nor disparage any known person or entity, living or dead.

Library of Congress Cataloging-in-Publication Data

Meyers, Susan V.
  Failing the Trapeze : a novel / Susan V. Meyers.
      pages cm
  "Winner of the 2013 Dorothy and Wedel Nilsen Prize for a First Novel."
  ISBN 978-0-9903530-1-0 (alk. paper)
  1. Family secrets--Fiction. 2. Circus performers--Fiction. I. Title.
  PS3613.E9857F35 2014
  813'.6--dc23
                                        2014027158

Cover Design: Liz Lester

For my family.

And in memory of Maxine Meyers,
whose stories will never be forgotten.

Acknowledgements

Twenty years ago, I promised my grandmother that I would write the story of her life. Although the present book is a work of fiction, I hope that I have captured the spirit of her stories in a way that would make her proud. Certainly, this book would not exist without the enthusiasm and generosity of her storytelling—and for that, I will be forever grateful.

In the end, no book is ever really the work of a single author. For their unwavering support and readership, I wish to thank a multitude of friends, family members, and former mentors: Beth Alvarado, Donna Bloechl, Michael Dennis Browne, Lightsey Darst, Cary Groner, Dana Hughes, Bill and Mary McClement, the entire Meyers clan (thank you *all* for the stories), Rick Monroe, Beverly Neubauer, Jodi O'Brien, Karen Rigby, Roxanne Sadovsky, Julie Schumacher, Ghida Sinno, and Rose Sweeney. And to my wonderful friends and colleagues in the English Department at Seattle University: thank you all for your love and support, past and present.

In addition, I wish to thank the editors of those journals where earlier versions of some of these chapters first appeared—*Cerise Press*, *Dogwood*, *Magnolia*, *Oregon Humanities*, *Per Contra*, and *Rosebud*—as well as those agencies that have offered me financial support throughout the writing of this book: the Squaw Valley Community of Writers; the Jentel residency center; the University of Arizona's Monique Wittig Memorial Scholarship; and the 4Culture organization in King County, Washington. As ever, I remain grateful to the Hedgebrook retreat center, where the bulk of this book was originally written.

My heartfelt thanks go out to Dr. Susan Swartwout and the entire staff at Southeast Missouri State University Press for their beautiful work on this book—and to Dorothy and Wedel Nilsen for their generous contribution to American literature. Thank you.

Finally, I wish to thank my parents, who taught me to love literature—and who taught me to believe that I could write it. I love you both.

Prologue, 1979

As soon as she saw him hanging there in the tree, Theresa Williams knew exactly who the dead man was. The light was good that morning, and had she thought about it, it may have surprised her that she hadn't noticed earlier that stray figure: a bit too much solid mass among the branches, a certain heft that shouldn't have been there. But the girl had been distracted, as she often was that summer after her father died; and she had come out, as she so often did, to spend the early hours reading beneath the family oak tree, crouched low and thick in their yard. The book she carried that day was a copy of *The Count of Monte Cristo*, borrowed from her father's shelf. She had started it the evening before, and was thinking still about Edmund Dantés and all of the injustices mounted against him. In this way, she had arrived at the tree without noticing the dead man; had lifted the leafy lower branches to duck beneath them; had straightened herself, as much as one can among the twisting branches of a low-lying, mature California oak; and had found herself finally at eye level with an alien object: a shoe, a boot dangling in the middle of the heavy foliage.

The body was strung high up in the branches, the tree itself being rather large: thick and sinewy and strong. Mercifully, then, Theresa did not have to see the dead man so much as become aware of him: noting the fine, thick tread of his boot soles, just inches away from her now, and those long, spidery legs traveling upward toward a torso, and—worse, she imagined—a face. The face of a dead man in a tree: this Lawrence, this perennial houseguest of theirs. But the foliage had cut her off from that deeper, more mysterious landscape of death. Nothing moved; the only sound was the twitching of dry, summer leaves, and the tight-knotted swaying of a rope some feet above her.

Of course, she understood why he had done it: Lawrence was not happy. He was a man who had failed at everything: God, commerce, love. Moreover, he was unwanted. And now that her husband was dead, Theresa's mother had gotten careless; she was a widow blown apart by grief. *You!* she might scream, rounding a corner into the kitchen to find the man stirring milk into his coffee. *What have you ever done for us? It should have been you! You should have died instead of him!* Her aimless rage filled the house for weeks: senseless, loud, and unforgiving. On and on. Until finally he had answered, choosing a good, sturdy rope from the horse barn. Answered, in one last terrible silence.

If Theresa had screamed, she would not remember it later. Nor would she maintain an exact impression of how long she had stood there, fear-stricken, staring at the dead man's boot soles hanging resolutely in her face. But it was enough time, anyway, to wonder, in the stunned way that young minds do, about the details of things—when, and how, and to what end?—and what they would mean for her own small life. After that, she was moving back toward the house—running, without the book. *Mother! Mom!* she shrieked into the breaking light. But her mother was not an early riser; Theresa was halfway up the first flight of stairs before Mrs. Williams had roused herself from her bedroom to stare blankly down at her daughter from the banister. There had been a moment, then: a single, slim instant of recognition between them. *Something terrible, something not right.* But when Theresa told her mother the fullness of what had happened, the reaction was not at all what she had expected or hoped for. A strange, hollow sound came out of the woman's throat: almost like a laugh, almost like grief. And then Mrs. Williams had collapsed briefly onto the floor, leaving Theresa finally, and utterly, alone.

Part I: Solo Acts

Theresa, May 1979

Chipped bark. A pungency in the air. The thrum of motors. These are the things that Theresa would remember from that early summer morning. It hadn't taken long. Her brother Nathan, having driven the hour south from Sacramento, had decided for them: the tree would be removed. It would disappear entirely. Chainsaws and rusted wood chippers: there was still an infinite variety of tools stored in their father's shed. Nathan had hired a boy from town, Tomás Quintanilla, to help him. From her bedroom window, Theresa could see them: a rented generator shuddering alongside the chipper as the two young men tossed in pounds of branches and bark. Within an hour, the air had filled with the ripe scent of a tree's secrets: sap and bark and resin and grit. The chipper clapped away all afternoon. Theresa set her elbows along the windowsill, chin on hands. When Nathan stopped by her room to check on her, she asked him about the tree. *We did it to spare you,* he had explained. As though that were possible. The grassless spot in the yard, a permanent indentation in the soil: even empty spaces now would be filled with constant reminders.

By then, the paramedics had come and gone. The police had taken measurements and photographs: scaling the unfortunate tree to look for signs of struggle. But there were none. Inside, two officers lingered late into the afternoon, wandering the spaces of the Williams' home. "Mrs. Williams," one of them emphasized. "There's been a death on your property—do you understand? We need you to answer a few questions."

Maxine Williams sat blankly on the living room sofa, staring forward without responding. Nathan had come to sit beside her. "Mom, this is standard procedure. Just talk to them."

One of the officers had a dark mole on his chin, like a spatter of ice cream. Theresa wondered what these men had had for breakfast. She wondered when they had started their shifts, and what they had told their wives before leaving that morning. What had they imagined their days would hold: prosecutions for petty theft, vagrants, street brawls? Had they imagined the death of the Williams man, dangling in a tree in the breaking morning light? Could they imagine, even now, the importance of this discovery to the girl sitting behind the banister of the second story above them?

"My mother has not been well recently," Nathan explained to the two men. "We just lost my dad a few months ago."

Four months already. Theresa's head bobbed forward, although no one had noticed her position at the banister. And it was true: her mother *had* gone a little bit crazy. There were good days: days when her mother sat quietly in the bathroom and put on her makeup, or went to the hair dresser's. Checks came from the government; they spent them. Food was purchased and heated and eaten. But there were also days when Maxine Williams forgot herself entirely: days when she screamed pulling up a carrot in the garden, or ran in from the honey hives panicked, in shock. *Something was missing—hands furious in hair—something was missing. What was it?*

"Mrs. Williams," the stout man with the mole cleared his throat again. Outside, the chainsaw rattled back into its work, tearing through another collection of branches. The police officer raised his voice; he spoke slowly and clearly, starting back at the beginning: "Are you aware that there was a man's body found in the tree in your front yard this morning?"

Maxine continued staring straight ahead. Her jaw dropped slightly, and something came out of her in a whisper that Theresa could not hear. The policeman leaned forward, "Mrs. Williams, I need you to speak up." The chainsaw screamed again from the yard. "I need to take your statement."

She sat stiffly, her body titled slightly to the left, propped against the healthy curve of the sofa's arm. "Dead?" she said more loudly over chainsaw's clatter and grind. "He's dead," she said again, with awkward finality.

The policemen looked at each other. "I'm afraid so," the other man said. Mrs. Williams did not respond. "It looks to be a suicide, but we'll have to wait on the coroner's report to confirm that."

Maxine Williams's head tilted backward to rest against the sofa's frame; her eyes shut. She didn't say anything more. From where she sat, Theresa could see the irritation building in the policemen's bodies. "Ma'am," the second officer repeated. "We need your statement. We have a few more questions."

Maxine did not move. "My husband," she said, without finishing the thought.

The man cleared his throat. "We know, ma'am. Your son explained all that." His voice was shaped long around the vowels, so that Theresa knew he wasn't from California. That voice, in fact, was not unlike Lawrence's itself, after he'd spent those few years living in Minnesota: the length of the syllables, the long yawn of a Midwestern drawl.

Maxine looked up, startled. For a moment, the work in the front yard settled into stillness. Nathan set a hand on the officer's arm; he was a much larger man than either of the police officers. "We could continue this outside."

But the more senior of the two officers shook his head. "We've got to talk to your mother. She's the only adult living in the house."

The Midwesterner cleared his throat. His voice came out tired. "Can you give us *some* kind of identifying information, ma'am?"

"I don't know anything," she insisted as the chainsaw growled back to life. *A vagrant*: that's what she called him. Some vagabond who used to skulk around their property.

"A vagrant," the man raised his voice to make himself heard. "Ma'am, why didn't you call this in earlier?"

"I don't know." She shook her head: *I don't know, I don't know.* Her head twisted almost violently; she caught it in her hands and held on. Nathan moved more assertively between his mother and the police officers; he put an arm around her, to stop the spinning.

Theresa grimaced. Her mother was being weak or stubborn; she didn't hardly know which. But the outcome was the same: other people had to step in. They had to pick up the pieces.

"So who called it in?" The Midwesterner wanted to know.

"My sister," Nathan's eyes flickered upward. "She's upstairs resting now." His voice boomed heavily in the low-lit room. "She called me," he clarified. "Early this morning."

The man stood dumb. "Your sister found the body?"

"She's fifteen," Nathan emphasized.

The senior officer's gaze shifted back toward their mother. "Mrs. Williams," he tried again. "This is your property. You're going to have to provide us with some kind of a statement." He let the room pause for a pregnant moment. "Or else I'm going to have to go upstairs and question your daughter."

Theresa turned away. She pulled her knees to her chest and shoved her face into them. She didn't want to answer those men's questions; she didn't want to talk to anyone. But she knew that she could, if she had to. She was good with crisis; this was something that she had come, recently, to know about herself. For weeks while her father had been ill, her mother had ignored the situation: Gerald's waning energy, his distant moods. When the idea to take him to the hospital had surfaced, it had been Lawrence himself who had suggested it. Maxine, by then, was too anxious to drive, but she would not have Lawrence there with them: *This is a family affair.* So she'd asked her daughter to do it, though of course Theresa hadn't had much experience driving: a bit here and there along the country roads by their house. But she hadn't passed any kind of exam, and she certainly didn't have a license. Her fingers had curled moist around the steering wheel, her eyes stinging and swimming stubbornly. Her father had lain uncomfortably in the back, his wide shoulders and long legs slipping off the vinyl seat, while Theresa had tried her best to keep the ride smooth. She'd glanced toward her mother, who held her head heavily in her hands, leaning against the window. *Left*, she'd directed, and Theresa had pulled them gently toward the highway.

Outside, the chainsaw sputtered and halted in the mounting

heat of the day. "Mrs. Williams," one of the officers started again, pressing the heel of one hand to the perspiration at his brow.

"I'll tell you one thing," she snapped, her voice coming suddenly into focus. "If you lay a finger on my daughter, I'll come after you with everything I've got."

The room went quiet again. The senior of the men sat down on the couch beside Theresa's mother. "Ma'am," his voice was tired. Impatient. "We just need information. To file a report. Nobody's going after anybody. We'll wait on the coroner's report, but it looks to be a clear case of suicide. We just need information to file the death certificate."

"He was spiteful," she spat. "He was ungrateful."

"Ungrateful for what?"

"He was adopted by this family," the other officer interjected.

Mrs. Williams stopped, just as Tomás, in the front yard, yanked the saw motor back into gear. She sat back against the couch. "Oh Gerald," she moaned, shaking her head. "Look what you've got us into now."

The saw screamed again as Tomás plunged into another hunk of branches. "Can someone get that fucking thing to stop?!" the man with the sweaty brow threw up his hands. His partner flashed him a quick look and slammed a notebook against the coffee table. "Mrs. Williams," he insisted. "Just fill in the gaps for us. You must know *something.*"

She looked up, her hands raised loosely, the fingers spread. She looked helpless, like someone who had been left dangling in mid-air. "No," she said again sadly. "I don't know anything that will help you."

* * *

Hours later, after they were gone—the police and Nathan and Tomás—her mother came heaving slowly back up the stairs. Theresa had, by then, retreated back into her room. Her mother was a woman who sought comfort from everyone, at all times. The girl braced herself as Maxine slumped red-eyed into the doorframe, though her expression was more calm than Theresa had expected. Her fingers rubbed against each other vaguely, as though she wanted something. "Theresa." Her voice was slightly hoarse: thready and loose, like you could hear the lining of it coming undone. "What are you doing?"

Maxine's gaze took a quick survey of the room. Theresa didn't answer; she sat motionless on the bed, her knees tucked upward, her back pressed to the headboard. Finally, her mother's eyes settled on her again. "What a day we've had," she said, too brightly. Theresa nodded slightly. "But they're all gone now," her mother declared. "All gone."

"Nathan's coming back," Theresa reminded her. "Tomorrow." Her own voice felt rusted, unfamiliar; she swallowed the light film that lined her palate.

Maxine nodded. Her gaze continued to flicker around the room, as though it was a place she had never been before. "It's not the worst thing," she said, "that's ever happened." She looked back at her daughter. "We've got to remember that."

Theresa's head bobbed slowly. *You wanted him gone*, she shivered. *Dead. You said so.* But she didn't speak the words out loud.

Maxine shifted toward the bed. Sat down at one end of it. Her fingers kept moving, and Theresa thought her mother might reach out to touch her. "Theresa," her breath rushed forward, as though she had just remembered. "Are you all right?"

The girl said she was.

"Good," Maxine folded her hands back into themselves. "Good."

Theresa watched her mother, and that troublesome thought kept echoing through her: *You made him die. It's your fault.* She closed her eyes. Shivered. It wasn't true—it *couldn't* be.

Maxine was still shaking her head. Theresa opened her eyes again; the expression on her mother's face was pained. "He never wanted to be here," she looked up. "It wasn't good for him—for anybody." There was real regret to her voice; in that moment, Theresa knew, her mother was not acting. Although Maxine Williams spent so much of her time engaged in drama—after a life like hers, how could you not?—in that moment, she was no longer on stage. "It never works," she concluded sadly. "Making people do things they don't want to."

Theresa waited. Then, in a rush, her mother came toward her, catching the girl up in her arms. Already, Theresa was larger than her mother; she had outgrown Maxine's narrow frame the year before, so that she was taller now, and wider. The physical reminder of that difference left her wanting. She was nearly sixteen, and pretty, although she didn't know it yet. The expanse of her body still confused her—hips and breasts and thighs growing into themselves. It had become difficult to know where she ended, and someone else began.

Her mother's fingers wound their way into hers. They were warm, thick fingers. All of Maxine Williams's body was trim and delicate, except for her hands. They were sturdy hands: short-fingered and wide-palmed. "It's not always easy," she told her daughter. "What happens in families."

Theresa let her body go lank against her mother's. For most of her life, Maxine had lived like a bull: rough and loud and single-minded. Her life read like a screenplay: brushes with death, gunfights and bar brawls, love affairs to break the heart. "My mother, Dollie Mae," Maxine reminded her daughter. "She also had other plans for herself, you know."

Maxine, 1926

Maxine's mother was famous in the way that young women on the circus could be: regional and whispered about. No one knew her name; she didn't expect them to. What they remembered was her act. Each time, it began gradually: Dollie Mae ascending alone up the towered ladder to the high wire platform in her plain white leotard with its simple tulle skirt, being careful to keep her body rigid and her limbs pressed tight against her. At the top, she stood narrowly in the light of the big top, her husband on the bullhorn below, announcing to the crowd the beauty and splendor of that solo performance. Such confidence and grace. There was no one like her, not in all the fourteen counties that they toured each season. Dollie Mae Richards: The Queen of Trapeze. As the crowd watched, she would toe the edge of the platform, as though probing the temperature of the sea, considering each time that same abyss beneath her. There weren't any nets; she didn't want any. Flight, she would always insist, depends on just enough fear to keep you up there.

But nothing in Dollie Mae's performance suggested fear. She was a smooth performer: lithe and sinewy and strong. As she readied herself, one of the catchers would hand her the bar, which she raised once sharply above her head, threw downward, and followed out above the crowd. Then she was flying, and you could see it finally: the plain white leotard that she had guarded so closely was studded with sequins and long, gauzy ribbons that streamed and shimmered as she moved. She was part cloud, part angel; the crowd drew its breath sharply.

"She can see us, can't she?" Maxine would want to know then. "She knows we're here?"

The girl's favorite way of watching her mother perform was to sit tucked at the base of the high-wire ladder, staring upward at her mother's confident shape, rising up into the air. Usually, her mother's sister, Della, or perhaps their mother, Mary, would sit there, too, having just completed her own trapeze routine. "What's it like?" Maxine wanted to know. But her Aunt Della and Grandmother Mary warned her that she was probably too little just yet. "You'll see in time," they promised. "Just wait."

But her mother hadn't waited. From her earliest days as a teenager on the show, Dollie Mae had perfected her solitary high-wire acts: flips and pirouettes and handstands. Few women, no matter what their age, were strong enough to do what she did. Her presence up there was like a dance: all improvisation, all art. Those performances kept people breathless; they never knew what to expect. In the circus world, a silent crowd was usually the last thing you wanted. People didn't come to the show to be on their best manners; a circus was a release. It was escape. But Dollie Mae was good at escaping, and people could see that. They could see it in her body, her wordless expression, the rigor and grace with which she shuttled around the trapeze bar. It was like a love affair. Whatever it was that Dollie Mae wanted in life, she had right there, in that singular trapeze bar.

Finally, as she began to lose momentum, she would complete a final sequence of tricks on the stilled bar, looping her body out and over, shuttling around it by her elbows and shoulders, slipping her body upward along the wires and stretching the trapeze into angled shapes as she shuttled along it, those silvery ribbons dripping endlessly from her costume. Then, when she had had enough, she would flip her body upright into a handstand and gaze downward toward the clowns below, her tulle skirt folding over her torso, and her legs, all in white, scissoring so gracefully, you almost forgot you were watching a person at all. That's when the clowns would know that it was time to get themselves ready, and they drew out the broad trampoline that they would use to catch her. Then, without warning, Dollie Mae would fold her entire shape in half, spin twice more around the bar, and plunge like a diver into the naked air, those silvered strands of tulle pressed around her like water.

Dollie Mae was a traditionalist; she relied on beauty alone. And for a while, it was enough. Back in those days, the flying trapeze was still fairly new, though it was quickly becoming the highlight of any respectable circus; and gradually, performers were learning that it wasn't enough simply to flip and spin and swirl. Competition became increasingly fierce. Near Atlanta, one young boy had begun to balance himself across the bar by his neck, swinging gradually back and forth as he played a solo on a little snare drum. Up in Chicago, another woman swung back and forth across the audience performing a strip tease down to her pantaloons. Then, the summer that Maxine turned six, a pair of sisters on a competing show, Miss Rosa and Matilde Richter, were performing a stunt that was astonishing audiences from Savannah to Baltimore. On two platforms across the tent from each other, they would take their bow. Then Matilde grabbed a trapeze bar swung out to her by one of the spotters and swung herself, suspended by her knees along the bar, out across the performance space; and Rosa, in a feat of bravery unmatched by then, climbed into a live cannon that had been hoisted to the level of the trapeze platform. Another spotter lit the fuse, and at just the perfect moment, Rosa came gliding out of the trapeze cannon, catapulted out into the air toward her sister, who would catch her wrists and hold on, swinging back over the breathless crowds.

But Dollie Mae was unimpressed. "Anyone can leap through the air," she shook her head. "That's not art. That's not real trapeze."

But art, it seemed, was no longer enough. Crowds were waning from the Richards Brothers show, until finally, even Dollie Mae had to admit: "We've got to do something." Her voice was small. "Before they forget all about us."

And that, to her delight, was where Maxine came in. They would go up together, both of them seated on the rung of a special trapeze bar that Dollie Mae had had engineered for just that purpose. The lines of her special, third trapeze were fixed to a scaffold at the top of the canopy, where a man up top wound the center crank to bring them carefully upward until he had them level with the two mirroring platforms, where Della and Grandmother Mary stood opposite, each of them holding a bar in hand. Three trapeze artists at once: that was the idea. Three sequined women spinning through the air, pressing and catching and turning—and passing Maxine, the littlest member of the show, among them over and over again. Della and Grandmother Mary would catch hold of her and carry her from platform to platform and back across the empty chasm of the air until, once again, Dollie Mae would catch hold of her daughter and send them both spinning magically through the air together in a perfect descent to the trampoline below. Beautiful, her mother promised. A beautiful, dramatic dance in air. People won't be able to get enough.

And she was right. As soon as they tried it before a live audience, the performance was an immediate success. They'd waited until summer, for a show with packed seats in a town just outside of Charleston. From behind the tent flap, Dollie Mae kept checking the head count: "Full house." Grandmother Mary nodded, and Maxine glanced upward, delighted. But something else had crossed her mother's face. Nervousness? Or sadness? Maxine tugged at the ribbons that lined her mother's costume. "Don't worry," she whispered. "They're going to love us."

And Dollie Mae nodded, distracted. "Yes, Maxine. Of course they will."

When it was time, they walked into the big top, all holding hands: the four Richards Brothers women. Then Della and Grandmother Mary split away and climbed the twin platforms across from each other, while the center trapeze bar was lowered down for Dollie Mae to seat herself with Maxine held cautiously in her lap. She locked her arms as they began to rise, drawing them up carefully from her sides, so as not to stir the magnificent ribbons that shimmered all along her costume. Gradually, Dollie Mae and Maxine were brought to the center of the ring, high up in the air, at the level of the platforms. And that is where Dollie Mae began to swing their trapeze bar, shifting her body in and out to make them glide upwards and outwards. At the same time, Della and Grandmother Mary swung back and forth between mirroring platforms, slipping graciously past Dollie Mae and intercepting the child, whom they grasped alternately by her wrists and ankles, passing her over and back again between them, theatrical and thrilled.

Throughout the trick, Dollie Mae, ever flawless, remained resolute, motioning toward the girl at turns and performing her strange set of solitary tricks while she waited for her daughter's return. Finally, Della swept past one last time, extending the girl to her mother again, and Dollie Mae grasped her, spinning the girl up across the bar. Maxine balanced there as her mother took one more swing forward, spun herself along the bar, and, grasping her daughter against her chest, folded herself over the girl, spinning forward into a triple somersault leap that landed them perfectly in the center of the trampoline below. From within her mother's careful grasp, Maxine could hear the crowd gasp, then cheer, as space, gravity, air—everything fell away. And for that instant—for that one magnificent instant—it was just her and her mother, spinning weightless through air. All the breathlessness around them was a slow, miraculous skip in time. And then there was the gasp, the cheer, and her mother flipped carefully out of the way, as Maxine felt herself toss forward once, twice, three times on the trampoline until the clowns caught them both and lowered them to the ground. Then her mother took Maxine's little fist and raised it while the crowd cheered around them and the girl beamed. *Yes, Mother*, she thought. *Yes, of course they love us. There's nothing at all to be afraid of.* And that was how Maxine thought of her family, and herself: invincible and fearless and forever loved.

* * *

But the truth is, Dollie Mae had never intended to join a show like the Richards Brothers Circus. At the time, she had been just sixteen, and it had been her mother Mary's idea. By then, Mary Bealin had had it with Texas. Life out on the ranch was dull, she told her girls; but after their father left, it was impossible. Mary had wanted more than ranch hands and poverty, and she guessed she deserved it.

After that, it hadn't taken Arthur Richards long to notice Dollie Mae; she was by far the prettiest girl on the show. So he waited two years, and the day she turned eighteen, he asked her to marry him. By then, he was thirty-two. But he loved Dollie Mae—loved her hard. Arthur loved enough for the both of them, so Dollie Mae said all right, as long as her family got a raise. And they did.

"Now, the best thing about being married," Maxine's aunt Della used to tell her, "was getting pregnant. Because that's how your mama finally got back to Texas." Like her sister, Della was handsome—except for a long red stain that curled down one side of her face like a ribbon. And unlike Dollie Mae, who kept her hair in the trim style of the day, Della wore hers in a slim black braid that she tossed forward over a shoulder to cover her disfigurement. In summertime it tanned; in winter it purpled. It was hideous and fascinating. Maxine looked up: the scar that day was bright as blood. "Tell me about my mother."

Those days before the birth, Della explained, what Dollie Mae had loved best were the tamales vended off the street. They were wrapped in dried corn husks, and she loved to listen to the crackling sound as Della peeled them for her. Every day around noon, she sat up straighter in bed and listened for the tamale man. "He'd come wheeling round his little cart with that silver bell ringing," Della remembered. "And she'd be pushing me out the door faster than you could spit.

"There was something magical about those tamales," she continued, her voice going low and conspiratorial. "And the effect they had on your mother. She relaxed. And you could see it, Maxine: you could see her skin start to glow and her muscles and bones loosen just like she had wings inside her. And that's when my mother, your Grandmother Mary, told me it wouldn't be too much longer." Della fell quiet for a long moment then, holding Maxine close in her secretive way; and the girl could smell her aunt's sweet, almost choking odor of unused woman.

"But the day before the baby came, the tamale man didn't show." It was Sunday, Della explained: his day off. But that hadn't kept Dollie Mae from craving those tamales—*Lord no*, Della shook her head. Her sister sat propped up like a princess in the window, straining her ears for that little silver bell.

Grandmother Mary, she said, had gotten cross. "You ain't getting none of that today, Dollie Mae, and you know it." Mary had never much appreciated her older daughter's stubbornness, so she fluffed the pillows back into place and laid Dollie Mae down in the bed.

"Stop it, Mama!" the girl screamed. "Lemme be! You got enough of my life all ready!"

And she didn't stop pining. As the day pushed on into afternoon, Dollie Mae was going crazy craving those tamales. Every few minutes, she'd start in sobbing again, and cursing the day and her husband and Della and Mary and the whole world for not bringing her tamales. Even God. She cursed God for making Sunday—Sunday without tamales.

And her mother Mary just sat there watching close. She knew the baby was near, and she started worrying that her daughter wouldn't calm herself; she thought it might strain the birth. So eventually she told Della, "You best go out and find that tamale man," which Della didn't like to hear at all, because everyone knew that the Mexicans all lived down across the river, and by then it was getting dark. But somehow she found them, the tamale man and his wife, and when Della came back awhile later, she had a hot cloth with a dozen husk-wrapped cakes in her arms.

It was nearly nine o'clock by then, and Dollie Mae hadn't eaten a thing all day, so she gobbled those tamales quick. Two of them— then three. Corn peelings started piling up in the bed, smearing peppers and salsa on the sheets. The whole room smelled like corn, the rest of the tamales spilled out across the nightstand.

It was about midnight when she woke up again. "Someone take those things away!" she shrieked, shoving the tamales onto the floor. Then she cried out some more—*oh! oh!*—like a crazy woman.

"I was scared," Della breathed into her niece's ear. "I'd never seen a woman give birth before—and here it was my own sweet sister."

Grandmother Mary, though, had stayed calm; she pulled towels from the bath, and extra sheets, and got basins ready for the blood. And then it was coming, that awful thing. And Dollie Mae was arching up in the bed, and it was the middle of the night, and the blood and tamales were getting confused, and bodies were getting confused. Grandmother Mary stood there, hard and firm, and even Della—sweet, meek little Della—was getting harder, impatient with her sister as she herself got more and more tired. And the room was growing rank with the stench of salsa and corn peelings. She grabbed a tamale in her fist and smashed it, flung it against that wall. And a pain tore through her like she'd never imagined. All of her pride was gone. All of her own wants for herself. She was gone, gone. And it was ripping her open like an egg. A hardboiled egg left too long in water. That was what she'd felt like, she told Della later. Like there just wasn't enough room; she was coming apart. And it would kill her, she'd thought. Oh God, it would just kill her.

And that's when things had started turning bad, because the top of the head—they could see it now—was a strange color. Right away, Mary knew that something was wrong. She slapped her daughter, telling her that she'd better push now, or she was going to lose the baby. *But don't you see, Mama?* Dollie Mae had wanted to cry. *I've lost already!* After all, this was not the life that she had wanted for herself. Still, she did it, just to get that screaming out of her face. She pushed and pushed, and closed her eyes, and waited for death to take her. She was sure she would, when the thing was finished.

But what happened a few minutes later is that she began to hear things again. She realized that for a while—who knows how long—she hadn't been aware of all the things in the room. And now she was hearing Della crying. And in the corner, she heard a hard sound, *clap! clap!* She leaned up. Her mother was holding a strange-looking bundle, and she was smacking at it with an even stranger, more frightening expression on her face. Dollie Mae looked down at the sheet, her legs folded over now and blood everywhere—blood and tamale salsa sticking the sheets together gluey and red. *Oh God*, she thought. *Oh God! What am I still doing here?* She looked again at her mother, slapping that strange pile of limbs. There had been a mistake! The baby was dead and she was still there. She felt like a fool; she'd been tricked. All that effort, and it was for nothing—nothing had changed.

And then, all of a sudden, it did. Because Maxine's grandmother had never faltered from what she was doing—smacking, smacking life back into that child. She had pulled the caul from its face and flattened out the arms and legs, and she was hitting it softly in the back, over and over, pausing briefly now and then to check the little girl baby's mouth and throat for blockages. It wasn't breathing. She wasn't breathing, but she wasn't dead. And then, after a few more moments, they heard a cry—a sputtering, coughing cry. A slow but living infant cry. And Grandmother Mary hugged it softly and thanked God, and carried the baby over to Dollie Mae, who took it with shocked arms, watching her mother in disbelief. Not sure whether to be grateful or furious. And Della, standing in the corner, was more jealous of her sister than ever before. Because now Dollie Mae had it all: beauty, talent, a husband, a child. A sweet little girl child just like her.

* * *

It was years before Dollie Mae took a real interest in her daughter, but finally she did: Maxine had made her famous again. All that summer of 1926, they continued doing the triplicate trapeze act, and the audience loved the spectacle of the little girl flying through the air, passed effortlessly through the hands of three beautiful women dressed all in white. Each time that Dollie Mae clasped her daughter and made that final leap downward, they would gasp and cheer, not sure whether to be excited or horrified. Meanwhile, Maxine's father made the announcement more and more elaborate, talking about the special bond between parent and child, and the endless devotion of motherhood. Those were the times that Maxine liked to remember her mother. When she would think about her, and all of the things that happened later, and how imperfect her love was to begin with, Maxine tried to remember the magic of those times when they had flown trapeze together. Because for all of life's accidents, there are still some glorious moments.

Afterward, everyone said they should have been more careful. "No nets?" one woman from Chattanooga, who had been there the night it happened, barked some days later to a *Circus Billboard* reporter. "That poor girl?" she'd shaken her head in disgust. "What were they thinking? What have they done?"

But who was really to say? *Fear. Flight.* During those brief moments, Maxine hadn't known the difference. Falling—*flying*—had been beautiful and solitary, like her mother had always known it was.

What she remembered was this: one set of hands reaching for her, and another one letting her go. The rhythm of the act was at its height by then: her mother and aunt and grandmother passing her from trapeze bar to platform and back again so rapidly that she didn't know, any longer, what to expect next. And who was to say, really, whose fault it was? Had her mother missed the pass? Had Della let go too soon? No one, in the end, could remember.

And even Maxine hadn't understood right away what had happened. That sensation—flight!—was just like her mother had said it would be. Fear, Maxine learned in that moment, had a kind of buoyancy to it, so that, even once she knew now that she was falling—*falling!*—there was still something almost exciting about it.

And then she was on the ground, looking upward. Her shocked little body didn't feel anything yet. Not pain. Not brokenness. Her gaze blurred, but still, she was able to see the spinning women above her: beautiful, though frantically now trying to still themselves. Della and Grandmother Mary had each swung to opposite platforms and were busily descending the laddered poles back to the ground. And above her mother, the circus hand at the top of the tent was winding the crank as fast as he could to lower her mother back down to the ground. But it wasn't fast enough, and as Maxine watched, a dizzied haze of lights above her, she saw her mother tuck into herself and leap forward, throwing herself into the air almost before the clowns had had enough time to react. Then from the blurred corners of her vision, she watched her mother bouncing once, twice on the trampoline, leaping masterfully to her feet, and running toward the tent flaps. She didn't stop; this is what Maxine would remember later. A look of horror had crossed her face. Her hands were raised to her head, those streaming silky ribbons at her arms, like a woman running steadfastly through the rain, until she disappeared through the side of the tent. No one saw her again for three days—during which time, they all assumed, she must have thought her daughter was dead.

But the damage, it turned out, was modest: a fractured clavicle, a few bruised ribs. "Oh Baby Mac," Della breathed later at the hospital, nervously holding the little girl's hand more tightly than she should have. "I was so scared we'd lose you."

Maxine's father shook his head. "Oh, Dollie Mae," he swallowed. "We never should have allowed it." Maxine looked up; his expression was still wide with panic. "Please," he turned to her. "Can you forgive her, Maxine? Sometimes, she doesn't know what she does."

But Maxine was too young to understand. What was there to forgive?

"She needs you to love her."

And Maxine nodded. She loved her mother; of course she did. Who wouldn't love Dollie Mae? She was so beautiful and lonely.

When she got back, everyone noticed that Dollie Mae was different. Heartier. She didn't ask for as much. She didn't complain. And she didn't perform trapeze any longer. But Maxine hadn't found all that out until later. Because she was out for the rest of the season, and by then it was decided that she should start school. So she didn't see her mother again until Christmas, by which time Maxine had begun inventing stories for the kids at school about how she didn't even have a mother. About how she had dropped out of the sky into her daddy's circus, but she didn't mind at all, because everyone there loved her and cared for her as if she were their very own.

Theresa, May 1979

"Theresa."

She looked up. Nathan's shape in the doorframe filled her recent memory in some way that she couldn't quite explain. It surprised her, after what had happened the day before, but she had slept deeply, almost decadently, filling long hours of the morning—and again later, in the afternoon. Nathan took a step forward. She blinked. "Theresa?" Her fingers moved loosely along the edges of the bedspread, feeling her way back out of sleep. "You all right?" her brother asked.

She nodded. Rubbed an eye. Nathan moved into the room and stood over her bed. "You've been sleeping all day?"

She nodded again.

"That's good." She didn't respond. He looked at her. "Still not talking much," he said. It wasn't really a question.

"Mom talks."

"Yeah?" he took a seat in the rocker beside the window. "What does she say? What did you guys talk about after I left?" He crossed his boots, newly polished, one over the other. The oldest of the Williams kids, Nathan was also the most successful. He ran a contracting business in Sacramento. Something about installing water mains for the city. Practical, unglamorous work that paid handsomely.

Theresa shoved an extra pillow under her head and flipped onto one side to see her brother more clearly. Sitting there, she knew, gave him a full view of the yard: the dry grasses extending toward the road, the length of the driveway, the missing tree. She blinked again, feeling her lashes catch against the pillow case. "About her mother," she answered. "About how she dropped her once."

Nathan's chin tilted downward until the skin folded into an expression that made him look suddenly much older than his twenty-nine years. "You're getting the circus stories."

She nodded. The drama of it: a woman dangling wordless from a canopy top, the entire circus crowd hushed in a moment of slow wonder. "I like them," she admitted. "I like to hear how crazy things were back then."

Nathan shifted his elbow onto the windowsill; he peeled at the paint like skin. "I'm sorry I couldn't get here earlier," he paused. "I should have been here earlier."

It didn't matter, she told him; she had been sleeping so much, anyway. Around them, the day, having climaxed in a bloom of early summer heat, held on muggy and warm. The large windows of Theresa's bedroom channeled it inward, leaving her perspiring faintly in the t-shirt and sweatpants that she had gone to bed in the night before. "Did you check on Mom?"

But Nathan's attention had caught, for a moment, out the window. "They pronounced it a suicide," he turned back, exhaling a plume of relief.

"What happened?"

"The coroner's report," Nathan pushed himself back and forth in the rocker, his feet still crossed, gripping the ground with his toes. "They did an autopsy, you know—to determine the cause of death."

"No, I mean—what *happened* to him?"

Nathan stopped rocking. He looked at her, concerned. "They took him away—you remember? The ambulance? the police?"

"No," she insisted. "Before that. What happened to him? Why did he do it?"

Nathan leaned back in the rocker, which squeaked stubbornly under his weight. "Oh, Theresa, I don't know," he shook his head. "He wasn't happy."

"You sound like Mom."

"Well, it's true."

"Lots of people are unhappy." She picked up a hand and spun it through the air for emphasis. "But they don't all kill themselves."

Nathan rocked wordlessly for another moment. The chair squeaked and grunted in the quiet of the house. Theresa wondered if her mother would hear them—if she would wind her way down the hall to see what they were up to. "I'm sorry you had to see that," her brother said.

"It's all right."

"No," his voice hardened. "It's not all right. A young girl shouldn't have to see things like that." Nathan had a daughter himself: a little girl who was just five years old. His ex-wife Michelle, who lived in Colorado now, had custody; Theresa knew how much this pained him.

"I didn't see much," she reminded him gently. "Just a boot. I really only saw his shoe."

But her brother was still shaking his head. "Mom should have been more careful." His voice edged: "She is not a careful woman."

Theresa sat quietly. She wasn't sure how to explain it, but the problem, she knew, wasn't caution or cruelty; it wasn't the body or the police or the reminder of the empty tree. The problem was Lawrence: the implication of what he had done. He was a man who had given up. A lot had happened in their lives, but that particular possibility had never occurred to her before: some people surrender; some people do not make it. It seemed criminal—it *was* criminal. Lawrence was a man who, for many years, Theresa had liked. Trusted, even. And now he, too, was gone. She felt angry—and had nowhere to go with it. So she decided right then that she wanted him dead; she thought he *should* be dead. This resolution left her feeling both urgent and guilty.

"It wasn't right, what happened to you," her brother slapped a weary hand against his cheek. Theresa could hear the grit of his beard rustle beneath his fingertips.

"It wasn't anybody's fault."

"She should have kept a better watch." Nathan shifted again, righting himself, pulling his body upward to its full, seated height. Like all of Theresa's older brothers, Nathan had this same wide, staunch build: large and intimidating, unless you knew him.

"It doesn't matter."

"Yes, it does, Theresa. It matters."

"But that's not it." Her voice pitched; she felt the air thicken slightly in her lungs.

"Well, what then? What was so terrible?"

For a moment, she gazed blindly out the doorway. Across the hallway, the banister ties folded into a U-turn of staircase. "I don't know," her voice went stale. Vague. "I don't know."

Her brother watched her for another moment. "We've got to sell this place." His expression twisted awkwardly; he knew that his sister needed something, but he didn't know precisely what. "It doesn't make sense anymore, the two of you living out here like this."

Her eyes circled upward. "Mom won't want to sell."

He slapped a thigh. "The taxes on this place are through the roof—they're eating up Dad's pension checks every month."

"It's all right with me," Theresa agreed. "I've wanted to go for months."

"I know," her brother's head bobbed, a bit too vigorously. He was older than her, and a man. He could leave on his own, and he had. But she had not been able to. And so she had been left behind—through their father's decline, and now *this*—quiet and unprotected, to witness all that she had seen.

* * *

"Nathan was here—did you see him?"

She had found her mother, after some effort, tucked away in the downstairs room behind the kitchen that had been converted, over the years, into Lawrence's private quarters. A hollowed-out annex, it had originally been something that Gerald had fixed up for Lawrence when the house was otherwise filled to capacity. But even in the years since, as Nathan and Theresa's three other brothers had slowly begun to slip away—to Phoenix and Portland, L.A. and Sacramento—Lawrence had kept himself there, preferring his private alcove to one of the upstairs bedrooms.

"Here?" her mother raised her head, distracted. Her hair was loosely matted beneath a kerchief; her fingers kept moving, sliding against each other and fumbling with the lip of the cardboard box in front of her. Lawrence's room was narrow and dimly lit. His modest clothing—charcoal and coffee-colored polyester slacks, a small variety of shirts with pearly buttons running down the front—hung neatly in the closet. The nightstand was carefully laid with comb and pomade and shaving gel. His was not a difficult life to disassemble.

Theresa told her the news about the coroner's report: "He killed himself."

"Yes."

Theresa paused. Her mother picked up a pair of pants, folded them in half, just once, and set them inside the box.

"Why?"

Maxine shook her head. "Life didn't give him enough."

Theresa peered inside the box at the dead man's filter of possessions: a thin nylon wallet without any cash in it, a pair of fractured reading glasses, a flask, a set of rosary beads. "Can I see those?" she asked, picking up the chain of rosary beads. They were pinkish in color and plastic, translucent. "He still had these?"

Her mother shrugged. "He was always hopeful," she admitted, clapping her hands across her thighs. "That's one thing he did have." It was one of her mother's better days, Theresa noted: One of the days on which her mind fit appropriately to the tasks that life laid out in front of them.

"Why didn't you talk to Nathan?"

Maxine turned. She stared meaningfully at her daughter. "He's angry with me, Theresa. This isn't my fault, but he's still angry."

Theresa ran a finger along the thin line of beads. "He's not angry—not really."

Her mother watched Theresa fingering the beads; she looked tired. "Put it back now," she said, gesturing toward the rosary.

"I want to keep it."

"*Theresa*." Her mother pointed to the box.

"Nobody needs this." She dangled the beads in the air, watching the mottled light catch them. Her mother grabbed hold of her hands. Theresa could feel the pressure of her fingers, thick and clammy warm. They were strong hands—stronger than you would have thought to look at Maxine's tiny frame. They pulled the rosary beads out of her daughter's fingers and tossed them into the box.

"What are you going to do with all this?" Theresa wanted to know.

"Salvation Army."

"You're getting rid of it all?"

"He's gone," she paused, then continued folding the man's shirts and narrow-hipped pants and laying them in a pile on the bed. The room was windowless and dim. What Theresa noticed here was the lack of things: space, light, sound. It was peaceful there, but anonymous. Not even any discerning fragrance. The closet was half empty; her mother sat carefully folding the clothes for donations. Already, there was almost no earthly reminder of the man.

"Won't there be a funeral?"

Maxine looked up. "A funeral," she repeated blankly.

"For Lawrence."

"A funeral," her mother said again. She pulled a pair of sleeves together, looped them behind the back of a checkered shirt, folded the entire thing in half, and dropped it on top of the boxed pile. "Who would come, Theresa? What would be the point?"

"We would."

Her mother's body stiffened. She set her palms against two sides of the open box. "Oh, Theresa," she sighed. "You're too fragile, that's the problem."

"I'm not fragile."

"You expect too much. You're like your father that way." Her voice was solid, certain of itself; she was so unlike the woman from the day before.

"Lawrence died," the girl insisted. "He lived with us, and now he's dead."

Her mother's head quivered back and forth. "That never should have happened," she said. "Neither of those things. It was a mistake," she looked squarely at her daughter. "It was too much to ask. What your father did back then—it was too much for us, and for Lawrence."

"And now they're both dead." Theresa's voice dropped its register. She was only fifteen, but already she had seen so much.

Her mother's fingers found each other, rubbing together slowly. "It's no good, Theresa. He wasn't right in the head—you remember."

"But it wasn't always like that."

"You were a child; you don't know."

"I remember—*I remember him.*"

Maxine studied her daughter's face. She seemed to feel sorry for her, though Theresa didn't understand exactly why. The girl leaned backward, letting her body shift away from the box and back down onto the floor. "Theresa," Maxine propped herself against the foot of the bed. "People sometimes get lost—for other people's principals." She considered for a moment, her thick hands smoothing the fabric of a shirt across her thigh. She fingered a button: pearlescent and trimmed with a delicate layer of aluminum. "Do you remember what happened with that elephant, Black Sapphire, after I got back from school the first time?"

Theresa eyed the gaping box of the dead man's possessions. "No," she lied. "What happened?"

"She was jealous, that's what." Maxine's eyes came to life. She pressed down on the bed behind her, locking her elbows and leaning backward to savor the memory. Beneath her small frame, the same checkered bedspread that Lawrence had kept for years lay neatly across the bed. He had risen in the middle of the night, Theresa considered: He had risen in the middle of the night to kill himself, but he had not forgotten to straighten the checkered bedspread, to arrange his toiletries neatly along the night stand.

"After all those months apart," her mother went on. "My daddy couldn't take his eyes off me. And Black Sapphire was furious. She acted just like a jilted lover."

Theresa spread her own hands against the floor. She had heard this story before: How the elephant, the star of their show, had begun acting out in quiet rage, refusing to be led back into her pen, throwing food all over the place, until finally, it had come to violence. One afternoon, she had gotten into a huff with one of the circus hands and had thrown him against a wall.

"Tore the man's arm right off," her mother remembered. "Just like that. Snapped it off and threw him across the yard. Broke four of his ribs and both ankles. We just about thought we'd lost him."

Maxine looked down impressively at her daughter. Then she eased herself up off the floor and moved toward the closet, drawing out another small pile of clothing and setting herself back down on the bed to fold it. Theresa leaned closer to the box. She let her fingers move casually along its lip, dipping further inside until they brushed along the piled fabric. "And then?"

"Well," her mother went on, "we had to put her down." She drew each article of clothing carefully from its hanger. "You just don't mess around with an animal that doesn't want to be tame anymore. So we decided on oranges because she loved them so much. Thought we could just poison a barrel of oranges and let her die peacefully."

Theresa's fingers moved gently through the top layers of Lawrence's clothing, motioning carefully until her fingertips pressed against the hard, cool surface of the rosary beads. Her mother was no longer paying attention. "But Sapphire was too smart for that," she shook her head to herself. "Lord, you should have seen the look in her eyes when she figured it out. Rage like you wouldn't believe." Her voice lowered for a moment, caught up with the drama of the thing. *She is not a careful woman,* Nathan had insisted. *You shouldn't have had to see something like that.* Theresa wrapped her fingers deftly around the beads, drawing them into a silent bundle in her palm.

"She picked up that barrel with her trunk," Maxine's voice wound itself up again for the final punch. "All those oranges in it and threw it outside of her pen. Just threw it, like you'd throw a worn out old baseball. I tell you, the circus hands went running after those oranges, rolling all over the place, worrying over the other animals eating them. The whole show could have gone down in one night. And me and Daddy just stood there, watching Black Sapphire. It was terrible, the way she looked at us. Like a person, an honest to God human being. I've never felt more cruel."

Maxine found her daughter's gaze and held it: so terrible, her expression said, the way things sometimes happen. Theresa drew her hand imperceptibly from the box of Lawrence's final belongings. The room was small—and getting smaller, as it emptied out. "So, Daddy went for his gun," she concluded sadly. "There wasn't anything else to do. And when he got back, she was just standing there, waiting for it. I don't know how many shots it took to fell her. The whole time, she never moved. Just kept watching and watching us. She must've been dead five, ten minutes before her body finally tilted over onto the ground. Afterward," she finished, "I asked my daddy if it made him sad. Of course, he said, but he was glad, because he still had his Baby Max. He said there wasn't anything in the world he loved so much as me."

Theresa nodded, flexing her fingers around her treasure: the rosary that had once belonged to Lawrence. And what did it all mean? Shot elephants and burnt principals and a boy half her age coming to live with her parents all those years ago, just after the war? Then killing himself, thirty years later? She closed her eyes, feeling the cool slip of her lids and the curl of her mother's voice still slipping its way into her brain: all those tangled histories, all the impossible lives that had come before her.

Lawrence, 1946

Gerald Williams had a deep, thick voice: "This has always been a temporary situation, Mr. Wells." He spoke slowly and firmly, like someone who is both very strong and very tired.

Perhaps, Lawrence thought, there had been previous discussions—phone calls or meetings between Gerald Williams and Lawrence's foster parents, Theo and Nancy Wells. Perhaps even Gerald's wife, Maxine, had come up, so that all four adults could come together to best discuss the circumstances. Lawrence didn't know. He was just a boy—orphaned, alone—and he didn't fully understand his relationship to either couple. Or his own history: how it was that he had been delivered, at two years old, into the Wells' willing hands; and how they had agreed, four years later, to let him go.

But whatever had happened, Theo and Nancy had clearly changed their minds. "If it's about the money, Mr. Williams," Theo's thin voice pleaded through the wall that separated the entryway from Lawrence's bedroom. "I'm sure something can be worked out." Beside the boy, Nancy's body tensed; she wrapped her arms more tightly around him.

"Mr. Wells," Gerald answered. "We need to think about what's best for Lawrence. He needs a regular family. He needs to get out into the world, play with boys his own age. It is true he hasn't been to school yet?" Nancy and Lawrence sat wordless as they listened to this new man and his heavy, unforgiving voice. He was a man who, unlike Theo, had been to war. This fact both frightened and impressed the child.

"Well, yes. But the war was such a confusing time. We were waiting until things settled down."

"The war *was* a very confusing time, Mr. Wells. But things have become much clearer since we've all come home."

"Yes," Theo's voice softened. "I'm sure they have."

Lawrence had been told that Theo and Nancy Wells were not really his parents. But what people say and what they do do not always agree. He was six; he believed what made sense to him. Largely, he believed in what he saw: the Wells' small life and his place at the center of it. It was a modest life: domestic and provincial. They lived nowhere special: a town called Selma, just south of Fresno, with long rows of houses all built the same. Theirs was particularly small, particularly poorly made. There had been a better house before. But that had been years ago—long before Theo's illness.

"It isn't fair," Nancy whispered, smoothing the crisp white shirt of the boy's new sailor outfit. "God help us, it isn't fair." She was crying harder now. She picked up a hairbrush, and Lawrence leaned into her heft, resting his head against her lap and slipping his hand into the loose pocket of her housedress. He lay there quietly as she did her work, breathing slow and making a quick, pulsing fist: squeezing and spreading his fingers to rustle the fabric and its curious lavender scent.

"What's not fair?"

Nancy let him go and set back against the chair. She eyed the boy carefully. "Just remember," she said. "No one will ever love you as much as I do. Nobody. Not ever."

Lawrence didn't know what to say.

"Do you promise to remember that?"

He promised.

Then she held him again, and he closed his eyes. Lawrence felt himself begin to tremble; he pressed his fingers against his thighs and tried to make it stop.

"Mrs. Wells!" Theo called, and Nancy straightened herself. She reached over, picked up the suitcase, and set it down next to the boy. "I'm sorry," she shook her head. "I just can't go out there."

Lawrence nodded: *all right.* And that is how he said goodbye to his mother, Nancy Wells: the only woman who promised to love him forever.

In the living room, Mr. Williams stood near the door. He was large enough to cut the light from the bright day outside, so that Theo stood in relative darkness. When he saw the little boy, the man smiled: "Hello, Lawrence."

"Hello," the boy answered. Already, without any help from Theo, Lawrence thought, he and Mr. Williams had greeted each other; they had met. And how strange it was to be on speaking terms with a man who had been to war! In the years that followed, as Lawrence grew up under the guidance of this man, the mystery of his experiences never left the boy. Even once he had learned that Gerald hadn't fought in actual combat, Lawrence still couldn't help fantasizing about what the man had been through. Whom he might have killed; who had tried to kill him. And what all he had done to survive.

Finally, Theo spoke. "This is Mr. Williams. Gerald Williams. You'll be going with him."

Lawrence swung around to look at Theo, the only father he had ever known. In the small, dimly lit room, Theo looked defeated. Lawrence thought he might just crumble to the floor: his narrow, polio-riddled legs giving way like kindling. He took the child's suitcase from his hands and handed it to Mr. Williams. "He doesn't have much." His voice was soft and heavy, like wetted bread. "We don't have much."

Gerald Williams nodded, taking up the suitcase in his strong hands. His eyes were wide and sad; they made the boy feel safer somehow.

Outside, Lawrence waved madly to Theo as Mr. Williams tossed his suitcase in the backseat of his Buick and buckled the child into the front passenger seat. Lawrence's stomach churned in a confusion of excitement and something akin to grief. He was leaving; he was going someplace new. He had no idea what he had done to cause this.

The car was large and heavy; it seemed like the kind of vehicle that Gerald Williams would have to own. Not impressive, but imposing. It tilted slightly toward the right, so that the boy's little body leaned against the door while Gerald's huge frame towered over him. But Lawrence was entranced. He couldn't remember ever having been in a private vehicle before, only buses and trolleys, and here he was sitting in the front seat, viewing the world the way the driver saw it. He thought things looked mighty fine from that angle; it helped him draw his mind away somewhat from what was happening.

Gerald Williams nodded, apparently to himself, grunting mildly as he shifted gears and gave the car more gas. His hands were tremendous, even for his hefty build. His skin was very dark and his chest pushed out like a drum. He was a beast, Lawrence thought. A huge, hulking man. He was the kind of man that one does not like to disappoint.

Finally, after more than an hour, they stopped at a small gas station off of Highway 80. A thin man in a white suit and cap came to the window and Mr. Williams told him to please fill the tank. Then Gerald turned to the boy. He seemed nervous. "What do you like to do, Lawrence? You like hunting? or fishing?"

"Yes," the boy lied. The air was strange. Lawrence had never smelled the thick, slimy odor of gasoline so close before.

"What else? You play baseball?"

"Yes." Once, he had seen some boys playing it in the neighborhood.

Gerald Williams nodded.

Lawrence coughed. Without the highway motion, the car was stagnant and hot. He was sweating in his little sailor suit. He could feel the heat coming off of Gerald's body. He was muscled and tan, with breath like eggs, sweet and earthy. "Look under your seat."

Outside, the sound of gasoline filling the car was like the sound of hard water, the way Lawrence imagined a powerful river would empty itself surging into the sea. He folded over and reached his arm into the darkness. When he came back up, there was a bright red toy fire truck in his hands.

"It's for you." Gerald cleared his throat. The little man in the white suit clicked off the gas pump and scribbled something on a piece of paper.

Lawrence looked at the toy. He'd never had anything like it. During his life with the Wells, he had been well-clothed and well-fed, but there hadn't been extra money for extravagances like this one.

"Do you like it?"

The boy looked up at Gerald, who was pulling limp dollar bills from his pocket to pay the attendant. The man's name, in embroidered red over the pocket of his shirt, was Mel.

"Yes," he answered, as Mel took the money and disappeared back into a square little box behind the gas tanks.

Mr. Williams looked back down. "Good."

He didn't start the car. He was waiting for something else. Lawrence fingered the truck, its slick red sides and shiny silver railings. Two little men stood boldly, clinging to the back by the hoses; another man sat at the wheel, driving.

He looked back up. "Thank you," he said, knowing that, by accepting the gift, he was agreeing to something. To staying with this man, this new father. And to forgetting where he had been, and what he had known before: Theo's slow tone sliding over the scriptures. The starched smell of lavender. Nancy's promise, and her infinite love.

Maxine, 1930

The thing that happened with Black Sapphire the elephant was only the beginning of their problems, but Maxine didn't know it yet. By the time she turned nine, they hadn't yet begun to lose the really important members of their show: Della and Grandmother Mary and even Maxine's own father. Circus life still seemed endless and essential; it was a diversion that no one ever tired of. Each year, the Richards Brothers show followed the same path through a series of sleepy southern towns, and each year, folks came out to fill the seats. People like to be fooled—that's what Maxine's father always used to tell her. They like to have their faith tested: two grinning girls with slanted eyes, joined at the hip; a woman so fat she couldn't walk; a Persian man who talked to snakes; another man the size of a child. Freaks and spectacles, all of them. At the entrance to the Richards Brothers show, they stood like something out of a museum, twisting torsos and rotating heads. The Siamese twins bickered for sport. The strong man heaved and tensed his muscles for the crowd. The midget giggled; the bearded lady cried. And audiences, speechless and amazed, paid their nickels in greedy wonder. But by the spring of 1930, those nickels were finally beginning to run out.

They had already come a long way that day, and had had a rough time of it: a tire going flat on one of the cars; Dinky, the fat lady, sick again with indigestion; the ponies skiddish and the lions irritable. And in the west, the clouds were growing dark and fat like ripened plums.

It was May, still early in the season, but Maxine's Uncle Cisco thought they were wasting time. California was Arthur's idea—a state nearly as large as Texas, rich and wide, and the old railway barons from the north rarely made it down there during the summer months. "We'll have our pick of towns," he had promised. "Folks will be lined up like it was doomsday."

But first they had to cross the Rockies. Maxine had never seen land like that—squirming and shoving its way west in a huge swirl of peaks and craters. It was slow going. The roads were steep and the crew was tired. Her father's silver canister of gas money jangled louder and louder as it emptied out.

"Shoot, Arthur. I told you this was a damn fool idea. What the hell are we crossing this damn pass for?"

"Cisco, please. There are ladies present." Maxine's father hated it when his brother Cisco swore; he said it wasn't civilized. But the little girl heard plenty. Lately, it had seemed like her daddy and uncle were always arguing. Unlike her father, Cisco wasn't a man who favored hard work, and in those days, that had gotten harder and harder to avoid.

But even though Cisco was a bit of a rogue, he was clever and outgoing, and the circus hands loved him. So when somebody spied smoke curling up out of the valley below, Cisco promised right away that he would fetch them a supper like they had never seen. "Folks that live out here just gotta know how to get us some meat."

He was right. The house was blazing inside: a heat so thick Maxine thought it might strangle her. And all across the floor, there were bear skins, black and shining like wet tongues. The fur was smooth and thicker than her toes, so she could shove her feet down into the slippery pelt and lose them, like planting roots. The man there told his woman what they wanted. Maxine thought the man's wife couldn't have been much older than her own father, but already the skin on the woman's face was tough and creased with lines like the boundaries drawn on a map. She slipped silently out behind the cabin to do her work—tearing apart huge hunks of meat, an odor like fifty grubbed pigs pushing its way back into the room. There were forty heads among the circus crew that night, not counting the darkies; and the woodsman sat quietly by the fire, calculating figures. His hair was a hard, bright red; his eyes green as a frog. And there was a scar like a hooked claw on one cheek. When they left the cabin, Maxine's father told her: Scandinavian. And she thought that must mean something magical, because she had never seen a man like that before.

It took a long time to cook that much meat. All around the huge, copper pot, the nighttime air behind the woodsman's house stunk like a hot, hungry prison. By the time they ate, Dinky swore she'd just about died of hunger. "But oh," she sighed, her breath rich and heavy. "There's nothing like a good meal to settle the stomach."

Like most of the crew, Dinky nodded off early that night. Maxine's Aunt Della and Grandmother Mary did the same. Arthur was still talking mildly with the woodsman, and Dollie Mae, as usual, was off someplace by herself. The only folks still awake were the darkies, sitting around their separate fire set off just a little ways from the main camp. Nobody said it, but Maxine knew it was forbidden to go to them. Hardly anyone ever talked to the darkies, unless it was to give directions about where to stake the tent poles or which one of the wagons needed loading. But nights like that one, she wanted to visit them: her belly comfortably full with a strange, new meat; her body tired, but her mind still moving. She wondered what they were doing that late in the evening: those mysterious black men who rarely spoke but who always seemed so jolly, winking at the girl Maxine on the sly and making the animals jump so she'd laugh.

The one called Steeley stood off to one side, his hands moving through the air; he was telling stories. The rest of them listened, sitting loose-legged and leaning in towards the fire. Across from Steeley, Ruthie was walking up from the creek, dragging a basin of water to rinse that night's beans out of her cook pot. Behind her, the girl could hear Priscilla running—Ruthie's daughter, who was just a year older than Maxine.

"My papa, he tol' me a few things," Steeley's voice sat a pitch lower than Arthur Richards's. He was a tall man and stringy, but strong; he sounded strong. "He tol' me about the slave life, and about the free life. The free life ain't much different from the slave life—that's what he said. Different men owned the plantation after the war: different men with different money, but they was all the same. My daddy was just nine year old when the war was won—so then he was free. 'Cept down in Georgia, ain't no such thing as free, not for no Negro man. You just go on working. They call you something different—they call you a man—but you're still working like the animals. They pay you, but you don't got much. You ain't got no house. You don' know how to read. You ain't going nowhere." The crowd around him murmured.

"So what we got, then? We got this here job, and we got the road. And maybe we get us a wife and some kids. That's what my papa said was the best thing—the best thing. You get yourself a wife and some little babies, is the best thing a black man could get."

The men rocked back on their haunches, a low murmur coming out of them. Then Steeley looked up. He saw the girl standing there. Smiled. Maxine smiled back. The fire light made his face light and dark at the same time. He asked if she had liked his speech.

"I didn't hear but a little bit, but it was good."

"You got yourself some parents?" His voice was flat, the story-telling rhythm gone out of it.

Maxine told him that she did.

"Good," he said. "Best thing in the world, family is. A mother and a father, that's a powerful thing. You hold onto 'em."

She promised that she would. Maxine loved her family, she told him, like they were the whole world.

Then, as though it had just occurred to him who she was, he asked: "You're one of them kids, ain't you? Arthur's kid?"

Maxine nodded. "Boss Richards is my dad."

He watched her for another moment, then walked over and helped her off the ground. He took the girl's middle between his two big hands and lifted her up, all the way up, until his elbows locked. The other men watched them; a couple of them snickered. But Maxine just watched Steeley, a line like a smirk crossing his face. What did it mean, she wondered—that smirk, and that strange, pinching lift? Or the little surge of fear that suddenly found her. She was frightened. What would he do? Hold her there like that all night? Dash her to the ground? Didn't he know it was uncomfortable, dangling there like that, his huge hands pressing against her ribs?

"Well," he said finally. "You tell your daddy that bear meat's a mighty fine thing. A mighty fine thing."

She looked for her breath. "Did you like it?"

Steeley's face got dark. "When I try some, I'll let you know."

He held the girl there for a while longer. Nobody said anything. A woman's low laughter flitted around the edges of the fire. Ruthie, she thought, still scrubbing beans from the cook pot. Her laughter made Maxine's skin do strange things. She felt the meat at the base of her stomach turning to lead.

Finally, Steeley set her back down. "You have you mama tell you a story before you sleep tonight," he said. "Remember what I told you about family."

She told him she wouldn't forget. Maxine loved her family. *Yes,* she told herself, her breath running shallow from the short distance she sprinted back to camp. She loved them all: Daddy and Della and Grandmother Mary. And even Mother, she thought: her mother, who had never stopped being afraid of her. Sometimes, Maxine thought she loved her mother best of all. Like she was trying to love double, to fill up the space between them.

But Dollie Mae was already sleeping, so Maxine went looking for her daddy instead. He was still waiting out by the cook pot. Smiling Ivan, the man who could stand barefoot on the backs of galloping horses, was holding out his tin plate. Arthur scooped up a heap of meat for him.

"Quite an appetite you've got tonight, Ivan."

Smiling Ivan flashed his gap-toothed grin. "Better than the normal fare."

Arthur's free hand found its way to the top of his daughter's head. His dainty fingers wound their way into her hair. "What is it, Maxine?"

"I need a story, Daddy. So I can go to sleep."

"A story, huh?" He talked down into the crown of her head. "What kind of story would you like?"

"I don't know!" She rolled her body into his so she could press her face against his hip. There was the sound of unclean metal clapping together as he scraped the side of the cook pot with his long-handled spoon.

"Do you want the one about Black Sapphire again?"

"No!" she was crying now. Her belly felt hard, twisted. She yanked her face up to meet his: "Daddy, I don't like bear meat."

"No?" He looked hurt. Right away, she was sorry she'd said it. But it was the closest that she could get. She couldn't tell her father that she'd gone to visit the darkies; she couldn't tell him what they'd said. The heavy feeling in her stomach turned to loneliness—a deeper, more terrible loneliness than she'd felt even during those months each year while she was away at boarding school.

"No," she answered. "I don't want to eat it ever again."

"Well," he laid the spoon back into the big, boiled-out pot. "You don't have to."

That was the first time Maxine ever remembered feeling something like regret. And that strange, new feeling tumbled around her belly like a stone, floating down to where the bear meat was. It stayed there for days—till long after they'd reached Arizona and were doing shows again. She couldn't get rid of it: a feeling like shame. Like there was some part of her that she didn't want, but couldn't change. She was just a girl, after all. Boss Richards's little girl. The youngest member of the show. A girl with hair so blonde it was almost white. A pretty little thing. Perfect, precious. Worth killing elephants for. Worth loving.

But the darkies believed something else about the circus, and her daddy, and even Maxine herself. She didn't understand just exactly what it was, but she knew that it wasn't good. They had a slick, laughing way about them—like they understood it all, but they weren't going to say. And all she knew was that she was special because she was her daddy's little girl and she lived on the circus and had a wild, wonderful life. But without these things, what would she be? That's when she started to realize that she wasn't just a part of things. *I am me*, she thought. *I am Maxine*. And someday Maxine might grow up and be something different, she realized. Choose different things. It was a new and terrifying thought. But underneath it, like water under thick ice, there was also a cold, swirling excitement.

Theresa, May 1979

Sheila, the realtor, was the kind of woman that Theresa knew her mother normally would have liked: well-dressed, slender, and chatty. Perfunctorily positive, she was a purely salesman type. "What a beautiful house," she beamed, pulling a notepad from her purse. "Very classic. Just look at all those *angles*."

But her mother, Theresa knew, was in no mood for social graces that day. Having filled two large boxes with Lawrence's belongings and put in a call to the Salvation Army for pick up two days before, Maxine had retired again to her room and would not come out. Earlier that morning, Theresa had carefully laid a plate of toast in front of her door. It had disappeared, but wordlessly. Her mother had gone dormant again.

Theresa watched as the woman began to scrawl a quick line of notes on her pad. She whistled mildly as she surveyed the windows and garrets of the upper story. Indeed, the house was quite elaborate for that part of the country: broad, gabled, and monolithic. It was an ambitious structure that could possibly have found its home farther south, in Marin County or the Berkeley Hills. Overwrought and slightly gothic, it was a house that had originally thought something of itself. But Theresa's parents had bought it decades ago for size, not aesthetic.

"My mother won't want to talk to you today." Theresa worried that the woman would want to come inside, though which possibility troubled her most, she wasn't sure: that Sheila would decide the chaos of the house, with its unkempt archive of the Williams last three decades, wasn't worth her time? Or that her mother, hearing a stranger's voice in the house, would emerge and create a scene? For the moment, though, Sheila was preoccupied with her informal survey of the size of the land, its proximity to the highway. "There's a lot of room here for growth."

"She doesn't want to sell the house," Theresa tried to make her understand. "We've been here forever."

Sheila put the pen down. Her brows lifted lightly into a perfect arch. The effect was not unlike one of the photographs in the house of a much younger Maxine: an expression half-haughty, half-amused, crossing her face. Sheila shifted her attention again to the upper stories. "This must be rough on you," she considered briefly, and her voice softened as a pair of fingers came to rest at the corner of her mouth. She shook her head. "What a lot of windows up there."

The upper floor of the house was nearly always flooded with light. The original owner, Theresa knew, had been a retired captain from the Merchant Marines, and it seemed that he had built his homestead not unlike a boat. The upper stories were light and airy, while the downstairs was stolid and forgotten: a veritable hull. The walls there were thick and wide, the masonry rising up a good two feet along the base.

Shelia's gaze trailed down the length of the house and then upward again. She pressed pen to pad. "Do you have any idea the last time the gutters were cleaned?" This woman, Theresa thought, must not have children. She was courteous but inattentive, bearing that kind of specific devotion that single people can have: so resolute within themselves that they cannot really attend to anyone else.

Theresa shook her head: Why would she know this? And besides, there had already been so much—*so much*—to keep track of since her father had died. On days like this one when her mother fared poorly, Theresa often found herself bicycling the two miles down the country road and back from Stevie's Stopover to keep the kitchen stocked. In between homework assignments, she kept the house going as best she could: boiling water and stirring sauces, or balancing the checkbook when her father's pension checks came from the government.

Sheila had approached the house and was now tracing her fingers along the crusted tin gutter. All around them, the yard yawned in expired disaster. Empty coffee cans marked the rough edges of the lawn, snug with dirt and struggling wildflowers. In other places, unclaimed poppies pressed their bright orange heads into the air. An umbrella next to the Williams' single lawn chair had been shoved into the ground and held in place with an inverted bundt cake pan filled with rocks and rainwater. Inside, the state of things was little better: a mild smell of moth balls and resin and flaking paint. The faucets dipped; a toilet ran. But Sheila seemed unphased. All around them, things interested her: the roof, the fireplace, the plumbing. She made neat check marks and notes on a little prefabricated list. In between inspections, she filled the silence of the house with friendly, innocuous questions.

"Nathan, isn't it? That's your brother's name? He's still planning on coming out today?"

Theresa nodded; she kept her voice low. "Are you really going to be able to sell it like this?"

Sheila clucked her tongue without quite responding; she did not look concerned. "I talked with Nathan earlier today. His name is also on the deed, isn't it?"

Theresa confirmed that it was; their father had been careful to leave the estate well managed. "He'll be here soon," she promised, holding her voice to a near whisper. "He called before you got here. He had to drop his daughter off at day care."

"You have a niece, then," Sheila said brightly. She gazed briefly around the entryway: scattered paper towels lining the stairs, the banister wound round with string, spare keys were kept on a shower curtain hook hanging by the door. There were scraps of newspaper and pictures hanging nearly everywhere, stuck on any available surface—the wainscoting, the walls, the staircase railing—overlapping into collages, one child's face pasted haphazardly over another. Along the living room sofa, thick-armed dolls—the kind with glass eyes and real hair—sat mutely in rows. Pillows were mounted over the tops of low-lying ottomans with packing tape. Sheila made a few extra marks on her list. "That must be nice," she said. "To have a child around."

"She doesn't live around here all the time," Theresa clarified, remembering the shy, lazy-eyed little girl who had visited them last summer from her mother's house in Colorado. She'd had thick lashes and a pouty mouth and spent most of her time quietly consumed with her coloring books: alarmingly pretty and self-contained.

Sheila turned briefly down the hallway that led into the kitchen. "It's good," she placed a hand absently against her jawbone, the nails painted neatly in a bright fuchsia color, "to keep your family around you at a time like this."

Theresa nodded carefully as Sheila clicked her tongue again and moved forward into the kitchen. The pantry there was full of things, mostly free, from restaurants and hotel rooms: powered coffee creamer, packets of ketchup and relish, instant oatmeal, and synthetic sugar in flat, blue paper packets. The cabinets were lined with rinsed-out paper cups from gas stations and burger joints. In the Williams' home, nothing was ever finished being useful: cellophane and paper napkins and used teabags. Sheila mashed her lips together and tilted her head thoughtfully. She pulled open a drawer: sample packets of shampoo and creamy peanut butter. She looked shocked, but only a little bit.

"Have you seen the boat house?" Theresa suggested, remembering the over-sized shed that sat out toward the rear of her family's property, a good quarter mile from the house itself.

"Excuse me?"

"It's out back," her voice pitched anxiously as she drew the woman back through the hallway toward the front door. She explained the story of the old sea captain and the large, somewhat nonsensical storage building that he had installed along the western edge of the property. All their lives, Theresa and her brothers had called it the boat house, imagining that the old man had kept any number of small vessels there. The building sat within a narrow field of dry grasses and clusters of deep green oak and sycamore trees. It was accessible from the highway: what used to be little more than a service road during the time that the old man himself had lived there.

Sheila looked intrigued. "That wasn't in your brother's description of the property," she answered, following Theresa carefully back outside, bending around to the rear of the house where the girl pointed out a set of tire tracks worn into the dirt: two thin grooves pressing their way through the long, dry grasses out toward the rear of the property. "Back there," she gestured, and Sheila cupped a hand across her eyes. The boat house was just visible, pressed up against the limits of their land, where the property line met with undeveloped county holdings. Behind them, a pair of ponies neighed through the narrow stables.

"A boat house."

"But there's nothing in there now," Theresa stared outward. Years ago, when she and her brothers still played there, it had been a space that she had loved. Tall-ceilinged and filled with lofts and spare lumber and the remnants of nautical tools, it had been exactly the kind of place to fascinate young minds. How nonsensical it was: a boat, locked in an over-sized shed, a dozen miles from the nearest stretch of sea.

"Well," Sheila said. "I'll have to make sure the surveyor got all that. It could add to the property value."

In the front yard, a vehicle careened into the driveway: Nathan's pick-up. A door slammed. She heard footsteps move toward the house.

"We used to keep lions out there," Theresa pressed, to keep the woman from heading back toward the house.

"*Lions?*"

She nodded sharply. "My uncle tried to bring the family circus back once, but it didn't work."

Sheila shook her head, flipping her gaze momentarily upward. "God above us," she breathed as Theresa kicked her sneaker into the dust. "What a history." She paused to take another moment to survey the land: strips of grassland, spotted with clumps of deep green oak trees. Then her voice shifted, going conspiratorial: "And where'd he do it? Where did it happen?"

Theresa didn't blink; she knew exactly what the woman meant. "In the front," she answered. "There used to be another tree out there, but my brother had it torn out. It's gone."

Sheila turned back toward the house, squinting into the blank expanse of front yard that was partially visible from that angle. Theresa followed her gaze; the woman's expression looked steady, but sad. "How awful," she shook her head. "Who was he, anyway? I heard he was a priest or something."

"Ex-priest."

They heard the front door of the house swing open and slam shut again, and Sheila whistled low and long. Sexy. She shook her head. "How did he possibly end up here?"

Theresa found herself responding—not, she thought, because the woman deserved to know, but simply because she had kept this information inside her long enough: "He lived with my family for a long time. From since when he was a boy."

"That long ago," Sheila tilted her head. Not far off, a foot twisted in the gravel in the front yard. "So, he was adopted?"

"Kind of. Maybe. I think his parents died in the war."

Sheila's eyes traveled upward. "How terrible," she mewed again as they saw Nathan's shape round the corner of the house, coming toward them. Her fingers moved absently across her purse strap. "And your family took him in?"

"But I don't think it was a good decision. It didn't work out very well."

Nathan raised a hand to them, and Sheila waved back. Her voice lowered: "So you grew up with him?"

"He left before I was born." Theresa shoved a fist down into her pocket. Her thoughts flittered briefly to the boat house: *Was it locked? Could they still get inside?* She hadn't been there in years, not since all that drama with her uncle's failed attempt to bring back the family circus. "But he came back sometimes, when things weren't going well."

"And how often was that?" Sheila's voice was breathless now; Nathan was within hearing distance.

"Not very much," Theresa whispered. "Until the end."

"Miss Reynolds?" Reaching them, Nathan extended a hand. Sheila nodded, shaking his hand once firmly and settling into their business about the house, the asking price, the timeline. While they talked, Theresa waited quietly on the stoop beneath the kitchen windows at the back of the house. It was shady there: dry and cool. The low light traced shapes along the skin of her arm: blurred, indistinct lines filtering down from the spaces between the eaves above her.

"You look tired." Nathan stood above her, shading her from the sun as Sheila's sharp-heeled pumps plodded back toward the front yard.

"Mom still isn't doing well today." Her brother's lips pressed together. "She doesn't come out of her room."

Nathan pressed his eyes toward the sun briefly, watching Sheila go. Then he reached over and gave Theresa a hand up. "Come on," he offered. "Why don't we go into town for a milkshake?"

Nathan's truck buckled through the gravel leading back down the driveway: past the empty pocket of tree roots, past the flushed clusters of poppies, flimsy petaled and over-bright. He pulled out onto the county road, passing the signs for Highway 80, which led out to Travis Air Force Base, where their father had spent his career.

"What were you two doing out there?" he asked after several minutes. "You and the realtor?"

"Talking," she answered lightly. "I told her about the boat house."

"Yeah?" Nathan reached a hand around the side of his head to scratch the stubble at the nape of his neck. "You liked talking to her?"

Theresa shrugged. "I knew Mom would make a mess of it today if she'd come out."

He agreed. "Thank you." After another moment, he added. "You need someone to talk to." He made the statement and let it sit there, expectant.

Theresa didn't respond. She asked instead: "Do you really think she can sell it?"

"That's what realtors do."

"But everything's such a mess."

"The listing won't go up for another couple of weeks," Nathan assured her. "It *is* going to take a bit of preparation."

They drove in silence for several minutes more, winding along the county highway toward town. "I've hired someone," he said eventually. "To help out with things—to get the property ready for selling. And to make sure you have everything you need."

Theresa was losing herself in the scenery: staunch oak trees bleeding a green so dark against the hillsides, it was almost black. "Ok."

"Tomás—you remember?"

She nodded. "He helped you pull out the tree."

"He's a good kid, hardworking." Tim, their brother who now worked with the highway patrol in Phoenix, had known his older brother in high school. "You can trust him," Nathan promised.

Her gaze shifted toward him. Nathan did not mention that the brother was gone now, having died in Vietnam. Or that Tomás, six years his junior, was getting to be nearly the age—just nineteen years old—that Nicolas had been when he was killed. Theresa thought that must feel quite strange to fold your life into the years that were stolen from an older sibling.

"You know I can't be here all the time. I'll do what I can. . . ." He left a pause in their conversation. "Julia's going to be here all summer." And Theresa could hear the way the name still melted over his tongue like something holy. *Julia*. His little girl.

"Call me," he said, "if you need anything, Theresa. Really," he held her eyes for a moment. "Anything."

They were pulling into town now, skidding past Holy Cross, the elementary school that all of the Williams children had once attended, and any number of slow-moving people pressing uncertainly toward work or home or, invariably, one or another of the local bars. "She wanted to know about Lawrence," Theresa said. "The realtor—she asked about him. About where he came from and stuff."

Nathan didn't take his eyes away from the windshield. He clicked his turn signal and moved them onto West Texas Street. "I don't know what to tell you, Theresa."

"But Mom must know." Theresa's gaze fell across the tavern where, she vaguely understood, Lawrence and her Uncle Ringling had once spent many evenings together.

"I wouldn't bother Mom about it right now."

"But don't you think we should know?" she insisted.

"Theresa," Nathan's knuckles whitened around the steering wheel, "it's better to just let all this go."

They buckled forward, pressing onward past the County Assessor's Office where, the summer before, Theresa had accompanied her brother to pick up an extra copy of Julia's birth certificate. The building looked unchanged: benign, bureaucratic. "That's what everyone says," she complained. "No one wants to think about him anymore."

"Because he's *gone*, Theresa."

The car slowed as they approached a stoplight at the corner of Beck Avenue. "Nobody loved him," she said suddenly. "He wasn't loved enough." She looked up at her brother, struck with the certainty of this new discovery.

Nathan pulled the car to a full stop. He looked over at her, shifting slightly in his seat. She thought he might lean over to press his hand over her own. "She loves you," he said. "If that's what you're worried about. She's distracted right now, but that doesn't mean she doesn't care about you."

"But what about Lawrence?" Through the window behind him, she could see the white-paneled facade of Nation's hamburger stand: clean and unadorned.

"That's different."

"Then he shouldn't have come here. Someone made a mistake."

The light changed, and Nathan eased them forward, turning into burger stand parking lot. "That was a long time ago, Theresa. There are probably things about it that we just don't understand."

Lawrence, 1946

Within minutes of their arrival at Lawrence's new home, Gerald Williams had already revealed the worst of the boy's secrets. "Thirty a month!" he bellowed at the entryway of the modest, rancher-style house. "Thirty cottonpicking dollars a month!" A small woman appeared in the living room, wearing an apron spotted in grease; she held her hands idly up in the air. She had bright features and delicate limbs; her hair was piled loosely in rollers. She watched them without comment.

Gerald slipped his work boots from his feet like hunks of lead. "They got paid thirty a month," he shook his massive head. "And they didn't even have the decency to send him to school."

Thirty a month? The slow train of the boy's mind shuddered and derailed. *Thirty a month? But how? From whom?* But Gerald made no further comment. He lowered his bulk into the soft meat of the sofa. "Jesus," he said. "That was a long drive." He looked at Lawrence. "I bet the kid's hungry. Aren't you hungry?"

The boy shook his head, instead watching Mrs. Williams, whose pretty face had twisted into a sour expression. "Skin and bones," she agreed. "What did they do with all that money?"

Lawrence peered down at his chest. The little red sailor tie had gone crooked during the long car ride to Fairfield. Wrinkles had worked their way into the fabric around his middle. He stood up taller against the doorframe as she approached, her slippered feet making a noise like sandpaper along the floor. She lifted the fire truck from his hands. "Did he like it?"

Gerald was unbuttoning his overcoat. Even in warm weather, Lawrence would learn, he had the unusual habit of wearing several layers of clothing. He deflected the question. "Do you like it, Lawrence?"

The truck dangled from Mrs. Williams's fingers like a bright red scream. The boy nodded.

"He doesn't say much." She set the toy on a wicker end table.

"It's those people," Gerald grunted, yanking off his coat and handing it to her. Mrs. Williams moved toward the hall closet. "Keep to themselves too goddamned much." He shook his head. "Pacifists."

Then Gerald beckoned the little boy to him. When Lawrence came forward, he clapped a hand over his shoulder. He looked pleased. "Well," his voice boomed, wide as boat sails. "We're certainly going to do you better around here," he gestured quickly around the room with it low lights and sagging, secondhand furniture, "that's for damn sure."

But Gerald wasn't Lawrence's real father, either; he made that clear early on. And when Lawrence asked who had paid the Wells and why, Gerald's answer was cryptic: "Someone who should have kept you, but couldn't."

"Then who are my real parents?"

The man shook his head. "The war was a very confusing time," he said again. "I'm indebted to some people; others are indebted to me. I promise to take care of you; that's all you need to know."

And that is where things laid, because the boy's stubborn memory refused to slip back beyond the ages of four or five—to a time before the world was at war, before he had lived with Nancy and Theo.

* * *

Gerald may not have been his real father, but he still wanted to get it right. He would teach his adopted son to be like him: hard and capable. In the following months, Lawrence learned how to play baseball and change a bicycle tube and examine the engine of a stalled sedan. These things were significant, according to Gerald; they were good, masculine activities. It was important to him that

Lawrence recognized their value: that he understood how the world worked. So there were trips to the park and the baseball diamond. Gerald tossed white-stitched balls and waited for Lawrence to catch them. He supervised carefully as the boy pushed metal trucks through the dirt. These were not activities that Lawrence was particularly fond of, but they satisfied Gerald. And, as it turned out, there *was* one thing that the boy was good at: precision. He could take aim; he could fire a gun.

"We're going to the carnival," Mrs. Williams's brother Ringling announced one morning. He was older than Lawrence—nearly a teenager by then—but easy-mannered and likeable. "Mac grew up on a show like that," he explained. "She loves it."

Lawrence had never been to a place like that: the long wooden stalls and red-tipped canopy covers, flooded with people; the midway rides and candy wagons and carnival games. San Francisco's *Playland*. Along one side, a tremendous wood-framed roller coaster sent screaming cars down a steep incline of tracks; and Laughing Sal, a gigantic, menacing clown, perched above the entrance to the Fun House. On the other side, people tried their luck tipping pins and lobbing ping-pong balls into goldfish bowls. Dimes and nickels clinked onto china dishes and colored vases with baubled necks. There were rings tossed around the slender shapes of Coca-Cola bottles, baseballs lobbed at large, cut-out metal milk containers, and pistols that you could fire at paper stars. The magnitude of the place was overwhelming. Lawrence felt his chest tighten slightly; he pulled loosely at Gerald's broad fingers.

But Mrs. Williams was unabashed; she led them briskly through the crowds, looking flushed and satisfied. During the war, she and Ringling had come here several times; it was the kind of place that could be depended on, even when the world had been filled with so much sadness and shame. In the Fun House, they marched past halls of mirrors and little glass cases of gypsy fortune tellers and mocking harlequins. They were menacing and maudlin; Lawrence shuddered briefly as Ringling put his hands out to touch them. He stared dumbly at himself in the distortion of mirrors, watching his belly pushing outward and his legs reduced to pencils. Afterward, there were caramel apples on sticks and wide, steaming bags of popcorn. Mrs. Williams and Ringling went off to ride the roller coaster, and Gerald stood beside his new ward on the Merry-Go-Round, shoving his hand gently along the boy's backside so that Lawrence wouldn't fall from his fabulously painted unicorn, its head thrown upward in a startled and permanent expression of surprise.

"Lawrence," Gerald asked as the boy slid from the lacquered saddle into his arms, "have you ever fired a rifle?" They were standing at the entrance to the games of chance; Lawrence could hear the clink and shudder of money tossed carelessly into the world.

"No." He shook his head.

"Well," Gerald answered with some satisfaction, "don't you think it's about time you tried?"

The boy nodded loosely, trying not to think too much about all those young men from the war that Gerald had once fought alongside, climbing carefully through the brush. Lawrence had seen pictures of them among Gerald's things: boys with sheepish expressions, grinning into the camera. Boys who never came home again. Gerald had explained the sadness of it all, but the tragedy of the war was not the aspect that troubled Lawrence the most. Because those boys were dead, he felt a kind of affinity with them. *One of them might be my father,* he had considered, thumbing carefully through Gerald's snapshots. *Or might have known him.* One of those dead boys from the war, he imagined, might hold some small secret about his past.

Gerald led Lawrence over toward the shooting gallery and paid the attendant there a quarter. The man filled the mounted rifle with BB pellets, and Gerald lifted the boy to the height of the counter. Inside, there was a series of small, stuffed animals with red and white painted bull's-eyes sitting next to them. The background was painted for nightfall; a few fake plants and boulders evened out the woodland scene.

"Go on," Gerald encouraged. "Get that squirrel." He pointed toward a small, grey-flecked figure with its tail thrust up into the air at too stark of an angle. Lawrence bent over the gun, touched its metal base. The thing was cold in his hands; he had no idea how to begin.

"Here," Gerald pointed out the sight along the top of the barrel and put on hand against the boy's back, easing him downward. "Get a good look," he instructed. "Just tilt and aim. That's all there is to it."

Lawrence tried, but the gun stuck in his hands. He couldn't move the metal trigger; he couldn't shoot. In his chest, he felt the familiar flutter of panic rising upward.

"Don't worry." Gerald shifted his weight against the counter and put one hand over the boy's. "Can you see the bull's-eye?" he asked. Lawrence tilted the gun slightly; he told Gerald that he could see it. "Good," Gerald answered. Then his hands compressed over the boy's, pinching them slightly, and the trigger went off. Lawrence could feel the gun lurch slightly forward and back—jarring and fluid in the same moment. A bright ping sounded in the woodland scene, and the rigid little squirrel tilted backward. A moment later, it lurched back up, wobbling slightly with its tail still thrust into the air.

"There!" Gerald shook the boy's shoulder proudly. Lawrence stared up at him and smiled. "You see?" Gerald beamed. "You can do it. Now try something over here." He directed the boy toward more targets, which he considered carefully and hit each and every time. He was good, Gerald said, at taking aim—good at following through. Lawrence nodded as Gerald shoved more money toward the little man behind the counter.

"Hey! You got any shots left?" By the time Ringling found them, his cheeks flushed from the crisp sea air and the thrill of the roller coaster, Lawrence had already felled a dozen of the little woodland animals, each of whom sprang back up afterwards, looking jittery and wild.

"This round's for Lawrence." Gerald pivoted the boy's body slightly so that he could take aim at a little red fox in one corner. Lawrence waited a moment, lining up the swirling red bull's-eye. Then he fired again and the fox tipped backward. Behind them, Lawrence heard Mrs. Williams jump.

"Gerald!" she gasped. "What are you doing?"

"Helping the boy out," he answered, setting the boy back

down on the ground. "Those people didn't teach him hardly any- thing useful."

Mrs. Williams looked sharply back at him, her excitement for the day's activities suddenly absent. "He's too young for this," she said bluntly. Lawrence was surprised. Until then, he hadn't seen her take any kind of special interest in him.

"He needs to learn how to be a man."

"But not now." Lawrence looked up; her voice had gone hushed and horrified. He felt his fingers curl and tingle from the effort of so much shooting. "It's violent," she said. "You shouldn't do this, Gerald."

Ringling looked up and shrugged. "It's just fun." He lined up the rifle and pretended to shoot. "It's a game, Mac."

But Mrs. Williams wasn't paying attention. She watched her husband. "The war's over, Gerald."

"This isn't about war," he shook his head, irritated. "It's about manhood."

Mrs. Williams tugged the boy down off the counter and held him to her. "He's just a little kid." Her arms dropped, winding around Lawrence, who could smell popcorn on her breath, warm and salty. It was a comforting embrace; he leaned into her.

Gerald stared back—angry, hurt. "The boy's good at it, Mac. Let him have that."

Lawrence could feel her shaking. "Let him have something else," she said. "I've had enough of violence."

They looked at each other: Gerald, the war veteran, and his wife, who had waited through three long years of war bulletins and news- reels. "You're going to stunt him," Gerald warned. "You're going to beat the man out of him."

Mrs. Williams shook her head again, and held onto the boy. Lawrence shut his eyes; he could feel himself begin to agree with her. It was difficult to imagine how he would ever become a man like Gerald: so big and imposing and unwilling to be wrong. The truth is, he didn't care if he learned how to shoot a rifle or fix an engine or crack a baseball out of its chalk diamond. The things he wanted were much simpler than that. More immediate—like those arms wrapped around him just then. All he wanted, he decided, was to find one good place in the world and to stay there—no matter what else he might be capable of.

Maxine, 1935

Every good story needs a villain, and in this one, it's Maxine's Uncle Cisco. He was the kind of man who knew how to capitalize on other people's misfortunes—and by the middle of the 1930s, there were certainly plenty of those. Gas prices had gone up; it had gotten more and more expensive to buy things like food and patched tires. So the Richards Brothers had had to start cutting back, taking on fewer shows and staying to the larger roads. Wages got sporadic, and some of the performers began to leave. The bearded lady was said to have run off with a homosexual from Tennessee. The Siamese twins headed north to go find a spot on the Barnum show. Their best slackwire girl found herself a rich Texan whom she didn't love but had agreed to marry anyway. Cisco didn't like to see the business failing; it made him irritable and sharp-tongued. Moreover, he still felt entitled to things: the best pup tent, an extra serving at meal times. It didn't matter to him that the rest of the crew was suffering. Cisco was smart; he knew how to get things. So he took what he wanted—though eventually, it seemed to catch up with him:

W. Cisco Richards Wounded, and his Show Postponed

Donthan, Ala. August 23, 1934. Westley Cisco Richards of Richards Brothers Shows was stabbed nearly fatally on August 14th, following a misunderstanding with a Negro employee on his show. In disagreement with her employer about certain handling of the staff, the Negro woman came at him with a concealed knife as he sat down to take his dinner that evening. She stabbed him twice, the worst of the cuts entering his spine just below the shoulder blade. Although Mr. Richards was seriously injured, the knife fortunately hit his ribcage, thereby preventing a more fatal outcome. At time of writing, Mr. Richards was resting at his family ranch. This unfortunate event has delayed the continuation of his show this season. Updates about future shows will be forthcoming.

Maxine remembered the little man from the *Circus Billboard* coming to visit her family out at the ranch near Pipe Creek, Texas, where they usually stayed during the winter months. He was a short, portly man with glasses, who couldn't stop grinning. His name was Mr. Chips and he was there, he explained, to ask a few questions. Did they mind so very much? Grin. It would only take a minute. Grin. Then he stuck his face into Cisco's sickroom, grinning even more to put the man at ease. Dollie Mae brought Mr. Chips a chair and set it by Cisco's bed. She whispered to her daughter that she should wait there with them, just in case: "You know your uncle's temper."

So Maxine did. Grandmother Mary had already explained to her what had really happened: "That girl, Ruthie's daughter, she's gotten to be quite a beauty, wouldn't you say?"

Maxine had nodded in agreement.

"Well, a man like Cisco, he's not going to take no for an answer. So he took her against her will, that's what he did."

Maxine was young; people hadn't said much to her yet about what a man can do to hurt a woman. But she tried to follow her grandmother's logic. Mary was someone who understood the darker pieces of life. "And the poor thing got pregnant," she went on. "But the baby died. They say the girl stopped talking; she just sits and stares at the wall. So Ruthie sent her to go live with some kin folks she's got back in Louisiana. Lord knows what will come of a girl like that." She shook her head, so Maxine shook hers, too. She still didn't know what sex was, but she understood that what Cisco had done was bad. Bad enough to ruin a person's life.

"So, Mr. Richards," the little man sat himself down and took out the tiniest notepad that Maxine had ever seen. "Tell me what happened on the afternoon of August fourteenth."

And Cisco did, describing the stabbing, and the good food that he was about to enjoy. He talked about the pain as the knife tore through him, and what the doctor had said afterward, and how shocked we all were that it had happened. Then, to finish off with a spark, he said: "I'll tell you, Mr. Chips, people have got to be more careful hiring Negros these days. Some of them are crazy. It's in the blood. I tell you, what happened to me, could happen to anybody. A circus boss or shop owner or whatever. You should put that in your story, Mr. Chips. How crazy the Negro people are."

And Mr. Chips sat there grinning and scribbling away. After a few more logistical questions, he spun his hand into the air, ever so casually, and asked: "I hear there was a girl, the woman's daughter. She was pregnant awhile back. That have anything to do with all this?"

"That?" Cisco looked confused. He considered for a moment, scratching his chin. "Well now, that was all just a misunderstanding. Because that girl, you see, she's not exactly the kind to keep it to herself, if you know what I mean."

Mr. Chips nodded again, still grinning. "What I thought," he said. "What I thought, Mr. Richards. Thank you kindly."

So the *Billboard* printed Cisco's version of the story, but Maxine's father wasn't fooled. "People are going to know what this means." He shook the folded *Billboard* pages over Cisco's sick bed a few days later.

"How's that, Arthur? You saw what that newspaper man wrote. Simple misunderstanding. She's lucky she didn't kill me."

Arthur scowled. "How could you do this, Cisco?" He tossed the newspaper across the room. Maxine had never seen her father angry like that. He argued with Cisco for hours that night, though she wasn't really sure what troubled him more: the loss of income or his brother's rotten morals. Money was tight, her mother had told her; even a few weeks off the line-up was bad.

"But what about the girl?" Maxine could still feel that cold night air, dark hands holding her, and a woman laughing. She had no real regrets about Ruthie. But Priscilla was young, like she was. "Aren't you sad about what happened to Ruthie's girl?"

"Of course, Maxine." Dollie Mae flapped her hand around the air like what her daughter had said was necessary but beside the point. "I've always known that man's a scoundrel."

* * *

Part of what was so troubling about Cisco is that he survived whatever happened to him: bar brawls and stabbings and brushes with the law. The man always sprang back, spry and listless as always. He didn't seem quite human, like the rest of them—felled by financial woes and bad luck and illness. Later that same year, Grandmother Mary died of a quick illness that was probably syphilis, but that everybody called brain fever. And Della, in sadness and financial strain, moved back to San Antonio where she took up work as a seamstress. Then quite suddenly, as though it was the grief that had done it to her, Dollie Mae was pregnant again. Everybody looked at her suspiciously; she and Arthur hadn't shared a tent together in years. But the couple just smiled sheepishly. It was true, Dollie Mae told her daughter. "I'm just sorry Mama won't be around to see it this time."

So a few months later, Maxine had a brother. They named him Ringling, for her father's friend John Ringling who lived up in Wisconsin. From the very beginning, Ringling was both adored and unlucky. He was a gentle baby—easy to care for and easy to love. He would be attractive his whole life: a round face and small, flashing features. He had a smile to win women's hearts—whether he was two years old or twenty. Dollie Mae thought he was perfect; so did Maxine. The trouble was, he trusted things too much. Not just people, but life itself; he believed things would always be all right. But before Ringling's first birthday, Arthur got sick. Tuberculosis, the doctor said. He needed rest; too much work might kill him.

By then, the circus was nearly gone, and the ranch in Pipe Creek had been sold off piecemeal to try to keep them afloat. There was no money and no place to go. But Cisco had a house. The only smart thing he'd ever done was to buy a piece of property and hang onto it: a little plantation up on the Florida panhandle, at a place called Pensacola. So close to the sea, Cisco said, that you could hear it— smell it. And he had a wife up there. He'd married her young and kept her there for years. "Belle will take good care of you all," he promised. "That woman's gotta be good for something."

So that's how Cisco convinced his brother to sell off the rest of the ponies and stock and split up what little money they got for it. "Think about your family," Cisco had said, and Arthur had agreed. Then Cisco went off and gambled his money away at the race track, and Maxine's family bought bus tickets for Pensacola. It was a difficult journey, and her father was the only one who wanted to go because, as Cisco had persuaded him, he believed that it was the only responsible thing to do. That was Arthur's fault in life: just like Ringling after him, he was too trusting. But Dollie Mae knew better. Dollie Mae, who had watched her daddy beat her mother, who knew what can happen to a family.

* * *

When they got to Pensacola, they found out that Cisco's wife was terrified of illness; her entire family had gone down in an outbreak of scarlet fever. So Maxine and Ringling were allowed to stay with her, but she insisted that Arthur move out to the little single-room cabin a few hundred yards off the main house. "It'll be more comfortable for him," she purred. "What with all the noise of the children up here at the house."

Dollie Mae looked carefully at her daughter. "Take care of Ringling," she said, grabbing up her suitcase and following Belle's housekeeper, who was rolling Arthur in a pushchair out across the lawn.

Maxine didn't go to school anymore. Instead, she helped with Ringling's care and brought food and fresh linens out to her parents. The latter barely spoke; her father was too weak. Maxine hated the disease that was taking him, and she hated whatever it was that was taking her mother. Dollie Mae sat there like a ghost, white-skinned and wordless, shifting quietly in her rocking chair. She didn't change her clothes or fix her hair or eat hardly any of what

Maxine brought. For the first time in her life, she looked ashen and ugly. When Arthur bloodied his sheets, she took them out behind the cabin and burned them. It was the only thing she did. And after a slow, terrible year of this, she had begun to lose her figure: her breasts sagged and sat low against her belly; her eyes grew dark and grayed around the sockets. When Maxine arrived daily, Dollie Mae only nodded, or held a finger to her lips. "Your daddy is sleeping— he's tired." But he was always tired; Maxine began to feel angry. She was fourteen years old, and life had suddenly gotten very heavy indeed. When they heard that Della had died from complications delivering a baby that no one had known she was expecting, Maxine thought she might just collapse, but she couldn't. She needed help, but there was no one: not her daddy, not Dollie Mae in her terrible rocking chair, not Della or Grandmother Mary, and not even Aunt Belle, who was, Maxine had come to understand, the worst kind of person: weak and useless without knowing it.

Belle wasn't unkind; she was just mousy and foolish. She was the type of woman who obsessed over dust on the staircase and fretted when the cream ran low, calling the delivery man in town for more, just in case Cisco came home and found the larder empty. But he never did—not once in the nearly two years that Maxine and her family stayed there.

Belle also worried about her looks. She was getting on in age now, she said—thirty-two—and she worried that she wasn't pretty enough anymore. She worried that, when her husband finally did come home, he wouldn't want her.

"Maxine," she called, fixing her hair in a fury of anticipation. It was raining; she was always more anxious when it rained. "Is it better up or down, Maxine?" She raised and lowered the lump of her hair. Maxine looked in the mirror with her. She was Dollie Mae's age. And, though not quite as naturally beautiful as Dollie Mae, she was handsome and well-kept. "It's much more classic-looking swept up like this," she demonstrated. "But he likes my hair down. See? It's just that now, I wonder if it doesn't show the lines on my face more when I do that." She tugged and pulled some more. "But maybe if I parted it to one side, like this. Yes, that's better. Don't you think so, Maxine?"

The one good thing about Aunt Belle was her library; the books numbered in the hundreds. Mostly they were novels of the gothic variety, about dark, winding staircases and sinister castles hanging over the sea. These were not at all the kinds of books that Maxine had read in school; they were much better. Often, she and Belle read together. The Brontes were their favorites; they read them over and over, swapping *Wuthering Heights* and *Jane Eyre* back and forth like party dresses. They loved the men in these books—their aloofness and their quiet charisma. Belle liked Heathcliff best, while Maxine preferred Mr. Rochester. She felt certain that she would love a man like that one day. It made her feel tragic: that she, too, would one day have a wounded love. Belle already did, but she swore it was the greatest experience on earth, remembering the one you love.

The problem with Belle is that she didn't know where the dream ended and the real life started up again. Toward the end of 1935, when Maxine's father was getting worse and worse—the fits so bad, he couldn't hide them anymore—Maxine tried asking Belle for help: "Maybe we should take him to a hospital? Or bring a doctor out?" But Belle was distraught. Her wedding anniversary had come and gone, and not a word from Cisco. She spent the whole week moping: "He didn't come. He didn't write."

Maxine's gut wrenched, listening to her. How could so much selfishness rise up in one small person? Secretly, her feared her aunt. Belle was someone who couldn't get through life on her own—not now, and probably not ever. But Maxine realized that she didn't have a choice. So she hated seeing her aunt's weakness. She hated her own knees buckling at the sight of her father's bloodied sheets.

One night, Maxine had had enough. The whole walkway between the house and her parents' cabin stunk of his burnt linens. Aunt Belle had been sobbing all day, and there wasn't any more clean bedding to be found. "Why do you love him so much?" the girl screamed. "Why are you worried so much about him loving you? Do you think he's a good man? Don't you know what he did, Aunt Belle?" And she knew it was cruel, but she told her aunt about the story in the *Circus Billboard*—about Ruthie and little Priscilla. "Can't you understand? Don't you care what an evil man he is?"

But Belle just looked back, terrified. She started to tremble. Then she turned to the cabinets, the counter. Noticing a stain on the table, she took up a towel and fingered it. "Brenda will have to clean this up tomorrow," she said. "She'll have to clean it up in case Cisco comes. He doesn't like a mess here—no, he doesn't."

Maxine could see the woman's eyes: they were hollow. "He's not coming back," she told her. "Maybe not ever."

Belle nodded, staring straight at her niece. "He always wanted things neat and clean. He told me that."

She was no better than a character in one of her books, but she was all there was. And the longer that they stayed on in Pensacola, the more Maxine felt herself beginning to lose track of things, too—time, and people, and things that she used to believe about life. And maybe because her fantasy life had become so rich, she was open to unusual persuasions. So when a visitor came one night, Maxine saw her: late in the evening, Aunt Della in her bedroom. She stood gazing out the window, a bright moon beside her. *Aunt Della!* Maxine whispered. The sheets were pulled tightly around Ringling. It was warm, but Maxine shivered anyway. Della was dead, she told herself; she shouldn't be here. Then Della turned, her eyes wide and sad with warning. She blinked once and stared at the girl in disbelief—as though *she* were the ghost. "I'm sorry, Maxine," she said, and glanced back out the window. Then she picked up her little suitcase, nodded once, and left. And that's how Maxine knew that her daddy was gone.

Theresa, May 1979

"Miss Williams." Mr. Patchett, the owner of Stevie's Stopover, the corner grocery store two miles from their house, slapped the counter. His eyes never left her. He was a difficult man to talk to simply because of how attentive he was. Theresa wanted to disappear, but she told herself to focus: her mother needed coffee. Yes, that was it: her mother would not get out of bed.

"Not so good on the home front, I hear." This was his favorite introduction: *Not so good in business, I hear. Not so good with the wife.* He had a specially attuned antennae for the town's less savory details. He knew how to draw out loneliness: people whose tragedies skidded along the surface, who never got the chance to talk about their despair openly. And Fairfield had plenty of those.

"They said it was a suicide," she told him, gripping her hand against a hipbone. She could feel the shape of the fluted bone, the socket. Wider now than when she was a child.

The man whistled, low and long. "That fella—a friend of your family, wasn't he?"

Theresa nodded.

Mr. Patchett's head bobbed. His tongue clicked against the roof of his mouth. "Terrible—what a tragedy." He paused. "I heard you found him," he said quickly. "Found the body."

Theresa's lungs felt stiff; she pivoted against her heel. "Mr. Patchett, where's your coffee?"

"Aisle two," he nodded, a bit disappointed. "About half way down."

She turned away quickly, pushing down aisle two, past the Ovaltine and the powdered milk. She picked up a canister of Folgers ground and an extra pack of filters. Her mother was so distractible. On the days she felt like leaving the house, she would grab a coffee filter like a tea bag, twist it up around some grounds, and shove it into a cup of boiling water to take outside. Ostensibly, she would visit the horse barn, although there were only two malnourished ponies left. The honey hives were in disrepair, and the garden had gone to seed.

"Must be getting real quiet down there."

Theresa set the Folgers canister on the counter. She nodded. It was true, of course, although this was not exactly how things felt. The less inhabited it became, the house seemed to swell around her. Light flooded in from all sides now; not even the old oak tree was there to cast its protective shadow.

Mr. Patchett picked up the canister and considered it: the red swirl of Folgers, the plastic lid lined with a film of dust. "Your mother doing all right?"

She knew he was vying for more gossip, but she didn't want to give him any. Her mother just needed some coffee, she explained, to help get her out of bed in the mornings.

Mr. Patchett nodded. "Quite a character, your mother. A real a survivor, isn't she? Lost her father, too, as I recall. Real young." He fingered the mild beard at his chin: the kind of stray hairs that a man his age could barely grow any longer. "Now, she's got some stories, your mother does," he grinned. "Her father dying out there in Florida, and then the rest of the family getting packed off to the sanatorium." He shook his head.

"They'd gotten sick by then, too," Theresa clarified, fingering a package of gum out of sight, under the counter. It felt mildly disloyal, the way her mother shared these stories with relative strangers. The world knew so much about them; it left her feeling less protected somehow. In her hand, the gum felt warm. Mr. Patchett rattled on, reminiscing about what he had heard of her mother's heroic months at the sanatorium, rallying Dollie Mae's spirits and keeping baby Ringling safe. Theresa pressed and flexed her fingers around the gum until the pack began to curve, taking on the shape of her own hand.

"A shame," Mr. Patchett was saying, "what all your family has been through. And now this," he paused, looking at her meaningfully. She knew he was talking again about Lawrence. "I guess you must be relieved—to have him finally gone."

She stared at him. "He wasn't so bad," she answered. Almost without her thinking, the chewing gum made its way quietly into her pocket, unnoticed. "He wasn't a bad person."

"Sure, sure. But difficult."

She fingered the counter. "People seem to think he was terrible, but he did some good things, too."

"Suicide's a private thing, Miss." Mr. Patchett shook his hands in the air, like brushing off water. "I don't make no judgment."

"It's not judgment," she said. "People just think the worst, that's all. But he helped us—he did." Her voice was speeding up, and she couldn't understand why so much was pouring out of her now, with Mr. Patchett, the gossiping storekeeper. Suddenly, she was telling him about her father's illness, how it had come on so slow and unnoticeable, just after his retirement. So strange, how his energy had waned, just weeks into his sixty-first year, insidious and sad, and how it was Lawrence who had finally convinced them of what was happening. It had been almost a year ago now, but she could still remember sitting there, hunched low in the yard by the front window, watching: her father lying stiffly on the sitting room sofa, not speaking, and Lawrence, that long-orphaned man who often stayed with them, arguing with her mother.

Mrs. Williams, he needs to go to the hospital. He's dying.

How dare you say that? Why would you say that?

Theresa had been surprised. Normally, Lawrence hadn't said much of anything; he had always been such a painfully quiet man. *Because it's true,* he'd added more softly. *He isn't getting any better sitting here in the house without proper medicine.*

Maxine had snarled at him, her hands fluttering through the air. They landed on her face like a pair of agitated moths. But at the hospital, the doctors had collectively shaken their heads: if only the Williams had come sooner. But Maxine had refused to hear it. *You're doctors*, she'd insisted. *For God's sake, do something!*

And so they had, putting Theresa's father into chemo, even though it was too late to hope for much. A slight slowing of the disease, perhaps. The tiniest remission. But after three weeks, nothing had changed. The cancer that had spread up from his colon was steadily eating out Gerald Williams's abdomen. And the treatment was painful; he asked them to stop.

Oh, Gerald, Theresa's mother had protested. *You've got to.*

But he had just shut his eyes and listened to the bang and clatter of patients down the hall. *It's too late for that, Mac.*

Up until that point, Theresa had believed that her father would get better. Finally, the idea of his death had begun to soak its way into her brain, like a towel lowered into a pool of water. Until the thought had become too full, too heavy, and she'd had to set it down.

Mr. Patchett's face had softened, "You've been through plenty, young lady."

But Theresa's head was still shaking. "Everybody's so worried about me, but I'm fine—really." She paused. "I just don't understand what happened. What made him do it? Why does a person kill himself?"

"He was a quiet fella," Mr. Patchettt conceded. "I didn't know him all that well."

"But he wasn't terrible," she insisted. "People think he was terrible."

The man nodded. He shoved the canister of coffee back at her. "Settle up with me next time, why don't you?" he said. "And tell your mother I said hello."

"Is it true?" she wanted to know. "Is that what people say?"

"About Lawrence?"

"That he was awful?"

"I don't think people say much of anything." He settled back onto his stool. "I don't think most folks noticed him much at all."

* * *

By the time she left the store, Theresa's head was screaming.

Outside, the sun was screaming, too. The handlebars and the seat of her bicycle itself were murderously hot. But she didn't care. She stood over the pedals and rode without sitting, her thumbs and forefingers pressed over the scalding handlebars, her elbows locked. She road that way for two miles, all the way back to her driveway. Coming up onto her property, she slowed slightly, shoved a hand into her jeans pocket, pulled out the stolen pack of gum, and tossed in into the indentation at the side of the road. The motion tilted the bike. She tried to steady it, but the bike pitched forward and came down, rolling over onto one side. She skidded, catching herself with a knee and one palm, the impact bruising her and shredding the skin of her hand. Her eyes pressed shut for a moment, and she lay there in the heat without moving. The pain in her hand felt not good, exactly, but reassuring: physical and grounding. The air around her packed itself full of heat, although the sun was nowhere near its climax yet. But there it was: hot air coming apart like cotton, moving in chunks around her, mildly flirting with the wind.

"Are you all right?" It was a man's voice. Or a boy's. A boy-man. She looked up. Squinted. It was Tomás, that boy who looked like her but had a Spanish name that Nathan had hired. The one who had torn out the oak tree. "You fell," he said, obvious as anything, and reached down to give her a hand. Theresa looked down at her own bloody one, and Tomás reached down further to pick her up by the elbows and shoulders, righting her and setting her back to standing in the sun.

"You're here to work," she said. It wasn't much of a question, but Tomás nodded. "I went to get coffee," she explained. "For my mother. She won't get out of bed." It was not until she spoke that she understood how tensed her voice had become. She cleared her throat—the strings of her voice struggling to untie themselves—and wondered what Tomás must see in her: buttons crossed wrong on the little seersucker she wore, her voice coming out strained and patchy, like wet dog's fur. But he just pulled at the bike, tugging gently to encourage her right ankle to pick itself up, cross over and away. She moved. Stood solidly on her own feet, the bag of coffee still dangling from a handlebar.

"You wanna go inside?"

She nodded.

His hand was at her back. She felt the insides of herself, all those molten jellies that make us human, sliding in and around each other, confused at the idea of balance. She tripped again. He stopped her. Looked her over. "You're tired," he concluded, as though he had been checking for liquor—or worse. Then he put his arm more firmly around her shoulders and led her inside. It was cooler in the house than she had expected. The fans were turning: *Tomás*, she guessed. Her mother, she knew, would still be upstairs, sleeping. "She needs coffee," she said again. "To get up." She moved toward the kitchen.

"Don't worry about it." He was tall and lean and stood over her like a lanky school boy she might have loved at some point. The hair at his cheek bones was a dark brown. He shaved, though not daily. Sometimes it came through in the thin outline of a beard: a gentle thickening of darkness that contrasted pleasantly with his china bone skin. "Let's get you cleaned up."

She sat on the lip of the bathtub as Tomás shifted through the medicine cabinet. He was adept; the clutter of the house did not seem to vex him. He pulled out a bottle of peroxide and took her hand and held it, palm up, over the cavity of the sink. Rinsed it. Poured a careful trickle of peroxide over it and let the medicine sit for a moment. She closed her eyes. The medicine stung mildly and brought a hint of dampness to her eyes. "Are there sleeping pills?" she asked.

"What?"

"The bottle of sleeping pills in the cabinet. Is it empty?"

Tomás picked up one prescription bottle and then another. Expired medicines for her father, or one of the boys. Years old. "I don't know," he said. "Come on." He picked her up. She was crying harder now, her head bent forward and shoulders heaving. She didn't have any more words just then to explain how things were: how her mother didn't sleep at all, or slept too much. How she herself had stolen those pills for several weeks after her father had died.

Tomás stopped at her bedroom door. "There you are," he said, gesturing a bit too widely. She looked up. He seemed embarrassed. "I'll go make some coffee for your mom."

She nodded, "Thank you." Then he moved away and left her standing there, her bandaged palm still throbbing lightly from the pain. And Tomás moved down the staircase, his tall form echoing the banister ties one after another after another.

Maxine, 1936

The day she found blood on her sheets, Maxine just knew she was dying. That's the way things happened in the sanatorium. She had seen it before. First you were just a little tired; you needed to rest. But then the coughing came, and the blood. *Oh Lord*, she thought, *I don't want to die!* It wasn't right. She felt fine—better, in fact, than she had in years. Because, finally, there was enough to eat. Finally, they were being taken care of: her and Ringling in the children's ward, and their mother in one of the private ladies' cabins built to the side of the main house. Maxine had begun to feel like there might be a future for her family. She and her mother still had their acrobatics skills. They could find work there in Florida, or maybe up north on one of the big railway shows. But it didn't matter now, because she was dying. She went to tell Sister Alberta.

Maxine took the stained sheet as proof and stood there crying at Sister's door, holding her wadded up bedding and shaking with the fear of death, which was primarily a fear of ghosts. Sister Alberta was a charitable woman, but she was the kind of person who doled out pity only when it was well deserved. "Oh, Sister!" Maxine cried. "Sister help me, I'm dying!"

There were a handful of Catholic nuns consigned to work at Mt. Carlisle sanatorium, and Sister Alberta was the one who looked over the young girl's wing. She cocked her square-framed head and looked at Maxine. "What have you got there, Maxine?" Her expression was doubtful, and a little severe. Around her face, the boxy black habit pinched inward, pushing her chin and cheeks forward so that she looked fatter than she actually was.

"Oh, Sister, it's my blood! I'm dying!" Maxine held out the sheet, sticky with a browning, iron-smelling stain. Sister Alberta took the sheet from her, shook it out, and raised the stain to eye level. Her glasses were thick; she took a long time considering. Finally, she told the girl: "Not yet, you're not."

Maxine stopped shaking, looked away from the greasy spot on her bedding and back to Sister Alberta. She asked if the woman was sure. Sister Alberta nodded firmly, the soft skin at her chin squishing down into a determined crease. "Do you know what this is, Maxine?"

"Blood, Sister. Like my daddy coughed up all the time."

"No," she shook her head, looking a little more kindly. "Not like your daddy."

So that's how Maxine learned about women's menstruation: from a nun at the sanatorium. She fetched the towels that Maxine would need, and explained how long it should last, and told her not to be too alarmed if things were a little irregular at first. But she also warned the girl to be careful: "No matter what someone might tell you, Maxine, you have a choice about things. And no amount of help from a man is worth getting yourself into trouble."

What she meant exactly, Maxine didn't understand just then. But somehow, she understood years later, Sister Alberta already knew how things would be—what would happen to Maxine's mother, and all that that would mean.

The days of her first period made Maxine thoughtful. She was relieved to be healthy—so thankful that she didn't really mind the discomfort or messiness or added work of scrubbing and ringing out her little ladies' towels. It was exciting to be a woman: to be able to make people. Surrounded as she'd been by death, this seemed important. Because now there would be a future—both she and her mother knew it. Their family would go on, and Maxine would be the one to make it so.

"Sister tells me you've got your cycle, Maxine. That's wonderful."

They were sitting in Dollie Mae's little bungalow, which Maxine rarely visited. Usually, she saw her mother in the dining hall or out on the grounds where they went for those short walks that the hospital staff said were so good for them. Mount Carlisle was a beautiful place, set just inland from the sea. On windy days, Maxine could smell the salt in the air. The rest of the time, it was scented with flowers; a retired plantation, the place was covered in gardens.

But that particular day, her mother had wanted to talk, so she'd gone to see her in her private room, which was little more than a steep A-frame roof set onto the ground—so narrow that even someone small like Maxine could only stand at full height directly below the apex. The bungalows had been added last, and in a hurry, after the main house had already been filled with hospital beds and dining facilities and nurse's quarters. But the patients kept coming. People were so poor back then; for many of them, the sanatorium was a better place than home.

"Do you know what I was doing when I first learned about women's matters?" Dollie Mae asked as her daughter lowered herself onto the empty bed a few feet away. There had been another woman there before, Judith, but she had suddenly disappeared—whether to health or death, Maxine didn't know.

The girl shook her head.

"I had a job back then," Dollie Mae explained slowly. "Down at Mr. Shaunnassy's theater in San Antonio. I learned everything from the other chorus girls." She sat propped against a pillow set behind her against the wall, her arms folded neatly against her stomach. Hearing her daughter's news, she acted stronger than she had in weeks.

"I had work," she went on, "whenever one of the girls went missing for a few weeks. Perfectly healthy girls suddenly disappeared. Some of them had boyfriends, but other ones had just been doing some man a favor. A show owner, probably. They were trying to get themselves a break by sleeping with a talent scout from New York or Houston. We all wanted to get out of San Antonio. But it was such a gamble; you could lose everything." She paused to take water from the little blue ceramic pitcher on the narrow table between the two beds. She swallowed and coughed once, lightly. "And a lot of them did. So I decided right then that wasn't the way for me. I'd wait for a husband."

Maxine was surprised to hear her mother talking so frankly about the world. Dollie Mae had always been such a private woman—she had never known her mother's real opinions. And she would never have guessed that Dollie Mae knew all that she did.

"So when Mama decided to take us on the circus," she coughed again, "I couldn't say no—even though it meant giving up everything I'd ever wanted for myself. But I had to. There were men who would have married me, sure, but none of them had any money. And the ones who did have money and wanted a girl—well, they were married already. The options for a girl without a job or a family just aren't very good."

Neither of them said anything about Maxine's circumstance—about the similar dangers that she might face if her mother didn't get better.

Dollie Mae took a sip of water from the basin next to her, choking against it as it went down. A tight little cluster of coughs followed. Maxine gripped the side of the bed where she sat. "Mother," she said, "it's ok. You don't have to talk now. Just rest."

"No, no, no," the woman insisted, shaking her head and shifting up higher so that she could see her daughter directly. "This is important, Maxine," she took a breath. "You're a woman now. There's some things you need to know." She stopped again to gather herself, and looked directly at Maxine. "You've got to be careful. Stay away from that Uncle Cisco of yours. He's a womanizer. It doesn't matter a whit to him that you're family. So don't you go back to see him—not ever."

This time, she was seized by a much more violent cough—the wicked, bloody kind. Maxine grabbed a towel and brought it to her. When it had ended, she closed her eyes and set back down on the pillow, breathing slowly. "I'm so glad," she whispered. "So glad you've grown up, Maxine."

But Maxine wasn't so sure how she felt about it. Her mother seemed all too relieved now, and Maxine could guess what she was thinking, handing her history and wisdoms over to her like that: her daughter was healthy, the family secure. So Dollie Mae could go. She could leave off from this life knowing that they would continue without her.

* * *

Maxine had already seen one family ghost, and she didn't want to see any more. So she told her mother to hang on. As often as she could, Maxine borrowed one of the hospital's little wicker push chairs and wheeled her mother through the lush sanatorium grounds. But Dollie Mae was less and less interested in these outings, and her conversation got gloomier and gloomier. After their meeting that day in the bungalow, the woman's energy began to wane. She wasn't sleeping well, she said. Sometimes she woke with nightmares, screaming. Or worse, woke without them and, not screaming, stayed up the rest of the night, coughing quietly and staring up into the tiny apex above her.

"Do you believe in God?" she asked suddenly one day.

"What do you mean?"

"Just what I said, Maxine. Do you believe in God?"

Maxine stared down at the top of her mother's head. Dollie Mae still kept her hair smoothly tied into a bun at base of her neck. "Yes, Mother," she answered. "Of course I do."

"Really?" her mother's voice was going dreamy, as it often did. Maxine found herself growing irritable with her mother, as she lost hold on the things of this world. "*Yes*," she said again.

"And do you believe that life turns out the way it should?"

The land up ahead of them was turning thick with vegetation: ground ferns and trees hung thick with Spanish moss. Residents were not permitted past this point on the grounds, where nature had begun to take back the land; soon, they would have to turn around.

"I don't know, Mother." The chair felt suddenly very heavy as Maxine dug it slightly into the ground to swivel her mother around. This kind of talk was making her tired.

Dollie Mae got quiet after that, nodding her head up and down along the uneven trail as her daughter pushed them back toward the hospital. Up and down, up and down. After a few minutes, Maxine thought that she had gone to sleep. But then the woman spoke up again: "Are you sorry that your father died?"

Maxine told her that she was—terribly, awfully sorry: "It's the worst thing that ever happened to us."

"Well, I'm not sorry," she said. "He wasn't a man of this world. He was too good."

Maxine wanted to agree with whatever her mother said, to make her feel better. And to make her stop talking—to stop saying such odd, inappropriate things. But how could she tell her that she was glad her father was gone? Or that she believed God had wanted him to go, and that He had some reason for taking him? "Things just happen," Maxine told her mother. "Sometimes there aren't reasons."

"There's always a reason, Maxine. Even if it's a bad one." Dollie Mae paused, choking on an intake of air. A moment later, her mouth opened again and the top of her shirt bloomed in bright petals of blood. Pretty and red as the little azalea bushes that were planted everywhere around the grounds. It made Maxine shiver. She wished her mother hadn't said those things: cold, faithless things. It was like her body was punishing her now, coughing up all those vile, hateful thoughts inside her.

* * *

The thing that Maxine and her mother did best together was love Ringling. He was a happy, easy child. As often as she could, Maxine went over to the little boys' ward to visit him, where he played enthusiastically with the other children and the nurses adored him. And, because she wasn't very sick anymore, they would let Maxine stay there with him—often for the entire afternoon—and she would teach him things about colors and numbers and all the other interesting things that he would learn when he got older and went to school. He was an uncomplaining little boy, and Maxine enjoyed doing for him whatever she could. And Dollie Mae, though she was getting too sick even for Maxine to take her for visits in the little wheeled chair, thought about him constantly. "How is Ringling?" she would demand when Maxine came in the door of her little room. "Is he healthy? Are they feeding him well?" He was fine, the girl told her. Always the same: a good, solid little boy with a bright future ahead of him. Dollie Mae nodded quietly. She agreed; they both knew that Ringling was the best hope they had right then.

Just before his second birthday, Maxine's mother showed her the jar of coins and dollar bills that she had rolled into an extra sheet and kept in her bedding. "Four hundred and ninety-seven dollars and seventy-two cents," she explained, as Maxine stared down at the tightly-rolled, musty-smelling money. She pulled one greasy dollar from the outside of the roll and handed it to her daughter. "Get him a cake. And a present. Make sure they do something nice for him."

Maxine gave the money to Sister Alberta, who sent the delivery man to get extra portions of sugar and cream and a little something extra from the five-and-dime shop. He came back with all the fixings for a birthday cake, as well as a pair of little tin soldiers that cost a nickel each. The following day, Maxine told her mother about the party, hoping that it would cheer her up.

"Did he say my name?" Dollie Mae wanted to know. "Did he ask for me?" Her face looked grayish, sunken in; she worked her fingers anxiously in the fabric of her bed sheet.

"He didn't ask for anything, Mother. You know how Ringling is—easy as pie."

Her mother nodded thoughtfully. "Maxine," she said slowly, "I need you to bring him to me. I need to see my son."

Maxine watched her mother carefully; the sick room was full of what the nurses called *contagions*. It was dangerous to bring a mostly healthy little boy in there. "I don't know if that's such a good idea, Mother."

"Maxine," she turned on her daughter, almost fierce. "You've got to do this for me. It's what I need from you."

When Ringling arrived at Dollie Mae's bungalow, he blinked once in the low light of the doorway and stood still. Maxine gave him a little push from behind: "Go say 'hi.'" Then he toddled up to the bed and put his flat, chubby hands on the bedspread to steady himself. "Hi!" he shouted, looking first at his mother's face, and then at her little round body under the bedspread.

"Hello, Baby," she said softly, laying a hand across the top of his head. He sat there quietly under it. "How's my baby boy?"

Ringling stared at her; he didn't have any kind of answer.

"He's doing good, Mama," Maxine told her.

"Is that right, Ringling?" Dollie Mae smiled. "Are you being a good little boy?"

Ringling nodded, shifting his mother's hand up and down. She lifted her arm and lowered it back onto her stomach. "Good, Ringling. That's good." Then she breathed heavy and sighed, closing her eyes. Ringling began to look around at the spare furnishings in the bungalow. He reached his hand up into the water basin; it came out wet. He giggled.

"Maxine," Dollie Mae asked. "Doesn't he know me?" Her voice had gone cold and airy again.

"Of course he does, Mother." She looked worriedly at Ringling. "Ring, say something to Mother."

He looked up blankly. Maxine pointed toward their mother. He followed the direction of her finger. "Say something nice," she instructed. "Say something to Mommy."

"Mommy," he repeated, and Maxine saw her mother shiver and smile, the lids folding down over her eyes. "Yes, Ringling. That's right. Mommy's here."

Except that she wasn't. For a long while after that, she didn't say anything. Ringling kept splashing the water in the basin above his head while Maxine stood in the doorway, watching nervously. After some minutes more, her eyes fluttered open again, and she beckoned Ringling to her. "Please," she said. "Come here, baby." Ringling stood still, uncertain. Dollie Mae flipped her eyes toward her daughter. "Just let me touch him," the air rattled in her throat. "Just once."

Maxine did what she asked, lifting Ringling and lowering him over their mother's eager face so that she could put her hands against his cheeks and give him a soft little kiss. "You're so sweet, Ringling baby. Such a good, sweet little boy."

It made her glad to hear their mother talking that way—about something warm and positive and good. She stood there with Ringling in her arms. Dollie Mae was so gentle with him, so affectionate. It made Maxine pretend that her mother had been like that with her as an infant. That she had loved Maxine, as well.

Before they left, Dollie Mae made her daughter swear that she would come back—and that she wouldn't leave Ringling. No matter what. "Promise me, Maxine," she said. "Promise me you'll never let him go." Tears were in her eyes. Outside, the sky was already losing its color. "My perfect little boy," she cried. "You can't let him go! Maxine!" She was shrieking now, tossing her frail head against the pillow—her skin so white and gray it looked almost translucent, almost like light. "I won't, Mother," Maxine promised. "I won't ever let him go."

By the time she had dropped Ringling back off at his room, it was already dark. Maxine knew that her mother was having one of her bad days, so she decided just to sleep there, in Judith's empty bed. "It's all right, Mother," Maxine whispered, climbing in between the sheets, the sharp angle of the roof slicing down the space above her. "I'm right here. Don't worry."

Dollie Mae sighed. "Thank God for you, Maxine. Thank God."

After that, she didn't speak. There were just mumblings and half-words that Maxine guessed must have come from sleep. For some time, she stared upward toward the slanted ceiling, where the two planes of wood came together in a tight, singular point. Outside, she heard seagulls rifling through the trash cans outside the kitchen. The slow buzz of fans wiggling their circular way in so many of the rooms up at the main house. And the gradually evening breath of her mother, slipping herself into sleep.

Around midnight, Maxine woke up again. She heard something: a low, rustling sound. But it wasn't the birds outside, or even the fans, or the wind coming in off the water. It came and went, slow and even at first, like a lake lapping up against the sides of a boat. And there was a smell, too. Recently, the bungalow had begun to smell mildly all the time. No matter how neat and tidy Dollie Mae tried to be, and no matter how often the nurses came in to bathe her, it was still there: an odor like overripe fruit. Like a big heap of bananas or oranges left sitting too long in the sun. And a burnt smell, too—an iron blood smell. Fruit and blood and something more. And then Maxine heard the sound again: faint, like a faraway wail, except that she knew it was right there in the same room with her. It was coming from her mother. Almost a whisper, but without any words. She tried to peer through the dark, but she couldn't see much. She could just tell that Dollie Mae wasn't sitting up in bed; she wasn't looking at her daughter. She wasn't talking at all. There was just that sound, sputtering and building, like water leaking through a dam. A moan. A long, wailing cry. It stopped and started. A patterning rhythm: chuck-achuck-chucka. She was breathing, but just barely. That's what it was then, Maxine knew: the death gargle.

She ran out of that bungalow faster than you could blink; she was bone-scared. Scared of her mother—scared of her father and Della's ghosts. She ran up to the main building and banged on Sister Alberta's door. "Come on! Come on!" she screamed. "Something's happening to my mother!"

Maxine was hysterical by then, shaking and crying—her legs almost collapsing under the pressure. Sister Alberta took hold of her shoulders to steady the girl: "Where, Maxine? Where is she?" Maxine said that she would show her, and Sister Alberta half followed the girl, half carried her, back to her mother. "Wait here," she said at the doorway, and shoved Maxine gently down into the grass, where she lay heaving and crying under the bright stars and dark night. And she never went into that bungalow again.

Part II: Better Angels

Theresa, June 1979

Tomás was long and lean. He was a tall man, like her father and brothers, but not nearly so broad. Instead, he was narrow, almost gawky: long-limbed and arched as he stooped to inspect the horse trough.

"They're going to have to go," he said, gesturing toward the ponies in their pens.

Theresa started; she hadn't realized that he had noticed her standing there behind him. "What?"

"No one's riding them," he looked up. "Your brother told me to get rid of anything out here that no one's been using." Then he bent a knee, hefting the trough of stagnant water, his wrists snapping back slightly with the strain, and shoved the whole thing out onto the ground. The water fizzed lazily against the hot earth, refusing to be absorbed.

Theresa moved closer. Tomás set the empty trough carefully back onto the ground. "Thank you," she said. "I just wanted to say thank you for the other day."

He turned toward her, clapping the dust from his hands. He stood a good eight inches above her; his head tilted slightly to the right and his lips bent into a faint smile.

"When I fell," she started to remind him, but Tomás nodded quickly and took a few paces away toward the back side of the house to gather a length of hose. He flipped on the spigot and pressed a thumb over the mouth of the hose to hold the water in. "Of course."

"I'm sorry," she ventured again. "For crying like that."

He came toward her, dragging the hose, his head tilted again. "You've been through a lot." Then he laced the hose carefully through the metal trellis that supported the trough and arced its mouth up and over the brim. The water thrummed downward with a bright, insistent urge. While they waited for it to fill, Theresa surveyed the slow destruction of her yard. Feathers wound into thin strands of chicken wire. Spilled honey, slicked over surfaces baked down into tarnish. The threads of tires, lying open-mouthed and idle. Sand baked into sand baked into sand. Fence posts that had lost their bearings long ago. Tomás gazed idly about the yard. Nudged at a rusted can with his toe. Beer. Probably one of her brother's, she thought; her father had usually stuck to whiskey.

"You're not in school," he said after a while.

"People talk too much," she nosed a sneaker into the dirt. "And the year's almost over anyway."

"Lawrence," Tomás agreed. "People *would* gossip about a thing like that."

Theresa looked up, encouraged. "Did you know him?"

"Knew who he was."

"He was here a long time."

The boy nodded.

"Off and on."

Tomás adjusted the hose, the water still banging loudly against the trough's thin metal bottom. The whole structure wobbled along the forked iron tresses that supported its frame. Beside him, the ground had begrudgingly begun turning to mud.

"Did you like him?" she dug her toe deeper into the dirt.

Tomás shrugged. "Didn't know him very well." He bent again to jiggle the hose into place, pinched his finger in the metal supports and swore: *Puta madre.* She blinked. He was white: his skin was white, and the way he acted was white, too. But he knew Spanish; his father had been sure to teach him that. So he didn't fit anywhere: not with his white skin, not with his Spanish name.

"But you knew him."

"A little."

"What did you think?" Theresa crossed her hands over her chest; she was getting excited now. "Do you think he was a good man?"

Tomás tilted his head again slightly. "I didn't see anything wrong with him."

Theresa turned. She slid the base of her sneaker more firmly into the dusty ground. "You're not answering the question."

"I don't know," he shoved the pinched finger into his mouth. "I don't know what kind of man he was," he said after another moment. "He was a lot older than me."

She was disappointed. "So, you didn't know much about him."

"What are you trying to figure out?"

Theresa looked back down at the dirt. The shape of her foot had swelled to nearly double its size from the constant thrum of pat and turn. "It's just that nobody talks about it much," she answered. "It seems important—that he killed himself."

Tomás agreed. "That *is* a pretty profound thing."

She made a face. "It's awful."

"Of course it is. Awful—and amazing. How does a person do that?"

Theresa swallowed. "He was crazy," she told him. "Toward the end."

"Crazy?"

"A little bit."

"So, that's what made him do it?"

But who knew what had made him do it? And what was worse, maybe they would never really know. It had been little more than a week since Lawrence had killed himself, but already he was lying in the ground someplace: unmarked, alone. It bothered Theresa, this understanding that no one was looking for him—no one would find him. It seemed wrong. Even if he *had* committed such a sin. Even if, at moments, the single emotion that flashed inside of her was a white hot note of anger, she still felt sorry for him. And mildly disturbed. Whatever had happened to Lawrence, it seemed possible that such a thing could happen to her—or to anyone. That a life could quite simply fail. That any single person could become so entirely forgotten.

"He wasn't wanted," she told him. In the trough, the hose had become submerged below the waterline, so that Theresa could no longer hear the sound of water thrashing against itself.

"I thought he lived here." Tomás shoved a hip slightly to one side and leaned against the frame of the modest little horse barn. Inside, one of the two mares whinnied.

"My parents took him in," she explained. "I don't know why."

Tomás nudged the hose. "They were probably trying to do something good."

She glanced up at him, curious. "I don't know—I don't think my mother ever wanted him to come here."

"No?"

She shook her head. And, surprising herself, she began to tell Tomás about the things her mother had been saying before the suicide. Caught in the gears of grief, Maxine had been looking for someone—anyone—to lay the blame on. *You!* she had screamed at Lawrence. *What good are you? It should have been you who died.*

Tomás watched her carefully. "That must have been difficult to hear."

She agreed. "It's like she made him die."

Tomás considered. "She was upset. People say all kinds of crazy things when they're upset."

Theresa stared back down at the dirt. She knew that he was right; she should forgive her mother. She wasn't sure quite how to do this, but she had begun to understand that so much of being an adult was knowing how to forgive. Not just to forgive, but to separate—not to need certain outcomes from certain people. Tomás was quiet; he didn't seem to need anything. She imagined that this was worth something.

"Her life hasn't been the easiest," Theresa admitted.

Tomás nodded. "She was on her own from an early age, wasn't she?"

"Sixteen," Theresa said, though neither of them commented on the coincidence of age. Or the two deaths within a year—for each of them. But after Dollie Mae had died, Maxine had had the luxury, Theresa thought, of moving on. What little money she'd been left was in a bank in central Texas. So she had gone back, taking Ringling with her. Land outside of Austin had been cheap back then. Up the highway out of town, toward an area called Old Bull Creek, her mother had paid three hundred dollars and gotten herself nearly an acre. But after she'd paid for the land, there hadn't been enough money left over to build anything, and work was hard to find. Eventually, she'd gotten a job selling burgers at a roller skate drive-in in town. But she'd hated those roller skates—hated the five dollars a week she got paid at the diner. By then, she and Ringling were sharing a bed at a bunkhouse for a dollar a week. She'd paid another two dollars each week to the woman who owned the place so that she would keep an eye on Ringling while Maxine went out to work. She had walked, even though it was more than a mile, because the bus fare was too expensive. And all the while, that land just sitting out there.

"Not easy," Tomás agreed. He stood staring at her for several moments without speaking. He was listening—waiting. Theresa guessed he would have stayed there for several minutes more if she had felt like finishing the story. "And now you," he said finally. "You've seen so much already. A dead body even." He studied her in a way that did not make her entirely comfortable.

"We used to talk," she said, to fill the space between his thoughts. "Lawrence was good to talk to."

"I thought he was crazy."

"Only toward the end. We didn't talk as much then. Not hardly at all."

Tomás nodded, his chin coming down over the adam's apple momentarily, like he was swallowing it. "So, what did he talk about?" He shoved a hip outward, waiting for her story.

"All kinds of things," she answered. "About God and other stuff. Like he knew everything, or was predicting it or something."

"You think he planned it?" Tomás asked.

"Dying?"

"Killing himself."

Theresa considered his question. In the days and weeks before the suicide, she couldn't remember much of anything from Lawrence but silence. And kindness. There had been certain things— dishes put away, a glass of milk poured, a pot of water set to boil. He had seemed to know things, before she even knew that she wanted them. "I don't think so," she said. "I don't know. He had a lot of ideas about things." She gestured toward the empty honey hives a few yards away. "Like once, he told me about bees."

Tomás glanced in the direction she pointed. He pivoted on a heel and turned slightly to face the vacant hives: a web of netted 2 x 4s and collapsed honeycomb and thin streams of petrified honey.

"He told me how they communicate and stuff," she went on, explaining what Lawrence had told her: the distances they traveled, the careful weightlessness with which they invaded flowers, the queen sitting at home orchestrating it all, and the magical dance that substituted for language.

It's all a script, he had told her. *Thousands and thousands of bees all in the same patterns. That's why it works.*

Why what works?

Everything. Their whole lives fit together because they do what they're told.

She had stared at Lawrence in silence. He was so curious, and he seemed to know things.

We're the same, don't you think? He had turned toward her.

But she hadn't understood. *What?*

Always wanting to be with other people in the right way.

Theresa had remained silent. Lawrence was full of riddles. But she decided that she liked him; no one else talked to her that way.

Are you happy, Theresa?

She had nodded; she was eight.

He'd kept watching her, his face folding into a soft, sweet expression. *Why? What makes you happy?*

A shrug had come off her shoulders before she could stop it. She'd wanted to hear more, so she'd said the only thing she could think of: *My mom says being a priest makes you special.*

Your mother is a good woman, but she only sees the things she wants to.

Theresa had thought that was right, but she'd never heard anyone say it out loud before. *Sometime's she's nice*, she'd told him. *But sometimes she says I make her sad.*

A bee had circled up near the wire meshing. Every moment, Lawrence had said, meant something in bee language.

That's because that's the way she wants it, he'd told her.

But Theresa had still been too young to understand how parents could want impossible things from their children. She'd kept watching him, realizing that she would never really know him; he was far too full of a history that she didn't understand.

"You understand quite a lot," Tomás said, "for your age." Theresa waited, but he didn't say anything else. After another moment, she emphasized again: "He was always like that—from the beginning. Like he understood so much that other people didn't."

"Strange." Tomás leaned against the water trough, the fresh ground water channeling a mild coolness upward. She noticed the fluidity of his arms, the way his back swept upward from his waist in the shape of a cello. She sucked down a breath. "He wasn't so bad," she assured him. "I just I wish I understood it better—what happened."

Tomás turned around and yanked the hose loose, tossing it back toward the shed and pivoting the wide, smooth expanse of his rib cage and shoulder blades. There was a certain grace to him. Other men—other boys—were jauntier. A bit more edgy and proud. But Tomás was neat and careful. His movements smacked of something familiar. *Skidded palms in the gravel. The sharp bite of peroxide as he had poured it over her palms.* "It would be hard, I guess," he offered, "to lose your vocation like that. Everything you worked for."

"But that's not enough—to kill yourself over."

Tomás paused; the hose water continued slushing against the dry ground several yards away. "Probably not," he agreed, shaking his head. "No." His mouth fit itself around the shape of that last vowel, holding it just long enough for Theresa to appreciate the shape of his mouth. She shook herself. There was too much grief for anything like romance to be happening to her. Already, her head was stuffed with so much loss and mystery; there simply wasn't room for anything else.

"I'm going to find out more," she promised. "I'm going to figure out what happened to him."

Tomás considered her again, the filtered light stretching cool shapes across his figure. "I bet you will," he said. "You seem like a smart girl. Whatever it is you're looking for, I imagine you'll find it."

Maxine, 1937

There are a lot of ways to sin. Maxine knew this. Sometimes, she figured, you mean to do things, even though you know they're wrong. You want something, and you take it. You say an unkind word because the old cottonpicker deserves it. Other times, there are accidents—things you never intended—and somebody suffers. Somebody gets hurt.

"You still want to marry me, Freddy Timberlake?"

She had just found out what it took in those days for a woman to get a bank loan: a man with good credit. Maxine didn't have a father—or a brother of legal age—so she needed a husband.

"I love you, Maxine." Freddy was a small man: small body and small mind. He was a man who bought cheeseburgers for lunch at the roller skate diner and proposed to Maxine every Wednesday afternoon. He didn't seem to think too hard about things. So if he was foolish enough to marry a woman who didn't really care for him, Maxine decided that that was his misfortune.

Still, she knew it was a sin. It wasn't nice to use a man for his money; mostly, it made people unhappy, like her mother Dollie Mae. But it wasn't Freddy's money that Maxine was after—working as a clerk over at the courthouse, he didn't have much anyway. She just needed his signature. So, she figured that wasn't as bad. And the way Maxine saw it, she was doing him a favor: Freddy wasn't the kind of man who would find a woman easily. His mother, for one, wouldn't have liked it; she was a controlling old widow who suffered arthritis and rarely let Freddy out of her sight. And though Freddy did seem like a decent man—sweet-mannered and pleasant enough to be around—there was nothing remarkable about him. When he laughed, he opened his small, puckered mouth and rolled his head back. No sound came out, but his belly punched in and out like he'd just heard the funniest thing on earth. Maxine figured that marrying her was just about the most exciting thing that had ever happened to him.

Still, just to be safe, she asked God's forgiveness right off the bat: "Please God, it's for Ringling's sake that I'm doing this. Just to keep Ring out of the orphan's home." She thought a sin shouldn't count for as much if you don't really want to do it. Most of what God warned people not to do had to do with their desires about things. All she'd wanted were good things: her family, her promise to her mother. Maxine wanted to do what was right. And Freddy was a lonely man. She would be good to him, she told herself. She would try.

* * *

The first night they were married, Freddy got them a room in a little hotel outside of San Marcos. There weren't many honeymoons in those days—or weddings, for that matter. Nobody had the money. Most couples did what they had done: drive down to the Justice of the Peace and signed their names in the book.

When they went next door to the hotel, Freddy was beaming proud: "Mr. and Mrs. Timberlake here for our reservation."

But the little clerk at the hotel was unimpressed; he saw couples like the Timberlakes all the time. And Maxine wondered if he could see through them: if he knew what disasters were in store.

"Mr. Carter will show you to your room." The bellhop smiled politely, lifted their modest luggage, and placed it on the little rolling cart. Everything at the Hotel San Marcos was perfect: narrow but plush, with high ceilings and elaborate decor. Long-stemmed calla lilies pushed their way out of stiff-necked crystal vases. A dish of candied ginger sat by the small, gurgling fountain in the entryway. It was elegant, majestic. Only once before had Maxine been in a place like this, and that had been years before, in Savannah, when her father had gotten rooms for the family as a special treat. Her mother must have been tired that day; most of the nice things they used to do were for her. Not that Maxine had minded. When Dollie Mae went into one of her moods, it usually ended in something lovely, like hotel rooms. Other times there had been restaurants or trips to the theater: whatever her daddy could think of that might take his wife's mind off of her disappointing life.

But Maxine had never been as good as her mother was with fabulous things and places. The Hotel San Marcos made her feel a little self-conscious. Here she was, just married, and all she had on was a secondhand skirt and a droopy-looking blouse with a hole at the collar. Her face was plain, and she hadn't had the money to get a permanent. Freddy asked if she wanted anything—dinner? a drink?—but Maxine felt terrible: her head reeling, her stomach in knots. She couldn't think of anything that would help. "Don't waste your money," she told him, and realized that that was the worst possible answer because then they had nothing to do but follow smug Mr. Carter up to their room.

"You're sweet, Maxine," Freddy breathed. He put his arm around her carefully, like she was made of glass. Maxine stiffened, and he didn't do anything more. There was something about him, she decided, that made her think distinctly of a woman. Freddy wasn't strong—not like her Uncle Cisco or her daddy. He had no physical prowess, no integrity. He made her feel sick, the way Aunt Belle had made her sick. Weak-spirited people always did, the way they fed off of other people: the ones who had spirit and drive. Already, Maxine could look at her new husband and know that she was worth more than him.

When they reached their room, the bellhop opened the door and neatly stacked their luggage inside: one, two. Freddy's old casement suitcase and Maxine's neatly folded handbag. Then he stood there, and Freddy fished a quarter out of his pocket. "Thank you, Sir. Madam." The man bobbed his head twice and was gone.

The room was pretty: lined with wallpaper covered in fleur-de-lis and long flocked curtains in an ornate design. There were little crystal dishes sitting on small, oak tables that turned down into three carved legs at the bottom. The dishes were filled with sweet-smelling oil, or toasted almonds, or matches. A small mirror in a spectacular frame stood above the armoire. Maxine considered herself in its reflection.

But Freddy wasn't much interested in the room. "Tonight is a night we'll remember for the rest of our lives," he promised. He had a pale-faced, weak little grin; when he was sad, he wore just such an expression, though tilted downward. Then he was touching her again. Maxine stood there looking into the mirror, with Freddy behind her. He was not a large man, but standing there like that, his hand fixed over her shoulder, she thought about how tiny she looked: the man behind her, the huge, ornate frame. And all of a sudden, she wanted her mother.

Maxine still didn't know exactly what sex was. She only knew that it involved being in bed with a man, and that it ended up in the having of babies. Sometimes dead ones. She had tried to imagine what had happened between her Uncle Cisco and little Priscilla. Where had they gone? But at the corners of her mind, she knew already: He wouldn't have taken her into his tent. And there were no beds like this one: soft, clean linens tucked in neatly at the corners, so perfect you didn't want to touch them. No, Cisco had taken her on the ground, in the dirt. Theirs had been a purely physical exchange. He had kissed her, his hot, sweaty lips against hers, like Freddy's were now. Maxine thought of how Priscilla would have turned away, how she would have struggled. And her uncle with his hands all over her, calling her awful names. *Nigger. Bitch. Little black whore.*

The memory of it made her cry—for Priscilla, and for herself. She was crying, and Freddy was trying to be gentle, but he had unbuttoned Maxine's blouse, and she stood covering her chest in her arms.

"Don't," he begged. "Don't cover yourself, Maxine. Don't you know how beautiful you are?"

But she was sobbing. "Turn out the light." It was all that she could think of to cut her shame. "Turn out the light," she cried. And he did.

Then he laid her down on the bed in just her skirt and sat

himself on top. His mouth was everywhere: her neck, her breasts, her waist. She was crying still. And she felt herself going slack. This was it: the punishment for what she had done. God saw her. He saw everything: the cold night air against her skin, the black men laughing. They had known this, too: how her daddy couldn't protect her forever.

The imagination doesn't need much kindling. Maxine had read a lot. She'd learned how to read through things. There was something hard pressing against her. Insistent. Freddy's hips were aimed at her. He groaned and shuddered: *How sweet, how sweet you are, Maxine.* Her body sickened. Her heart was racing and thudding. She hated him. She hated what was happening between their two bodies. How he reminded Maxine that she was a body—and how this made her vulnerable. She didn't have space in her life for weakness. She didn't want to be a woman, and she didn't want to be married. Maxine's mind spun out: there must have been another way; she just hadn't tried hard enough to find it. She thought about Sister Alberta. Nothing, she had said, was worth this. But she hadn't been thinking about Ringling—sweet little Ringling. Nobody had. Nobody without a child of their own, Maxine thought, could understand that there truly is something worth giving yourself up for.

Now Freddy was groaning as he slapped himself against her thighs. He parted her. And parted himself inside her. There was a tearing pain. And when it was over, he fell on top of his wife and kissed her again, with those big, sick lips of his. He was still crooning: *Oh god, Maxine. Oh god, oh god. I love you.*

Afterward, Maxine washed herself out with vinegar, the way she'd heard once from Della. And then she prayed. She got down on her knees and asked God to forgive her for what had happened. Now she knew what could be taken from a woman. And she told him again that she hadn't wanted to do this. That it was just for Ringling that she had let it happen. Just for little Ringling, and couldn't he understand that? How sometimes things just had to be done? Maxine prayed that she wouldn't have a baby. She just knew it would die, like Pricilla's. Babies born out of sin would have to die like that, she thought. And then what would happen to her? Would she go crazy, like Priscilla? Maxine guessed she would; she felt halfway there already. This was her punishment, she thought. And she was so scared. *I can't go crazy*, she told God. *I just can't*. Somebody had to look out for Ringling. And she didn't trust Freddy; he was too weak. *Don't you see, God?* her mind was screaming now. *There's nobody else that can do this but me.*

But of course there was no answer, and so there was nothing else to do but lay back down along the side of the bed. She turned her back against Freddy, but he pulled her to him: "Did you like it, Maxine?"

She didn't answer him. She grabbed her skirt and pulled it over her to hide her nakedness. The room was dark. She shut her eyes.

"Maxine, I love you. Maxine?" His hands were on her again. She tried to shrug them off.

"It's sinful, Freddy."

"But you married me, Maxine."

"It's still a sin," she shook her head, sobbing again. She told him about Priscilla—about what God does when he's angry. "If God puts a dead baby in me," she snapped, "I'll know it!"

But no babies came; that was one mercy. And the other mercy was Freddy's demanding old mother. "I can't leave her," he moaned. "Not yet." Apparently, she was the jealous type. And apparently, the bills for her rheumatism medicine were alarmingly high; they didn't leave Freddy with much extra money from his paycheck. So they wouldn't be able to live together right away, he told his wife. Freddy cleaned his fingernails nervously as he explained the situation.

"But I'll work it out," he promised. "Soon, Maxine. And I'll visit you. Don't worry."

But Maxine just shrugged, gathering up her things so. "Don't trouble yourself on my account, Freddy."

And truly, all those years later, she still wished he never had.

Lawrence, 1948

Lawrence was too young to understand all that he saw, but he saw plenty: friction between the Williams, catching and slipping like sputtering gears. Some days were good. They went out together, the four of them—Lawrence and Gerald and Mrs. Williams and her charming brother Ringling—to a movie, or ice cream shop, or park. But other days there were arguments. Fights that never resolved. Gerald made all the decisions; he ran the house as a man should. But Mrs. Williams, Lawrence learned, was a woman who couldn't sit still; she didn't have the patience or concentration for sweeping every speck from the kitchen floor, or planning out a week of hearty meals for her family. But neither was she a busy woman. There were times when he found her sitting blankly, staring at the wall. There were days she didn't get out of bed at all.

"It isn't right," she said absently one day, not exactly to him. They were alone—Ringling at the baseball diamond, Gerald in San Bernardino for his weekend with the Reserves. By then Lawrence was growing used to Mrs. Williams' moods: the times she talked to herself out loud and hardly noticed him. He watched her carefully. Was he supposed to say something in return?

But she just shook her head, the hair pinned back in a roll as it always was, though not quite as neatly that day as it was when Gerald was home. "Lord," she pulled one of her husband's cigarettes out of an apron pocket and put it to her lips. The last time she'd had one, Gerald had smelled it on her breath and scolded her in their bedroom for nearly an hour. She picked at the white rim of the paper, rolled the thing back and forth between her fingertips. Then she turned to him: "Lawrence, what do you think? Shouldn't we hire a girl to keep house? It wouldn't be so hard." Now she bent to light the cigarette. She held it, burning, between her fingers for a moment. "I could get a job, you know, to pay for it. You and Ringling help out good with some things, and we could get someone to come cook and clean." She took one long sip on the cigarette, blew it out, and looked at the boy, almost accusingly. "Do you know how much I made down at the shipyards during the war?"

Lawrence shook his head.

"Twenty a week. Twenty a week!" She took in another drag.

He stood silent; his stomach grumbled. When Lawrence stayed home alone with Mrs. Williams, they often forgot to eat. He stared dumbly at the roasting edge of the cigarette, the brightness eating away at the paper, the way, holding something sweet in your mouth long enough, you can feel the little crystals of sugar spill out like sand.

"You don't care, do you?" she watched the boy narrowly, sucking in again and spitting out the smoke like a bad egg. "Don't you care what happens to you?"

He shrugged his shoulders, confused.

"Well," she said, "if I were to go to work, I wouldn't be here to look after you kids. Ringling is used to it. He's older, and that's what we had to do, anyway, during the war."

Lawrence put the palm of his hand against the rock where she was sitting. It was pleasantly warm, with the slight granite cool below. Around them, the small, square lawn behind the Williams' home rustled high and green in the low wind.

"I'm okay," he told her.

"Gerald doesn't think you are. He thinks you're too used to all the attention those other people gave you."

Lawrence shrugged again.

"You liked them, didn't you? You were happy there."

It wasn't even really a question. But Mrs. Williams looked so miserable, he didn't want to make her feel any worse. "I like it here, too."

She smirked, pinched out the cigarette against the rock, and tossed it into the unmown lawn. "Well, at least you're smart, Lawrence. You'll be all right." Mrs. Williams slouched backward, looking up into the sky: wide, blue, and unbroken. Weather in the valley was stagnant, uninteresting. "What women do," she announced after another moment, "is take care of people. I was never very good at that." She looked down at the boy, a bit expectant.

"That's okay."

Then she leaned back again, open hands against the rock. "My mother wasn't very good at it, either," she paused. "So there you have it. I'm a good promoter. Even had my own bar back in Austin. Built it myself, up on Old Bull Creek Road. We called it Bella Vista, on account of the view." She traced the little charred circle on the rock where she had stabbed out her cigarette, but didn't say anymore. There were many things about her past that Mrs. Williams didn't fully explain—so many things about her that Lawrence would never fully understand.

"Anyway," she continued, straightening. "I can keep things going in a business sense, but don't come running to me with your nightmares and bloody knees. I don't barely know a bandage from a fruitcake."

He told her again that that was all right. Then he asked: "Mrs. Williams, did you know the Wells?"

"I met them once. They're good people."

Lawrence supposed they were, and he supposed he loved them still. But even so, the world had grown confusing so quickly: the people who had loved him most had kept him for the wrong reasons, and the people who treated him right didn't really seem to want him.

"They were good to you, weren't they?" she asked. "Don't you want to go back to them? Don't you want Gerald to let you go back?"

The boy nodded; he didn't feel very good at the game they were playing.

"See, of course you do. And you could go back and grow up with them. They loved you so much, Lawrence."

And that is how he understood that Mrs. Williams did not love him. That she could not. Lawrence made her sad, though he didn't know why. He thought she seemed as lost in life as he was.

* * *

What held Mrs. Williams in life at that time was the Catholic Church. Going to mass was a habit that she had picked up during the war, and it had stayed with her; the mass was one thing that she could do apart from her husband. So she took Lawrence and Ring-ling to Holy Cross parish each Sunday. When they were there, she seemed sorry for things, Lawrence thought—big things—though she never said exactly what. She was an earnest participant: nodding along with the hymns, bowing her head low, and breathing roughly through her nose in concentrated excitement. She was such a small woman to begin with that when she knelt and bowed her head, she became like an infant, tiny and curved. Like a pinto bean. He thought sometimes, watching her tremble with the emotion of the thing, that she might just keep growing smaller and smaller until she vanished under the weight of God's thumb.

Faith in this way was a little bit frightening, but there was something in it that Lawrence liked: a kind of security. The guarantee that, if you listened hard enough, someone would tell you whatever it was you had to do. But when he asked, no one knew the exact translation of what was being said at mass, though Mrs. Williams assured him that it was something important and holy: the word of God. Lawrence was fascinated with this new riddle of religion—a God who spoke his own private language. Later, he learned that there was a name for God's language: Latin. But that information didn't turn out to clarify much because, the nuns at Holy Cross Elementary explained, it was a dead language: the source from which all other words sprung. So Lawrence began to imagine the speech of the dead—spiritual and ghostly. And words everywhere began to sound strange and wonderful. Latin words. English words. Spanish spoken on the bus. Lawrence wondered what made different people choose a language. And why one set of sounds meant something while another did not. He wondered why God had made things so complicated. Why couldn't Lawrence understand the immigrants in Chinatown, or the Catholic mass, or his own origin, like a word whose history cannot be traced to anything?

The other question was the mystery of the choir. Everyone in the congregation was silent. At the altar, the priest and his assistants walked carefully through the mass, partly obscured by a slim velvet curtain that fell to the ground from a railing perched several feet in the air. Intermittently, they heard a second group of voices: the thick, slow tones of the priests, and then a high, careful one responding. *Angels*, he thought. *They must be angels.*

But Mrs. Williams told him otherwise. They were boys, she said, just like him. "Altar boys," she explained. They were good, special boys; God had picked them out himself.

This, however, Lawrence could not believe. He looked around himself at the boys in school and Ringling's friends at the baseball diamond: all of them loud and dusty-kneed and ill-mannered. How could these be the same sweet voices that haunted the vaulted church? That sent chills into the tips of his fingers as he sat dumbly beside Mrs. Williams at mass?

To Lawrence's good fortune, Ringling was well acquainted with the small disobediences of boyhood: switching street signs and skipping class and letting dogs out of their yards without getting caught. So they left the house early one Sunday to attend the seven o'clock mass, sneaking past Mrs. Williams and the smell of burnt batter coming from the kitchen. When they arrived at Holy Cross, Ringling pulled Lawrence with him toward the front of the church, to the narrower line of pews on the left-hand side. From there, they had a better view of the church altar: a plain ivory table spread with a green silk cloth. Behind, the tabernacle, decorated with a bright golden cross, waited patiently; and further back, a flocked curtain marked the entrance to the mysterious chambers of the sacristan. As the priest approached, Lawrence felt his ears go hot, then his mouth and cheeks and neck; it was like seeing the inside of a play: all the theatrics that normal people had no access to. After another moment, a small boy entered from the side of the sanctuary and rang a little set of golden-colored bells. They tinkled quick and neat against the heavy silence of the church, and then he placed them on a red velvet pillow to cut the sound. Ringling elbowed Lawrence as ten or twelve other altar boys filed out, some of them carrying books or little boxes of incense holders, all of them dressed in plain white robes cinched neatly at their middle with a dangling cord. And these were indeed the same boys that Lawrence knew from school. There was Matt McGregor and Steven Hillsboro. And Cal Winston. On the playground, they were raucous and uncouth. But here, they opened their mouths together and a simple, chime-like song spilled out: three lines sung over and over until one of them raised again the little golden bells and tinkled them into silence. Lawrence felt something shift inside himself. He wanted to be part of it: those voices, all working as one, repeating hymns that no one else understood.

And that's when it happened: in the boys' silver-throated song, in the repeated call and answer of the priests. Suddenly, Lawrence understood. Not the words themselves, but their larger message: *You could do this.* He heard it through the spaces between notes, in the strange half tones and the click-clack clanging of the bells. *You can do this,* it came again. *You might do even better.* Like the Wells had told him so many times. Whatever they didn't like about the world—war, politics, corruption. *You're better than this, Lawrence.* These men drowning themselves in war, governments throwing armies together like dice. *You, Lawrence, are something set apart.*

He waited for more. He hoped for an explanation, but there was none. After the service, Ringling took him out for ice cream with a quarter he'd gotten from Gerald. He asked how Lawrence had liked seeing the altar boys. "Nothing to it, huh?" he grinned.

"Yeah," Lawrence nodded. "Boys just like us." Though he didn't tell Ringling what had happened—what he'd heard and what that meant. Once again, his life had shifted unalterably. Like Gerald's war photographs and his memories of a family that had loved him more than anything, Lawrence was haunted now by another kind of history that would not let him go.

Theresa, June 1979

"Did you sleep well?"

The next morning when Theresa came downstairs, her mother was fully dressed. She stood in the kitchen, making eggs and frozen sausage links. Her metal spoon clattered against the skillet in a quick scatter of sound. Cheerful. "Sure." Theresa watched her mother carefully, as she scraped a portion of the food onto a plate.

"Good," Maxine answered brightly. Then she announced, "I'm going out," pulling off her apron and letting it slump over the back of a chair. Theresa stared at the plate of food in front of her. Her mother hadn't gone anywhere in more than a week, not since the incident with Lawrence. Now she stood smartly in the middle of the kitchen, dressed in a fitted jacket, an A-line skirt, and pumps. She dipped her hand into a pocket and the car keys jangled.

"Where are you going?"

"Oh, here and there. I called the principal at St. Ann's this morning. She thinks you're smart." Maxine left the comment hanging there in the air, as though Theresa should corroborate it somehow. "She says you can finish your school work from home for the rest of the year."

"It's only two more weeks." Theresa had no intention of going back to that school where prim girls in checkered skirts—even the ones whom she had once claimed as friends—watched her uncomfortably from the corners of hallways, forcing smiles and holding their books tightly to their chests. *They treat me like something broken*, she had told her mother. Ever since Theresa's father had died, her peers had had little idea of how to act around her. The thing with Lawrence, she knew, would only make things worse. And her mother did not argue; this was one detail of her daughter's life that she seemed to understand.

"It's good they know you're smart—that you can finish up on your own."

Theresa gathered a forkful of eggs. "Like Lawrence," she offered. "He was good in school, too."

Her mother's fingers stopped smoothing the plastic tablecloth. She reached over and grabbed Theresa's wrist. "Don't you *say* that," she demanded. "Why would you say that?"

The fork clapped against her plate. "Because it's true." She looked up, confused. "He was good at school, wasn't he? When he was a boy? You told me that."

Her mother's fingers loosened, but her voice remained urgent. "Theresa, I don't want you to be thinking like that. It's not the same. He was different. He wasn't like you."

"All right," Theresa eased herself away from her mother's grip. "Ok—I'm not like Lawrence."

Maxine's head bobbed lightly. "That's right, Theresa. You aren't anything like him."

She watched her mother loop out of the kitchen doorway and listened to that familiar, non-linear flurry through the hallway and living room to the front door as her mother stopped here and there to check her face in the mirror or straighten her dress. For such a small person, Maxine Williams was gifted at taking up space. When the front door latched behind her, Theresa sat up straighter, looking down at her eggs: mealy and over-cooked. She pushed at them with her fork, then got up to make herself a piece of toast. Whether her mother would be back that afternoon or the next, she didn't know. But almost certainly, it would take awhile. These sudden, unexplained excursions nearly always did. Theresa imagined her mother driving up the coast on 101, the windows of the station wagon rolled down in a rush of briny air. She would be chasing the sunset; she would be clearing her thoughts. More often than not, she would return long hours—even days—later, bearing gifts or stories or strange artifacts from another time and place. Once, during the summer that Theresa had turned eight, her mother had come home with a bar and cabling that she ordered two of her sons to string up in the back yard. She had decided that all of her children should learn trapeze. And the boys had been good at it. Muscular like their father, they'd swung easily from the bar, tossing themselves zealously into the pile of hay bales they'd set up a few feet away. *See? You're natural performers*, their mother had clapped her hands. She was telling them stories about the tricks she used to do on her father's show—bird's nest, double traps, two-legged Russian roll— all the things she would teach them how to do. *It's so easy*, she had promised, *because you've got it in your blood*.

But Theresa had proved the theory wrong: she wasn't a natural. The bar was too big around in her stubby fingers. She hadn't been able to lift herself—to find any kind of momentum.

Oh, don't worry, Theresa. It's easy. Her mother had stood behind her, holding her torso to swivel it back and forth. *Like this. Can't you feel that?*

But all that Theresa had felt was stuck dangling there in the air. Why did her mother insist on this? Her body ached; she had wanted the lesson to end. Then her mother had pressed back against the bar for momentum and given her daughter one final push, and Theresa had let go the bar, relieved, and plunged down onto the hard-packed dirt. Her mother had screamed: *Theresa!* And her hands had gone to her mouth. *Why did you let go?*

Theresa had looked dumbly up at her. What could she have said? It never worked to tell her mother when something was impossible.

* * *

Once she was certain that her mother had gone, Theresa got up and looped behind the kitchen to Lawrence's room. She opened bureau drawers, checked beneath the mattress and along the top shelves of the closet. But there was nothing left: no speck of paper left in a drawer, no stray shoe box lying in the closet. So instead, she went upstairs to check her parents' room: her father's pipe tobacco, the rough leather of his work boots, a faint hint of sweat. They were all still there, the small odors of his life, months after his death. She pulled boxes from the closet, filled with letters from the war. Mementos and old clothes. But nothing that related to Lawrence. No certificates suggesting his origin. Finally, she went outside and curled back around toward the shed. The house loomed large and stocky: few decorations except for elaborate gabled details along the top. She thought again of the ephemeral sea captain and how curious it was that the top stories had been so artfully attended to, while the bottom sections were forgotten, as though he really had expected them to remain submerged.

"What are you looking for?"

"Tomás!" her head jerked upward, startled.

He flipped on the switch by the doorway. A low light buzzed on. Theresa raised a hand to her forehead. "Is my mother still gone? Is the car there?"

He looked at her curiously, setting down his motorcycle helmet and a bag from the auto shop store in town. "No," he said. "Nobody's here."

Theresa sighed, shoving back onto her haunches. All around her, a splay of objects scattered the floor: more plastic-sealed boxes of war letters and photographs. She had uncovered boxes of hoses, popcorn makers, and used cameras, their blind eyes staring upward. But nothing, it seemed, that related to Lawrence.

"Find anything good?"

"Not much." She clasped her fingers more tightly over her thighs. There was nothing, it appeared—not in the house, not out back in the shed—that could tell her anything more about their strange visitor or his unfortunate decline. No letter or clue to help her straighten out the story in her own head. Nothing to grant her some kind of definitive closure.

"What's this?" Tomás came toward her, picking up a metal rod that Theresa had set beside one of the boxes.

"Just something that I want to get rid of."

Tomás picked it up: a thick metal rod about a yard long with a bit of cable wrapped around it. "What is it?"

"A trapeze bar," she answered, getting to her feet. She clapped the cold from her fingers and moved toward the door. Despite the hot day, the concrete floor of the shed had chilled her. She squinted into the sun, expectant.

Tomás waited, but she didn't explain anything more. He watched her standing in the doorway, tilting his head in the mildly charming manner of his that she was becoming used to. "You're interesting, Theresa Williams."

Tomás took the trapeze bar and the bag of auto parts with him and followed her back out into the yard. He stopped by the side of the sporty Mazda car. "Trapeze," he said, sliding his hands along the bar.

"We set it up over there." She pointed to the sturdy sycamore tree a few paces beyond the shed.

"The circus reborn," he grinned.

"Pretty much." And she explained her mother's insistent coaching, their failed attempt at the trapeze. Despite moments like those, though, her mother could be generous when she wanted to. With strangers, her mother would often brag about her, exaggerating Theresa's accomplishments until her stories sounded like another person entirely: someone strong and resolute, a girl that Theresa could never imagine becoming. But with her mother, these things had seemed possible: her future career as an equestrian, or a violinist, or an acrobat. *We're going to get her the most fabulous costume*, she had once told a woman on a bus coming into Berkeley. *I saw it in a magazine advertisement: a blue-sequined leotard with a matching head piece. Very classic. And Theresa looks so nice in blue.* Theresa hadn't seen the picture—if there really had been one—but she had understood instantly just what it must have looked like: trim and bright and glittering. It would make her beautiful, she felt sure. It would keep her mother loving her forever.

Tomás squeezed the bar again. He tested its weight and wrapped his long fingers around it. Stretched around the trapeze bar like that, his hands seemed quite broad, almost out of proportion with the rest of him. "You were eight," he considered the bar. "What did she expect?"

Theresa laid her elbows up against the roof of the car, stretching herself out in the sun. Despite its warmth, the faintest chill ran through her. "My mother grew up doing tricks like that. She doesn't remember what it took to learn them."

Tomás nodded, dropping the bar and the bag of auto supplies onto the ground and jimmying open the tired hood of Nathan's old sports coup—the Mazda Z model that he had driven wildly up and down the county roads until he got married. Tomás whistled mildly, toggling the keys in the ignition to get power. Once the radio shuddered on, he wound the dial until it clicked onto a station that spat out some kind of accordion-heavy music with a strong, regular beat that Theresa understood was Mexican. Tomás whistled and whistled, checking the power on the dashboard and coming back around to consider the engine. After another few moments, he asked, "Where'd your mom go?" He leaned back against the frame of the car, pulling a small bag of pistachio nuts out of his front pocket. Then he squeezed one between two fingers, emptied the meat in his mouth, and tossed away its bone-like shell in one neat gesture.

Theresa watched him, shrugging casually at his question. Long before she had been born, her mother had stopped pretending that she could be a good housewife. Organizing kitchen shelves, frying chicken with a certain finesse, ironing sharp folds into her husband's shirts: these simply were not Maxine's specialties. She belonged to the world instead. So they had left whenever they could: taking trips down to San Francisco to buy Gerald's pipe tobacco or choosing the long bus route back from Sacramento, just to take in the scenery. Once, when Theresa was five, she and her mother got into the car and drove all the way to Canada. Maxine had had two hundred dollars in her pocket; they were gone three weeks, sleeping at highway rest stops and campgrounds and church parking lots. For the Williams girls, this was normal. Most often, their adventures were sudden and directionless; Theresa never knew exactly what had inspired them. When they came back home, her brothers pouted; they had stayed home, in school. But she had still been young, so her mother had taken her along. It was the best evidence of affection that Theresa ever got.

"She's probably at the bank or something," she suggested. "Trying to keep them from selling the house." This was possible, she knew, and the thought left her feeling reckless. Tomás was cracking open another pistachio, the trapeze bar still angled loosely at his feet. "What's the worst thing that ever happened to you?" she wanted to know.

He ran a finger along the dusty rim of the car's headlight. He did not hesitate. "My father died, too. He had a heart attack when I was nine years old. I remember him less and less." He looked at her meaningfully, extending the bag of pistachios. She took her time cracking one open, the startlingly colorful flesh rolling salty against her tongue. Oddly, she found she had nothing to say. She felt she *should* have had something to say, as one half-orphaned person to another. But it seemed so different: what had happened to Tomás, what had happened to her. His story was like a distant flash. A camera snap from years ago. She pulled the trapeze bar back up off the ground and rolled it between the flats of her hands. "What do you know about him?"

"He was an engineer—a pretty good one, actually. He came from a good family. But when things go bad here, they're even worse in Mexico." He paused, cracked open another pistachio. The green and purple sheen held her attention for just a moment. "He came up here in the forties, after the war started. America was recruiting. There were so many soldiers leaving, they needed somebody to take their place."

"He came to work."

Tomás nodded, the dark curls at the nape of his neck faintly damp from the heat of the day. "But not like you think of it now." His voice sounded mildly bruised. He had told this story before, she imagined, in less sympathetic company. "It was legal. He had a desk job. He married an American." Tomás shoved the pistachios back into his shirt pocket, turned, and pressed his palms over the frame of the Z car, locking his elbows.

"And that was worse," she pressed, "than what happened with your brother?"

Tomás bowed his head over the engine. His shape, arced like that over the yawning mouth of Nathan's old car, was elegant in a way that she had tried not to notice. "It's worse when you're young.

You need more." He pulled his gaze back up to meet hers, "The first one's always the hardest."

She stood silent, filtering the sensations of salt and guilt against her tongue. It was Lawrence who troubled her most. With her father, the agony had been clear and profound: a terrible ocean of grief so pervasive that, for a while, she really had believed that she might lose herself. Except that her mother's suffering had waxed louder and more bold. At least one of them, Theresa had decided, had to keep herself pulled together; and so she had. But with Lawrence, things felt different. Unresolved. Fractured in a way that wholly did not make sense. She turned the trapeze bar over in her hands. "I don't know if my mother is going to recover."

"It hasn't been very long yet," he reminded her. "She'll get better. Don't worry."

"You don't know her." Theresa tapped the bar against the metal disc of a hubcap. "She's stubborn."

"People have their limits," he insisted. "Even with grief."

The bar clattered again more loudly against the frame of the Z car; she let it go. "My mother doesn't forget things," she told him, "when she doesn't want to." After her failure with the trapeze, Theresa had felt ashamed, but she'd kept listening to her mother. There was still the promise of the blue-sequined leotard; there was still the chance of becoming beautiful. And Maxine, for her part, had decided that the boys could have the trapeze; she would train Theresa, instead, for high-wire performance.

"Tight rope?" Tomás's eyebrows knit carefully upward. He crossed his arms over his chest in attention, pulling the fabric of his shirt neatly at the shoulder seams. Even working there in the yard, he wore shirts that fit him precisely, tucked neatly in at the waist, his belt a soft leather strip with wide, metal eyelets that stretched smoothly around his middle. His presence standing there, waiting for more of her story, made her conscious of her own image: flushed cheeks, the hastily bound ponytail, a thin cotton seersucker, and jeans that had recently gone pleasantly snug through the hips and thighs.

"We practiced over there," she gestured toward a patch of hard-packed dirt and shade that ran several yards along the rear of the house, feeling the slip of her hair swing upward with the movement. "It's wasn't too hard at first," she explained. "You just lay out the cable and practice following it with your feet, over and over. Until it feels like a part of you."

"A high-wire girl," Tomás's expression cracked into a grin, his hand tented across his eyes so she couldn't tell quite what he was thinking.

"But it didn't work," she shook her head. "It was all right at the beginning, when she had it up only a few inches. Slack wire," she said. "So it bowed down in the middle; it was easy. But then she took it up higher, I couldn't do it."

The hand fell away from Tomás's brows, and Theresa saw something like sympathy painted there. *I just don't understand!* her mother had finally wailed after the failed acrobatics training. *It's like you aren't even my daughter!* And Theresa hadn't been sure what that was supposed to mean, but it had made her feel bad enough to die. She wasn't ever going to be a circus performer. She wouldn't get the lights and costumes and applause. She wasn't going to be beautiful like her mother and grandmother. There was something wrong with her. Some internal lack of balance. It beat against her blood.

Tomás tilted his head thoughtfully, "She's a challenge, your mother." He ran his fingers through his dark hair so that it shifted slightly against his brow. Boyish. Around them, the June heat pressed in almost palpably.

"She wants things that don't made sense," Theresa agreed. "She always has."

Maxine, 1937–8

Much of Maxine's life hadn't made sense up until then, so she didn't worry too much over the fact that she was married now. Or that her husband stayed in town with his clerk job and his mother while she moved up Old Bull Creek Road to build her bar. During the Depression, life was big and hard to manage; most of them left romance to the movies anyway.

Once she got her bank loan—Freddy's signature neatly, dutifully scribbled next to hers—she was busy every day running supplies up to Bella Vista. The loan was modest, so she had to be careful. Anything she could do on her own, she did: building tables and chairs, painting signs, and putting in a garden. The man that she contracted to help with the building itself did things on the cheap. The boys he hired were young and quiet, but he got them working. Most of them came from the charcoal burning families further up the road. They were squatters and vagrants—people with lives worse, even, than an orphaned circus girl's. So, within a matter of days, she had a pit boss and a work crew of squirrelly teenage boys out pouring concrete for the foundation, raising beams, and hammering in supports. And not too long after that, she got some company that she hadn't been expecting.

"I'm called John," the girl said, one knee pushed forward and her soot-stained fingers stamped across it. "I come to work."

Maxine stared. John was a skinny little muscle of a girl. Young. All sinew and bone. Not a lick of hip on her yet, and tiny little breasts that didn't look like they were going anywhere too fast. She was so scrawny and little, Maxine didn't know how she could even pick up a hammer. "What kind of qualifications you got?"

"I ain't lazy."

Maxine laughed; that much, she supposed, she could believe. The girl's clothes were near threadbare, but she was clean and neat. She wore a mealy looking hat over a pageboy cut tucked behind her ears. Her eyes flicked up toward the workmen. "If I was a man, I'd have a job like that. With a company," she said. "But I ain't. So you can have me."

She was direct and fearless, and Maxine liked her immediately. "But I haven't got any money to pay you."

She shrugged. "You will."

Maxine looked her over again. John wore oversized men's pants and undershirts, and steel-tipped work boots stuffed with batting at the toe to make them fit. She kept her hair tidy, and her face was thin but well-shaped, with freckles like a Bartlett pear. Her teeth cut short, like little white eraser stubs that never came in fully, and she got ruddy from outside work but never fully tanned. She was pretty—or would be, one day—and she had a loose way with her body: moving like water, so you were never sure if she was staying or going.

But John stayed. After a few days, she didn't even bother going home at night anymore. "What about your family?" Maxine insisted.

"They won't miss me."

But Maxine was a girl on her own, too; she knew that there were limits to things. "Or friends?"

"Naw," she shook her head. "It don't matter."

"What about school?"

That question made John real quiet—which for her was a chore because she was so unconversational already. "They don't want me at that school no more."

It was the first time that Maxine had seen anything like fear in her. "All right," she decided. "Don't worry. As long as you want, you can stay here with me."

So they set to work together building the little caretaker cabin alongside the bar where they would live for the next several years. They grubbed stumps and put in a garden and painted signs and generally brought the place to life. John was only twelve years old, but Maxine had to admit that she was a strong worker. She never complained, and she was up working most mornings before Maxine herself was out of bed. "I don't care what they say about your age, John," she told her new partner. "Once we get this place running, you're gonna be my best bartender. A real top kick."

John let the compliment roll off her shoulders, the way she did most things. "Most people don't think a girl like me is good for much," she said. Maxine waited, but that was all. Throughout those years that Maxine knew her, John always did have a funny way of starting statements and leaving them unfinished.

* * *

With John there, Maxine found it much easier to manage Freddy, who did come up on occasion. She still kept the little bottle of vinegar by her bedside, although it was hardly necessary anymore. He felt awkward with a child around, he said. And, most of the time, he was too sullen and antsy anyway. His mother's demands were getting him down; mostly, he came up to talk. But Freddy's bad luck in life didn't impress Maxine. She supposed a better wife would have had some more sympathy. But she was busy getting her business started, and, so far, life hadn't been easy for her, either.

"I don't get it, Freddy. If you're so unhappy, why don't you just leave her?"

"Oh, I couldn't, Maxine." He tilted his head down and shook it, quick and furious. "Her health, you know. She needs me."

Maxine figured that Freddy must like feeling needed; it was, perhaps, the one thing in life that made him feel important.

"But you're not even living, Freddy."

"Oh," his body shook, silent and hard, like when he laughed, "I know, I know. You're right, Maxine."

"She'd be fine, Freddy. Believe me."

He raised his head. "How do you know?"

"Because she's got a mean streak," she snapped. "Mean people always know how to take care of themselves." She knew it was a terrible thing to say, but other people's weakness made Maxine short-tempered. That was always the way it was between her and Freddy.

John was no fool: "You don't much like your husband, do you?"

"He's more in love with his mother than he is with me."

John gave that some thought; even for a charcoal burner, there were limits. But John was easy-mannered and, in her way, broad-minded. "S'pose he's not so bad as men go," she said. "At least he doesn't sass. I hate a man that sasses."

She was right, Maxine admitted; Freddy wasn't all that bad. But still, she didn't like him. He was monotonous; he never had anything new to say or to be excited about. And nothing that he promised would happen ever did. They'd been married half a year, and his mother still didn't know. That promotion he always talked about at work never came. If Maxine had been a more anxious bride, waiting for their new life to begin, she figured she would have left him by then.

"He's spineless," she told John.

"What's that mean, exactly?"

"He doesn't have any ideas of his own."

John shrugged. "Well, at least you won't be having no fights. Man like that don't know how to say 'boo' to a woman."

Maxine nodded. John was young, but she knew some things; Maxine had to give her that. One afternoon some days later, she stood abruptly, squinting into the sun. "Boys can fight," she said, "but girls cain't." As usual, John's observations came without much warning or explanation. They were leveling the garden, and she'd stopped for a moment to watch the work crew, shadowboxing during one of their breaks.

"Why I can't go back to school no more," she said, and then bent back over her hoe.

Maxine waited.

"Taught 'em a lesson, though," she grunted, pulling up a weed.

That was John: fewest words that Maxine ever heard come out of a woman. After another minute, she asked her why.

"Tried to steal my knickers."

Maxine stared at John; there was plenty already that had happened in her small life, but Maxine hadn't ever been hurt by some-body outright. She watched John for another moment and wondered what else there was about the girl that she didn't yet understand. But mostly, Maxine would have to guess at things because John didn't say much. And in the nearly four years they lived together out at Bella Vista, they didn't have many philosophical discussions, but Maxine knew where her young friend stood: most people in life will hurt you if you let them. The best you can do is find somebody like you and stick by them. And the person John had picked, Maxine understood, was her.

* * *

Bella Vista was a white-washed pole barn with matching shut-ters and two stubby steps leading up to the front door. The floor was unfinished—covered with sawdust—and the tables and stools were handmade and wobbly. Maxine rented a jukebox from a company down in town, the ice man fronted them the first week's product, and beer came on consignment. They weren't what you'd call busy, but they drew enough business to pay their bills and eat and keep up Ringling's tuition down at the school. Most of their custom-ers were men from the dam project up at Bastrop, or C-core boys who were out building trails and planting sign posts in the state park nearby. But they got other folks, too: people who came up from town on the weekends to swim at the lake or take in the view. When there were enough of them, they pushed back the tables and stools and turned to dancing. Those were nights that Maxine loved, twisting her feet to the Charleston or Lindyhop. But John never joined in; she was athletic, but not terribly social. Most nights she kept behind the bar, cracking open bottles of beer and making sure the boys paid their nickels.

Still, even with her short haircut and men's clothing, John was becoming a beauty: those dark eyes of hers sunk deeper into their sockets as time went on, her cheekbones rose up like well-planned architecture, and a pair of pouty lips filled in more and more, taking on a certain shine. She didn't wiggle her hips or bat her eyes that way most of the girls did, but that didn't keep the men off her any less. They were in love with her; they were entranced.

Pete Whittier was the one who liked her best. He came from one of the better families in Austin. *A real humdinger*, Maxine said. She could tell: *He dresses up and talks so nice.* And he was handsome, too, the way boys with money can be: pale and sharply dressed. He was no laborer, but still he cut a fine shape as he passed through a doorway or slipped off his shirt for races down at the lake. John was the fastest swimmer there was; no one could beat her. Slim Pete was the only one who even came close. Once, he swore he'd reached the finish line first, but John denied it. His pack of friends drove off that night hollering all the way back to Austin, and by the next evening, they all knew about it.

"John! What on God's green earth are you doing?" A crashing sound had come from the bar. Maxine had looked over, and there was John, leaned over with a broken beer bottle in her hand, holding off a pack of three or four boys.

She looked back, furious and wild: "That one tried ta kiss me!"

Pete stood a few feet away, looking amused. "Aw, come on now, John. You owe me, and you know it. I beat you fair and square."

John raised the bottle and flung it across the room. "Liar!" she screamed, and that glass shattered against the far wall behind Pete. She picked up another bottle and held it ready.

"John!" Maxine bolted toward her. "Stop it, now. Come on, John—that's just what boys do."

"Certainly," Pete said, venturing a step toward us. "Specially on account of pretty ladies like you."

John raised the bottle again, looking fierce. "He's lying," she snarled. "I ain't no lady."

"Sure you are, John. You're about the prettiest girl in here, if you'd just get that scowl off your face."

John twisted her wrist and flung another beer bottle at the boys—Pabst Blue Ribbon fizzed across the back wall. "John!" Maxine screamed again. "That's enough!"

Somebody pulled the cord on the juke box, and from the back of the room, Maxine heard the loud screech of bar stool legs as a man got to his feet. "Ladies!" he called, clearing out from the table and making his way through the crowd. "Let's just hold on here a minute." The man coming toward them was tall, dark-haired, and self-assured. Older than most of the boys there by at least a couple of years. But Maxine didn't like the idea of some handsome stranger taking control. "I don't need your help, sir. I know how to run my own bar."

The man looked her over; then his eyes flickered briefly between John—her bottle still raised—and Pete's group of friends, standing quietly at his sides, their mouths twisting with amusement. "On the contrary, Miss. It appears you do."

Maxine turned back for a moment. *Williams*, she thought. That was his name. He was a leader of one of the C-core crews: a polished, broad-shouldered man who always rode a silver-colored stallion. When he spoke, his voice was commanding. "Pete," he belted, and Peter blinked. Maxine couldn't guess how the two men would have known each other, running in such different crowds as they did, but Pete Whittier listened. "You let up on that young lady," Gerald Williams commanded. Then he bent over and whispered something into Peter's ear. Pete stood awkwardly for a moment and threw another glance at John. "All in good sport," he shrugged, and shuffled off. After that, they didn't have any more problems on account of John. But neither did Gerald Williams say anything else to them that night. He was just about as quiet as they came: sitting calmly in a corner drinking his beer and keeping a watch on his boys.

"You love him," John whispered later on that evening. She had the habit of stating obvious facts about life that otherwise shouldn't have been mentioned.

"No," Maxine shook her head. "I'm married."

"But you don't love your husband."

"That's different." Maxine insisted, flickering another glance over at Gerald Williams, who was tossing the last of a Pabst Blue Ribbon down the thick column of his throat. He set the bottle back down on the table and continued to watch the crowd, which was just picking up into a lilting Jitterbug Stroll. "It doesn't matter." The truth was, now that Maxine had her bar, she didn't want to be married to anybody. Not ever. And this was one thing that John could understand.

"Woman don't need no man," she said. And Maxine nodded slightly, feeling the electric lick of her spine tell her something different: something that she'd never expected to feel at all. Not after Freddy. Not after what she had learned could happen between a man and a woman, and how awful it could be.

"No," she shook her head emphatically. "Not these two, anyway, John. Not you and me."

Lawrence, 1950–52

Lawrence waited until he was just ten years old before announcing his call to the priesthood. By then he had stood two solemn years behind the velvet curtain with the other altar boys, shifting hymnals and ringing bells, answering incantations in a language that none of them understood: *dominus-in spiritum-benedictum*. In this way, it was a slow accumulation: this movement toward his life's work. But by the end of those two years, Lawrence felt sure. He had watched the priests with an aching sense of longing. All their secrets were slowly becoming his: what they did while the congregation rose and fell, skittering along in their hymnbooks, feigning translations. The raised host, the crack of wafer, the promises made on quivering lips. Words repeated for centuries. Over and over. Until it didn't matter anymore, the precise meanings of things.

Gerald was looking over a pile of slate-blue papers, real estate forms, marked in red ink. Two days earlier, he'd made an offer on a house—the first that the Williams hoped to own themselves. He held a glass of iced gin in his thick hand. "Now, how do you figure that?"

"Because God called me," the boy answered. "I'm called."

"He called you?" Gerald was still fingering morosely through the forms, as though looking for some kind of specific revelation.

Lawrence nodded. "Yessir."

"How?"

"In church."

He shifted the slow liquid in the glass, considering. "Listen, boy," he said carefully. "You don't want a life like that. Wouldn't be much different from the army. I'm telling you. You don't want a bunch of men like that telling you what to think and do."

The boy paused to consider: the church worked liked a clock, tipping its spheres of time toward feast days or the celebrations of saints. The rhythms of ritual did not change; they were constant as the gentle click of gears spinning out across time. It was a pattern that Lawrence admired: it was something consistent and real. At home, their lives were different. Gerald fell headlong into his work, still trying to forget the war. Ringling had started high school; he was chasing a new girl each week. Even Mrs. Williams was rarely home; she had finally gotten herself a job as a camera girl down at a nightclub in San Francisco. In the mornings, she slept long, and by the time Lawrence got home from school, she was already gone. So he was lonely, and he was still waiting to hear from God. But *He* didn't speak. Eventually, Lawrence took that silence as consent.

"Listen to him, Gerald." It was Saturday morning, and Mrs. Williams was getting ready for work. Even freshly laundered, her uniform still smelled of cigars and cologne: a sweet, smoky odor that Lawrence had begun to associate with goodness because, since taking the job, Mrs. Williams had been much happier.

Gerald gave her an angry look; his wife's good moods always seemed to make him uncomfortable. "Listen to what?"

"The boy says he's called by God. How're you going to deny that?"

"He'll probably change his mind."

"No." Lawrence felt sure of this. "I won't."

Mrs. Williams sloughed her smoky jacket onto the couch. She straightened her vest and poked hatpins into her hair, smiling at Lawrence conspiratorially. In the early light, her make-up was less crisp, but she was still pretty: rosy and smooth. Her uniform was tight and smart across her little frame. She folded at the waist, giving Gerald a prim little kiss on the cheek. "It's not his decision, Gerald. It's God's."

Gerald slammed his glass against the table. "God! God's got all the answers, huh?" He looked at his wife and at the boy, and at the real estate forms spattered with gin. "If God's so bloody smart, why doesn't he tell an honest working man what he's got to do to get himself a house?"

Mrs. Williams was unfazed; she settled down onto the armrest of Gerald's chair, laying her thin arm along his shoulders. "Is this really what you want, Lawrence?"

He told her that it was.

"Well, then, I don't see why not."

Gerald shook his gruff head, half-buried in his wife's embrace. "Baby, it's an honor."

"So's shooting a Jap."

She clicked her tongue. "Gerald, someday you're going to have to come back to the real world."

"I'm not the only one," he said, looking at her morosely. Gerald made decisions, and he expected his family to comply. He ran the house the way a man should. He tried to do what was right. Everything he decided on was deliberate and well-intentioned. His wife had little room to argue.

But she could escape to Fernando's night club four nights a week. She had another life now—one that none of them knew much about. The people there were rich and glamorous, she had told Lawrence. And they liked her; she was good at her job. "You've really gotta hustle to be a good camera girl," she had explained. "It isn't easy. People don't even know that they want their picture taken, but they do. So you've just gotta be the one to help them realize that." There were new girls every month, and most didn't last. But Mrs. Williams stayed on, bringing her tips back in thick, creased envelopes. "Folks say I'm the best little camera girl that ever worked taking photos at Fernando's."

So Mrs. Williams had gotten good at showing people what was in their best interest. Even Gerald. The louder he got, the calmer and sweeter she became. Some days later, he stopped grumbling about the boy's decision. There were more important matters at hand. He marched glumly around the house with his folded real estate forms. They had lost the house. But there would be other houses, his wife promised. And in the meantime, she'd convinced him that the seminary would be cheaper than the tuition at St. Thomas Elementary. "Don't worry," she winked at Lawrence. "I've got it all worked out for you."

Those few years before Lawrence left for the seminary were the most gratifying of his life. In those days, priesthood brought with it its own kind of fame. The nuns at Holy Cross were pleased: there was a future man of God among them. In class, they made an example of Lawrence: how well he did on his spelling drills, they noted. And his handwriting was so gracious. It was because he was so close to the Lord, they told the other children. At home, too, Mrs. Williams treated him with special attention. "God works in mysterious ways," she beamed. Finally, he had made her proud; it was the first and last time that this would ever happen.

But the boy's celebrity life ran out abruptly one day when the camera disappeared. There wasn't any kind of announcement. He looked up at the shelf, and it was gone. Mrs. Williams was in her bedroom, resting. No one said anything. Gerald looked severe, but more relaxed.

Ringling was the one who explained it: "There's going to be a baby."

Lawrence had no experience with infants, but he knew that they were gifts from God. So God, apparently, had blessed them.

But Ringling didn't think his sister was very happy about it.

"Why not?"

"Because now she can't do things."

Lawrence asked what kind of things, and Ringling nodded toward the empty shelf. The camera, for one. "And other things that she used to do before," he said.

But Lawrence didn't understand. The world was still large and outside of him. He didn't think about what other people's joys were; he was still too busy establishing his own.

* * *

"You can't tell Gerald about this." Mrs. Williams made the boy promise. "He thinks I got rid of all of this stuff years ago."

But when she lifted the lid, it was difficult to understand what

Gerald might object to. There was a lot of junk there, none of which Lawrence could guess the names or uses of. Something that looked like clothing, and some cables and tools. These items were greasy and a little damp; they smelled of work that had long ago been completed. He looked at the items in the box: they were old, used up. But Mrs. Williams was enthusiastic.

"Look, Lawrence," she picked up the suit, which was made out of a thick, padded material, and pressed it into his hands, grinning like a girl. "Isn't it heavy?"

Her voice sounded conspiratorial, and Lawrence understood that he was sharing in something important. He could see her straining to make good with him, to be his friend. She wanted to get it right, even if just as Lawrence was planning to leave. And he understood that she hadn't meant to be a bad mother; she just hadn't known what to do. Even Ringling lacked the qualities of having been nurtured. He was always restless; he loved people too hard, too much. Already, the girls at school were breaking his heart—even though he was beautiful and adored by all of them. But he wanted something that they couldn't give—that they didn't yet have within themselves at sixteen, seventeen years old. He loved them blindly, madly, a different one every few weeks. And their ability to take it wore out quickly.

Lawrence could see, too, that a space had opened inside of Mrs. Williams: a bit of uncertainty. She laughed, holding the awkward fabric up against her: "Wouldn't fit me now!" She pressed it to her, so he couldn't see anymore the slight roundedness of her belly. "I used to wear these every day during the war. My leathers. You had to, welding down at the docks. They had rules and things. But I was happy." She explained it all matter-of-factly, like she was reading out of a book.

Then she picked up a metal object, round and pointed at the end, like some kind of weapon. "This is my stinger. We used it to weld metal for the boats. You could do flat seams or horizontals," she said, moving the stinger in imaginary loops. "Verticals were the hardest, because you had to keep the stinger held so straight in the air. My leaderman said I was very good at verticals."

134

She handed it to him; it was also quite heavy. Lawrence imagined the tight beam of light coming out of it and Mrs. Williams holding it steady to a wall, melting two pieces of metal together in quiet precision. She sat there smiling. The boy could tell that she had liked this work; it was something she still felt proud of.

"When the war finished, they didn't need so many boats." The stinger was back in her hands now, its long electrical cord wrapped around its body. "We walked off with these things, and nobody said a thing. I thought maybe my children might like to see them one day."

She made no mention of Lawrence, whether or not she considered him one of her children. But either way, her eyes stayed sad. "Gerald doesn't like it, though. He's stubborn. He doesn't think women should have to work." She lowered the stinger and the leathers back into the box, and they would stay like that in the basement, stacking up more and more years until somebody—maybe one of her children—finally took an interest in all that history. "My husband is a good man," she said, nodding to herself. "Family is important."

Lawrence said he thought so, too. "I'm going to have a family in the Church."

"Yes," she looked down at him. "That's a good thing. I'm glad you're going to be a priest, Lawrence," she smiled briefly. "That's something important."

Theresa, June 1979

A car door slammed; Theresa bolted. Her mother had come back—of course she had come back. She always did. Without thinking, she grabbed Tomás's hand, tugging him away from the Z car. She shoved her chin in the direction of the path that led away from the house, out toward the boat house. "Let's go," she urged, and he followed her back toward the taller grasses. The path they took—the same worn pair of tire tracks that she had always followed out to the back of the property—was rutted and dry, though grown so tall with weeds, they felt themselves half submerged. It made her feel safe, hidden. In the distance, they could hear the motion of her mother climbing the stairs to the house, opening the door and shutting it again.

"You don't want to see her?" Tomás walked alongside her now, hefting the length of the trapeze bar with him. He had a habit, she thought, of saying out loud what they both already knew. She dropped his hand. "She needs too much," she told him. "It's complicated."

Tomás neither asked nor reflected aloud on what those things might be. He followed her silently, walking carefully through the weeds, yellowed by now but still pliable in the early summer heat. There was little shade in the flat expanse of land behind the house. To the north, small clusters of oak trees sat muscled and green where the land buttressed up against the highway, but otherwise, there was little out there. Stray sycamores. Sometimes the faint smell of burning. Within a few brief minutes, they had crossed the quarter mile distance to the boat house: the only structure out there beyond an abandoned burn pile that Gerald had once used to slough off excess lumber when he changed out fence posts or repaired a worn stretch of shingles.

"So, what happened?" Tomás wanted to know.

"After the trapeze?"

"And the high wire."

Theresa sighed. They had stopped walking. A few yards in front of them, the boat house sagged, weary from years of disuse, though it was still intriguing. High-ceilinged and almost window-less, it was an opaque structure, though well ventilated along the top with grated air shafts that channeled the breeze in and out without permitting rain to enter. As a child, she had climbed an old set of planked steps up to a loft-like space along the vented eaves, where she might lie for hours while her older brothers shot marbles along the concrete floor or whispered over magazines that she was never allowed to see.

"I got mean," she told him, and the answer surprised her: the truth of it, and the sudden ease with which she had shared it with Tomás. Her head snapped upward. "To the kids at school, mostly," she clarified. It had been so easy to do. The children at Holy Spirit Elementary were serious and dutiful. They came from good families—*the best*. So they had been easy to pick on because they were quick to trust; they hadn't yet learned how unforgiving the world can be. After each small ingression, they had stared at Theresa with wide, unclasped eyes—the tearful lining of disbelief building up at the corners like stale milk.

"They were small things." She had started out the way that children do: testing the boundaries of things. How much could she get away with? How far could she press her own young sense of guilt? *Amber Higgins doesn't have real front teeth.* She had told people's secrets, pretending not to realize that they had been shared in confidence. Or she'd spoken openly about things that other people tried politely to cover up: *It's too bad Samantha can't go on to fourth grade with us. It's only because she has that problem so she can't read. It's like a disease; she can't get rid of it.*

Tomás's expression softened. He tapped the trapeze bar against the ground, tamping down a bit of loose topsoil. "But that's normal, Theresa. Kids do stuff like that."

His response was disappointing. All those years ago, during those months of her meanness, no one had seemed to notice much. At home, her brothers were coming of age and moving away; her parents were busy somehow—impossibly—falling in love with each other again after many years. So no one had minded her small experiments in wickedness; no one had seemed to care.

She pressed further. "Once," she explained. "I told my mother that I hated her." That event, at least, had been noticed. "When my dad got home that night, I knew he'd found out because he told me to go into his study with him. Nobody ever went in there."

Before his physical decline, Gerald Williams's study had been a narrow, windowless room stacked neatly with books and flavored with the rich scent of tobacco. The rows of volumes that lined the walls were mostly series of history treatises, poorly written and sold cheaply as box sets. They touched on wars and presidents. And although Gerald never read many of them, preferring most often the daily newspaper or *Reader's Digest*, Theresa understood that they comforted her father: that proximity a more important world.

Children don't hate their parents. It had been a statement of fact, not a scolding. *It's not natural.* Theresa's father had always been like that. He seemed to understand the world: what was possible and what wasn't. For him, life had seemed to fit together very evenly— except that other people were always failing him, forgetting how things worked.

Theresa, he had put a hand on his daughter's shoulder, trying to get her to look at him. *Why don't you love your mother?*

Theresa had shrugged, but he'd kept looking at her. His face was square and severe. She had expected it to grow red like it did when they were in traffic: flushing out from the jaw in cottony clumps like fish scales. He would breathe hard and shallow at moments like those: his eyes coming small and angry all at once. He was tragic, but in the quiet, sweep-it-under-the-rug kind of way. Not like her mother, whose upsets were always loud and painfully apparent.

You don't hate her, Theresa. It had sounded like a plea—something that he was asking her not to do.

So she had shaken her head.

Then her father had done something that surprised Theresa: he put his arms around her and held her gently. She had waited; he had never done that before. But suddenly, it had all been so easy. So she had folded herself into his lap and stayed there, smelling the thick odor of pipe tobacco in his clothing and another scent that she hadn't known yet: whiskey. He was a lonely man—his whole life he'd been lonely, no matter what he was doing or who he was with. Afterward, Theresa could not remember how long they had stayed like that. It had been a strange and lovely moment. *Oh, Theresa*, her father had breathed. *You're worth so much more than you think you are.*

"He was a good man," Tomás said simply. He approached the boat house, and she followed. Then he curled his fingers around the knob, and she watched him toggle it back and forth to see if it was open. She remembered having heard that her father had helped Mrs. Quintanilla find a job—a secretary position down at Travis Air Force Base, where Gerald worked—after her husband had passed away. He had always been like that: idealistic, philanthropic in the small-scale ways he was capable of. "He had a lot of principles," she echoed, as Tomás spun the knob.

"Good principles."

She shoved her fists into her pockets, the knuckles cramming against the plastic of Lawrence's rosary beads, still sitting there from days before.

"That's a good thing, Theresa," he grunted softly, leveraging his weight against the door. "You had a good role model." He shoved his hip more firmly to the door, pressing and jangling the knob until finally the door gave in a squeaking rush. Tomás steadied himself and peered inward. "Dark," he said. "You want to go inside? You want to see?"

Theresa sunk down into a patch of low grass nearby, her knees bent and her calves tucked beneath her. Her head twisted vigorously. "Not right now."

"No?" He sounded surprised.

"Go in if you want." And she left it at that.

Tomás glanced inside once more, training his eyes for a moment in the low light. He coughed briefly on the musty air and carefully pulled the door back shut. "Someone needs to air that place out," he said, taking the trapeze bar back up in his hands and needling it along the dry ground like a blind man's cane until he came to the place where she had sat herself down. He joined her.

"You're not mean now," he said, speaking into the daylight the things between them that were already clear. "Something must have changed."

She sat quietly for several moments, considering the empty boat house and the bright day shouting around it. Somewhere inside the house, her mother would be humming faintly to herself, rustling through pans in the kitchen or pasting an old pile of photographs into an album. Coming home again after being on the road nearly always left her in good spirits.

Theresa turned to Tomás. The answer again was sudden and palpable. She remembered the Friday masses at her school: how Father McDougal had warned her class about the possibility of the devil getting into their hearts. He'd said this sometimes happened without people even knowing it. This had made Theresa feel better: maybe it wasn't really her fault. So she'd thought about the devil being in her heart the day she'd withheld Mary Jane Price's lunch from her until she could sing backwards the entirety of the National Anthem. Every time she missed a word, Theresa had thrown some small piece of it into the trash. The girl was in tears by the time she had finished. And Theresa had felt sorry for her: It was terrible, sometimes, the way things happened.

So when the man from the Church had come to live with her family and Theresa's meanness stopped, she had assumed that her theory had been correct: something about the proximity to good-ness had stamped all the badness out of her.

"Lawrence?"

She nodded.

"So he *was* a priest."

"Sort of—or something like that. But he stopped eventually. I don't think it was what he expected."

Tomás leaned backward, digging his fingertips into the soil. "I wonder what makes that happen."

"I don't know," she said, watching the shape of Tomás's hand curl against the ground. "He was so hard to understand."

One day, she told him, they had been in the kitchen together. Lawrence was splitting open bread for a sandwich. He had a certain reverence about the way he did things: moving slowly, considering his body and its relationship to things. Even then, he had seemed not quite part of this world.

Theresa had stood there quietly at first. She had wanted him to notice her, so she'd said the meanest thing she could think of: *My mom says you used to work for God. She says it's shameful to do that and then stop.*

He had looked up and nodded slowly.

Is it true?

Is what true?

Did you used to work at church?

He had shrugged.

But not now.

No, he'd answered, spreading a slow layer of peanut butter across one half of the bread.

Well, isn't that a sin? she'd insisted. *If you're supposed to do that, and you don't?*

He'd picked up a jar of marmalade and nodded again. *Yes, I suppose it's quite easy to sin.*

This had surprised Theresa; back then, she didn't expect people to agree with her. But he hadn't said anything else; he'd just kept his gaze on her, even but distant. She'd felt something in the center of herself shift. This man was different from the other people she knew.

Finally, she'd asked, *Didn't you like it?*

Yes.

Then why'd you stop?

Because God was through with me. He had left off the sandwich and was watching Theresa carefully; it made her nervous.

At school, we go to mass on Fridays, she'd blurted then. His head had bobbed carefully up and down. And because he hadn't said anything else, she'd added: *I don't like it.*

Nothing had happened.

I think the priest says weird things, she'd gone on. *Like he said we have to be careful not to let the devil get inside us. But that's dumb, don't you think?*

Lawrence had held the sugary knife lightly in his hand and looked up toward the wall. *I used to wonder where sin came from,* he'd said. *And punishment. Now I know that they're the same thing.* Then he had carried the knife to the sink, rinsed it, dried it, and laid it carefully back inside the drawer. Theresa had stared at him. He was a man who thought big things: big ideas and big hurts. Already she could tell that he was either very smart or a little bit crazy.

"That's sad, Theresa."

"It's just—that's how he always was." She swallowed to keep her throat from closing and blinked once, hard. She did not want to cry in front of Tomás—not again. Especially when she could not be certain what she was crying over: Lawrence, or her father, or her mother. Or maybe it was some other small bit of herself that had died alongside the rest of these tangled losses? She sat up, flipping her head in the direction of the house. "Nathan's car," she asked. "You going to fix it?"

"Going to try."

She shifted her legs out from under her, drawing her knees upward and holding them against her chest. "How long's it gonna take?"

The corners of his mouth curled upward. "You want to go somewhere?" he grinned. "You got big plans?"

"Just into town. But it's too far to bike from here."

"You know how to drive?"

"Enough."

He pulled himself up off the ground, taking the trapeze bar with him. "Where?" he asked. "Where you wanna go?"

"It doesn't matter. Nothing far. I just want to check on something."

Tomás shoved his weight onto a hip and stood there, staring down at her. The perspective gave her a renewed sense of his height: those long legs leading up toward a slim torso. He stood there for a moment like that, resting his hands one over the other, two hands on one end of the trapeze bar, which stood nearly to his waist. "You're still curious about him, aren't you? About Lawrence?"

"Does it matter?"

"No—no, I guess it doesn't." He tapped the bar against the toe of his work boot.

"So you'll help me? To get into town?"

"We'll go together," he offered, meeting her gaze head-on.

"Friday," she suggested. "You can have it fixed by then?"

"I can sure try." Tomás dragged a sleeve across his forehead. "Hot," he said, digging the pistachio bag back out of his pocket and crunching solidly on a kernel. He shook his head, as though to suggest the pure illogic of life: a hot day like that one, two half-orphaned teenagers, and a broken down sports car. In the near background of their lives, the haunting memory of a dead man hanging in a tree. The slow collapse of cancer; a heart bursting in the night. Tomás tilted his head, then shuffled the trapeze bar upward through the grip of one hand off the ground, and carried it with him several paces to the sycamore tree that marked the border where the Williams' property bled into undeveloped county lands. Theresa followed him curiously, posting herself in the shade of the tree as Tomás squinted into the sunlight, considering the distance. Then he lifted the trapeze bar high over his head and flung it outward as far as he could. The bar spun forward in an arc, looping like a baton in its private orbit. Then it fell, a hundred yards out, thudding briefly against the ground. "Gone," he said. And she nodded, sheltering her eyes and staring into the long expanse of grasslands to the place where that one single memory had finally disappeared.

Lawrence, 1953

Galt 1953 wasn't anywhere in particular. A little blip of highway. A pause in the thick, blue-yellow stream of Central California. Nothing but burnt ground and cows, their udders hanging grotesquely from years of over milking. Train tracks running crisscrossed. A pile of tin and rubble fenced-in from some unknown threat. And to one side, just where the sun hit across a square grove of eucalyptus trees—their long, peeling bark smelling wild and strangely medicinal—stood St. Pious X's seminary for boys.

This, thought Lawrence, was the perfect place for holiness: the austere grounds, the modest, U-shaped chapel, the long barrack-like buildings flanking each side, one for classrooms and one for dormitories. A narrow steeple pressed up toward the sky. And, like all seminaries at that time, St. Pious was a model of steadfast, plotted ritual and routine. The boys were up at five to wash and ready themselves; mass was at six, and then there was breakfast; lessons stretched until five at night; and afterwards they had chores, and two more sets of prayers. They lived in shared dormitories, twelve boys to a room. Homework was done in the library between dinner and bedtime. There was no private space—there was little time for anything personal. But it didn't matter to Lawrence. He wasn't himself anymore; he belonged to God now. In those early days, this was still an easy thing to tell himself.

But thirteen-year-old boys, he also learned, did not behave graciously—even if they did belong to God.

"Hey! Where'd you come from? A hyena's ass?"

That was Frankie Morlin, the second-year mentor assigned to Lawrence. It was Frankie's job to orient him—to be the role model for his new life. "Better watch out, little turd. Tonight's not going to be easy."

Frankie, as it turned out, was right. So much of the seminary was not as Lawrence had imagined. The boys there were neither somber nor refined; they were, more than anything, human. When the new class filed into the refectory, they found hordes of older boys eating like animals: stealing from each other's plates and inventing unsavory rumors about the food.

"Qui-*et*! This is *Gawd's* house!"

The silence that first night was immediate. Lawrence was stunned. He had never heard a priest take such a tone. But Father Luke did not apologize. He was the school's Dean of Discipline: 6'2", 250 pounds and an ex-paratrooper. "You're in the Lord's presence," he bellowed again. "For *Gawd's* sake."

No one else spoke. Lawrence stared at the other priests: they stood wordlessly against the wall, like statues. It was 1953. The world had come out of a war; things were not the same. But the Catholic Church remained intact. It was a reminder of history: things that had worked for centuries and went on working. For this reason, the boys at St. Pious would learn how to blend in with their surroundings. Everything had already been determined: the motions that their bodies would make, their postures, their words. The opinions that they should report on this or that matter. Things did not change; it had been this way for five hundred years.

"You gonna carry on like that in the presence of our Lord?" Father Luke continued glaring about the room. "Not on my watch, you're not. *Gawd* has rules. You're gonna do things the way *Gawd* wants them done." The other brothers watched on without comment: Bogotá Bob, the missionary; Father Gregory, the theologian; Father Benedict, the rector, who monitored the halls and bathrooms in resolute silence; and Father Justinian Pierce, who taught Gregorian Change and scolded boys' fingers with the edges of his cassock belt if they missed as aspect of their lessons.

After that, the crowd finished their meal in relative quiet, the older boys sniggering softly, and the group that had just arrived casting their eyes about in confusion and dread. When they were done, they were led to the dormitories for another lecture from Father Luke.

"Don't worry," Frankie elbowed Lawrence. "His bark is worse than his bite."

Frankie knew things—such as which rules to keep and which ones you could break. St. Pious was, after all, a school like any other: notes were passed in class, homeworks copied, tests rigged. And the forbidden nature of things only made them more urgent. "It's also possible," he whispered, "to see girls." He conveyed this news with especial aplomb. Frankie was the kind of boy, Lawrence grew to understand, who always wanted to be the center of attention, but seldom was. The sixth of seventh children, he attended St. Pious with two of his older brothers. This connection to the more advanced class accounted for much of his wisdom.

"My brother Victor even kissed one once." He looked Lawrence square in the eye, as though he should be deeply impressed by this information.

"But we're supposed to be men of God," Lawrence whispered.

Frankie shrugged. "Sure. But everybody gets tempted, right?"

Lawrence nodded slowly, but the truth was, he wasn't thinking yet of breaking vows. He didn't yet understand that temptation works best when there is something waiting to be filled.

* * *

They went home twice each year: two weeks at Christmas and a month during the summer. Most of the boys looked forward to these times. But for Lawrence, the experience was jilted. On that first trip home, he found that he had been replaced. The little boy's name was Nathan. He was a long, plump baby who looked startlingly like Gerald. Mrs. Williams thought he was the grandest thing on earth. She was entirely changed now, staying at home all day without complaint, doing chores—anything to be close to the baby. Already, she was talking about getting pregnant again. By the time Lawrence finished high school, the Williams would have four little boys: one for each of the white-washed rooms of their newly purchased home.

The thing that struck Lawrence about the Williams during that Christmas season was that their marriage seemed much safer now. Gerald had bought his house; Mrs. Williams had borne her son. They had each given each other something important. And there weren't nearly as many fights; the couple had become happily distracted. Ringling saw it, too. "They're good people," he said, "but they've got their family now." He looked meaningfully at Lawrence. Some part of their lives was over; Lawrence wondered if Ringling had seen it coming. The two of them were orphans, after all; they would have to grow up fast. In two more years, Ringling would swear allegiance to the nation. He would be sent to Korea, where he would perform bravely and leave without a scratch. That was Ringling's life: beautiful and protected.

In the meantime, Lawrence knew that he was right. The Williams didn't ignore him because of anything that he had done. It was simply the fact that he wasn't the little baby lying in the crib. He wasn't *hers*. Not the way that Nathan was hers: born out of married love. He had saved them.

But Lawrence hadn't saved anybody; he was still too busy searching out salvation for himself. And always, he was dumbfounded when things left him: "Don't you love me anymore?" The Williams were traveling to Texas for Christmas, to introduce the new baby to Gerald's family. But the bus fare was expensive. Ringling and Lawrence weren't going.

Mrs. Williams smiled gently. "God loves you," she said, lowering her head over the crib, lifting the little boy into her arms. Lawrence looked at the baby and thought about how much he was wanted. But Lawrence knew, also, that jealousy was a sin, so he tried to make himself stop. He felt his head nodding in spite of itself. *Yes-yes-yes. Of course. God loves you.* As if that alone should be enough.

* * *

The following spring, when the weather turned fine again, Frankie invited him to the riverside, which was really little more than a stream, sandy in parts, and at other junctures generous with reeds and cat tails. It wound its way through the valley just to the west of St. Pious—walking distance, though they rarely had the time or made the effort. But when the offer came, it came quickly; there wasn't time for deliberation. "Come on," Frankie encouraged. "It's Saturday. My brother and his friends are going. This is your chance to learn something."

But what Frankie hadn't mentioned was what they would learn about. When they arrived at a particular, predetermined bend in the stream, shaded finely by a willow and an oak tree, four girls were waiting for them, looking bored with the effort. "What took so long?" one of them, a girl with a cleft on the right side of her upper lip, challenged as they appeared.

Frankie's brother Victor moved to the front of our group. "The Lord moves in His own good time," he answered, and the boys sniggered. The whole family of Morlin boys was there at St. Pious's, like a gamble: perhaps one of them would stick it out. But none of them seemed interested.

The cleft lip twitched and the girl broke into a wry smile. "It's warm already," she said, stretching out her legs. They watched as she slowly unrolled a knee-length sock, unbuckling her shoe and tossing both articles to the side. Then she flexed her toes so they could see her clean white calf buckle and muscle along the damp embankment. She tossed her head. The other girls began to twitch, moving hair from their faces and stretching out their bodies in the grass.

The girls in Galt were small town country girls—farm girls. They came from large families, many of them Catholic, and they had never been given much attention of their own. They had little room to voice their complaints against life—such as why they were still there in Galt, going nowhere, while girls up in Sacramento were going out in powder blue cars with boys smelling of pomade. They were listless girls with a ruinous fascination for the priests-to-be: here was their one chance to tempt fate. And the boys lent themselves to it: foolishly and hopefully. Already, Lawrence thought, so lost to God.

What happened that day was no different from the encounters that pass between any such group of adolescent boys and girls. Rocks were tossed into the water; grass was pulled up by its roots and shredded, lazily, across girls' laps. Small conversations about not much of anything passed between various couples. There were seven seminarians, and at times two boys went off with a single girl. The taller grasses moved. There were exposures of skin. Splashing. Somewhere amidst all of it, Frankie disappeared, and Lawrence was left to himself, sitting there quietly along the riverbank, startled by his own desires: those girls with their little hips and butts and thighs. Smooth and pink and entirely different from him. He had always loved motherliness, but now he had another idea about womanhood. The giggling and rustling around him had opened up something that he couldn't put back.

"Hey," a short girl with a thick waist called over to him. He looked up. She had stubby teeth and brown, unshaped hair. Her nose was mousy and her hips jiggled slightly as she walked. She took two firm steps toward him. "What're you doing?"

He felt briefly stunned. "Nothing," he told her honestly. Another boy, Victor's friend, was standing nervously at her side. She paused for a minute, uncertainly.

"Aren't you bored like that?"

Lawrence shook his head.

She stared back, almost hateful. After another moment, she put one hand on a hip and flipped her body around, sauntering off down closer to the crick. The boy followed. He was a smallish adolescent who was already seventeen and, from the looks of it, would never become very attractive. He shivered against the light springtime breeze. When it seemed that no one else was watching him, Lawrence stood up and moved away from the twittering and giggling and made his way back to the seminary grounds.

* * *

From among the many mentors at St. Pious, Father Gregory was Lawrence's favorite. He taught theology, which made him an expert on things—the most important things. A man not unlike Gerald, he was somber and withheld, and the things he said were final.

But despite his wisdom, Lawrence could not bring himself to tell Father Gregory about what was going on down at the creek. "Lawrence," the man asked, "why are you here?"

Lawrence stood blankly. In the back of his mind, he could still hear the splash of the cool water. A giggle. The fresh scent of grass.

Father Gregory leaned back in his chair, a leather ledger opened in front of him, where he was working on his sermon. He asked more pointedly: "Why did you come here to St. Pious?"

Lawrence blinked. "Because God called me, Father."

But Father Gregory just shook his big, mangy head. He wasn't especially old—fifty at most—but his face was already covered by a thick, creamy beard. His head was balding from the front; he had eyes the color of olives. He sighed and shook his head: "The ones who think that never last."

Lawrence knew better than to question Father Gregory, but man kept watching him, holding those steady olive eyes against his without flinching. He tried again: "Father, I love God."

Father Gregory tapped the stem of his fountain pen against the ledger. Lawrence felt his mind begin to spin: What was happening down at the creek? What would it all mean? "You feel special being here, don't you?"

The boy tucked his hands together and nodded. "Yes, Father."

"Well, it's not being here that counts," he said. "It's staying. You must commit yourself to God every day. Over and over. It's the only way."

Father Gregory had been at St. Pious for more than a decade. He knew that many boys would leave, and some would stay. He knew which ones would make which decisions. Lawrence was a good child—an eager child. "Yes, Father," he answered. "I'll work hard. I will."

The man shook his head. He smoothed the hairs along the back of his index finger, his mind seeming to move elsewhere. "It's not about effort, Lawrence. It's about openness. Receptivity."

Holiness, then, must be like emptiness, Lawrence thought. So he would work hard, he decided, at releasing all that he could.

"You'll know God when you chose to do whatever He wants, even though it's the last thing you want for yourself," Father Gregory concluded. "Sacrifice, Lawrence," he reminded the boy. "That's what you need. But you haven't hardly lived yet, so what do you have to give up?"

Lawrence had no idea.

"Exactly. And until you figure that out, you won't really know what you're meant for."

But that didn't seem quite fair. Father Gregory was right: Lawrence didn't have anything. So far, the things in his life had been taken from him, or had fallen away. He only had the experience of losing things, not of giving them up.

Theresa, June 1979

On Friday morning, the light was long. Her mother slept late, but by nine-thirty, Tomás still had not arrived. Theresa worried; she wanted to be gone and back before her mother roused herself enough to notice her daughter's absence. In the downstairs rooms, there was no evidence of her mother's purse. No checkbook, no car keys. Nothing that Theresa could borrow to get herself to town. Outside, a fastidious sun was pulling up into the sky. Even from her cool perch in the shade of the front porch, Theresa could feel the building pressure that would be the heat of the day. She crossed her forearms around her tented knees. "He's not coming," she said, and listened to the pang in her stomach, like snared wire. She was not in love with him—*she was not*—but still, it hurt. In truth, his absence pained her more than the inconvenience of having to ride her bicycle into town alone.

The breeze was soothing, at least. She pedaled as fast as she could, keeping the air moving around her. She had little idea of how long it would take her to reach the assessor's office downtown: that stoic-looking storefront along West Texas Street. One hour? Two? She passed Stevie's Stopover and kept on pedaling. In front of her, the world split into two colors: yellow grasses, blue sky. She rode along the shoulder, trying to avoid the snags of gravel here and there, and the occasional thrum of traffic that sped past her. The highway was lined with metal scraps and the outlines of half-built houses. Fairfield was too far south for vineyards, but the hills were golden, and the oak trees were a dark, vicious green. They lived in groups, never alone, speckling the dry hills in hunkered victory.

By the time she arrived, she was winded. Ten miles? Twelve maybe? She stood outside the assessor's office, waiting for her body to cool. Nearby, there was a service station and the church, Holy Cross, where she and her brothers had gone to the parish school years before. There was a supermarket and a bank. The town was grid-like and slow. Fairfield was not a place where people rushed. Men of different skin colors and backgrounds ambled the streets between taverns. Not many people there showed much evidence of an inbound purpose. Theresa sucked down a breath—hot and spoiled, now that the air had taken on the character of the sun—crossed the street to the assessor's office, and went inside.

"Where do I find death certificates?"

A man near the door fanned himself with a folded newspaper and gestured down a narrow hallway. He mumbled an office number, and she left him, counting stale little rooms until she found it. Behind the counter, a woman with a heavy face and blonde streaks tucked into her hair wore a chalky expression. Young, Theresa thought. Twenty? Twenty-five? Not old enough to look like that, anyway. Her hands puffed out. Her eyes swelled; they looked like that had been borrowed from someone else entirely.

Theresa slid her high school ID across the counter as proof of herself. "I'm looking for information," she cleared her throat and her voice caught mildly; these were the first words that she had spoken all day. "About a man who died a couple of weeks ago."

The woman did not react.

"Out at the Williams' property, by Highway 80," she paused. Nothing. "A man killed himself," she swallowed. "Didn't you hear about that?"

The woman blinked. "Hanging," she said. And left it at that.

"Yeah. I want to find his death certificate. Or anything else you've got on file."

"You next of kin?"

Theresa swallowed and decided to nod.

"What's the full name?"

She paused. "That's the part I'm not sure about."

"Gotta have a name."

"I know but—I thought since it was such a recent case . . . I thought someone here might remember."

The woman looked down at her fingernails, which were long and plastic. Theresa could not guess how she ambled comfortably through file folders or entered new forms into the typewriter. "I'm the only one here," she said. "And I need his name."

Theresa sighed. "Williams. Try the name Williams."

Several minutes later, the woman came back empty-handed. The heft below her chin wobbled slightly. "No one named Williams on file for last month."

"But can't you look by date?" Theresa felt her voice crack. "The most recent entries? His name was Lawrence—first name Lawrence. Date of death, May twenty-fifth."

"I need a full name to draw a file," the woman repeated.

"But you know what I'm talking about," Theresa's chest cranked up. "The suicide."

The woman looked at her skeptically. "Why isn't your mother here?" she asked with sudden interest. "Or your father? You aren't eighteen, are you?"

"There's no rule about who can order certificates," Theresa snapped. She had no idea whether or not this was true. "I'm old enough."

The woman retreated back into the room of files and forgotten lives. How many, Theresa wondered, would have been from the war? All those young men who had died—younger even than Lawrence.

When she came back ten minutes later, the woman was still shaking her head. "Gotta have that last name," she sighed, "or I can't find anything."

Outside, the sun blazed all the more intensely. *Record-breaking summer temperatures*, she had heard recently on the evening news. Now, even the breeze seemed to have stopped; she felt her body slump. "I can't do this," she whispered, pressing a hand over the small bulge in her jeans pocket: the rosary. Her palm was warm, damp, even through her clothing. She squinted upward toward the sky, then around the streets in front of her: angular and nondescript. There was so little to recommend this town. So little. It was an after-thought from the war: a necessary swelling of population near the shipyards. Although, of course, Theresa did not understand this quite yet. She only knew that it was not the kind of place where people stay—not if they want to have any kind of forward-moving life. That conviction created an urgency in her belly; it moved quickly upward, catching itself in her throat. They should move to Sacramento—that was it. She and her mother. They would be closer to Nathan then, and he wouldn't have to worry about them so much. It would be good for them, this change, she decided; it would take care of everything.

"Nathan." She'd found enough change in her pocket to make a call at a phone booth across the street which sat, mercifully, in the shade of a corner drug store.

"What is it, Theresa?"

But of course she couldn't tell him what she was doing. It would trouble him: her stubborn curiosity, her refusal to let go. "Just saying hello."

"How's school?" In the background, she could hear the keys of a typewriter, the quick murmur of office voices.

"Mom got the materials," she told him, "earlier this week. I'm almost finished."

"You're quick." His voice was heavy and solid. Reassuring. "That's good, Theresa. You'll finish the year up on time."

"Nathan," she blurted. "What's happening with the house?"

"The house?"

"You're still going to sell it?"

Her brother cleared his throat. "Mom has to be the one to sell, but I think it's a good idea. I've found some developers who are interested. All that land along the highway—we could get a good price. You guys would be very well taken care of."

"Developers?"

"They'll build services there or an off ramp. There's been a lot of building going on up north of town."

Yes, she agreed. *Of course.* The land would get sold off piecemeal. Chopped up into gas station lots and strip malls along the highway. Maybe an outlet center or a church. Leveled and parceled and reconstructed. The landscapes that they had known would disappear entirely.

* * *

By the time she got back home, she was exhausted: perspiring and panting, her legs heavy from twenty miles of riding. The day had crescendoed into early afternoon. The woman from Human Statistics was probably back from her lunch break by then, sitting quietly at her desk, scanning names and dates to enter into her typewriter without attaching any particular feeling to them. Theresa glanced up at the house. She waited: nothing. Perhaps her mother hadn't registered her absence; perhaps she was too distracted that day to care. Theresa passed Tomás's scooter and marched around behind the house.

"You weren't here," she accused. "You didn't come."

Tomás was stooped over Nathan's Z car. He straightened, cramming a fist into his pocket. "You didn't wait for me."

"You said you'd be here at eight." Her gaze was hard but bleary-eyed in the heat of the day; her eyes pricked. Tomás had not come, and, worse, finding her missing at home, he had not ridden his scooter back along the highway to find her.

"My mother wasn't feeling well this morning." He stood aside the raised hood of the car, resting his elbow its rim. "What happened?" he wanted to know.

"Nothing happened."

"Did you find what you wanted?"

No, she told him, she hadn't. Lawrence had disappeared so quickly into the world; she didn't know how to find him. And now the land around them was about to be transformed. Their lives here would be completely forgotten.

"What did you try to do?"

She told him about the failed attempt at the assessor's office. He thought for a moment. "Maybe the Catholic Church," he suggested, "would have some kind of records."

"I don't care," she slumped down onto the lawn. It was hot—terribly hot—and the front yard no longer offered any shade. She missed the oak tree. Missed that simple reading spot, missed the life she'd had six months before: nobody dying, nobody killing themselves. "It's not worth it."

She looked back up at him. He was handsome, it was true. And he looked concerned. Theresa imagined that this was the same expression he had worn that morning, finding his mother, her arthritis flared again, unable to climb smoothly out of bed. He had chosen her—of course, of course he had chosen his mother!—over Theresa. The iron-toothed pang from that morning found her again. She pulled away from him.

"Why does it matter so much to you?"

She looked at him, helpless: she didn't know. *Goddamit*, she didn't know. That was the whole point, wasn't it? How would she understad the importance of things until she found whatever it was she was looking for?

"He wasn't adopted."

Tomás looked surprised. "Really?"

"His name wasn't Williams."

The boy's left eyebrow arched upward.

"He didn't really belong to this family." As she said it, she felt a door closing within her: he wasn't theirs; he wasn't one of them. That slim conclusion, the more she registered it, became alarmingly significant.

"But he was here with you—he was like family."

"No," she made herself say. "He wasn't one of us." The tenor of her voice sounded like someone else entirely. Tomás was slightly taken aback. "It's not worth it," she said. "Whoever he was, whatever happened to him. He wasn't one of us, anyway."

Tomás stretched out the fingers of his left hand and considered them. They were long and tapered. Well-shaped fingers. Attractive. Theresa turned away. She didn't want to talk about Lawrence any more. She was tired and still damp from her ride.

"Is it working now?" she nodded toward the car.

"The Z?"

"What else?"

Tomás ignored the bite in her voice; he said it was. She looked it over and climbed inside. Tomás watched her settle into the driver's seat, slammed the hood shut, moved around to the passenger side, and got in. The keys were already in the ignition. Theresa tried the motor; it sputtered and didn't quite catch. But she knew how to flood the engine, so she flipped the ignition again and gave it some gas, revving the Z, her left foot still pressed down hard over the clutch. Then in one quick movement, she popped the clutch and moved the car several meters forward. It rolled under the shade of the sycamore tree, and she stopped, sitting there with the engine running.

"Nice," Tomás said. "You really *can* drive."

"Four brothers," she reminded him.

Tomás grinned.

"But I haven't been out much by myself."

"You're ready," he sounded quite sure of it. "I think you're ready."

Theresa looked down at the steering wheel. Maybe, after Tomás finished tinkering with it, Nathan would let her have this car. Maybe she would take the next government check that came in for her mother and buy a tank of gas and drive south. Drive to Mexico. She had never been to Mexico. It seemed wildly adventurous. It seemed like a good idea.

She reached over and turned off the gas. The car purred back into silence.

"Don't you want to go anywhere?"

"No. Not right now." Her eyes slid shut, her right hand slipping off of the gear shift and resting against its base. Tomás sat staring at it, inches from his thigh.

"I'm sorry I was late."

"You said you'd come," her voice was getting tired.

He was quiet for a moment. "I thought you would understand, Theresa. Your mother," he reminded her. "She needs a lot, too."

Her head snapped upward: "She likes the attention." Her lids felt heavy, but the slight breeze coming through the windows of the car was cooling. She knew she was being difficult, but she didn't care. "She likes to keep me close by," she said, "so she's got someone to listen to her."

"Maybe she's just trying to protect you."

She shook her head fiercely. "She doesn't need to do that." Then she turned her face against the leather headrest. Her voice cooled. She tried to concentrate on the air pooling up around her body. She tried not to pay attention to Tomás' eyes, moving across her. "Sure she does," he said. "She's worried."

"Worried?" her face shifted toward him.

"About this," he said, slipping a hand into the strands of hair at the top of her skull. His fingers felt delicate against her. He moved them slowly against her skull, the hair there light and warm and slightly greasy from the day's ride. She froze beneath them, like an animal. Tomás's fingers moved gently through the strands of her hair, the same slow pattern several times over, as though memorizing some new terrain.

Theresa turned toward him, and the shape of his face relaxed; he was watching her. She looked away again. His hand was on her arm, moving downward from her shoulder to the tender space inside her elbow. He touched her gently. His hands, she knew, were rough from work. But touching her, working their way along the lines of her bones, they felt soft. Now his hands were at her chin, lifting her up to him. The kiss was mildly chapped, but warm and slightly audible. Quick. And another one. She barely moved. Tomás kept his eyes closed, turning toward her and moving his hands down the shape of her shoulders. They felt tremendous—huge—those hands. Like an elegant bird, taking her inside its mouth. Swallowing her. Her eyes shut; she barely remembered how this had started. There was a silence inside her: a sound like a broken voice, coming more deeply unfastened. Tomás's hands were shifting her frame, turning her slightly toward him. His lips were surprising: cool and warm at the same time. It startled her, how much she became aware of her own body by tying it to someone else's: the cool flavor of the inner lips, the textured surface of a tongue. She tried to determine how best to breathe, and faltered.

"Do you want to stop?"

She shook her head. He kissed her again—longer this time. She moved her lips against him, and he responded. Responded with his whole body. Tomás—light-boned and elegant. There was a sudden weight behind his mouth. She could barely see what was happening, but she could feel it. It was like a script being acted out. Her body startled her: what it knew implicitly how to do and what it already understood. Tomás was leaning into her, his mouth on her, with an unmistakable vigor that shook her. A hunger. A man's appetite, and her own. She took another quick breath.

By the time she went inside, it was nearly dusk. Tomás had gone, slinging a leg easily over the side of his scooter and clipping the round red helmet over his head. He had smiled sweetly at her: a brief, boyish excitement taking over his face long enough for her to know that it wasn't out of pity, what he had done. What *they* had done, for hours all throughout the afternoon: exploring the folds of each other's arms, fingers, necks, waists. Moving from the Z car to the dry grass below the sycamore tree; following each other's rhythms and pausing intermittently to whisper together more stories from the past. Theresa had waved as he'd ridden away: this new love interest, this new distraction. For a long while, she stood there watching the space where he had been. *Tomás.* A man from two worlds. A man without a world. Her face felt dry, mildly chapped from the moisture of his lips; her cheeks and arms and hips still felt the shape of his hands. *Tomás*, she mouthed the word over and over. *Tomás Tomás Tomás.*

"Theresa." The lights were low. Her mother's voice rounded the corner of the kitchen. Theresa moved into the room. Her mother was standing by the speckled kitchen table, her arms hanging loosely at her sides. Theresa's eyes flickered through the room. There was nothing: no half-prepared meal, no freshly washed dishes. "What were you doing, Theresa? Where have you been?"

"Outside. Mom, don't you remember? Nathan hired that man Tomás to come help out."

"Tomás," she repeated. Her eyes shifted into recognition. "Tomás," she said again. "You were with Tomás."

Theresa nodded slowly. "He's cleaning out the horse barn. And fixing the car. Nathan hired him."

Her mother's head tilted mildly to the left. Her gaze angled out past Theresa, to the dying light. "It's getting dark," she said. Theresa reached over and flipped on the hallway light. Her mother started, blinked. "You're not being careful." Her mother's fingers played distracted along the vinyl edging of a kitchen chair. "You've got to be careful, Theresa."

"Mom," her voice frilled with an edge of anger that she recognized was still left over from the conversation outside. One brand of disappointment rolled over into the next. "He's just here cleaning. I was helping him."

But her mother was still shaking her head. "You don't know, baby," she warned. "You don't know what all can happen."

Maxine, 1939

Maxine told Freddy about the divorce through a letter. Three weeks went by and she hadn't heard anything, so she started filing the papers. She hadn't seen Freddy in months anyway; she figured he'd finally given up.

But she was wrong. It was a dry day when Freddy finally showed up at the bar. A Sunday, and she wasn't expecting anybody. When she heard footsteps out in the gravel, she figured it was John, coming back from her bath at the creek. But it was Freddy, looking tired. He must have hitched, she thought, watching him from the window, except that there wasn't any sound of a car. "Freddy," she called, stepping out into the sun. "Hey Freddy, did you walk here? Couldn't you find a ride?"

He shook his head. "Didn't want a ride," he said. "Wanted to walk." He looked bad: haggard, dirty. She felt sure he hadn't slept. And he was drunk. Walked seven miles from town, but still he was intoxicated.

"What happened, Freddy? What's wrong?"

He looked up at her with those big, foolish eyes of his. "She knows, Maxine," he whined. "Mother knows."

Jesus, Maxine thought. *She had read his mail.* Freddy was shaking now, his whole body shifting back and forth, punching around like when he laughed. He looked almost comic like that, his movements slowed from the liquor, his gangly arms and legs trying to get themselves under control. "She can't abide it," he cried at last. "She can't abide it, Maxine."

Now, that did make Maxine feel bad. As much as Freddy tried her patience, she had never meant to cause him grief.

"Come on, Freddy," she told him. "Come on in here and get out of that sun."

When he stumbled inside, she sat him down on one of the stools by the bar. Freddy looked around; they had done a lot with the place since he'd seen it last: polished walnut floors and wrought-iron electric lights and a smooth maple wood bar with a great big, heavy-framed mirror behind it. But Freddy didn't say anything—whether he was proud of his wife, or jealous, or what.

"I'm gonna get you some water," she told him. "You're gonna have a helluva headache when you sober up."

Freddy turned to her; his eyes were wide and desperate. "Maxine," he blurted. "We could make it, you and me."

She shook her head. "Oh no, Freddy. I told you. It won't work."

"But I love you, Maxine."

"Love's not enough, Freddy." She made a move to leave, but he held down her hand; his grip was stronger than she would have expected.

"Don't you love me, Maxine?"

"I told you, Freddy. It's a sin. God's going to punish us."

"Yeah," he let her hand fall away. "That's right. God's going to punish us."

He was such a sad, failed man. "I sure am sorry, Freddy."

"But you do love me, don't you?" he insisted. "Say you love me, Maxine." The way he looked was just the same, pathetic look that her Aunt Belle wore on rainy days. Like you need someone else's blessing to make you whole.

"No, Freddy. I don't love you like that. You should find some-body who does."

He slouched lower on his seat.

"Freddy," she said again, "I'm going to get you some water."

He looked up; his expression had shifted. "Who is he, Maxine?" His voice took on a dark edge. He looked around the bar suspi-ciously, like he might find some kind of evidence. "Is he here?"

She shook her head. "There isn't anybody, Freddy."

"Is he handsome, Maxine?" He threw a hateful look her way. "Do you love him?"

Maxine slammed the flat of her hand down on the bar; inside, the nickel tray and polished glasses rattled. "I don't love anybody!" she yelled. "I don't need *anybody*!"

Freddy pulled his angered expression together and looked back accusingly. "Everybody needs to be loved, Maxine."

Maxine stomped outside. He was crazy, she told herself. Just crazy. Pumping water into a bucket to keep her husband from making himself sick, she hissed under her breath: "Not me, Freddy Timberlake. I've had enough of that kind of love."

The weather that day had been bright and stifling. John was down bathing at the creek. Maybe Freddy had heard her, Maxine figured later; maybe he'd known that they had only a little time alone. She couldn't guess know how much he had planned, but it is true that he knew how Maxine ran her bar. He knew where she kept things: the jar of nickels, the key to the juke box, and her daddy's old silver pistol hidden up underneath the bar counter. And that's just what she found, stepping back inside and adjusting to the dimness of the bar: Freddy was standing there, checking the loaded chambers of the pistol. They looked at each other, and down at the gun. "Freddy," she said, setting down the water bucket, "put that back. Don't be a fool."

But he wasn't listening; he pointed the gun toward her and fired. The gun coughed and bucked in his hand. The shot flew wild, lodging into the walnut flooring several feet from Maxine. She leapt back. Freddy looked surprised.

"Freddy!" she screamed. "Put that thing down!"

He looked up again and fired. Missed. He was crazy, Maxine thought. And he meant it: he wanted her dead.

It didn't take her long getting out of there: racing down the steps and out toward the road. They had made good progress on the building by then, but not much of the grounds had been cleared; all around them, dry woods and thick grasses pressed inward. Maxine tried to keep to the thickest parts, moving herself through the trees behind the bar and cabin, and on out towards Old Bull Creek Road. She strained to hear a car coming, but there wasn't any such kind of sound: it was Sunday, and early. All she could hear was Freddy's long, drunken footsteps lagging behind her, and the skittering whistles of birds, distant and high up and unimpressed with their racket. It was possible, she thought, that not even John would hear them. Their bathing spot was on the other side of the road, down an embankment where the water surged slightly around a bend.

"Maxine!" Freddy called, dragging his feet wearily behind him. He fired another aimless shot. It whistled past her, closer than before. She dashed quickly behind one of the thicker pine trees and stayed there. From her position, she could see the road, some two hundred feet off. In between, though, the vegetation thinned; even if a car did appear, she recognized how risky it would be to run for it.

"Maxine!" Freddy barked. "Come out!"

She pressed herself against the tree and yelled back: "What the hell do you think I'd do that for, Freddy?! Put that gun down!" she screeched. But he didn't answer. "Come on, Freddy. Throw it over here and let's talk. You wanna stay married?" she demanded. "Ok, we'll stay married."

He didn't say anything; she couldn't hear him moving. "Freddy?" Her heart thudded stronger. "What are you doing?" But there wasn't any kind of answer. "Freddy, I swear I didn't step out on you."

Nothing. She waited. Finally, he answered: "Talk, Maxine? You'll talk to me?"

She bent her head around the tree. He was a hundred yards back, his shoulders slumped, squinting low in the sun. "You're so beautiful, Maxine."

"Freddy, throw the gun on the ground."

He shook his head. "You're mine," he called. His eyes were hollow. She thought he'd fallen into some kind of stupor; the gun had almost slipped out of his fingers. Maxine moved slightly and he remembered himself, grabbing up the gun and firing. *Damnit!* she breathed, leaping forward and flattening down into the brush.

It was long and thick and dry; overhead, she heard the fir trees bending, their knotted insides creaking slightly. Freddy yelped out once more: "Maxine!" she heard another shot. Then another heavy sound—then nothing. What was he doing? Crazy Freddy. She waited for several seconds more, her heart grinding inside her. *Jesus,* she thought. *Jesus Christ. Where are you now? Didn't I tell you?* Her pulse thudded; the sweat on her brow dripped over her lids, stinging. *Didn't I tell you I never wanted to marry him?* Silence. She didn't move; she tried to think straight. How long had it been since he'd fired that first shot? How long could it possibly take John to run up from the creek. Five, six minutes? She told herself to wait it out. She tried to count—one, two, three, four.

The next thing she heard was John's voice. John was still a far ways off, but Maxine heard her calling: "Maxine!" She was running. Maxine heard her over and over. "Maxine! Where are you?!"

But she was too frightened to move. "John!" she yelled back. "John, be careful!"

John got closer, and her voice stopped. Maxine couldn't hear her running anymore. She didn't hear anything. Then John yelled: "Maxine?! What happened, Maxine?"

There was no other sound: no more Freddy. Something inside Maxine snapped; she breathed heavily, pulling her knees to her chest and crying in dumb fits. The grass moved around her; she felt John staring over her. She peered downward, her hair wet and her expression blank. All she wore was a pair of coveralls, slung on in haste as she'd scrambled up the bank. "Are you hurt, Maxine?"

Maxine shook her head. John looked her over. "Well, come on, then." She pulled her friend up out of the grasses dragged her back to the place where her husband had fallen. Freddy was laid out in the grass, his eyes open, staring up at them. His mouth, too, was open into that same round, soundless shape that he made when laughing. There was a little hole over his chest, punched into the fabric just above his heart. "Oh!" Maxine gasped, and pulled her weight onto John's shoulder. The bib of the girl's coveralls shifted, exposing the neat little rise of new breast beneath it; John tugged the fabric back into place. Then she bent down and studied the hole in Freddy's chest. It was small and round as a marble, without even that much blood. John put a hand to his neck to test the rhythm there. The tip of her tongue slid thoughtfully out one corner of her mouth. She looked concentrated and gentle, like tending to some kind of worried animal. Then she stood up. "He's dead," she said bluntly. "Fred's dead." She was so cool about it that Maxine thought to herself: *She must have seen dead people before.* But not Maxine. She hadn't really seen bodies—not killed ones, anyway. And it scared her, all of it: Freddy, and God, and the law.

"John," she gasped, trying not to look too closely at her dead husband. "What're we going to do?"

John was wiping her hands on the coveralls. She shrugged.

"They're going to come asking questions, you know."

She shook her head. "Naw. People's too busy with other things," she said.

"But how's it going to look? That's my pistol—and he's the one dead."

But John had already turned to walk back toward the bar. Maxine scrambled to catch up with her. "We'll just tell 'em what happened," she said after a while.

"How do you think they're going to believe us, John?" Maxine looked at her: she was a nobody, as was Maxine. "They might put us in jail."

But John shook her head again. "Not women," she answered. "People don't like no attention on women." She turned and glanced the hundred yards back toward the spot where Freddy laid; one quick shiver ran through her. Then she sighed and grabbed up a fist of hair and wrung it out thoughtfully over the grass. "Nobody's gonna worry too much about old Freddy, I guess," she concluded. "Men like that." She turned and spit into a corner of dirt. "Men like that."

Part III: Burning Paradise

Theresa, June 1979

"Theresa." Her mother's voice was sharp. Alert. "Theresa, let's go."

Around them, the light was barely breaking. It was early—too early. "Mom, what's wrong? What happened?"

"Theresa, it's time. Get up."

Theresa sat forward, squinting in the low light. Her mother stood above her, shifting her weight in all directions: pulling the covers off of her daughter, surveying the nightstand, the closet. "Theresa, we've got to get you ready," her voice was becoming breathy with excitement. "Where's that duffle bag you used to have?"

"Where are we going?" her own voice was stale and throaty. Tired. "I thought Nathan was coming again today," she reminded her mother. "With the realtor?"

"Come *on*, Theresa," her mother motioned toward the closet. The deflated duffle bag hung from her hands in protest. "Get dressed." Her mother would not stop moving; she pulsed like a June bug throughout the room, pulling together fresh clothes from Theresa's dresser, a spare pair of sneakers, her sunglasses, and a coat.

"Mom, wait a minute."

"We've got to go," she looked up. "Theresa, get dressed. I've got everything else in the car. Come on—it's getting late."

"What about my school work?"

"You can finish it when you get back," her mother's voice was exasperated. "Or you can bring it with you. Either way."

Light crept low and gray into the room. It couldn't have been much more than five o'clock. "I could stay here," Theresa suggested. "To help Nathan out."

"Don't be silly." Her mother bent over Theresa's laundry bin, yanked out a crinkled sweater and some used socks, and shoved them into the duffle bag.

Outside, the station wagon thrummed. It still smelled like her father's pipe: a dark-toned smoky flavor that clung permanently to the upholstery. Theresa found it soothing. She closed her eyes. The trunk slammed shut. Her mother slipped into the driver's seat and banged that door closed, as well. "All right," she breathed.

"I don't want to go." Theresa was awake now, although her mouth was barely washed, and her hair still clung to her head. She wore, in resistance to her mother's impromptu journey, the same faded t-shirt and pair of sweatpants that she had slept in. Her fingers crept up one side to tug her bra into place.

"Theresa," her mother's eyebrows folded inward. She was pretty. Even at sixty years old, Maxine was inordinately pretty: wide brown eyes and fluted cheek bones. Her hair was white, but combed and curled perfectly. She was smartly dressed in a two-piece suit with skirt and blazer. Theresa imagined that she had not slept at all the night before. "Theresa," she insisted, "this is important."

* * *

The highway opened out in front of them: oak-topped hills widening into plains, the ocean pulling farther and farther away. They drove north and east, up through Sacramento with its glistening towers and the river sipping through its streets. Nathan wouldn't even be awake yet, Theresa thought, staring out at the pooled lights of the freeway. Then the land around them shifted into indiscriminate plains. Her mother plugged onward, pushing past dry fields and hills into the remnants of gold country. The scents of rich dust and sage blossoms filtered past them. They were climbing. Pine forests and sudden creeks. The sky was an interminable blue.

Maxine flipped on the radio and began whistling softly as she drove. They stopped at highway marts and bought fizzing sodas with straws sticking straight out of them. She told her daughter how, in Mexico, people drank these beverages out of plastic bags, not even enough money for bottles. Theresa listened, imagining Tomás holding a plastic bag of soda pop, carefully as a heart. She watched her mother sip and suck. Being on the road agreed with her mother. It always had. "I'd like to know," she asked, "what we're doing."

"You needed a break. You were getting so sad there at the house."

Theresa shoved her empty soda bottle into the gap between her seat and the passenger door. "I was feeling better."

"You needed this." Her mother placed a hand gently over Theresa's knee. She smiled. It was still early. Theresa laid her head back and listened to the thrum of the road beneath their tires. There was no plan, no purpose. They were just driving. Driving until the little foil-wrapped roll of cash in her mother's purse ran out. Driving until the road blurred nostalgia into a dull paste. Driving until some grey lining of the past shook them awake again.

* * *

By the time Theresa woke up the next time, the sun was nearing its zenith. Her mother was still humming: old, big-band songs that channeled somehow, amazingly, through the dry air of Highway 99 and caught the radio wires: "Dancing Cheek to Cheek" and "Stormy Weather." Theresa breathed; a crisp, pine air had filtered through the car. To the north, Mount Shasta came steadily into view, breaking up the distance. Just ahead, a sign for Yreka appeared, passed. *Fifty miles.* Maxine reminded her daughter: "Ringling used to do one of his shows up here." Her voice was sad and pointed, as though she expected Theresa to appreciate that defeated history. For close to two years, Maxine's brother had traveled northern California with a sideshow, trying to bring the family circus back to life. But Theresa knew they hadn't been very significant. They had set up at highway rest stops or hired on as entertainment for car dealerships, sidewalk sales, or supermarket grand openings. The elephants and lions and billy goats all braying in the hot afternoons of Redding and Fresno and Weed.

"He used to do that with Lawrence, didn't he?"

Maxine stared straight out the windshield. Her hair was

mounted neatly in a twist at the back of her head. *Pretty*, Theresa thought, without meaning to. "They were friends, I suppose," her mother admitted.

Around them, the land was moving upward into mountains and crags: the gray-brown earth going iron and black, the sky taking on a jeweled tone as they climbed. And there was green—the deep green of fir trees all around them. Verdant and bold.

"Do you think Ringling knew? Did he understand how bad off Lawrence was?"

"Oh, Theresa," her mother sighed. "Some things are so simple, they're complicated." Her voice punched a bit breathy, "Lawrence was always a bit lost." Her fingers stretched themselves around the steering wheel.

"He used to say things," Theresa offered. "Strange things."

Her mother fell silent. She thrummed her fingers against the steering wheel and hummed lightly for a moment: *Don't sit under the apple tree with anyone else but me—no! no! no!* "What kinds of things?" she asked lightly. "What did he say to you?"

Theresa considered. "Philosophical things—religious things. He had a lot of big ideas." Once, she remembered, when she had upset her mother, she had gone to Lawrence looking for forgiveness. *Will God forgive anything you ask?* she'd wanted to know.

If you ask it with a pure heart.

And what if your heart isn't pure?

He had smiled. *Then you're human.*

Theresa had gotten quiet then. She knew she wasn't a good girl. She'd had the devil in her heart; maybe, she thought, he was still there.

Don't worry, he'd told her. *God forgives most things before you even ask.*

"He was considerate," her mother agreed. "And sad." She drove in silence for several moments more. The land around them shifted into increasingly vibrant palettes. "There are some people who just aren't cut out for this world."

Theresa gazed out the window; the mountain peak was a perfect triangle of white. "Are you saying it was his fault? He was hopeless?"

172

"I'm saying life is complicated, Theresa."

* * *

"We're in Medford."

By early evening, they had stopped at a diner along the highway in southern Oregon. Maxine had gone inside to get them a table, and Theresa circled around back toward the restroom until her mother was out of sight. Then she had gone to make a call at the payphone.

"*Medford?*" Nathan's voice spiked.

"In Oregon." Theresa cupped her hand around the phone. The highway traffic would make it difficult, she knew, for him to hear her.

"I know—I know Medford. But what the hell are you doing up there?"

Theresa shrugged against the side of the building; she felt a fleck of paint detach and catch against her sleeve. "I have no idea," she answered. "She just wanted to get us out of the house."

"Good lord."

"I know."

A semi-truck pulled into the lot, leaning toward her with its tremendous tonnage and angling out the sun for the slow moments that it took to move forward.

"Theresa?"

She waited until the truck had passed. "We're all right," she told him. "I just wanted you to know that we're all right."

"I'm glad you called," he said. "Tomás didn't know where you were, either." Then, as an afterthought, he asked. "Is she drinking?"

"*Drinking?*" Their mother never drank. "No, she's not drinking."

Nathan was silent for a moment. "Look," he said finally, "if things get too weird—if you're uncomfortable—I'll come get you. I will."

She imagined a thin note of jealousy in his voice: *They were having an adventure, she and her mother. They were out on the road together going somewhere—anywhere.* "I'm not uncomfortable," she promised.

"You know what I mean."

She did. But despite it all—the illogic, her mother's willfulness—there had always been a certain pleasure to these excursions: a secrecy, a freedom. "I'll be ok," she promised, and hung up. There was the startled cry of plastic on plastic. She took a few steps forward and glanced in the window of the diner. Her mother sat quietly at a booth, applying a fresh coat of lipstick, her mouth cupped carefully as she traced the lines. Then she smacked her lips together and turned back to the menu. The door jangled as Theresa entered.

"Look at this!" her mother gestured impressively at the diner's offerings. "Lemon pancakes! Can you imagine? Lemon! We might practically be in France!"

Theresa slid into the booth opposite her mother. It was six-thirty in the evening.

"You have no idea," her mother mused, "the kinds of meals we used to eat out on the road." Her fingers thrummed along the tabletop as she considered the menu.

"Bear meat," Theresa confirmed.

"That's right!" her mother beamed. "You know, baby, we could go *anywhere* tomorrow."

Theresa glanced at her mother's purse: a tightly wrapped coil of aluminum-wrapped dollars lay inside. Theresa had no idea how much was there.

"The coast," her mother suggested. "Or maybe there's a county fair some place. Or Bella Vista," she pursed her lips, the fresh coat of red peeking like a bright *ping!* from the middle of her face. "We could go visit Bella Vista."

"Mom, we're in Oregon."

"I still have claim on that land, you know." Her mouth pressed inward, slightly indignant. "We could look up the records. I bet you I still have claim on that land."

The waitress came back to fill their water glasses. "Hello!" her mother grinned at the woman. "Are you still serving off the breakfast menu?"

"All day."

Her mother ordered the lemon pancakes and Theresa asked for a cheeseburger with a salad.

"This is my daughter," Maxine announced, before the woman could slip away. "She's going to college."

Theresa looked up, alarmed. The woman looked her over, and her eyebrow rose, mildly surprised. "Well," she said, "good for you."

"She's going to be a doctor," Maxine pressed. "Or, what else, Theresa? A teacher? She's smart," she told the waitress. "You'll see."

The woman smiled politely and left to go put in their order.

"Why do you do that?" Theresa demanded, gripping the edge of the table. "Why do you tell lies about me?"

"They're not lies."

"They aren't true."

"But they will be." Maxine took a careful sip from her coffee cup; the hot liquid ate away her lipstick, creating a little moon of colorlessness. "Eventually."

"You don't know that."

"Sure I do. You're smart, Theresa. You could do a lot," she paused, considering her daughter across the table. "Don't you want to? Don't you want to have a big, important life?"

Theresa watched her mother: all those stories behind her. A big life, certainly, but a haphazard one. "I don't know what kind of life I want yet."

"Well," her mother leaned back, "you'll see—you will."

Theresa sat in silence. She poked at the thin tablecloth, plastic and checkered along the top, and felted white on the underside. "Mom, I want to know more about Lawrence."

"You know plenty," she answered briskly. "You know how he was."

"But I want to know what happened to him."

"Oh, you don't really." Her mother sipped her coffee again, a wider and wider moon-space opening up along her top lip. "You're just worried," she concluded. "Like it's going to infect you, or something." Her eyes focused on her child, holding her in a single frame. "But it won't, baby. I promise."

"He lived with us."

"You don't have to be like him." Her hand came over Theresa's.

"Why can't we talk about this?"

"And ruin our vacation?" Her mother flipped a hand through the air. Her brightness that day simply did not cease. It *would not*.

Theresa ran the edges of her fingernails across the textured rise and fold of the tablecloth. As the waitress returned with their meals, there was a sweet-noxious smell of lemon and grease. They fell silent for a moment as the woman—her name, the embroidered scrawl over her left bosom told them, was Patti—clinked their plates into place. After she had left, Maxine explained to her daughter. "Sad things stay in the past." She forked a square of lemon pancake and aimed it toward her mouth. "That's the one good thing about them."

Maxine, 1941

"Heard you had some trouble." The man on the silver stallion was back. Maxine shoved a garden spade into the dirt and peered up at him. But that was all he said: stating what was already apparent. Everybody in town had heard about her trouble with Freddy.

"Yeah," she answered, smacking the soil off her hands. "It's taken care of." The law, as it turned out, could be quite sympathetic to a pair of unprotected girls like her and John.

He nodded. "That's what the sheriff told me." He was handsome, and sat atop the stallion loose and confident, like the farm boy he was: his back held straight and well turned, sloping down into a narrow set of hips. Now that she knew what sex was, what men and women did together, she could understand better what passion was. But Maxine didn't think she wanted any more of that. It was too painful—quite simply too much.

"I suppose you'll be opening up again soon," he went on. The blacks of his eyes did pretty things in the sunlight.

Maxine nodded. It had taken several weeks, of course, for her and John to recover.

"That's good," he said. "My boys—they've been getting thirsty. Maybe you can help us out."

She shoved a hand onto her hip. "Williams," she said. "That's your name, isn't it?"

He tugged his hat down lower against the sun and nodded slightly.

"Well, Mr. Williams," she told him, "you bring your boys by, and you'll all get what you pay for."

Gerald Williams chuckled. His head bobbed forward again in the sun. "Yes, ma'am. I expect we will."

* * *

Within a few weeks of Bella Vista's reopening, Maxine and John were hosting crowds like they'd never seen: ranchers and businessmen; clerks, college kids, and small time politicians; union leaders and crowds of CCC boys. Everybody within twenty miles wanted to come out and meet the two girls who had survived a madman's attack. So business was good; and before too long, Maxine was making all kinds of friends: men and women her own age who thought Maxine's life was just about as romantic as they came. The girls kept her abreast of all the news in town, whispering heated rumors in the corners of the bar, and the boys took her out occasionally for fried chicken or walks along the creek. Maxine was getting just what she wanted: small town notoriety, a bit of flirtatious attention. Back then, it was easy to go out with boys and not love them. The early 1940s were not a time for intimacy and heart-squeezing love affairs. They had fun up at Bella Vista collectively: taking rides through the country when someone had a car, or floating down Old Bull Creek on patched inner tubes when they did not. Other times, they'd spent whole days fishing down by the lake, or holding swimming matches. By night, most of them were back up at the bar, practicing their two-step. Those had been good times for Maxine—some of the best; she hadn't figured there was much that she was missing.

But Gerald Williams thought otherwise. "So what's next?" He sat loose and easy on a bar stool by the juke box. "You sure have made this place a success," he gestured around the room, bustling with couples rolling along to the Charleston.

Maxine shrugged. "Nothing, I guess. I'm happy here."

Gerald's eyebrows rose ever so slightly, but she didn't guess she cared what he thought. He'd been missing for weeks, anyway, coming and going just as casual as you please. People said most likely he had a wife and family down there in Smithville, where he always went to visit. So Maxine didn't figure he had much authority in the matter: what kind of life Bella Vista was. "I got my bar," she told him. "John likes it here, and my brother's getting his schooling with the nuns down at St. Ann's. It's a good enough life."

"Good enough," he said again, without taking the comment further. Gerald had been successful too, she knew. Although he didn't come from anything more than farmer's stock, he never let the college boys and their fancy talk get to him, and he didn't apologize to anyone. People respected Gerald, and that was just as well for Maxine and her bar. Whenever he was around—which, after about the first year, did amount to more evenings than not—they didn't have to worry about any rough-housing or nasty language or men throwing dice. Women liked him, and men did too. In that small world, he was important: a quiet, charismatic man who had done well with the government jobs. Gerald was a man who believed in progress: the world was changing, he said. Work was changing, and the ways you found work. There was a certain security to being a part of something, he told Maxine. An institution. A group of people. She shook her head. "I belong to myself," she told him. And he grinned.

* * *

"Mac!" John was standing in the doorway, her bathing suit and towel slung over an arm, expectant. It was a Tuesday evening in July. Balmy outside. The bar had been open for more than an hour, but there weren't many customers.

"Swimming?" Maxine asked. "Tonight?"

"Couple of the boys got a car." John pushed her chin in the direction of the door.

Maxine glanced back at Gerald, who sat idly at one of the high-standing bar tables.

"Mac?" John was turning to go. She was still so young—not even sixteen yet—but she would have hitched herself a ride all the way to Canada if the mood had struck her.

"Better go keep an eye on her," Gerald nodded lightly.

"And you?" Maxine asked as he pulled himself up from the table, looming a good two heads above her at his full height. He shrugged: "Didn't bring a suit."

"Then you can chaperone," she told him briskly, making her way out to the shed to gather her things.

The light down at the lake was good that night: the scattered park lamps coupled with just enough moon to make the water navigatable. Not that John hardly needed it. She was a natural swimmer: long-bodied and strong, she lifted herself smoothly in and out of the dark water like a slowly dipping oar. By the time that Maxine and Gerald had made their way down to the dock, John had already slipped into her suit and was haggling with the boys about the stakes for that night's race. "Best of *three*," she was insisting. "I ain't giving you fools no more chance than that."

Gerald laughed, moving away from the crowd, down toward the water's edge. "Now that's a woman who knows her mind."

"She's no woman *yet*," Maxine insisted, watching carefully as John stood, hip out, and the boys stole surreptitious glances at her. She barked orders out there at the lake the same as she did up at Bella Vista—never noticing or caring about the way her smooth thighs and neckline picked up the moonlight.

"It's good you look out for her," he said, picking his way through the underbrush.

"We look out for each other."

"As you should," he nodded, leaving the little gravel path and making his way through the slight underbrush toward the embankment. "You don't ever know what's coming down the pike."

Arriving at the edge of the lake, he stood for a moment, his broad back turned toward Maxine, and considered the night, the moon, the ring of swimmers a few hundred yards away, pairing off for their matches. "You sure don't ever know," he shook his head and sat down along a grassy space of waterline. The first two swimmers pushed off into the water, and Maxine moved toward him, standing there beside him for a long minute, watching the racers lengthen in the water, a long thin wake floating after them. Gerald didn't invite her to sit down with him, but eventually she did, choosing a flattened patch of grass a couple of feet away. Then they watched the rest of that first race in silence, the moon skittering along the water and the dark breezes filling the spaces between them.

After another moment, Gerald looked up. "My daddy killed a man once," he said abruptly. Maxine started—not sure if she was more shocked by what he said or the fact of him saying it. This was more than she'd heard him share about himself in more than a year. "We had us a little gas stop on the edge of our land. Trucks came to fill up, you know?" She nodded. "So this fella tried to rob us one day—took a whole week's earnings out of the till. He would have got away, too; he had a car. But my daddy shot him. I watched him do it."

Gerald was staring out at the black water. The moon was so bright, it seemed to fill the lake with movement, touching down in different patterns where the eddies shifted.

"What happened?"

Gerald bent his head, drawing his knees up underneath his chin. He was such a large man, and so quiet. Maxine felt herself almost fretting about him, as though something terrible was about to happen. "Nothing," he said. "He was a convict, it turned out. The car was hot, so the cops were glad enough to find him dead." Then he paused to toss a couple of stones lightly into the water, pivoting backward and sloughing them off so they skipped twice along the surface of the dark water before disappearing. The moon was ripe above them. In the background, they could hear blurred voices: girls cheering their fellas, and John still arguing details of the race results. From a distance, in the matronly woman's swimsuit that she had inherited from some other girl and taken up with safety pins, John looked even skinnier than she was. Long unshaped legs, and just a hint of breasts. It was the kind of budding temptation that the boys loved.

"Things happen," Gerald sighed, poking around the soil for another flat-shaped stone. "You don't ever know what."

"I got a pistol," Maxine reminded him. "And I know how to shoot."

He nodded. "Sure, Mac," he answered, finding a suitable stone and tossing it sideways across the water. "I know."

Maxine nodded to herself, thinking again about Freddy: that little hole punched right over his heart. So small and neat you wouldn't have thought it could get a man dead—you just wouldn't have thought that at all.

Gerald was shaking his head again: "But you sure don't ever know what's coming down the pike."

"I can handle myself," she assured him. "Me and John both."

He spread his broad fingers through the grass. The smell coming off him was like shaved wood. It smelled good—whiskey and work and something sweet. Maxine watched him, wordless, for several minutes, wondering what it was about this night—the lake, or the moon, or the hollering boys in the distance—that had opened him up so. Part of her was grateful, and part was disappointed. He wasn't asking her nearly as much about herself now—not hardly a damn thing.

"He was a good man, my father," Gerald said then, looking up.

"Did he die?"

"Last year," Gerald nodded. "Got him in the ground just this past September. He was sick for years."

"My daddy was a good man, too," she told him. "Just a bit foolish is all. He thought such good things about the world."

"Nothing wrong with that," Gerald said, staring blankly out across the water.

Maxine narrowed her eyes and watched him, remembering her mother, the desperation in her eyes as she'd said goodbye to Ringling; and her father, so noble and good and overly trusting. She shook her head. Maxine had decided that she wouldn't be like either one of them. She would survive, no matter what the cost—to her or to anyone else.

Gerald was still staring up at the moon. "What happens to a girl like you?" he asked, though mostly to himself. Maxine watched his profile, sharp cut and handsome as it was, and noticed the slight lines forming at the corners of his eyes. There was something about him, she thought, that he didn't let other people see. And right then, she wanted desperately to know what it was: all those secrets he kept, and whatever it was that he thought of her.

"Well," he sighed, rocking his weight backwards, hands wrapped around his knees. "You're smart, Maxine. I guess you'll figure it out."

"That's it?" The words came out before she had even realized that they were there. She looked wildly around at the moon and the lake and the swimmers beyond. Some small night creature scurried past them. A slight wind came up, and with it, dust, erasing the stars. It was as romantic an evening as she had ever known. "That's all you can say?"

"Well?" he answered. "What else did you expect, Mac?"

She didn't respond, and after a moment, a slight smile lifted his lips, replacing that other, more mysterious expression. Maxine shook her head. "I don't know."

"Oh," he said, grinning wider, "I think you do." He watched her for another moment. "You ever loved anybody, Maxine? Did that Freddy teach you anything?"

She stared back at him: that confident man, so smooth and secretive and sure of himself. "My husband tried to be a good man." Her voice was stiff. "He just didn't ever get it right."

"Well," Gerald said. "That's a shame, Mac. Because you're quite a woman—and I guess he mostly left you out to dry."

And then he did it, just like that: leaned over and swept his arms around her, pulling her to him. The kiss was cool and creamy and lasted a long moment. When he finally released her, Maxine fell backward, her hands cutting against the dry grasses. "How dare you?!" she belted, brushing a burr off her palm and slapping him against the cheek. "You're married!"

"Married?" He looked amused, tucking a hand over the space where she had hit him. He kept it there almost tenderly, as though he was holding onto something that he didn't want to lose. "Now, whatever gave you that idea?"

From across the lake, the shouts filled out the air in a triumphant burst as someone else pulled, victorious, up to the shore. "But you're gone so much," she insisted. "Down in Smithville."

He nodded. "That's true enough," he answered. "When the camp will let me go."

"The girls say you got a wife down there," she went on, pointing a finger loosely across the lake. "That's why you go off so much. Everybody knows that."

He let his hand fall away from his face, shaking his head again. "You shouldn't listen to everything you hear, Mac."

But that just made Maxine even more furious—he had humiliated her not once, but twice. "Well, you still can't just go around kissing girls like that, just because you feel like it, Mr. Williams."

Gerald's eyes winked in the moonlight. "Not even when the girl wants so very much to be kissed?"

"San Antonio!" She jumped to her feet. "I never met such a heel!"

"Oh, Mac, come on now." He drew himself slowly up to stand beside her. "Don't tell me there aren't half a dozen boys over there who you let do the same." He nodded toward the swimmers, slightly hunched and shivering now that their match was over.

This was true, but she wouldn't give him the satisfaction of hearing her say it. "Least those boys don't go sneaking off all the time without letting anybody know what they're up to," she snapped.

Gerald frowned. "All right," he said. "You want to know what I got down in Smithville? A couple of spinster sisters ten years older than me, that's what. And my mother, who can't do hardly anything now that my dad's gone. So don't you think I go down there and check on them? Don't you think I try to be a good son?"

Maxine watched him, her eyes still narrowed. "If you're such a hero, why don't you stay down there with them, then?"

He shook his head. "Because a man's got to have his own life," he answered carefully. "You, too, Maxine. It's a real good thing you're doing for Ringling. A real good thing. But he's not going to be around forever."

She stared at him, hard: "I love my brother more than anything in the world."

Gerald nodded. "Sure, Mac, but he's just a kid. They grow up and leave. That's what kids do."

She shook her head. "Ringling won't leave me," she assured him. "He *won't*."

"Oh, Mac," he sighed, shaking his head in the near darkness. He didn't say anything else, but the way he looked at her made Maxine angry: like he had the whole world figured out, and she was just struggling to get started.

"I *like* my life," she told him. "I like what I got here."

"This?" he gestured toward the lake, the stars coming back into focus, John shivering in her swimsuit, reigning victorious again. "This is just about as pretty as it can be, Mac, but it ain't gonna last. Things like this never do."

She shook her head. Gerald was so damn serious. And maybe he *was* right; there wasn't much of anything in her life that had lasted. But she decided she didn't care. She turned away and started moving back around the edge of the lake toward John, swaggering victorious along the shore. Most of the boys were dressed again and starting up their engines. "Don't worry about me, Gerald," she called over her shoulder. "I'll get through things. I always have." And he followed her up along the narrow path around the edge of the lake, nearer and nearer, until they could hear their voices again: the excited fizz of young people inventing life, moment by moment. "Sure enough, Mac," his voice echoed behind her. "Sure enough."

Lawrence, 1965

It was the spring of 1965 when Frankie Morlin decided not to become a priest. Instead, he would marry Ginger, a woman he'd met in a bar just off Market Street. Lawrence couldn't think of anything worse.

"It's just a choice, man. You gotta make up your mind what's best for you." Less than a year away from being ordained, and Frankie wasn't at all reticent about the change.

"God makes that choice," his friend reminded him. "We're *called*, Frankie."

Frankie slid a hand across Lawrence's shoulder. "God makes a suggestion," he said. "It's up to us to figure out whether or not it's right."

But Lawrence knew that he was fooling himself. If Frankie left the Church, it meant he wasn't chosen; he hadn't ever really been called. This kind of thing happened all the time: God didn't make mistakes, but people did. Even back at St. Pious, parents had occasionally arrived to reclaim their trembling sons. "So sorry," they'd tell the parish brothers. "My boy thought he'd heard God, but he was wrong." Out of a class of forty-five, they were down to twenty-nine by high school graduation. The numbers were even lower by then, down there in the city—three hours from St. Pious with its strict brotherhood and only the most rural of distractions. But in San Francisco, they were so close to everything: the ports, the televisions, the budding political rallies. Everyone their age was busy experimenting—with drugs, sex, politics.

Even the Church itself was full of new ideas. For three years now, the new decrees had been rolling down from Rome: the *Ad Gentes*, the *Optatum Totius*, the *Christus Dominus*. Detailed regulations for bishops, missionaries, and the training of priests. Finally there was a day—one modest week to the next—when the entire liturgy was interrupted: the altar uprooted, prayers shifted from Latin to vernacular. Suddenly, they were breaking bread over rented folding tables and speaking in a language that everyone could understand. The change was immediate and painful: priests forgetting the new translations of things, altar boys missing their cues, hymns sung shyly or not at all. The congregation didn't know what to do with their eyes; all at once, they had to face godliness head-on.

"I feel betrayed," Lawrence had confided, but Frankie didn't understand. By the time Vatican II was dealing its final blows, Frankie was already taking classes at the regular university. "That first day," Lawrence had tried to make him understand, "delivering the new liturgy, I almost couldn't breathe." He had found it terrifying: no more cloaks or Latin prayers to hide behind. And worse, God seemed suddenly absent. There was no great, dominant mind controlling them any longer; there was no plan.

"It's just logistics," Frankie answered reassuringly. "It doesn't change your relationship with God."

"But people can *see* you up there," he'd insisted. And it was true, he thought: they could see right through you.

Ginger's friend Sylvia was a person like that. "You're looking for something." That's the first thing she said to Lawrence. He was standing in a corner of Frankie's new apartment, drinking a beer at the engagement party. His fourth.

"Yes," he nodded. "Something important."

Sylvia was tall and slender. Her features were distinct: a long face with a sharp chin and nose. She had a full chest, but narrow hips, which jutted out slightly against the lines of her dress. "What?" she wanted to know.

He told her: "God."

"Oh," she chuckled. "You must be one of Frankie's priest friends."

"Not yet," he said. "Not for another year."

"So what do you do, then?" Her eyes narrowed. They were light-brown, almost camel-colored.

"Study," he told her. "And apprentice. It's a very intensive process."

"I see." Sylvia watched him for a moment, seeming amused. "Tell me," she said, sipping wine from a paper cup. "What's it like, believing that a man could be as powerful as God?"

"It's very intimate."

"Yes," she considered. "That would be. It must excuse you from a lot—humanity, the fall." Her hand flipped through the air; the fingers were long and fluted and moved in a charming, selective way. Lawrence could tell that she was a woman who usually got what she wanted.

"Yes," he agreed. He supposed it did.

* * *

Lawrence had never seen a woman's body in that way before: a bright, sudden nakedness. Until he was with Sylvia, there in her apartment after Frankie's party, he had never completely understood lust: what exactly it is that a man wants. He had only known a craving—huge and nameless and unformed. But that first night with Sylvia, it was all so immediate: hips and stomach and chest. Her narrow arms, the curve of her calf. Her smell. The slightly acrid taste of her mouth. And those dark, crinkled nipples, pink points like stars—twin nail heads, fastening together some fleshly architecture. She was exactly what he had wanted, without knowing. Their bodies, he realized, were engineered for each other. It came to him as a shock—something bitterly human. He thought about his creator; he stood in awe of such a perfect betrayal.

When they made love, hours after the party, Lawrence wasn't drunk anymore. So it wasn't foolishness—it wasn't even seduction. If anything, it was despair, he thought, as she removed his clothes, and then hers. After that, she laid him down on the bed and took him in a way that he hadn't known about: his own body splayed out on the bed, waiting to receive hers. Very slowly, she traced a hand over the flat of his stomach, a small rise of chest, and then of thigh.

Her expression was so uncertain, he imagined a tenderness passing through her. Lawrence's heart threw its weight irresponsibly around his chest; he felt himself begin to sweat. Sylvia fluttered her hand gently along the surface of his erection, and he thought he would collapse under the pressure. But she was particular—intent on this specific physical preparation, like a ritual. He didn't know what to do. She wasn't kissing him, or even speaking; she just kept touching, examining. And what did she see, he wondered? Was a priest like other men? Was there some kind of special satisfaction for her in this? His heart moved again, rattling against its cage of anticipation. What was he supposed to do? There was no script, no specific answer. Right then, intimacy felt just about as terrible as the new mass—that tight restriction, this feeling of being watched. Lawrence sucked and sucked at the air like his lungs just couldn't wrap themselves around it fast enough.

When she was ready, she lifted herself—the sweet division of her legs, those twin white thighs opening themselves like the mouth of a bird—and hunched over him again, making him wait a little longer. All this time, her eyes didn't leave him; she didn't speak. Lawrence's heart moved more slowly now, and his thoughts—rugged, complicated pieces of myth and history—locked and unlocked themselves into wieldy, uncomfortable patterns. He wanted badly to be rid of them—rid of something. His mind or his body; he didn't care which. It was simply too much, this living in both worlds together, all at once.

Then she was on him—over him—and he was inside of that careful mystery. When he came, it was loud and unforgiving, like a fire. Like something sacred had knelt down and touched him, but only for an instant. Lawrence's head flung itself back in a gesture of defeat, and he felt her hand darting quickly downward. She held him there, riding him for another moment; and he kept his gaze someplace else. When she had finished, Sylvia groaned once, and let him go.

Afterward, in a very clichéd way, she smoked. This was part of the luxurious way in which she experienced herself. To Lawrence, it was a disappointment—not the fact of the cigarette itself, but its sad banality. By her bedside, she kept a low stool with an empty Coca-Cola bottle and a dried sprig of columbine, a law book, and a split mollusk shell. On the floor, more books were piled: Kierkegaard, Kafka, Camus.

"Do you like literature?" he asked.

"Only the kind that makes you think."

"About what?"

"Life," she shrugged. "Losing things." She looked at him. "Nothing's worth very much unless it hurts first."

He told her that wasn't a very uplifting outlook.

"Philosophy," she answered, "wasn't designed to make people feel better."

"Then why do you read it?"

"Because it's honest." She twirled the cigarette gently between thumb and index finger; it glittered and fumed. "And logical. It's something you can rely on."

Lawrence nodded, carefully.

"Don't you think that's important?" she insisted. "Reliability? Something to count on?"

"Yes," he agreed. "Of course."

Sylvia held the cigarette deftly away from the bed, extending her long, white arm. Intermittently, she tapped the debris lightly into the mollusk shell.

"Lawrence," she snuffed out the cigarette and flipped over, pushing herself up onto an elbow, "what's the worst thing you ever did?"

He told her truthfully: "This."

"And you think your God will forgive you for it?"

"I hope so."

She leaned over and pulled a speck of something from her bottom lip. Then she turned back coyly, looking up through the tops of her eyes. "I don't believe you."

* * *

They went on like that for two months. "Are you worried?" Sylvia gestured broadly about the room: their bodies wrapped through the bed sheets, her piles of unshelved philosophy books, a two-burner and a crock pot sitting in one corner. "Does anybody know?"

190

He shook his head; he wasn't worried. He was not, after all, the only seminarian who had given way to carnal need. Even if Frankie or one of the others found out, it wasn't likely that they would tell.

But what he did feel was lost.

"Of course you do," Sylvia's voice was crisp. She was not, Lawrence had to admit, the kind of soft-hearted woman that he had hoped for. "The worst thing about living is that we do it alone."

Sylvia was smoking again; she always needed something in her hands when she talked about big ideas. "For instance," she took a drag and held it for a moment, "everybody knows they've got the power to destroy themselves—or to go on living. It's something we decide every day." She looked at him seriously. "That's Heidegger, by the way."

Sylvia contended that everyone has to make choices; that's the fate we're condemned to. The worst choice she'd had to make was moving there to San Francisco. Even with the full university scholarship, it had been difficult. "My father said if I left, I'd better not ever come back," she traced a finger gently around her kneecap. "He told me it was shameful, my being a woman and going out to be educated like that. But I'm going to law school afterward, too. My father doesn't think women can become lawyers. But I will. I'll do better than that. I'll be a judge: the first woman judge in California."

She reached over and took a sip of something from a flask at her bedside. "Do you think I can do it?"

Lawrence looked at her; he felt sure she was capable of just about anything. It was what thrilled and terrified him most about her. "Of course," he told her, and she grinned, leaning in to him. She pulled a tuft of hair at his temple, looking pleased. He was handsome, she had told him, though he didn't do too much with it.

"What about you?" she asked. "What do you want most?"

The priesthood, he told her. He wanted to become a priest.

"So why are you doing this?"

Lawrence shook his head: "It's complicated."

"Nonsense." She sat herself upright, her legs tucked underneath themselves and her naked chest warm and round. "Desire's not that complicated. People just say that to make themselves feel better."

She took another sip and swallowed, hard. "I'll bet even your Christ had something to say about that."

He took the liquor from her and held it for a moment.

"Well?" she insisted. "What did he say?"

He sniffed the flask and took a drink. Then he told her the story of Christ in the wilderness, perched with Satan on a cliff overlooking the most beautiful kingdom imaginable. He told her how Satan had offered it to him—all of it—if he would renounce his father: *All the power in the world can be yours*, the story goes, *if you will just bow down before me.*

"And what did he do?" She reached again for the whiskey.

"He refused."

She took another swig and whistled, bright and shrill; it was not a sound that he had expected from her. "All the power in the world, and he turned it down?" She paused briefly. "Would you want to be all-powerful like that?"

"No," Lawrence shook his head.

She set the bottle down and lay back on the bed, stretching her body out in four directions. Her back arched, the nipples punching upward toward the ceiling, still sharp and red from their sex.

"Well then, what do you think about me?" She considered her body pleasurably for a moment. "Do you suppose I could be all-powerful?"

"No one can do that except God."

"But he turned it down," she said, unfazed.

"Yes," Lawrence admitted.

"So it's still up for grabs."

Theresa, June 1979

The light was lengthening by the time they left the diner, and Theresa wanted to know if they would be spending the night there in Medford. It had been a long day already, and she was tired. Her mother considered their options: the gas station, the weary diner, and an even shabbier-looking motel across the street. She smacked her lips together, smearing around a fresh coat of color. "And waste all this good driving time?" She checked her watch; it was nearly eight o'clock. "The roads will be mostly empty by now," she chirped. "We could get ourselves up to the coast. Find some place to camp. A day at the beach—you'd like that, wouldn't you, Theresa?" Then she clucked at the price of gas and announced that they would stop some place further down the highway. Theresa watched the truckers in their box-cut denim pants mill stiffly about the gas tanks; inside, Patti would be collecting their plates, leaving them in a pile for the dish boy. They pulled away, lurching back toward the freeway on-ramp, and Theresa guessed she could forgive her mother's small indiscretions. They were leaving; they were moving on. But it would be temporary; it had to be. Eventually, the aluminum roll of cash would run out; they would go back, like they always did. And Tomás would still be there, wouldn't he? Her eyes pressed shut: the feel of his mouth, the shape of him, just becoming distinct to her. There were girls at school who had cousins or older siblings who remembered the summer of love and talked big talk about sexual matters. Theresa's brothers were not like that; they didn't talk—at least, not with her. She didn't know anyone who was free with their body. But the buzz was around her still, and she could see the shapes of things ahead. It seemed inevitable, like a promise: these things that would happen to her. For her. *Love and the body*, and whatever other unnamed future, were still out there, waiting.

The façade of the station where they stopped next was paneled in knotted wood. The attendant wore a full uniform with stripes running down the legs of his pants and his name embroidered in cursive below his lapel. The air around them had thinned even further. Theresa concentrated, pulling deep breaths into her lungs.

"When my boys were young, we used to come here every summer," her mother was telling the attendant. Theresa shifted forward in her seat and strained her ear out the window. Her mother stood by the pumps, chatting excitedly with the gas attendant. It was nearly night time, but the filling station was one she recognized. *The Siskiyous*, she thought. *Siskiyou National Forest.*

"That man remembers me," her mother said brightly, sliding back into the driver's seat. "Can you believe that? All those years ago, when we came up here with the van and the whole bunch of you kids. He's been working here this whole time—isn't that remarkable?"

"Are we staying here, Mom?"

Her mother gripped the steering wheel, her elbows locked. She considered the slow-moving world of cars and attendants beyond the windshield. Her mood sank; she looked mildly baffled. "Will you just hold on a second, Theresa? Give a person a minute to figure things out."

Theresa set her mouth. She shut her eyes again and the smell of gas overtook her: strong, ravenous, and invisible as the odor of the sea.

* * *

The modest grocery near the park entrance was nearly as Theresa had remembered it: a small affair, but complete. They could have hotdogs or hamburgers, her mother announced. She was forcing a bright, inexhaustible enthusiasm again, grinning in self-satisfaction because she had thought to bring a skillet, a knife, and cooking utensils: "We can eat like kings." Theresa responded that either option was fine, and her mother looked at her a bit sourly. She took a breath, grabbing hold of one of the wire-framed baskets at the front of the store. "So," she started again. "You'll be getting out of school soon, Theresa. Have you thought about where you'd like to go to college?" No one in the family had been to college. Maxine rounded a corner into the narrow aisle with refrigerated products; Theresa followed.

"Probably somewhere in California."

"Oh!" her mother glanced back, horrified. "But everyone in your class will be going someplace in California."

Theresa shrugged. She liked California; there were plenty of good schools right where she was.

"Oh, Theresa," Maxine tossed a package of ground beef into the cart. "You'll never get through life like that." They turned onto the aisle for condiments. Ketchup, relish, and a generous line of pickles. Theresa sighed. She wished her mother wouldn't insist on cooking something as elaborate as hamburgers; it always left her moody. Maxine hated slapping those little pink patties into shape. Usually, Theresa did it for her.

"You've got to be more creative," she was saying. "How about Texas? You've got your roots in Texas."

"I've never been to Texas, Mom." Theresa stared at a surprisingly long line of pickles—big and green and overwhelming.

"I know, baby, but I can tell you about it. I could even go with you." She considered: sweet, or dill.

"You're always telling me things. Why can't I just do something for myself?"

"Well!" She grabbed a jar and dropped into the cart, where it thudded against the meat, so little pink bubbles foamed out along the styrofoam edges. "I didn't know you were so ungrateful." She pulled the little basket closer to her body. "After all I've tried to teach you."

Then there was silence. Always, there was silence. That was her mother's favorite way of letting her know how she'd disappointed her. So it wasn't until they got to the check-out that Theresa found out just what her mother was thinking: "Girls are so complicated."

She set the down their groceries with a thud. "I raised four boys—but girls are another thing entirely." The man at the register nodded. He looked down, and Theresa could tell he figured she'd done something awful. She didn't look at him. She crossed her arms and stood there without saying anything. She didn't think she was complicated; she didn't know what was so difficult about wanting to go to a school in California instead of Texas. She looked at her mother: *You're the one who's complicated.*

* * *

It was getting dark by the time they had pitched their tent, but the air around them still held the memory of summer warmth. Theresa laid down on a blanket by the campfire, tenting her knees in the air and tucking her arms below her head.

Her mother lifted her head, gazing up at the sky. "You can't see stars like this in Fairfield," she mused. "It's too close to the city."

Theresa turned to consider her mother; the firelight cast strange figures across her face. She got up, moved around the campsite, kicking at the dark ground to scare up more kindling. She was dressed in tight linen pants and a flannel shirt. Her hair was braided, lying against her back in a thin cord that reached almost as far as her shoulder blades. Her foot came across something and made it snap; she bent over to retrieve the branch.

"When are we going home?"

"Don't worry about it, Theresa."

"I'm not worried; I'm just asking a question."

Her mother tossed the extra branches in the fire. They popped and hissed. "You always want to know everything ahead of time. Your father was like that, too."

Theresa turned slightly, watching her mother bend over the fire, and imagined briefly what that earlier life in the Austin foothills must have been like: bathing down in the river, catching trout for supper, cooking her meals over a fire. Maxine sighed. "A person just doesn't always have everything all figured out ahead of time. Life doesn't work that way." *But a person*, Theresa thought, *might at least try.* Her mother stooped over the fire, the flames sending fingers of brightness up across her chin and cheeks. She gave off poking the fire and tossed another thin branch into the flames. Sighed. "It's so hard, being a mother," she complained. "It's not for the faint of heart."

Theresa toed the ground, stirring up a small ant that scribbled in confusion across her foot and up the back of her calf; she reached down to brush it away. "I have a strong heart."

Maxine's sharp nose tilted up toward the night sky. "Oh, baby, you're so sweet. Of course you do. You've always been very big-hearted. Sometimes you remind me so much of my Aunt Della."

But Theresa knew about Della. "No," she said. "I mean I'm *strong*."

"Sure, baby," her mother answered, and went back to stargazing. Theresa had learned not to argue with her mother; it rarely paid off. She looked upward again. There were holes left in the sky, in the spaces between trees. Sage, and salamanders shifting against rocks. The air was still hot, even at night. Theresa's skin smelled mildly of charcoal and insect repellent. She breathed: despite the frictions with her mother, this was a place she loved.

"You know I had husband before your father." Her mother made this announcement without introduction or apology. But Theresa had not known this; it made her shudder. Just when she thought she understood her mother, Maxine's history would shift again, opening into a whole new set of tragedies and circumstances—forcing her daughter to question everything that had come before.

"He died. Killed himself, actually. Though I wasn't planning on staying married to him anyway."

Theresa lay there, holding her body as still as she could, to keep that information from touching her.

"He was a sad man, and I didn't love him. He didn't love himself, either. That was the problem." Her mother poked the fire. "It's important for a person to love himself. You shouldn't forget that, Theresa."

Theresa shook her head against the dirt. She could feel a tightness against the back of her skull: *She wouldn't. She would not forget.*

Her mother sighed. "Sometimes you just have to do things. In those days, I would have done anything to keep Ringling with me," she explained, yanking back up to attention the memory of her early heroism in the wake of their parents' deaths. "*Anything*," she swore again. "That's the kind of person I am." Then she turned toward Theresa: "You should know that about me, baby."

But Theresa did not want to know this—not any of it. Her mother's life was too complicated; it seemed they would never be finished with it.

"It's not easy raising somebody. I really didn't think I'd do it again. Not even after I married your father."

Theresa wished she would stop. It seemed there must be some way of making her stop, but she didn't know what it was.

"Life just doesn't turn out the way you think." The poker in her hand came loose, sliding away from the fire. She got quiet for a moment. But Theresa knew they weren't finished: "Why'd you do it, then?"

Her mother shrugged, tapping her stick against the ground. "You find out what you're capable of."

* * *

When they decided that it was time, Theresa followed her mother through the half-empty campgrounds down to the restroom, used the toilet, and rinsed her face. She stared for a moment at her reflection in the warped mirror. Her face came in and out of focus, like someone was trying to line her up for a photograph. *Pretty*, she thought. *Pretty enough*. Her mother had unzipped a generous cosmetics bag and was carefully lifting out her long chain of skin care products. "I'll wait by the door," Theresa told her, and moved back outside, shuffling a few paces down a bark path that led to a little picnic area. She sat down atop one of the tables, her sneakers propped on the bench below. The air was cool and fresh. It was a dark night; the sky was without a moon, so the stars felt increasingly close. Beautiful and alarming. Behind her, the river was talking. Theresa leaned her head back and stared straight upward at the canopy of fir trees and galaxy. She shut her eyes, drinking in the smell of cedar and soil and rushing water. She stood for a moment without moving, imagining that she might hear the wingdrop of a hoot owl, or her mother's cosmetic bag finally snapping shut in the empty hollow of the restroom.

There was a sound, but it was a several yards away, further

toward the river and down the embankment: a dull sound, a rustling. Theresa kept her body still; a silent explosion of fear spread quickly through her, like a match igniting and cooling within the space of a few seconds. She imagined thieves, drug deals, or animals. Maybe there was a mountain lion prowling the territory. Or even a bear.

The stars moved over the relative calm of the river without comment. A woman's voice groaned. Groaned again. Theresa's head shifted to the left, although she couldn't see anything. The rustling in the underbrush shifted its pacing, picking up speed. The woman groaned again. She sighed more loudly and was followed by a man's thick breathing. They weren't trying to be subtle now. Theresa sat on the hard, smooth surface of the picnic table, her body flushing in the darkness. She could feel the heat of her embarrassment spreading itself through her chest. But she could not move. Or would not. The woman was moaning with such exaggerated pleasure, Theresa wondered if anything that sounded like that could be real. She threw her gaze back across her shoulder, picked out the light from the restroom and waited a moment: no motion. She could barely believe that the sound of the couple's lovemaking had not reached her mother. Her mother, who might never know lovemaking again; and Theresa, who had not known it yet. The thought made her shudder; she closed her eyes. Her hands slipped between her thighs, pressed together palms inward. She brought them up against the trunk of herself and held them like that, without moving. The pressure of her hands; the rustle in the underbrush; the woman's loud, expectant pleading. Then there was a dull grumble—a man's hushed, incoherent voice.

The night came silent again, and Theresa was alone, sitting on a picnic table at night, some place in southern Oregon, her hands pinched together in wary anticipation. Double-edged: desire and alarm. She picked herself up and walked back toward the campsite. Half way there, she heard a sharp creak: her mother thrust the bathroom door open and let it swing shut behind her. She moved toward Theresa in the near dark, not noticing her daughter until they nearly collided. "Oh!" she exclaimed, and Theresa could see the careful outline of her eyes, the sheen of her cheeks, waxy and scented from her nightly facial. "Theresa! Where were you?"

"Right here," she promised. "I was just waiting for you. I didn't go anywhere."

Maxine, 1942

They were living in an ordinary time; nothing big and important had happened in several years. It was a good time to be living. Money was coming back slowly; jobs were coming back. All throughout the country, people were gradually becoming hopeful again. So when Pearl Harbor was hit, nobody could quite believe it. Out on the road climbing up toward Bella Vista, they had thought it was a joke: somebody screaming the news from a passing car. Maxine and Gerald ran with a raucous group in those days; people made jokes like that. But by the time they had made it back up to the bar, they'd found John listening soberly to the radio. Outside, another car skidded into the gravel. Maxine's friend Doris and her boyfriend rushed in. "The Japs!" the guy was panting. "They bombed us! The dirty Japs!" Maxine looked at Doris and nodded loosely. Her best friend from town, Doris was three years older than Maxine, and sharp-minded about worldly matters. On the airwaves, President Roosevelt was giving instructions to the nation to stay calm. The attack had been isolated, he said, and targeted military holdings. They watched each other carefully. None of them knew where Pearl Harbor was. They tried to imagine what a row of sunken ships in Hawaii must look like: metal rims and popping embers smoking amidst sandy islands full of palm trees. A burning paradise. The whole thing was so foreign, and so unbelievable. But the news spun onward, and the group of them listened quietly to the click and buzz of the radio. There was FDR talking over the lines: that same smooth, reassuring voice that had delivered fireside chats and opened up WPA programs for years. Now he was telling them that they would not back down. America was a strong nation, he declared; they would stand united.

Nobody said anything. They paid attention. Decades later, Maxine could look back and remember how all of them knew right away how much that event was going to change their lives. They couldn't see the particulars just yet, but the power of the thing was clear. The hole punched into the pit of their stomachs was collective: they had been hurt together, all at once. Next to her, Gerald must have been feeling it, too. "My God," he breathed, and she felt the tips of his fingers wind their way absent-mindedly into hers. It was the first time that their two bodies had ever touched in any kind of tender way. Even the kiss they'd shared had been different: strident and sexy. But in that moment, Gerald held onto her with such a simple intimacy: as though they had known each other their whole lives. The way the war affected him—quietly and profoundly—moved Maxine almost to tears. She hadn't thought what it would be like to find a man who felt things, but didn't talk about them. Freddy had always crooned on about all his unmet wants in life, all the ways the world had failed him. There was no mystery about him, nothing dynamic. But Gerald was different. There was a capacity in him—for feeling, and for some kind of other, more invisible strength—that she was only beginning to guess at.

Things changed quickly. Within days, there were rally centers and lines for enlistment. The courthouse downtown began to fill with weddings. New songs came on the radio, almost overnight. News coverage, too, went on for days and days. The president was quick to decide: they were going to war. Everyone became patriotic. They each did what they needed to do: enlist or donate or volunteer. After such a long time without a common cause, they finally had one. Just like that, they all felt part of the effort; each of their small lives was suddenly worth something.

And in just that same way, it took a war to make Gerald Williams clarify his intentions with Maxine. A little more than two weeks after Pearl Harbor, he showed up at Bella Vista with a small silver ring. He was already enlisted; most of the C-core men were. Not a month into the war with Japan, government projects were being suspended: the trails, the park, the dam up at Bastrop.

"I'd like to marry you, Maxine."

That was just how he said it: no romance, no charm. Just the straight, unadorned truth.

But Gerald had misread her. Maxine wasn't looking for marriage; she was just trying to keep her life going. And that small chore had gotten more difficult: there were fewer patrons coming up Bella Vista, and less to celebrate.

"And what about me, Mr. Williams?" she snapped. "What about what I want?"

Gerald was taken aback. He stared dumbly for a moment, and cleared his throat. "I figured you'd want the best things for yourself," he answered. "A solid life. A family someday." His head tilted to one side, like he was figuring something. "You don't really mean to spend your whole life out here selling beer?"

"It's a good life."

Gerald's chin buckled downward into a slight nod. "Sure, Mac. But not for forever. Not for a woman like you."

He didn't say what kind of woman that was, and Maxine didn't ask. It was enough that he was staring down the barrel of his intentions at her, his dark eyes silty and glittering. He was a beautiful man, just as he'd been on the first day she'd seen him. But a lot had changed since then.

"I'm off marriage," she told him. "I tried it once, and it didn't stick. Maybe that's the kind of woman I am—not the marrying kind."

* * *

"What're we gonna do?" John was worried; it was the first time that Maxine had seen her like that. But ever since that day they'd come back to find her locked in place beside the sputtering radio newsreels, something in John had shifted. She wasn't so cool and unconcerned anymore; there was a larger world, now, that mattered to her. "What're we gonna do, Mac?"

Maxine shook her head. "Nothing, John. We're fine—just as long as we can keep Bella Vista running, we'll be ok."

John turned toward her with a curious look in her eyes, like a whole new part of herself was opening up. This was nothing unusual for a sixteen-year-old girl, Maxine supposed, but those were not usual times. "What's gonna happen?"

"It's a war, John. I don't know. But we'll be all right here, you and me. And Ringling, too. We just gotta dig our heels in and get through this thing."

But John wasn't interested in heel digging. "It ain't right," she declared, pulling herself around the edge of the bar. Now that she was getting a little older, her body was catching up with those natural good looks of hers. She had a set of low, lengthening hips and an unusually long torso; they made her movements slow and seductive, whether or not she wanted them to be. "It just ain't right."

"People fight sometimes, John. You know that."

Her gaze shifted, moving slightly inward. "Still don't make it right."

Maxine felt bad for John, imagining that the world's war had brought to the surface all the things she'd been trying to forget: abuse, conflict, people's needless suffering. But that still didn't change what was happening. "This time we've got to, though," she reminded her friend. "We've got to clean out those dirty Japs."

John didn't answer. For all her roughness and shrewd living, Maxine hadn't ever heard John say anything mean-spirited about anybody.

"Don't you want our boys to go get rid of them?" she insisted. "Don't you hate them, John? What they did was terrible."

But John shook her head. She was the only person Maxine knew who hadn't taken an immediate disliking to the Japs. "Never met one," she concluded simply. "Can't hate what you don't know."

But Maxine had found plenty to resent in those days. The Japs, whether she knew them personally or not, had interrupted their lives in ways that Maxine felt sure not even they had imagined. As the country got ready for war, civilian gas stations started running out of stock, rubber got rationed, and people's extra money went in for war bonds. There were fewer and fewer cars making their way up Old Bull Creek Road. The prospect had her worried; at this rate, Maxine didn't see how they would make it through six months of war.

John, for different reasons, was worried, too. She had stopped sleeping. One night when Maxine got up to use the outhouse, there were lights on in the bar. She found John shuffling nickels through the juke box, spooning them out the other side and playing the songs over and over again: sad, romantic love songs.

"John," she asked. "What's getting at you? Is there some fella?"

For a moment, John didn't answer. Then she turned around. "People hurt each other," she said. "They always doing that."

On the table next to her was a flattened out newspaper from December 12. "John, what are you holding on to this for?"

John watched her with glassy eye. "Gotta do something, Mac," she said softly. "A body ought to do something."

"John," Maxine told her. "You're just a girl. This isn't your war, and it's not mine. The best thing we can do is buckle down and survive it."

But she shook her head. "There's always something to do." And that's when Maxine understood how much she'd misread John. There was a flash of idealism in the girl: the kind of impossible goodness that gets beat down inside of a person when enough bad things happen to them. A hopefulness that, when it finally surfaces, is out of proportion because of how long it had remained dormant: like an invalid going down with chest pain in November, coming back out in June, still wearing his winter coat. John didn't hardly know what to make of the world anymore; it had been such a long time since she'd done anything but follow along with Maxine.

"They got girls," she said. "They got girls who do things."

"Those girls are older," Maxine reminded her. "A lot of 'em older even than me." She was twenty by then, but she didn't see how she could go out and join the Red Cross, become a nurse, and follow the boys out to the battle lines. "I got Ringling to worry about. And Bella Vista. What am I going to do?"

Gerald, of course, saw that answer clearly: she should marry him. He continued coming out each week to remind her. But it worried her, too, to think about leaning on a man again. Even one as good as Gerald.

John didn't understand: "I thought you loved him."

"I do," she admitted. "But that's not enough, is it?"

John shrugged; unresolved things tended to leave her speechless.

"Well," Maxine said, "I don't think it is. There's got to be something more than that."

John watched her carefully, chewing a small cud of tobacco. "Like what?"

"I don't know," she shook her head. "Something solid. Like this life I got here." She gestured loosely about the room. "I got my own things to worry about." John stared back blankly, like she couldn't imagine what kind of things. "You and Ring," she told her fiercely. "And my bar."

But John didn't seem convinced. "You don't gotta worry about me," she answered finally, shrugging again in that same easy-boned way that she always did, like water coming off a rock.

Maxine shook her head. "I know it, John. But you understand, don't you? He can't just expect me to give all this up."

John shrugged. "Things might go away anyway."

"I know," she sighed, remembering some advice that Doris had given her once: sometimes you don't know how heavy your burden is until somebody offers you a place to set it down.

"So, what're you gonna do?" She stepped out from behind the bar, her slim fingers curled around a cigarette. The fellows always gave them to her—more than anything, for the entertainment of watching a woman smoke. "Gerald Williams," she said. "He's a good man."

Maxine nodded.

"You gonna marry him?"

"I don't know, John." She covered her face in her hands. "I just don't goddamned know."

* * *

"It's getting pretty desolate out here, Mac." The week before he left for Basic Training, Gerald came back to the bar one last time. He found Maxine hunched over the floor, picking bottle caps out of the sawdust. "Aren't you tired of all this?" he asked, gesturing around the all but empty bar. In a back corner, a few stray customers sniggered over a game of dice. She sighed, getting to her feet. In fact, Maxine *was* getting tired: tired of the noise and the uncertainty, the mud and the hustle, men taking fist fights out into the yard, and broken-hearted girls crying on her shoulder. She was tired of doing things that she'd never thought she could do. A person gets fed up with being brave all the time, she realized, when they finally have time to sit back and think about it.

Gerald glanced around the bar at the empty stools and the blinking jukebox. "Where's John?"

"She left."

"Left?"

"Signed up with the Red Cross. Two days ago. They shipped her up to Houston for the training."

Gerald was visibly shocked. "But she can't be anywhere *near* eighteen."

Maxine scattered a fist of bottle caps across the tabletop and beat the sawdust off her palms. "You gonna say 'no' to someone like John?" She stared at him, setting her hands against her hips and flipping her eyes around the empty bar. "So, yeah, I'm alone again."

Standing there in his uniform, Gerald cut an impressive shape against the light in the doorway. His voice lowered, so the men in the corner wouldn't hear them. "You don't have to be, you know." He watched her seriously. He had gotten them an appointment, he said, to be married the next day at the courthouse. Appointments, Maxine knew, were hard to get; there were so many other couples like them. "They're going to move me soon," he warned. "I can't keep waiting forever."

Goddamnit, she thought, slumping onto a stool. *Goddamnit, Gerald. And John, too. Why was everybody in such a goddamned hurry?*

"John thinks she can save the whole goddamned world." Her breathing picked up speed, tears pressing against the backs of her eyes. "But you can't," she told him bleakly. "You can only just save yourself."

"Oh, Maxine." Gerald came at her softly, putting an arm around her shoulder. "Come on now, Maxine. Come here. It doesn't have to be like that."

She turned to him. "She wasn't any trouble," she choked. "She didn't have to go."

Gerald bent over and pulled her into his arms, pressing her up against his thick chest, her head neatly tucked beneath his chin. "Oh, Maxine," he breathed. "It's going to be all right."

She stood rigid for a moment—motionless. But she felt his body relax into the moment, warm and solid; and, slowly, hers did, too. For the first time, Maxine felt herself physically connected to a man. Not even sex, she thought, had been like that. Nothing about Freddy had even come close. She felt consumed—caught on the edge of something that was both reassuring and startling. Her body went limp. In the back of her mind, she could still hear that mountain wind beating against her years ago, and the sound of men chuckling. For such a long time, the world had held her up and examined her. *The cold wind against her face, and a huge pot of something cooking, boiling over.* The natural dangers of the world were all around them. But she didn't feel frightened of them anymore—not nearly as much. That was the one mistake that Gerald had made about her: she wasn't afraid of things; she was just tired.

"You need to rest," he said, and she nodded. "I'll come back early tomorrow," he promised. "We'll get you a dress; get your hair done. Anything you want."

"No!" she pushed herself away from him, shaking. It was a mistake. He would be disappointed with her in the end—she felt sure of it. "Gerald, look at me," she cried. "I'm just an old scrap. You don't want to marry me. Really—I'm not the person you think I am."

Gerald stopped; he was not a man who dealt well with frustration. He looked down at her, and his expression folded into itself. Maxine thought he might yell or storm off, and she guessed she deserved it.

But he didn't. "Of course I want to marry you, Maxine," he said. He looked hurt. This was a mood of his that Maxine didn't know yet but that she would become much more familiar with after the war. After he was broken more—her fine, handsome man—as they all were. All of them damaged, somehow, by the end of it. "I love you," he said quietly. "I thought you knew it."

Maxine's eyes stung; it was the first time that she had ever heard him say it. "*What?*"

"Since the beginning, Maxine." He pulled her back to him. "I've loved you since back when you were married, and all the time in between."

Maxine stared at up him—all those nights in the bar he'd spent dancing with all those other women. And all those other nights when he hadn't even been there. For weeks, months. Was it really true? Had he been out there in the world somewhere, thinking about her? "How am I supposed to believe you, Gerald? You never said so. You never told me anything at all."

He looked at her, seriously. "Maxine, how could a man not love you? You've amazing. You're almost too much."

She stared back at him. No one had ever said that to her: amazing. Her mother, her father, Della, Grandmother Mary: they had all been amazing. All of them glamorous and gorgeous and wonderful. "Goddamnit, Gerald. What took you so long to say it?"

"Because I had to wait," he answered carefully. "I had to wait until I knew you'd be listening."

Lawrence, 1965

Six months after Rome's announcements, the mass was unrecognizable. Mortar had to be drilled out and the huge stone slabs of altars rearranged. Velvet curtains were being removed from altar rails, and the rails themselves were packed up and put away. During the ceremony, there were still awkward lulls before hymns and the alleluia. More prayers were being translated, and in the meantime, parishioners sang uncertainly out of temporary, stapled hymnals. Most difficult of all was the homily—the part of the mass when the priest delivers his own understanding of the gospel reading to the people. They had no idea how to construct such a speech. All their lives, they'd been listening to God; no one had ever asked them to listen to themselves.

Sylvia was intrigued: "What will you do?"

Lawrence told her he didn't know.

"But that vow—you could still take it?"

He told her he could, if it was still what he wanted.

"I thought that's all you've ever wanted."

He moved his head carefully up and down.

She traced a finger slowly along his chest. "So then," she challenged, "do you feel bad about this?" Sylvia was beautiful. Her body was new and perfect, like his own; there were no errors.

Lawrence shook his head. "No Sylvia—not this."

"And that's sinful, too, I suppose—not regretting it?"

"Yes," he agreed. Of course it was.

Sylvia studied him for another moment. "You know," she smiled narrowly, "I could love you. If I decided to." Her lower lip pushed out, shoving the smoke off to one side. "How would you feel about that?"

Frankie had told him that loving a woman was the best thing there was. "It keeps you human," he'd explained. "Remember Christ, how much of himself he had to give up just to love people. There is no bigger sacrifice."

Lawrence watched Sylvia suck again at the base of the cigarette, carefully drawing her cheeks inward around the thin substance of it. She exhaled slowly, and Lawrence motioned for a drag. Her eyebrows lifted slightly, but she handed it to him, and he held the thing delicately between two fingers, like she did. The flame glittered, eating at the paper in a slow, premeditated way. "Well, hurry up, Lawrence. You're going to get ashes all over the bed."

Lawrence shoved a hand underneath and continued to watch it burn, tilting the hot fag slowly downward so the smoke ribbons traveled straight up. He held it like that for a moment, distended above his upturned hand. Then he brought it closer and closer to his skin, the thin strings of smoke traveling inexhaustibly upward, winding into the air. He held it there until he felt himself begin to sweat, the heat of the cigarette biting down into the creases of his palm. Pain held on a threshold, careful as pleasure; sometimes, the divisions between things could be so indistinct. Lawrence clenched his jaw; he didn't cry out. But Sylvia grabbed the cigarette back, in a quick motion like jealousy. Her eyes were steady. She took another drag. "You really are a strange man, Lawrence."

* * *

Nothing at St. Pious had changed. There was still the simple, shingled pair of buildings: the study halls and dormitories, and the windowless refectory down at one end. The brothers' voices wandered out from austere classrooms, laying out instructions on scripture, Latin, and chant. At the refectory, the same two childless women stirred together steaming vats of donated food. And Father Gregory, close to retirement now, sat quietly in his front office, presiding over it all.

"He won't speak to you." Father Luke's voice was hard. He was a hard man.

Lawrence shook his head; he didn't understand.

"The changes," he said. "They've been too much for him."

The young man gazed out at a group of boys funneled into rows, heading toward the chapel. "It doesn't matter," he answered. Father Gregory was still the holiest man he knew of. "I need to see him."

Father Luke's eyes were sad but brazen. "He's not a role model for you anymore," he warned. "You need to understand this; he is not someone to emulate."

"Yes, Father."

"I just want you to know what to expect."

"All right, Father."

What they found was an earnest man writing furtively at his desk. He had the same thick, close-cut silver hair, and a beard that needed to be trimmed. When they came in, he did not look up. His brow was seamless; one hand looped effortlessly through the calligraphy of ecclesiastical Latin. "His sermon," Father Luke nodded, taking a chair from the far wall of the office. "He starts over every day, but it's always the same." He set the chair down for Lawrence, across the desk from Father Gregory. "Remember what I told you, son. It's over. Leave him your blessings. He doesn't have anything for you anymore."

After Father Luke left them, the old man's pen continued moving across paper without pause—as though he was channeling something. The rhythm with which he worked suggested an internal confidence, as one who knows each word intimately before committing it to paper. Watching him, Lawrence couldn't help but think of emptiness: an alarming vacancy.

"Father," he swallowed. "I have sinned, Father." Lawrence's voice was small; he didn't know what to do. It was like the new liturgy, or sex: it came without instructions. So he offered up his sins plainly, all of them: the physical trespasses and lapses of mind. He had fallen in love, he confessed. He had failed his calling.

But nothing happened. Father Gregory sat quietly, going over his sermon, the same one he wrote every day. Again and again— eternal and devout. His mind was not absent, but it was limited: refusing to lift itself up off the single track it inhabited, to adjust its course to the world they now lived in.

"It hurts, Father," Lawrence pleaded. "I don't know what to do now."

But the man didn't shift; he didn't say anything. His head tilted carefully as he moved across the page, the heel of his left hand picking up ink from the quick blur of words. Father Luke had been right. The old priest he didn't respond; he didn't say anything.

And then, because he didn't know what else to do, Lawrence began to pray: *Pater noster qui es in coelis, sanctificetur nomen tuum.* Quietly, and without intention, repeating the old prayers over again: *adveniat regnum tuum.* Those familiar currents— *fiat voluntas tua, sicut in coelo et in terra*—he let them fall over his tongue, his throat. His lids slipping shut with the effort of it: *panem nostrum quotidianum, da nobis hodie, et dimitte nobis debita nostra.*

When he opened his eyes again, he recognized that one ritual had interrupted another: Father Gregory's hand had paused inconclusively over his sermon, his lips taking up the same smooth patterns. No sound emerged, but his mouth was shaping itself around the words—that old comfort. *Sicut et nos dimittimus.* His lips kept moving, his eyes sharply focused on something beyond the physical limits of the room. They had turned hard and unflinching. *Debitoribus nostris.* Lawrence shuddered. *Forgive me, Father, please.* And he explained everything again—he made it worse than it was. Not one woman, but ten. Twenty. There in the church: a hundred women, a thousand. *Et ne nos inducas in tentationem sed.* A whole huge congregation of them, with longing eyes. Waiting their turn. *Libera nos a malo. Amen.*

When they had finished, Lawrence knew there was nothing left of the man. Prayers kept tumbling from his lips: *Gloria Patri, et Filio, et Spiritui Sancto.* Salted prayers. *Salve Regina, Mater misericordiae.* He wanted to catch them, scoop them up in his hands, and shove them back into his mouth. To make him stop. *In nomine Patris, et Filii, et Spiritus Sancti.* He felt desperate, almost violent. "Father!" he shouted. "Father! Forgive me—I have sinned!"

Then Luke McAllister was at the doorway again, his broad-shouldered form surveying the damage between them. Father Gregory still sat hunched in his chair, mumbling soundless Latin.

The pen on his desk had trailed over the words: sermons in the old style that no one would ever deliver because that God didn't exist anymore. Things about holiness and emptiness and all the tangled possibilities of redemption.

* * *

"Well, what happened?" Sylvia knew about the trip to St. Pious; she knew how badly Lawrence needed to set things straight. When he arrived at her apartment, she was leaning up in bed, reading a book of Sartre. Her semester exams were starting the following week.

"It felt like talking to God," he told her quietly. "He didn't say anything."

She looked at him, stretching out her legs and laying the book casually across a thigh. "You know," she said, "if you keep going back to the same people, you're going to get the same answers. Maybe you should try something different."

Lawrence shook his head. "This wasn't the same."

Sylvia's brows bent skeptically toward the middle of her upper nose. She looked angular and pretty, like she always did. Outside, the weather was creeping carefully toward summer. Sylvia wore a mini-skirt so that, lying out along the mattress like she was, her legs were almost entirely exposed. They were smooth and newly shaven. She flexed, bending them like a giant pair of commas. "Oh, wasn't it?"

"No," he insisted. "Father Gregory is ill. He's deaf—or dumb. Or both. He doesn't speak. Not since April."

"So then," she flipped a hand through the air, "you're not forgiven."

"I don't know," his voice was tense. He lowered himself down onto the bed.

"You either are or you aren't, Lawrence—there is no in between."

He regarded her carefully. "It's not like that, Sylvia."

She picked up her philosophy book and tossed it on top of the piles that sat at the foot of the night table. "Well, then, what will you do?"

The vow, he told her. He still wanted to take it. "Maybe I'll try missionary work," he said. "Africa. Or South America. There's plenty of need out there in the world; maybe I can do some good."

Sylvia looked disappointed. "You'll lie to them," she answered flatly. "You're not letting them know how it really is."

"It's *not* a lie," he insisted. "I confessed. I told him everything."

"But he didn't listen, Lawrence," she said, pulling herself up onto her haunches. "He didn't even hear you."

Then, without another word, she began to undress him: first his shirt, then his belt, and pants and undergarments. He felt grateful for her silence—grateful for that human touch. Once she was naked, too, she knelt lower beside him and bent over to put her mouth on him. He felt her breath, and then her lips, and tongue: the sudden, unmistakable gift of it. "Sylvia," he gasped. Again, and again. Her tongue floated over him: moist and warm and ungoverned. After another moment, she righted herself and looked down at him—elbows locked, palms on thighs. "Finish it," she said flatly.

"What?"

"Do it yourself. I want to watch."

Sylvia's urges were sudden and inexplicable. She picked up Lawrence's hands and placed them over his penis. "Don't you trust me?" She brushed the tips of his fingers along its skin, but the sensation was awkward, almost painful. Flits of pleasure pulsed against the sides of his body—confused and directionless. He was unfamiliar with himself. Having spent so many years unlearning his own desires, he didn't know what to do. His heart thudded; he felt divided.

"That's not the way other men do it." Sylvia licked her palm and swiped it across him. Then she put her hands back over it, and squeezed. "Like this," she said, moving them together up and down over the terrified throbbing of his penis. Pleasure began punching its way back through again—bright and confident and separate from him. It was like a thing that he was witnessing instead of feeling. "Keep going," she said, shifting her weight up onto a thigh to get a better handle over their work. She held her hands over his, moving them for him, her breasts swinging easily with the effort of it.

"Keep going," she said again. And he wondered suddenly if she had met another man—if she was in love with someone else. But just as quickly, he knew that it didn't matter. He only hoped that she would mount him soon. He needed her—that spontaneous richness of her body. The ease with which she could lift goodness out of him.

"Don't stop," she breathed.

"Please," he said. "Put yourself on me."

"No, Lawrence," she grunted. "You can do this." There was no particular motive to her voice. He could see her perspiring—sweat building up against her brow, her breasts hanging pendulous and unbeautiful now, slapping against her chest. Her face was blank, measured.

"Sylvia, please." The heat of the thing was burning him: the sensation twisting, both aroused and painful by turns. But she wouldn't stop: *You can do this.* She kept squeezing him, pulling his hands up and down. And he couldn't think now what exactly it was that he had wanted. Just this complicated desire: to couple himself with someone—anyone—no matter what the cost.

He was crying softly by then, but Sylvia didn't seem to notice. When he came, it was sharp and short and finished: a bright blast of joy that mocked him. "There," she said, satisfied, wiping away his cum from the heel of her hand. "That's all there is to it." Then she rolled back up onto her haunches and watched him, like staring out at someone from over a cliff. Lawrence looked back at her, his temptress, and knew that she would leave him soon. Of course. And it would be his own fault. Because he hadn't loved her enough, because she was not the one that he had chosen.

Theresa, June 1979

Theresa stared out at the waves. After three days of hiking in the Siskiyous and shaping hamburger patties over the fire, her mother was finally growing weary. Arriving at the coast that morning, she had lain down on the sand, her skirt pushed up a bit too far past her knees. She wasn't being as careful as she usually was. But it was early; there was no one around. Theresa slipped off her sneakers. At their backs, the bluff melted into a system of wooded trails and camp sites. Rabbits on the trails stopped to bask in the sunlight; salamanders flickered in and out of the early light. They were surrounded by curved, petrified wood and a subtle network of shells. Theresa knew that they would keep moving until the money gave out. Today the ocean, tomorrow—perhaps a cityscape. Portland. Seattle. The Canadian border. It was impossible to say. Her mother was still such a romantic: always searching, always waiting to be found.

But for now she had fallen asleep, her camera at her feet. She had been taking pictures of the sea. Theresa wondered if there was film in the camera; it would not have surprised her if there wasn't. Her mother made a habit of photography, but it was primarily the activity of lining up the frame that thrilled her. The click and whirl and another fresh start. In an earlier life, she had worked as a nightclub photographer. That had been after the war, after Theresa's father had come home but before they had started a family. *They wanted their jobs back*, Maxine had told her daughter. *All those men coming home. Once the war was over, they wanted to be the ones work-*

ing at the shipyards, taking home the government pay checks. So we had to give it up—the jobs, the freedom. All of it.

Theresa yawned and turned to face the sea: such an open expanse of possibility. Lawrence, she thought, could have died in a place like this. Her mother didn't want to talk about it, but there was still so much—Theresa could not help herself—to consider. He could have taken the car, for instance, driven down to the city and thrown himself from the Golden Gate Bridge. Or borrowed her father's shotgun and driven to Point Reyes to die along the ocean. There were so many things that he could have done. But he had chosen the tree. *Her* tree. He must have known—he *had* to have known what he was doing. He had put himself there for a reason; he hadn't wanted to be alone. This, she understood, was the principal betrayal: *He wanted me to find him.* And now those dangling boot soles: she could never forget them. Her palm brushed restless against a thigh, up and down, until the sensation at her fingertips melted into a blur of denim. The girl's eyes flickered along the beach: no one. *You've got to be careful*, her mother had told her time and again. But she was tired: tired of waiting to go home, tired of the world's secrets flushing around her, tired of Lawrence's story, pressed like a film at the back of her mind. She wanted to wash it all away. Wanted to be rid of him. Her mother dozed on the sand, one arm flung above her head. The camera lay at waist level, hunched harmlessly in the sand. Theresa set her shoes carefully by the edge of a large block of twisted driftwood. Who knew how long ago it had washed out to sea—and washed back? She peeled the socks from her feet, and then her jeans, rolling them carefully and setting them beside the shoes. And then her shirt.

In the water, she was weightless. There was hardly a wind. It was cold; her skin prickled to attention, her jellied insides thrumming blood into her capillaries, her outstretched fingers. The water buoyed her; it was easy to keep afloat. She laid her head back and felt the sea film slip into her ears. Her eyes shut. She was nearly sixteen years old and washing out to sea. She ran her fingers along herself: the way the body changed from ten to twelve to fifteen. She had little concept, still, of its relative beauty or worth. But she was curious.

Tomás had noticed something; that much she knew. As she laid there, eyes closed and the water filling her ears with the empty-saturated sound of ocean intimacy, she imagined Tomás's hands moving across her body. Imagined those delicate fingers. His lips. The story in her mind frightened her as much as it excited her.

So little had been said when Theresa's body had started changing. Almost without a word, pink-lined packages of sanitary napkins had appeared in the upstairs bathroom, while other things were removed: her brothers' rusted razors and deodorant sticks and sharp-smelling bottles of aftershave. Her mother had set herself resolutely to the task. She'd cleaned out drawers, fixed cabinet handles, and kept Theresa supplied: aspirin and tampons and clinking canisters of hairspray. Some days, Maxine had come home with filigreed boxes of cosmetics and perfumes: lovely and feminine and without instructions. Womanhood, it seemed, was something that should come to one intuitively.

With her father, things had been even more disappointing. For years, he had welcomed Theresa into his study—ever since Theresa had told her mother that she hated her—where they would sit quietly, reading newspapers and comic books and staring up at the wide collection of military histories that Gerald bought through the mail. They were leather-bound and handsome and remained almost entirely untouched. A person could learn a lot from those books, he had told his daughter, and they had stared upward, imagining all those other circumstances that were not their own.

What do you want from life, Theresa?

But Theresa had never thought about things in those terms before.

You should know, her father had insisted. *It's important. Women usually don't.*

Mom knows what she wants.

He had shaken his head. *But she never asks for it.*

Even back then, this had been true. Apparently, some kind of rough geography had carved itself out between her parents. They acted, each of them, independently—without seeking permission.

It's better, Gerald had rested his great head in his hands, *to know yourself first. Things go more smoothly after that.*

Theresa had liked her father's wisdoms. His lessons were always stern but encouraging; it felt like a privilege, hearing them: like her father understood certain things about the world—things that not everyone was able to see with such shocking accuracy.

But even her father had had his limits. Once she had gotten her period, they didn't go together into his study again. *You've grown up,* he said, taking a seat on the living room sofa and picking up a newspaper, as though she didn't need those wisdoms anymore. As though he had nothing left to offer her.

"Theresa!" her mother was rushing toward the water—her arms moving at some kind of inordinate clip. "Theresa, what were you thinking?"

Theresa climbed out of the water and stood dripping against the sand. "It's warm enough," she insisted.

"You're naked!"

Her voice flattened. "I'm in my underwear, Mom."

Her mother's frantic gaze scanned the beach.

"Nobody's here."

"What are you *doing*?" Her mother's voice pitched again.

"I didn't have a bathing suit."

"This is ridiculous, Theresa. You're going to catch pneumonia."

"It's sunny." Theresa shifted slightly, running her fingers along her skin. Sand stuck across her legs, her chest—her bra and underwear becoming a network of cotton and grit.

"You're trying to spite me."

"I went *swimming*."

"Good lord." Her mother's eyes lifted toward the sky. The air was so bright, so sunny, that the scent of brine and recycled earth was overblown by freshness. Theresa didn't answer. They moved back up the beach, toward the camera and her neatly folded pile of clothing. "Nobody's here," she said again.

Her mother looked her over sourly. "You need a towel." Their car was a good ten-minute walk through the forested bank behind them. Maxine told her daughter to wait, thrust her hands into her jacket pockets, and started walking. By the time she got back,

Theresa was shivering, pitched forward on the petrified log, her arms shoved over her chest. "Here." Her mother wrapped the towel around her, and Theresa sank down onto the warm sand, her skin softening through the fabric as the sun pulled itself into the sky.

Her mother plucked idly at the camera. "Your father knew a lot about the sea," she mentioned, unsolicited. Theresa shut her eyes and listened. She knew these stories, too, but she liked hearing them again. "He was posted out in the South Pacific during the war, you know. Island after island. He said they all began to look the same."

She pressed her shape more fully into the outline of warm sand. "What did he tell you about it?"

Her mother snorted. She unzipped her jacket and sat down in the sand beside her daughter, shifting her bottom back and forth until she was comfortable. "Not much. All those men back then—they didn't listen. They didn't tell us anything. GI husbands." She moved her fingers through the loose, warm sand. "The worst part is that you couldn't ask about it; they all wanted to pretend like it never happened. But you can't ignore a history like that," she looked meaningfully at her daughter. "You just can't."

Theresa leaned backward, laying the bath towel beneath her and letting her legs stretch out over the sand. She could feel the dampness of her calves picking up a riddled swarm of sand. Her legs felt long, elastic. She stretched the broad angles of her body over the sand, listening to her mother spinning more history around her.

"Your father would be up crying half the night." Maxine's hand smacked down against the sand. "And I just held him. When he got up in the morning and went to work and made decisions about our future, he felt better. They weren't always the best decisions, but I let him. I talked to a lot of women back then, and they all said the same thing. So we just figured it was something we had to put up with for a while, until the men got readjusted."

"But you loved Dad." Theresa pressed her gaze upward, where it caught in the light as the sun pulled past the tree line behind them, dripping more fully into the sky.

"I loved what he thought of himself. I loved the fact that he *had* an idea of himself; it was sort of romantic. I'd never had that; I didn't have the time."

"So you did—you loved him."

"He was the best man I ever knew. He just didn't trust me. All throughout the war, he wanted to know everything I was doing. He was jealous. We both were, I guess. Sacrifice can do that to a marriage. Especially during a war, when you're both willing to give each other up so easily, for a higher purpose. It damages the love somehow. Nobody ever warned me about that, but it's true."

Theresa sat quietly. Her mother was so curious: waxing suddenly into these little sound-bite wisdoms. Her legs, caught in the steaming sand, rubbed against each other to loosen the debris.

"Your father was good in the war; he was very principled," she went on. "But principles can be dangerous when they get in the way of real people."

Theresa shoved up onto an elbow. She remembered the shut door to her father's study and a hand at the back of her shoulder, leading her out into the living room. "Did he hurt your feelings?"

"He did."

Theresa considered. "But there was a war—it wasn't his fault."

"No," her mother agreed. "That wasn't the real problem. It was because he didn't mind. He was out there fighting the good fight, and that was enough for him."

Theresa twisted again, feeling the grit between her toes.

"They weren't easy, those war marriages," her mother continued. "But if I had to do it over again, I suppose I'd do the same thing, because the options would be the same."

The girl dug her fingers into the sand. She felt the undersides of her nails jab full of grains, but she pressed down further—all the way down, until she could feel the level where the sand became moist, as the sea seemed to penetrate the land beneath them. "Mom," she asked quietly, "what's the bravest thing you ever did?"

"Huh!" Maxine laughed. "Just that—marrying your father."

All those things—dangling high wires, building bars, welding shut the hulls of ships—and this is what she chose. "That's *it*?"

"Lord, Theresa," her mother turned onto her side, basking in the building light, "that's the bravest any of us gets: putting your life up next to someone else's. I don't know anything harder."

* * *

By evening, her mother was exhausted. They had stopped at a drug store, bought a package of the sleeping pills that her mother so often relied on. Next, she wanted someplace comfortable to sleep. "Theresa," she motioned toward the lobby of a motor lodge somewhere off of Interstate 5. "Go get us checked in, would you?" Her chin sloped downward as she held the roll of aluminum foil loosely toward her daughter. Theresa thought instantly of taking inventory—of counting the wadded bills and calculating how much longer they could afford to stay on the road. If they went back soon enough, Tomás would still be there working, she thought, walking toward the reception area and fingering the sharp, light creases of the tinfoil.

The man at the front desk looked her over carefully. His expression wasn't lewd, but it was, she thought, more interested than it should have been. He was nearly her mother's age, and he moved deliberately, as though he didn't entirely trust his body. In the narrow lobby, the thin whir of air-conditioning colored the silence. There was no one else around. The man's face was flushed: the same patched ruddiness that her father's face had sometimes taken in the evenings. She understood that he had been drinking.

"You want a room?"

She told him she did, and he made her sign the register. She moved her pen quickly through the lines. Her hair, still crusted lightly with sea salt, was pulled up into a bun; she scratched lightly at her temple, and set down the pen. She wished he would stop watching her. "How much?"

The man stood gravely for a moment, like one of those damaged men from the war. He smelled mildly of antiseptic, and his fingers fumbled slightly as he collected the registry sheet. He told her the price, and she pulled several bills from the aluminum roll. The man said nothing. He handed her a key, his eyes never leaving her. Moving away from him, back toward the door, Theresa decided it seemed reasonable, what her mother had said: how her father had been the kind of man who took his suffering inside himself, and suffered all the more because of it. Maxine herself was the opposite: nothing was ever planned; nothing happened quickly. But she moved; she was always going somewhere. And her father, Theresa supposed, must have sensed this about her mother: that there was something inside her that would never break. That would never stop spinning.

In the parking lot, though, there was stillness. Her mother's figure was shadowy in the front seat. She was asleep: her body tilted slightly to the left, her head bent along a shoulder. Theresa thumbed the scratched outline of the key fob that man had given her. She could feel the braised outline of the numbers—311—under the pad of her finger. It was a reassuring motion, so she continued, rubbing her fingers in a rhythmic motion until the texture of the words, *Umpqua Valley Motor Lodge*, and numbers blurred past distinction. There was a bite to the air now that it was night. She pulled her sweater around herself and sat on the nub of pavement in the adjoining parking spot. She wouldn't wake her mother; she didn't want to. There was plenty that she had left to consider, there on her own: her father, those silences that had held him to his life. In this way, he must have understood Lawrence, she imagined. Lawrence, a man who had asked for so little and hoped for so much. They would have been well suited to each other, as father and son. Except that they weren't—they couldn't have been.

"Theresa." The heavy creak of the station wagon swung open, and her mother's feet dangled outward, child-like in thin canvas loafers. The rest of her followed slowly, pulling together a complete shadow. She moved uncertainly, almost like the man behind the reception desk. "Theresa?" Her voice wavered.

"Over here." Theresa stood up, dangling the key toward her mother. Maxine turned, started. "We're in 311," Theresa said. "It's just up the stairs."

Her mother's eyes shifted, adjusting to the weak light coming from the stairwell. She was tired—so tired now. Her hand leapt upward, pressing itself against her blouse. "Oh, Theresa," she gasped, staring blindly for a moment, and Theresa could imagine the indignant silences that had managed to win her father's heart. There was her mother: clearly so ensnared by love, and so wounded by it. "I thought you'd gone," she breathed. "I thought you'd never come back."

Maxine, 1943

In those days, it took seventy-five dollars to get an abortion. Even on a good salary, that was a month's pay. Maxine had no idea where her husband had gotten the money or the address. But she had followed his directions, and there she was, standing outside of a storefront on Market Street, amid the scream and bustle of downtown San Francisco. Dr. Mahyer's office was on the fourth floor. Nearby, a barber shop radio was playing the new hit song, "Shoo-shoo Baby." Maxine's eyes flittered nervously around the crowded street. What she was doing was illegal, of course, but no one paid her any attention. She was dressed in plain clothes, like Gerald had instructed. If anyone asked, he had told her to explain that she was going in for a fitness exam so that she could get a job down at one of the shipyards.

For six months, they had lived together: first in a training camp in Missouri, and then at the base outside of San Francisco. Gerald was a good man, and smart; he was already on his way to earning a rating. Rated men often got permanent positions in San Francisco or New York or Washington DC. Maxine had told her husband that she didn't care where they went, just as long as they stayed together. But now he was telling her that it was no use; he was getting shipped out to Hawaii—and who knew, after that? *They're just going to keep moving me*, he told her, *until they run out of world*. In the meantime, Maxine had herself and Ringling to worry about. *I don't want my wife to be raising babies on her own*, Gerald had said. He was a good man who was right about so many things. He had promised Maxine a better life, and she had made a promise, too: to trust her new husband to keep her safe, no matter how invisible the means.

* * *

Dr. Mahyer's office was a clinic like any other: the lobby sparse and tastefully decorated, the attending rooms clean and filled with clinical instruments. Maxine had nothing else to do that day, but she lied: she asked for the last appointment on the schedule. Maybe the little register would fill up, she thought; maybe the doctor would run out of time. Already, she knew that she wouldn't come back the following day.

The receptionist nodded, writing down the name that Maxine had given her—not her own—in the little appointment folder. "Four o'clock," she said, slipping Maxine's downpayment into a locked drawer at the desk. "No refunds," she reminded her. "So don't be late."

But of course, Maxine had nothing to do, so she just walked down to the docks and stared out across the water. Alcatraz was out there, and the two big bridges on either side. Ships large and small were moving through the harbor, pushing along goods and war supplies. Maxine wasn't used to seafaring towns. To her, San Francisco felt transient: everything shifting constantly, even the weather. Nothing stayed put in the city—not people, not feelings. Just months before, she had felt immeasurably in love with her husband. She had trusted his every decision: enlistment, marriage, even the meager sale of Bella Vista. But now she had begun to wonder what it was that she had agreed to.

Crossing from one street to the next, she stopped to watch a rally where volunteers were selling war bonds and auctioning other items: tea kettles, briefcases, cosmetic supplies. Anything that would raise money for the war effort. She watched a potted geranium go for forty dollars. The crowd cheered, passing the basket of flowers back to a man in a long overcoat. Maxine could smell its thick, metallic scent as it passed just above her head.

Up two more blocks, she passed a new Red Cross station. Out front, a woman was waving an American flag and handing out brochures about the uses of V-mails: where to buy them, the cost, and how quickly one could expect them to arrive. Inside, there was also a list of instructions about how to write to the soldiers. Short, upbeat letters were best, it recommended—and lots of them. A soldier's livelihood depended on such letters. He will want to know about home, it said—what's happening, what is going well. The Red Cross volunteer was dressed in a smart two-piece suit with a kick-pleat skirt. She smiled at Maxine: "Do you have a man across?"

"I will."

"Well," she brightened, "you'll want to starting sending letters now, so they'll be there when he arrives. I'm sure he'll want to know how you're doing."

It was true. Gerald wanted to know everything; he'd already said so. That's what he had made her swear to: *You've got to tell me everything. Every single thing you do. So that we can stay close.*

Maxine nodded and thanked her: this woman who talked to so many soldiers' wives. She was a young woman, like John. Maxine winced slightly, and the woman smiled back. Didn't she know how difficult it was? Maxine wondered. And how unlikely—her and her husband, and a hundred thousand more? They weren't locked together now by anything more than a war and a piece of paper.

* * *

The nurse checked her in at two minutes past four. The woman's name was Maryanne—such a sweet, unremarkable name that Maxine had wondered if it, too, had been invented. She was pretty, with large, round cheeks and a healthy complexion.

"Will it hurt?" Maxine wanted to know, as Maryanne lifted her arm gently to check her blood pressure.

She shook her head. "Not to worry," she promised. The doctor would administer something to numb the pain; she shouldn't feel much of anything. "Just a little pressure. Anything else is in your head."

And she was right; as the doctor began his work, Maxine could feel a heaviness, dull and throbbing. It felt to her like a stone beating laundry, instead of the other way around. She felt layers of herself coming away. And there again that pressure thudded and thudded against her, insistent. Pressing itself harder—reaching its way into real pain. She yelped out, and Maryanne offered her hand. Maxine squeezed her eyes shut. Yes, she thought, it was painful, having her husband's baby torn out of her. Thick and aching and sore—like her body had suddenly grown fangs inside of itself and was lazily gnashing its teeth. She moaned again. "Gerald," she cried, and Maryanne moved closer. "Miss," she whispered. "You're all right. It's almost finished." Her voice sounded such a long, far ways off.

No, Maxine wanted to tell her—she was wrong. They were all wrong. Gerald, too. This time, he hadn't known what kind of decision he was making: not his, but *theirs*. And the truth was, Maxine had wanted that baby. She didn't care about the work or the war or the problems with money, she told herself. She just wanted something to love in a big, unquestioning way. There had been so much—so much!—of her life that wasn't certain. All she wanted was this one thing—this one little piece.

Afterward, the world was very fuzzy. The painkillers wore off slowly; she found it difficult to walk. Maryanne helped lift her up off the table and walked her out into the empty waiting room. At the end of the day, the woman's uniform was wrinkled, but still clean. She was a woman careful with appearances. She was also good with details; she had taken notice of her patient's ring.

"Is your husband in the service?"

"Yes." Maxine told her that he was a second lieutenant already.

"Oh, you must be quite proud."

Maxine nodded, her eyelids drooping.

"Keep your eyes open please, Miss. There, that's better." She put her hands flat against Maxine's shoulders to keep her in place. "Now tell me, what does your husband do, exactly?"

"The supply," she told her. "He's in charge of the supply."

"Well," Maryanne answered. "He must be a very important man. And how long have you been married?"

"Six months."

"Is he going overseas, then?"

Maxine nodded again; her head felt light as a balloon. She raised a hand to her forehead; it was still clammy. She shivered.

"I'm going to get you something to help with that. You just stay put, okay? Eyes open, please."

She came back a minute later with a small glass. "Drink this," she offered. "It will make you feel better."

Maxine lifted the glass toward her lips. The odor was sharp: whiskey. She stopped, shaking her head.

"Trust me," said Maryanne. "It'll keep the pain down—and help you sleep some."

Maxine nodded, and sucked at the fiery liquid. She coughed and tried it again. Just then, there wasn't anything that she wanted so much as to trust someone. And she thought Maryanne must have understood that. Day after day, these women came in, putting their false names in the register and responding wearily when the time came. So many of them were married to soldiers or had been with soldiers. And these same men were being sent away. The sea was separating them from their lives.

* * *

The stairs were difficult. Maxine's legs were still tingling. She had to look at them—one foot and then the other—and tell them, carefully, to march on down toward the street. At her core, she felt the anesthesia wearing off. It felt strangely heavy, that much emptiness; it made keeping balance difficult. She gripped the thin metal handrail; no matter where she put her weight, she hurt. Landing finally out on the street again, she turned wearily to the left. In her hand, she had the address that Maryanne had recommended. Fortunately, there wasn't far to go: four store fronts; four high, narrow buildings. Just half a block, that was all. Even so, she had to keep herself pressed up against things, moving carefully from light pole to sidewalk bench to news cart to stairwell. The business day was finished, and the streets were flooded with people: stylish women with their hair shiny and trim, their silky legs batting at their kick pleat skirts, or a hat set rakishly to one side, fastened with a pin.

And the men: there was a whole sea of green and grey uniforms. So many people, Maxine felt sure that someone would notice her, clobbing her way awkwardly down the sidewalk. Drunk—that's what they'd take her for. And just like that, she understood the whiskey: If she got picked up, it would be for the liquor on her breath. No one would ever suspect the little clinic upstairs. That's what Maryanne had intended. Another little spot of sadness opened up inside of her: even that kindness had been bought and paid for.

Maxine wouldn't remember very much from there. A few minutes later, she reached the hotel, where someone handed her a key and guided her up to her room. The building was pierced with a narrow elevator shaft, the kind with a rickety wrought-iron box and no walls, that climbs, screeching and complaining, between floors. Maxine was registered on the sixth floor, which was for women only. Each day, the management filled that gloomy hallway with the whiskey-breathed women from the clinic. Sleepy and shivering. All of them quieted from the experience—relieved or broken-hearted, as the case may be.

* * *

Even before she noticed the light in the room—silty, early light—Maxine felt the wet sheets. There was a strong odor in the room: sharp and sickening, like iron. She could barely click her brain along its gears—the clinic, the stairs, the baby that was gone now. She couldn't remember pouring a glass of water, but there was one. She tried lifting her head for a drink, but it was still screaming from the whiskey from the night before. Lying back down and pressing her hands into the bed, Maxine knew that she was lying in a drying pool of her own blood. She spread her fingers out away from her, the starchy stain expanding and expanding until she began to cry from the sheer fact of it. Her eyes swam. All around her, the hotel room rose steep and narrow. Small. Barely enough space for a pair of feet next to the bed. The walls were painted a deep green—a poor choice, she thought, for such a gloomy city. And the door was a grimy white, with swirled shapes carved into the wood. The only furniture apart from the bed was one lonely armoire, missing a drawer. It stared back at her: a big gap-toothed thing, like a squarish pumpkin.

Some hours later, when she woke again and tried to right herself, it was not as difficult as she had expected. Emptying the water glass, she stood and put a hand on the doorknob. It was cold to the touch—narrow and oval-shaped, and both pock-marked and smooth from decades of use. On the bed, the blood stain was wider across than her own body. It didn't seem possible that one little person could have that much blood and tears in her. There was so much within her: strength, daring, resourcefulness. *I could have raised that baby*, she thought. But her husband wouldn't believe it; he assumed she was fragile, like other women. He thought things about her that were sweet and devoted and impossible, and she loved him for that. But still, Maxine began to realize as she lifted her tired body off the bed and out of that terrible, iron-smelling room, there were limits to what a woman could give up for her husband. Limits to what he ought to ask of her.

The hallway was mostly dark: no windows. Just a few flickering bulbs on wrought-iron stems, curving up from the walls. No one was there, so she left her room unlocked and made her way down to the lavatory. In the small, heavy-framed mirror Maxine could tell that her face was blanched. There was an extra oil lamp with matches, but she didn't bother to light it. She preferred the near dark anyway, as she stripped off her clothes and rinsed what she could—the sink basin going dark almost immediately. Her skirt, she washed and wrung out as best she could. The other things—underwear and a pair of stockings—she threw into the trash basin.

Out on the street again, she moved more quickly. It was Saturday, and later than she had imagined, but the streets were much emptier than they had been the evening before. Maxine followed again that set of directions written in her husband's hand: left out of the building back onto Market Street, up two blocks, then another left. She felt hurried, though she couldn't say exactly why. Ringling was fine, staying with a neighbor woman; there was nothing, really, to rush back to. *Maybe it's just the coast*, she told herself. The places where she'd lived before hadn't had this anxiousness about them—crowded, brisk, trying to fill up all available space. But San

Francisco was a huge place: more city than Maxine had ever known. It moved quickly, as did all the people in it.

Up three blocks more, Gerald had written. *Then a quick right. Look for a bus stop there.* Seeing none, Maxine asked a woman where she might find one. "The bus should be one coming by here any minute," she nodded and coughed. She was middle-aged, maybe fifty years old, and black. The two women didn't say anything else to each other. But when the bus came, they both got on, funneling toward the empty seats at the back. The bus was more full than Maxine had expected for such an early morning ride. Passing the other customers, she hoped that no one would detect the terrible stink of rinsed blood on her clothes. Or her blanched cheeks, the dark patches circling her eyes. She pulled her overcoat more snuggly around her.

The woman sat down next to her. In the seat in front of them, she had noticed someone that she knew: a black man, also in his fifties. The silvery curls wound their way into darker ones. His face was broad, and his features prominent. He breathed audibly through his nose, especially while laughing.

As the bus rattled forward, Maxine felt her strength begin to fail her. She worried that she might miss her stop. "Can you let me know, please, when we get to the transfer for El Cerrito?" she asked the woman.

"Sure, Miss."

Maxine thanked her and leaned her head against the rickety glass, her teeth rattling as they mounted another hill in downtown San Francisco. The city still seemed so impossibly constructed: its steep rises and plunges. Not calming or endearing, but certainly exciting: a fitting place, she supposed, to spend a war.

Reaching the crest of another hill, the bus threw itself down the adjoining street until they petered out by the wharf. Then they bounced along more smoothly until they reached the Bay Bridge. And of course, Maxine was a country girl. She didn't know bays, and she didn't know ships. But they all knew by then what a transpacific liner looked like: those massive vessels that carried our boys across the sea.

"Does anyone know," she asked groggily, "if there's any ships scheduled to go out today?"

The man in front of her nodded. "Sure, Miss. Two, I believe. Bound for the Pacific."

"Well, then, there's one," she told them, pointing. And that's when she understood—Gerald's anxiousness about the appointment, his urgency to get it done. "There goes my love."

And the woman, because this is what women do—across ages, races, faiths—patted Maxine's shoulder reassuringly. "Don't worry," she promised. "He'll come back. He will."

Part IV: Shooting the Lions

Lawrence, 1974

It had been such a long time since God had said anything, so when Ringling had an idea, Lawrence listened: "Brother Ringling's Traveling Menagerie." That was his vision: resurrect the old family show. Get themselves some animals—an elephant and a peacock; ponies, llamas, and black-horned billy goats; a giant iguana—train them, and take them on the road. His sister knew people; it was still possible to get wagons, animals, canopies. Ringling had a bit of money left over from the decade he'd spent in the army, so Lawrence had agreed. When you're trying to salvage a history, you don't think too much about details. It is something that operates on the level of myth: the trapeze tango, the hanging perch, the aching iron jaw. "It's possible," Ringling had promised. "You can do it—you *can* recreate the past."

And Lawrence had agreed. In the end, he'd never been ordained; he'd gone on missionary work instead, leaving the country as quickly as he could after the affair with Sylvia had finally ended. But after seven years working in Chile, the Church had sent him home. For so long, his work there had gone well; the faith in Chile had been an older, more traditional faith. Embalmed bodies, the knuckle of a saint, fault lines in the seams of buildings: almost anything physical could be prayed to. But suddenly, there had been a military coup; foreigners were asked to leave. The change, Lawrence told his friend, had been sudden and brutal; by the time people understood what was happening—the government dissolved, politicians and intellectuals disappearing from their homes—it was too late for comment. Public buildings were emptied out: schools, theaters, the National Stadium. Stories circulated about what was going on at those places: fingernails pulled from fingers, knuckles broken, an eye smashed into its socket. People broken, for no particular reason, there in the rooms where an orchestra used to tune, or soccer players had readied themselves for the game.

"Life can get pretty awful," Ringling agreed. He had been to war—two of them—in Asia.

"There wasn't anything you could do," Lawrence admitted. "The Church forbade it—I couldn't say a word."

His training for war, Ringling claimed, had been the same. "We weren't supposed to talk about it, right? They taught us that real good. I didn't think. I just threw a grenade, and then there was one less enemy. They weren't separate, like people—it was just one big idea. A little more, a little less."

But coming home again, their hopes had amounted to so much more than this: exhausted animals and nauseating highway hours; overheated engines and jack-knifed trailers; an occasional contract at a used car lot or supermarket grand opening, a summer sidewalk sale, one or two elaborate birthday parties. Money came in slow and sporadic; there was never enough. When things got worse, they took their show to the open road, parking themselves at wide freeway exits and staking down handwritten signs: *Brother Ringling's Roadside Zoo, exit ½ mile.* People came in fits and starts: bored families cruising north on Friday afternoons, out for Sunday drives or down to see somebody's in-laws. The men set out seats for them, umbrellas to get out of the sun. Those were long, boring drives along I-5 and I-99; people were grateful for an excuse to stop: some place to let the kids run off their energy, to pet a donkey, or see a real elephant up close. And what Ringling asked him to ignore, Lawrence ignored: out behind the vans and trailers, a card table, a certain set of mirrors. When the men stomped gruffly back to meet their wives and kids, having lost half a week's salary in a few crummy rounds, Lawrence didn't question his partner. But even that foolery wasn't enough. There was always gas to be purchased, meat to be bought, animals to be endlessly fed. They couldn't survive. What Ringling had hoped for was useless: the past stayed where it was; it didn't come back.

So, eventually, the animals began to disappear, drifting off easily to special collectors, animal protection groups, and private zoos. The twin monkeys, Patsy and Elvira, went north to a rich couple in Sacramento who bought them as pets for their eight-year-old daughters, and Ringling just shook his head. He could see it already, he said: a pulled tail, the monkey's clean teeth slicing through skin, a razor blade scar. Screaming children, and the parents' stern, unforgiving faces. The veterinarian wouldn't have any other alternative. He would put them down, the rich parents dragging their sobbing children off to the doctor's clinic for vaccinations.

"Damn people got all these fancy notions," Ringling balked. He pushed his lips forward and dug into a pocket, pulling out five crisp one hundred dollar bills. He was just back from an all-night trip to Klamath Falls and back, to sell the elephant to an enterprising farmer and his wife. "That elephant'll be dead within a year," Ringling swore. Forty-four years old, and the ruddiness of youth was finally leaving him. He had a sallow look. There was alcohol on his breath—an odor like fear. Ringling was giving up.

It was a Sunday in June. A morning like cellophane: plastic, sticky. The house was empty. Gerald had gone down to San Bernardino for one of his Reserve weekends; his wife and kids were camped out some place in southern Oregon. Ringling shoved three of the warm bills into Lawrence's hand and motioned him back toward the truck. Together, they hefted the trailer off its socket, leaving it there in the front yard by the garage, then they rode jauntily back through the long lot behind the house, a quarter mile back to the boat house.

All that was left were the lions: sickly, unwanted, and underfed. It was a delicate situation. After almost two years in the damp, earth-bottomed barn, the wooden beams had grown soft, and the aluminum meshing was rusted and weak. The lions—Sasha and Sophocles—were each tethered to the ground by a light chain tied to a railway spike and cinched to the collars at their throats. The men knew their job had to be done quickly. One shot—then two. Fatal and brief. Lawrence looked toward Ringling, who was slipping the safety off his rifle. He was a soldier, after all; at least there was that.

But the first shot lodged itself instead into the woodchips just under Sophocles' nose. Immediately, the lion reared back and roared. Lawrence's eyes flipped to Sasha, sitting farther back in the cage, heat-ridden and undernourished. His body cinched, but he stayed where he was. Even in their compromised states, the lions were elegant, imposing creatures. Lawrence had visions of them both rising up: twin lions bursting through a collapsed heap of metal and splinters, lunging toward the men in their anger and aching need.

Ringling fired another poorly aimed shot. And another—shattering open the air beside Sophocles and making him wild. The lion roared louder, pacing and tugging in fury at his chain. Sasha's eyes were perked, his eyes swimming in their thick pools of paste. "Ring, what's happening?" He fired again and again, his body loose-jointed and shuddering, the bullets pummeling wildly around the lion. Sophocles was screaming now, his matted hair on end, prickling up along the bony curve of his back—stirring that terrible lion stench, which several weeks earlier had already begun to smell like death.

Ringling was bent over his gun, reloading. The cat neared the front of the cage, giving him a low, threatening growl that rattled deep in his throat like a motor full of marbles. He switched his tail, yanking against the chain, his head lowered and ears flat. But the next moment Ringling was on his feet again, pointing the rifle down into the center of the cage. Sophocles buckled back, spreading his jowls as far as they would go; he'd been hit, finally, just below the shoulder. Then he leveled his gaze with theirs, pawed the ground, growling and screaming in turns. Ringling let the gun go slack; he stood there trembling, staring dumbly at the lion cage. Another roar, and the lion had pulled the rail stake from the ground, charging the cage and banging against it with his uninjured side. Ringling blinked and dropped his gun. The men backed away—twenty short, stumbling paces, until the far side of the barn met their backs. Sophocles was yowling. "Please, Lawrence," Ringling gasped. "Finish it."

"But Ring, I don't know how."

He shook his head. "You do, you do." He was weeping wildly now. Lawrence stared down at the gun that lay a few yards away. It was a bright day, but still dim in the barn; the overhead lights had burned out months ago. "Please," he whispered. "For god's sake, Lawrence."

For God's sake. Lawrence nodded. *All right, all right.* He would do it—he would do what he had to do. Lawrence picked up Ringling's gun and pointed the long barrel at Sophocles, who had turned his predatory glare on him. The air in the barn was thick and unforgiving—dank and hot and rancid. His fingertips slipped against the rifle as he brought it to a shoulder and fired. The gun burst backward in his hands and fell away. The lion roared again. But he reached over and grabbed up the weapon again. *Oh God*, he breathed. *Oh God, oh God.*

"You've got to get closer," Ringling whispered. "To aim."

Lawrence glanced back briefly at his face—it was white—and approached the lion's cage, standing five feet from it. As he pulled the trigger again, he felt its force screaming out of the body of the gun, but he held on, like Gerald had taught him. Holding on—for years and years now. He moved closer—some old, reckless feeling in him that he couldn't quite identify. Blood was still matted against the cat's shoulder, but there was more of it now, coming from his nose, his ear, his muzzle. Lawrence had hit him in the neck, though he was still fighting: whining and rolling over in the stale wood-chips, trying to right himself. Ringling crouched in the corner, crying and begging his friend to hurry—swearing that the cage was going to give. Outside, Lawrence could tell a rain was coming: a thick, summertime monsoon rain. Muggy and stale. Sophocles rolled onto a side, but he couldn't stand. Lawrence moved as quickly as he could under the long, awkward weight of the rifle—steadying it against a shoulder and spreading his feet wider apart to prepare for the punch. He fired again, as close to Sophocles's head as he could. It worked. In a clap of bullet, the cat was dead. Shot three times—in the shoulder, throat, and head. Lawrence felt the bile surge up in his throat. His shoulder ached. It was terrible, what they were doing; no god had to tell him that.

Sasha hadn't moved yet, but he sat tense and hunkered down, hind legs drawn under him and the meat of his shoulder flickering. Lawrence walked around the side of the cage, closer to him, and he backed away, head low and a gurgling in his throat like a low death growl. Without moving his eyes away from his hunter, he sniffed the body of his compatriot and let out a terrible, human-sounding yowl. *God forgive me*, Lawrence thought, and fired: foolishly and poorly, missing him altogether. Then the cat charged him head-on, the spike slipping easily out of the ground and his body slapping against the side of the cage so that the whole structure pressed outward.

"Lawrence!" Ringling was almost breathless, back still pressed against the barn wall. He moved fumbling into his front pocket. "Do you need more ammunition? Lawrence?" The box of bullets dangled loosely between his fingers; he made no motion to come toward his friend. Lawrence glanced back fiercely and shook his head. *No*, he didn't need him. He didn't need Ringling, or God, or anybody.

Sasha watched on and growled more loudly. Lawrence's second shot hit him, but the cat barely reacted. Crazed from weeks of half-starvation, Sasha lunged again, rattling the cage and sending Lawrence's guts into a frenzy. He fired again and again, hitting Sasha once behind the ear. The animal fell back in a roar. "Lawrence!" Ringling was sobbing in his corner of the room. Lawrence ran up to the cage and shoved the rifle between the chicken wire mesh, right at the base of the lion's skull. Sasha's head had rolled into the dirt, but he could still see the gun; he knew what Lawrence was doing. Knowledge, Lawrence thought, could be such a terrible thing. And Sasha just lay there and took it as Lawrence fired, and the gun kicked backward once more, and it was done.

When it was over, Lawrence dropped the rifle and sank down onto his knees. The smell of gun powder and iron and animal sweat was in the air, filling up the windowless barn so he couldn't get his lungs around anything else. It was repugnant; he breathed through his teeth. "Lawrence," Ringling had come up to him now, his hands at his back—gentle, worried. He held his friend up to sitting, and Lawrence collapsed into him, spitting and choking against his sorrow and his shame. And they knelt there like that for several minutes more: two grown men, crying over a lion pen. Holding each other and grieving for everything they'd lost, or never quite had.

Theresa, July 1979

"You're back."

She nodded.

"I thought you might not be coming back."

"We always come back. My mom leaves sometimes—she does that. But we always come back."

Tomás was wearing thick leather work gloves, a rusted length of barbed wire stuck across his hands; he was carefully tearing apart the old chicken coop. Inside, her mother had gone upstairs to rest, claiming exhaustion. None of their luggage had been put away. The tin foil was balled up inside her purse. *Tell that boy he can leave now,* she'd told Theresa. *We all need some rest.*

"My mother says you can go home."

Tomás tossed the barbed wire into a pile of scrap that he was accumulating by the door of the shed. Theresa followed the gesture, taking a quick survey of what had changed since she had been gone. The Z car had been washed and parked along the side of the house, the ponies were missing, the hives had been relieved of their stagnant honeycomb, and the shed door swung open to a sensible file of boxes, organized in rows. Tomás pulled the gloves from his hands methodically, finger by finger. "Your mother's pretty well done with me."

"No," she blurted.

Tomás looked up, the edge of his eyebrow hunched upward. "She doesn't like me—or haven't you noticed?"

Her voice pitched: "We need you here."

"You want me to stay?"

Theresa pressed her foot downward into the dirt, deepening in the dust. "I didn't have a choice," she said. "About leaving last week."

Tomás tossed the leather gloves next to the scrap pile. A faint line of something like hurt creased across his face. *Does he love me?* The question pressed itself into her brain and she shook it away.

"Where did you go?" He stood, expectant, a hip jutted to one side to hold his weight. Lanky. Loose. Theresa glanced up at the house: no lights, no sound. "Let's walk," she suggested, moving toward the twin tire tracks that pressed their way through the grasses beyond the house. Some years before, Theresa knew, on a hot day like that one, a pick-up carrying Lawrence and her Uncle Ringling had rambled along these same tracks to the boat house to bring an end to their dreams of resurrecting the past. Now, the circus animals were gone, and so were the men themselves. Tomás made no comment; he followed. When they reached the boat house a few minutes later, Theresa noticed that the door swung slightly inward in the fading light. Tomás took a step forward; he pressed his fingertips to the door and shoved it gently open: "It needed some freshening up in there."

Inside, the air was still salty and damp; there were undertones of wood and iron. It reminded her strangely of the ocean: the ripe air, a musty odor of animal energy and loam. Along the floor lay broken cages like half-bare skeletons: the jaw line or rib cage of some heroic beast. Theresa shivered. Years before, this had been a place she'd loved: the recycled boat house, a veritable arc. She eased herself down onto the bark-chipped floor—it was cold, but dry—and Tomás followed. They leaned backward against a pile of salvaged lumber, noticing darker patches sprinkled among the bark chips where the door cast light from the day. *Sweat, urine, blood.* Baby elephants and lions and pythons and billy goats. Theresa shook her head with the memory of it all. "It's tiny," she said. "When you think about it—what all they had in here."

Tomás agreed. There were reasons—good ones—why the venture hadn't worked out. "It's hard," he said. "People always want to, but you can't do it—you can't bring back the past."

Theresa's eyes flittered toward him. The low light stretched shadows across his face. He looked older in that setting. Not the boy Tomás, but something different. "What will you do," she asked, "when you're finished here?"

The bark chips beneath them were soft and dry, but spongy somehow. Cool. The heat from outside hadn't made its way inside the boat house. Tomás breathed deep, drawing that stale but sea-like air into his lungs. "I'm good with motors," he said. "When things get better, I should be able to get a regular job again. Maybe downtown somewhere, at one of the shops," he got quiet. "Or over in Vacaville—some place."

"A mechanic."

"Something like that."

She was silent for a moment.

"You'll do more than that, I know. You'll go to college."

She looked up. "That's not what I meant."

"But it's true," he said. "You've got all kinds of things ahead of you. Nathan will make sure of that."

She picked quietly through the woodchips. A jolt of sadness flooded her. It was like a mild betrayal: his conviction that she would leave eventually, and that he wouldn't try to stop her. The grief she felt was grayed and sodden, like the boat house itself: the warped walls, the burnt siding. In this place, she thought again, two lions had died. Lawrence had shot them. *Lawrence. Shot them.* She shivered. "He told me about what happened to the lions."

"Who did?"

"Lawrence—before he went to Minnesota. He told me about how he killed them. Because my Uncle Ringling couldn't stand to do it."

Tomás sprawled on the bark beside her, staring up at the high, wood- beam ceiling. "How awful for him. He didn't seem like a violent guy."

She shut her eyes and leaned back against the pile of used 2 x 4s. In the silence, there was still so much history clanging around her ears. She breathed deeply—musk and iron and loam—and exhaled into the cool air. Her mind moved back to Lawrence—it was impossible not to—picking up the gun and taking aim. That man, her one-time friend, had disappeared into so many layers of sadness, it had become impossible to bring him back. A shallow tremor passed through her; she pressed herself more firmly against the pile of bark and building materials at her back.

The next sensation was Tomás's warmth: his lips coming down over hers. His tongue moved slowly against her lips and teeth. She let her breath unfold into his mouth, grateful for it, and tried to let all the other things fall back out of her mind. Tomás's fingers were winding their way into her hair; she let herself slump backward into the bark. *Does he love me?* The boat house rafters shuddered mildly from the breezes that made their way into dry corners and crevices. The building was not air-tight; this made it more bearable, coming here, years after it had been shut down. She breathed: salt and loam and history. And Tomás. She breathed again. She liked the breadiness of his breath, the smooth tone of his skin. She kissed him harder, and his body came closer, closing the gap between them. She let herself slide more fully onto the floor beneath him; it was cool and textured. He slipped a hand beneath her head. "Where did you go?" he asked again. "Where did your mother take you?"

"Nowhere," she told him. "She never goes anywhere. Just drives and drives."

"Drives?"

"She's like that; she can't stay in one place."

"I suppose that would be hard," he answered after a moment. "Her whole life, she's been moving."

His weight was on her; she felt herself small against him. *Small. Against him.* Tomás's body was not thick, but it was broad. Expansive. He filled space in the way that a man should. It was startling, the way this so clearly appealed to her: a thought that held on and would not let go—like a weasel. She felt corrupted and emboldened, both. Whatever her mother had feared, it did not matter.

"Do you think she had something to do with it?" he whispered. "With Lawrence's death?"

Her body went lank, listening to the wind, the stray branches brushing the surface of the roof. She sighed; there was Tomás, always naming out loud the things that she was thinking.

"I'm sorry," his breath came at her warm and hurried. "Sorry I asked."

She told him it didn't matter, and their hands found each other in the darkening shed. They came together again: all of the inevitable energies between them, tracing the shapes of each other. She swallowed. And swallowed again. Something between lust and terror catching her and holding on. Her hands were in his hair, moving across his arms, his back. Under his hands, she felt the shape of her breasts, her ribs, the flutter of her shoulder blades—all of it, coming into clearer consciousness under someone else's notice.

His mouth traveled down her neck, her ears. She heard his breathing: *Tomás Tomás*. Nearly a week they had been gone, but her body still remembered this. The rhythm, the careful give and take. She felt reckless and famished and wildly alert. Frenetic. His leg slid against hers. Each piece of him was active. Alive. It was almost too much. She tried to concentrate on one thing at a time: her hands, her mouth. She blew into his ear. He laughed. She tried the lobe, the space behind the ear. His skin was salty there. His hair smelled fresh; it curled darkly at his temples and at the base of his neck. "*Te-re-sa*," he said, his voice folding consciously into another accent. His hips shifted; he pulled himself up alongside her, lodged an elbow beneath himself and stared down at her. "Do you want this? Is this what you wanted?"

She stared back. In the falling darkness of the boat house, they were nearly invisible to each other. She could not stop that iron smell from mingling, already, with her memory of that day. *Is this what you wanted?*

"Do you really know Spanish?" she asked impulsively. He nodded, startled. "*Say* something." And he did. He said it again. She smiled. It did not bother her that she did not know what it meant. Instead, it was a kind of relief. She asked for things, and he gave them; and that was enough.

He took the fingers of her hand into his own, squeezed them gently and kissed her again. *Do you love me?* The question kept rattling against her skull. *Do you love me? Do you?* Her fingers tightened around his shoulders, still not entirely certain how to navigate tongue, teeth, breath, voice; but Tomás responded, drawing the full length of himself onto her, bearing down slightly, gently, answering the confused complexity of her longing.

"*Eres bonita*," he said

"What?" she gasped. "What did you say?"

"*Eres bonita*," he grinned. "*Siempre lo pensaba.*"

A quick shadow crossed her face. "You don't have to keep doing that."

He stared down at her, surprised. "I thought you liked it."

She nodded. "What did you say?"

"I said you were pretty," he answered. "I always thought so."

She didn't move; she felt something draining from her body. "Since when?"

Tomás laughed lightly. He shrugged. "I don't know. It's just a nice thing to say. And it's true." He caught her shape and encouraged her back downward. A hand passed briefly across her breast; the arousal of it all left her feeling breathless and parched and mildly drunk.

She dropped her arm from his back. In the slim light, she could see the small line of freckles that dotted through the hair at his neckline. "Were you watching me?" she demanded. "When did you start thinking that?"

"What?" he pulled himself slightly upward. He took her fingers into his and held them. She breathed harder.

"Were you watching me?"

"What are you talking about?"

"I don't know." She gasped quickly, sucking away a brief sob that startled her. "I don't know."

"Theresa." He moved his face closer to hers. His breath was comforting. Familiar. "Don't worry so much. *No te preocupas.*"

She shook her head again. She would not worry—she would *not*—and let her head collapse onto the bark. Tomás kissed her cheek. She put her fingers to his hair, rubbing slow circles against the scalp. He found her breasts and rubbed his face against them. Kissed the skin of her blouse there. His face pressed against hers again, then her neck. A hand slipped beneath her shirt. She could hear him pausing between kisses, drinking in her smell, rubbing a cheek against her neck. She breathed deeply. *Tomás Tomás.* More of his weight came onto her. A leg slipped between hers. His lips opened wider, more and more of him coming on to her, full and generous and wanting her to respond. Her hands were at his back, her mouth moving against his. She wanted this; she *did.* But her brain was still clicking away: a pair of lions, the scent of gunpowder, ice clinking along the rim of a Minnesota lake. Bear meat and trapeze bar and pistol smoke and ships pulling out to sea. And something more. "Stop," she breathed. "Please stop." He paused. She rolled over onto her side, away from him.

"Theresa? What happened?"

"They shot lions here," she said again. For a moment, her eyes fell shut.

Tomás rolled her onto her back and peered down at her, curiously. "Theresa, what is it? What happened?"

She looked up, shaking her head.

"With Lawrence," he said, his voice lowered in conviction. "Something happened."

"No," her voice was thin, teary. "Nothing happened."

He tried to put a hand to hers; she flinched. "Theresa—something happened."

She shut her eyes and lay there for several moments. "It's all right," Tomás breathed. He held her fingers loosely, and they breathed together into the cool night, which was nearly upon them now. The scent of history crushed around them; a breeze had risen up behind the boat house and came crackling through the rafters. It swayed and scattered against the roof, nested alongside some other, more distant movement: a sifting of gravel and grassland. A flurried motion. Theresa sighed. Waited. They heard it coming closer. The beam of a flashlight trembled sporadically through the open doorway. They heard footsteps coming softly through the grasses. Then a voice: "Theresa! Theresa, where are you?!" Tomás's hands froze; he shifted his weight carefully. Silent. "Theresa!" History echoed strangely around them: *the slug of a bullet, an indignant roar.* Tomás was moving away from her; he was getting to his feet. When the light found them, he was bent over her, helping to steady her. His hands grabbed onto hers, urging her upward. "Theresa!" her mother gasped. The light played wildly in the near pitch of the boat house. The loam smell was softening into the cooling night air. Her mother took a step forward and tripped—nearly losing the light altogether as it cast blurred shadows across the stray loft and the old foundations of the lion pens. Tomás bowed near her again, and then away. The sharp scent of iron pressed around them. Damp. Insistent.

"Mrs. Williams," Tomás started. And stopped.

"Theresa!" her mother gasped again.

Theresa was trembling, her hand damp against the ground. She started to get up and felt her palm smart from where a thin sliver of bark had worked its way under her skin. She paused, flinched. Drew the damaged skin to her mouth and sucked at it quickly. "It's all right." Her voice was breathy. "We're fine."

Tomás shifted near her for a brief moment. He pressed something into her hand. Something cold and metallic. A key. *The Z car,* she thought, and slid it automatically into her pocket. Her mother's eyes turned on him, emblazoned. "Out!" she screamed. "Get out!"

"Mom!" Theresa shuddered, desperate, watching him turn to leave. "Tomás, don't!" He glanced backward, somber, but kept moving. "Mom, he didn't do anything wrong." She could still feel the pressure of his hands light against her hips and breasts. The key was weightless in her pocket. But Tomás was already leaving; he was already gone.

"Oh, Theresa," her mother gasped. One hand was at her throat; the flashlight sagged wearily in the other, casting the light downward, watery against the floor.

Anger flared inside her, replacing grief. Replacing lust. "Mom, I'm fine," she insisted. Confused at first, and then weary. Exhausted. "Goddamit—I'm *fine.*"

"Oh, Theresa," her mother breathed, steadying the flashlight beam. Behind them, the slow crunch of gravel echoed beneath Tomás's footsteps. Her voice shifted sadly. Carefully. "You're more like me than you think you are."

Maxine, 1950

Maxine had already put up with a lot: the move to Fairfield, instead of back to Texas; the endless nightmares; the permanent, unanswered mystery of what had happened "over there"; and her husband's fingers pressing into her in the middle of the night—desperate, like a child's, but stronger. Maxine woke up sore, spotted with the small, accidental bruises he'd left there, clutching her in his private terror. She was willing to love her husband through quite a lot; she already had. But he was a broken man; he didn't know how to trust his wife, or the world. He was busy setting things right: perfecting inventory procedures down at Travis Air Force Base or teaching Ringling the finer points of manhood. When he brought the new boy home, however, Maxine finally understood that things would not change. This was the first sign of real commitment that Gerald had made since coming home—and it was not a commitment to her. It was important, he said, to do the right thing: the boy needed a home; the Williams would be responsible for him. It was as simple as that. And that was when Maxine first began to worry that things would not, as she had hoped, shift back to the way they had been.

Buddy Maxwell seemed to know it. "How's life on the home front?"

A decent man, Maxine thought, wouldn't ask about that; a decent man would mind his manners. "You've got no business asking me that, Mr. Maxwell. No business at all."

"A man can't ask a pretty lady how she's doing?"

"You're a rascal, Mr. Maxwell. That's what you are."

"Yes ma'am," he grinned in the low light of Fernando's night club. "And you love every bit of it."

It was terrible, Maxine knew, but he was right. Buddy was the kind of man who was so sure of himself, that even though he was playing hard for her, he remained alluring and seductive—as though Maxine were the one playing for him.

"Those men aren't going to change though, you know." Buddy's voice was smooth and convincing, like he'd been trained how to use it. "They've been to war; they're different people now."

"You know right well that I waited three long years for my husband to come home, so you can't imagine that I'm going to start being untrue to him now."

Buddy tipped a glass of scotch toward his chest; he peered into it. "I expect that you're the kind of woman who is true to herself."

"And what, Mr. Maxwell, is that supposed to mean?"

"Call me Buddy."

She glared at him.

"It means, Mrs. Williams, that your husband has been back two whole years, and you haven't gotten him started a family yet. You aren't home to cook his meals. It doesn't seem you're barely home to sleep in his bed."

"How dare you, Mr. Maxwell?!" She reached right over and slapped him.

"Buddy," he grinned, holding a hand to the sharp blush of his cheek. "Now see there? You're a woman who takes what she wants, Maxine. Just knows how to step in and take exactly what she wants."

* * *

What she had wanted was a job and a little society—a bit of life outside of her strained home. And something purposeful that she knew she could be good at. She found those things at Fernando's, one of the most notable nightclubs in San Francisco during the late 1940s. It was a wide, single-story affair with plush seats, low lighting, and a live piano bar. The people who visited were luxurious, even mildly famous. Some old money and some new. The war was over, and people were getting used to the idea of enjoying themselves again. But beyond the first few weeks of celebration—full of open doors and block parties, shared liquor and free kisses—it took money to entertain and to enjoy. So happiness got contained to clubs, bars, and dancehalls. Places that, as a married woman and still mostly poor, Maxine never got to go—until the job taking pictures at Fernando's.

"Do you think that man loves me?"

Joe, the photo developer, spent most of his time in the tiny darkroom behind the coat check, but he always knew what was going on inside the club. He was a quiet man—the only Japanese that Maxine had known since the war—and he paid attention. During the war, he and his young wife had been sent to the Manzanar internment camp. Now he was back in San Francisco, making pictures come to life under the red lights of his cramped studio: quick, permanent flashes of the fun people were having outside. Those images were as good as any window.

In the developing tray, Buddy Maxwell's whole body was bathed in revelry. He was unquestionably handsome: trim, narrow-hipped, and broad-shouldered; his chin and cheeks were so smooth and well-cut, they could have driven tears from a runway model. The shapes of his fingers were long and liquid and almost unboned. His skin, when he ran his fingers along a woman's shoulder or the inside of an elbow, was soft to the touch. His overall physical presence was so neat, so close to frail perfection, it inspired a kind of majesty. He was someone that a person wanted to take a picture of.

When Maxine did, though, she hadn't meant anything in particular. That was simply how she made her living: landing herself in the middle of a tangle of guests and taking a shot or two at the height of people's mirth: raucous laughter or a pitched line of eyebrows at the punch line of some good slip of gossip. Then it was off to the darkroom for a quick minute, and when she got back, folks were so tickled at their own spirited faces in those prints, they bought up every one. So it hadn't really occurred to her that she was inviting anything additional when she flashed her bulb in Buddy

Maxwell's face. He was a popular, important man, and Maxine hadn't pegged him for someone who could get easily distracted—especially by some little camera girl like her. But then, she was married; she had never imagined that she could get distracted, either. Maxine snapped her shutter again and Buddy's friends roared with laughter, slapping him good-naturedly across the back. Somebody grabbed the box and shoved her into the crowd for another shot: Maxine and her neat little uniform, tossed up against Buddy and all his friends. In the big flash from her camera, they all came white and still for a moment, like everything might suddenly be revealed.

She and Joe watched as Buddy's face came slowly into view under the warm lights and the chemicals: first an outline, like a ghost, then shadows and light around him. Joe sifted the pan of developing solution so that it spread itself, watered and greasy, over him, blurring the image for a moment; and when it came back, Buddy's features rose up again, so that you could tell what a well-shaped, attractive man he was. The faces of everyone around him were caught mid-gesture, shouting and carousing, but Buddy faced the camera head-on, grinning mildly, like he wasn't surprised at all. A few seconds more and they could see all of him—all the minor details of his expression. And they just knew that what they were seeing was a man in love.

"What his name?" Joe asked.

"Bud Maxwell. He's a producer from Hollywood."

Joe nodded. "Yes, I think I know Mr. Maxwell. He good-look man, Maxine."

Maxine swallowed. "I know it, Joey."

* * *

So Maxine found out that an unhappy woman can only resist so much temptation. Buddy was gorgeous and seductive, and her husband was anything but perfect. Gerald still wouldn't talk about the things that kept him trembling; he wouldn't tell Maxine much at all about the things that he'd done in the war. But Buddy talked—he talked all the time. He told Maxine the things he would do to her, if she would let him. He sailed her around the dance floor like that, whispering curious little love-making tricks in her ear—things that should have embarrassed her, but didn't. As they danced, Maxine thought about the photographs that she had found tucked inside her husband's footlocker: the grinning Kentucky boys, the small, twisted bodies lined up at the mouth of a gigantic hole, and the prim, white-faced geisha ladies linking arms with the GIs. There was so much that she still didn't know for sure. But Buddy Maxwell was one certain thing in her life: twirling her through the hall like that, he made her palms moisten and her knees begin to ache. And she was sure he knew that: it was working. Maxine wanted him. She wanted that slim, sure-footed man.

"What does it matter?" he whispered in earnest, the two of them finally nestled secretly on the back steps of Fernando's club. So many marriages had broken up after 1945. The war had been another time, Buddy said; the promises they had made back then shouldn't count anymore. "Don't try to be such a hero, Maxine."

But there was still Gerald, waking in a sweat beside her: that great block of a man heaving in tears, curled next to her. Needing her. "You don't know anything about it," she told him.

But his hands were in her hair: smooth fingers pressed up against her skull, moving rhythmically from nape to crown. He held her carefully like that—like she was precious. With his other hand, he moved around Maxine's waist, drawing her to him. "What don't I know?"

"War. And what happens afterward."

"I was here too, wasn't I?" Instead of kissing her, he just held her close; her body ached for him.

"You were down in Hollywood, making movies. That's not real life."

"But it sure helps the real life keep going. Don't underestimate the power of film." Then he lifted her, setting her in his lap. She didn't stop him. Against the back of her thigh, she could feel his thickness. He tilted her head back and kissed her, slipping his tongue, thin and pleasant, inside her mouth. It was sweet, kissing Buddy Maxwell. His breath was fresh, his silk shirt cool against the night. Maxine's hands went around his neck, her lips taking it, whatever he had to give. And for a long time, they stayed there together, sitting on the cool alley steps behind the club, the buttons of Maxine's blouse coming undone, her one-eyed camera sitting stupidly at her feet.

Love hits you in all kinds of crazy ways, Maxine decided. And she guessed she deserved what she got. *If you want a quiet life*, she told herself, *you don't go on like I have.* Before she left that night, Buddy made her say it: he made her tell him that she loved him. And she did. Then he paid her taxi home, all the way out of the city to her husband's house in Fairfield. It was late when she finally made her way up the stairs, carefully, her heart thick and her fingers shaking. And there was Gerald, asleep: that huge bulk of a man in their bed. Barrel-chested, thick-limbed, and all muscle. But she wasn't afraid of him. He was never quick about anger, anyway; he had to think about things first. Always. Maxine shook her head: *Oh Gerald, how did you ever manage to make it through a war?* She felt sorry for him, really, as she pulled a needle from her sewing kit and slid open the drawer where he kept his rubbers. She took up one small envelop and then another, slipping the point of her needle gently into each package, again and again and again.

Lawrence, 1974

Fairfield, California: a mixture of races and histories and tangled, unimportant lives. Lying north, just beyond the vibrant influence of San Francisco, it was a forgotten town, with forgotten sorrows. The homeless managed there the best they could. It was not sacred ground; no one asked them to leave. Buildings were square, unimaginative, and badly painted. Many of the shop windows had been boarded up; so many invisible details had already been discussed and sadly agreed to. It was a depressed area, and it was depressing to be there. But the men of Fairfield collectively migrated to the bars along Beck Avenue to drink for long hours and eye the women. These were low-roofed, windowless places with cracked vinyl seats. Booths you could sit down and get lost inside of. No one asked you to move on. No one asked you much of anything—not even the women who came in late at night, staring back at the men, unashamed. They were dressed in the kind of clothing that one would expect of a woman who is selling her body: nipped and darted and low-cut. Their make-up was exaggerated; they had dark, unforgiving eyes. Lawrence had never seen women like that— almost not like women at all.

"I was thinking," Ringling traced the outline of his pint with the neat tips of his fingers, "maybe we could get a candy wagon. Take it out on Larry Davis's show. Carnivals, man. That's more secure, you know; you got more to go on."

Lawrence watched his friend steadily: Ringling was caught in some kind of despair and endless hope; he wasn't sure which of these was more dangerous. All around them, other men had bottomed out. Ringling knew so many of them—from his army days or even further back to high school. No matter how ruined his life had become, Ringling was still loved. "We could make it," he was saying. "You just need vision. That's mostly what you need."

Lawrence's gaze trickled across the solitary women, stationed near the bar. He stopped at one in particular: a young girl in her early twenties, a bit plain-looking and less lewdly dressed than the rest of them. Her expression was fixed. She stood there waiting; there was nothing more.

"Lawrence?"

He blinked.

"What do you think?"

Lawrence flickered his eyes back toward the table. Gerald, he knew, had other plans. He had found jobs for them—in Minnesota. *Someone owes me a favor*, he had told the two men, and right away Lawrence understood that this "someone" was from the war: yet another person that Gerald had at one point saved.

But Ringling was unconvinced. "I gotta get back to Juno," he went on. "I had a girl up there, you know?"

Lawrence nodded—yes, he knew about the girl in Juno. Once Ringling was out of wars, there was still enough left of him to fall in love; he still needed something big and impossible in his life. He was stationed in Alaska by then, where there weren't a lot of women. But when he found her, he had loved her hard. *That's what a man does*, he had told Lawrence, laughing one of those high, staccato laughs of his that was almost pretty.

But things had changed. "She cheated on me—cheated and then left." Ringling shook his head. "I've gotta go back there. I'm gonna get her back."

Lawrence nodded again. The girl by the bar was watching him coolly. He swallowed; the air got thick and uncomfortable in his lungs.

"What about yours?" Ringling tilted the pint glass to his mouth. "What was her name?"

"What?" Lawrence felt the surfaces of his hands melt against the plastic lining of his seat.

"Her name, man. Don't tell me there hasn't been a woman or two."

"I'm a man of God."

"Still a man. I don't care what you say. Men need women—we need them so much, we can't ever let them know."

In the restroom, Lawrence gripped the narrow shelf of the sink, elbows locked. The space there was small, no bigger than a closet, and it reeked badly of urine. *It was true,* he thought: he was a man; he shared those self-same cravings. But he had given it up. Not since Sylvia had he been with anyone—*anyone.* Lawrence gulped the air. He could feel that now familiar pulse at the back of his head, how the whole backside of his skull felt simultaneously absent and severely weighted. Like it was just about to fall away. His shoulders, too, and the meat of his back began to unfasten, sinew by delicate sinew. He felt his eyes gel and loosen in his head. *This is what has become of my life*, he thought. He was crying into the sink of a washed-up country bar. The kind that sells the same cheap, sturdy beers for decades and doesn't take care of appearances. Inside, the surfaces of things don't matter; nothing does. His chest by then was a factory of despair, pumping and grinding. His body was so heavy, it was lifting off into nothing. This is what it means, he thought, to move beyond sadness. This is what it means for a man to lose hope.

When Lawrence came back from the restroom, nothing had changed. The universe was still as it had been: the men in their place, loud over their beers, flicking intermittent, half-interested looks at the women. They wouldn't yet commit to their intentions; they were a take-it-or-leave-it kind of crowd. Lawrence felt like a ghost walking toward them. He felt like he could slam one of these men's faces down onto the table and scream at them for some kind of grave infracture that he couldn't even name. He felt like he could slide quite easily out of his own life.

He sat down again at the table, feeling the perfect, insistent detail of the slit vinyl seat against his pant leg: waxed and worn, slightly unpleasant but reassuringly physical. A man has needs. Certainly. He needs those small reminders of his own humanness: how concrete the world is, how made up of individual details. Because, taken together, the whole thing could quite simply overwhelm.

* * *

Mrs. Williams's scream echoed through the hallways, down the stairs, and over to the tiny sunroom behind the kitchen where Lawrence slept. "He's dead!" she bellowed. "Ringling's dead!"

By the time Lawrence had made it up the stairs, there wasn't much left to see. Two of the Williams boys were crouching by the bathtub, pouring cool water over their uncle. In the doorway, Gerald's huge, bulky form took up most of the space. He was struggling with his wife: "Stay out in the hallway, Maxine. We can handle this." But she was inconsolable. She looked wildly around, catching sight of Lawrence by the banister and her daughter staring wide-eyed from her bedroom down the hallway. From where she stood, halfway down the hall, Lawrence didn't know if the little girl could see what he did, narrowly, through the spaces between bodies: Ringling, lolling limp in the bathtub, his eyes closed and his face grayed and sallow-looking. One flaccid arm dangled over the side.

"Call the police!" Mrs. Williams shrieked. "Doctor! Doctor!"

"Get a handle on yourself, Maxine!" Gerald grabbed her so firmly by the shoulders, Lawrence thought a lesser woman might have snapped in two. But she just stared back fiercely.

Gerald left her, roughed his way past his sons and bent over the soaking man, pressing a finger to his throat.

In the hallway, Mrs. Williams waxed hysterical. "Gerald? What are you doing?! What are you going to do?"

"He's just passed out is all," her husband growled. "We need to get him some air." Then he rolled up his sleeves and pushed his arms into the bath around his brother-in-law. There was the sound of agitated water—and for a moment, Lawrence caught the girl Theresa's gaze from down the hall. "It will be alright," he told her. But she was too smart for that. "No," she whispered hoarsely. "No."

"Get out of the way!" Gerald had Ringling out of the bath now. He stood elbowing his wife aside, who was following them from the bathroom, tossing towels to cover Ringling's nakedness. "Don't fuss, Maxine," he said sternly. "The man needs to breathe."

She stopped, turning her attention instead down the hall, to where Theresa stood watching. "Oh!" she shrieked. Her eyes leapt alarmed between her daughter and her naked brother. "Don't look!" she screamed, and slammed the door in the little girl's face.

* * *

It was nearly a week before they saw him again. By then, Gerald had decided that Lawrence should go on to Minnesota alone. He had bought a ticket for the fourth day of the following month. "And Ringling?" Lawrence asked.

"Ringling needs rest. We'll keep him here with us." Gerald wanted Lawrence gone; he put on a meaningful expression. "We've got to keep things organized around here."

What Gerald didn't say is that they were bringing Ringling home to die. Six days after the bathtub incident, a formal prognosis was announced. "Six months!" Mrs. Williams shrieked; even Lawrence knew about the promise that Maxine had made to her mother: to keep her brother safe forever. She stared in disbelief. "But Ringling!" she gasped, as though he'd had some kind of say in all of this. "You're too young, baby. You're too young!"

No one disagreed, but the doctors said there was nothing to be done. The cancer was a pancreatic strain: efficient, quick. So they had sent him home, to make him more comfortable.

During the two remaining weeks before Lawrence left the Williams home for the last time, he had occasional dreams of himself with a rifle, hunting through strange city landscapes, shooting at a man just ahead of him. The man was always laughing; when Lawrence caught him, the man never died.

The girl, too, was disturbed. She sulked about the house quietly, skipping school. "God has a plan," Lawrence told her. She was the only one who still had a habit of listening to him. But even she didn't believe it. "No," she answered. "I don't think he does." She had a certain streak in her, Lawrence had noticed: a kind of willfulness that marked her as her mother's daughter.

"But you know that your uncle might die?"

She nodded.

"Aren't you afraid?" Lawrence looked down at the girl's hands, which were twisting themselves together. They were large hands for a woman—square and strong.

"No," she said. "He might not even die. My mother says she's going to get him fixed."

Lawrence sat there quietly; this girl, he recognized, had so much more resistance than him. And more future. She was getting prettier all the time: her pale, freckled skin and round cheeks and bright, questioning eyes. "Theresa," he told her quietly, "people can't always save each other."

She shrugged, turning away from him: "But sometimes they can."

Theresa, July 1979

The engine caught once and died. Theresa tried again, gunning it before disengaging the clutch, the way her father had taught her, to flood the car with gas. It caught again, bucking forward before smoothing back out along the hard-packed dirt. The motor thrummed. Better—Tomás had made it better. The Z car eased slowly through the pot holes of the back yard and out toward the front of the house. Her eyes flickered toward the house, but no lights came on. She breathed more deeply. This, she supposed, was what he had intended: a key pressed into her palm, and her mother's sleeping pills, finally shutting down the anxious sea of her thoughts. *He's dangerous, that boy.* Her mother's words on the way back into the house the hour before still scalded her.

No, she had fired back. *No, he's not.*

Men like that, Maxine had shaken her head, mounting the front steps. *Men like that.*

No, Theresa had insisted again, certain that whatever other griefs might be upon them, Tomás was certainly not to blame. *No—it isn't him.* She had watched her mother funnel into the house and climb upward toward her bedroom. *It doesn't have anything to do with him.*

* * *

It was the same fold of highway that she and her mother had just traveled: out and back. Theresa recognized the exits, the names of things. She knew that she was driving north—toward Oregon, Canada, Sacramento. That singular direction could have taken her nearly anywhere. There was half a tank of gas. This seemed like a good sign, though she had no real idea how far that would get her. She had no more than some loose change with her. No tin foil roll. No check book. She had less of a plan than her mother had had.

Is this what you want? Do you want this?

The night was balmy. She rolled down the windows and let the wind chase through her hair. The air sliced past her. She shoved one hand into her pocket, winding the fingers into the rosary beads that she had lifted from their hiding place in the dresser. Along the highway, she noticed the shapes of grape vines appearing. The air smelled good: clean and open in a way that filled her brain so she felt drugged. At that hour on a Wednesday evening, she found herself nearly alone on the highway. She pressed the gas pedal until it tapped against the floor. Fifty miles an hour—sixty, seventy. The Z car spun through the empty night.

Galt. After another half hour, the sign flashed by in a thrum of recognition. *Lawrence*, she thought. *The Church*. When she came to the exit, she took it, shuttled several miles down the country road, and pulled the car, finally, onto a gravel shoulder by the entrance to *St. Pious X Seminary for Boys*. The gates, of course, were closed; it was nearly ten o'clock at night. The lights were dim. And what did she expect them to tell her, anyway? A fifteen-year-old girl, trembling in the darkness of a summer night. What did she expect to find here? Or the assessor's office, or anywhere? Origins and heartbreak are not always the same. What *was* it that she wanted to know? *Do you love me? Do you?* It wasn't reasonable—it *wasn't*.

She cut the engine and got out of the car. What did it matter—Lawrence, Tomás? The taste of the latter still on her lips. The muscular sound of those words in her ears: *Eres bonita. Bonita, bonita*. Already, she knew that he would not be back. Nathan would complete the job himself. Or he would hire day laborers from down by the hardware store and wait for them like a flock of hornets to finish clearing the land. Then Sheila would come back with her clients, and her mother would cry against the unfairness of it all. Their other brothers—in Portland, Phoenix, Los Angeles—would barely register what had happened.

She moved toward the wrought-iron gates, testing them with her fingers: cold and rough in patches where the paint had begun to flake away. Through the bars, she could see the outline of the chapel and the hallways of dorm rooms. They looked smaller than she had imagined. All these years, the seminary had stood no more than an hour from their home in Fairfield, but, of course, they had never come here. This place was a coda in their lives. In Lawrence's life. What had he found here? A place where people had understood him for a time? A place where life had still seemed possible? She didn't know; she was running out of questions. She turned a hand back into the front pocket of her jeans, pressing the knuckles against those little plastic beads. She felt tired. *I don't want to hear anything more*, she thought. *No more.* Not Tomás's tongue at her ear fringe: *bonita bonita*. Not her mother's panicked plea: *Get up now, we're going. It's time.*

A plug of air filled her throat and swelled. She choked against it, her eyes catching, too. Then her body pressed itself against the cool gates, which clanged mildly against her weight. She let herself slide downward onto her haunches, arms extended above her, and felt herself begin to cry: a brief, powerful sob that surprised her. She grabbed more firmly onto the gates and let it come, her throat catching for a moment, and then there was that exaggerated trumpet of anguish. A sad, lonely cry—gasping and rough-edged—that did not sound like her at all. Then another. And another. Embarrassing, the way her voice bled uncensored into the night. But no one heard her; no one came. She let herself slump further down onto her haunches, her arms still strung up above her, her hands holding onto the gate. Thin. Those wrought-iron bars felt so thin and inconsequential. Nothing—she would find nothing here. No archives; no one who would remember Lawrence enough to shed some kind of light onto what had happened.

He had been too quiet; that was part of the problem. Lawrence had been the kind of man who didn't leave a strong impression on most people. Being with him, Theresa had learned that she didn't have to say much if she didn't want to. He had appreciated her silence, her company, almost without comment. At certain moments, he had told her things—stories, for instance, about his former life as a priest. How he had loved the rhythm of the liturgy: the hymns and incantations. And he had told her, too, about Chile: that far away country where people spoke Spanish and the mountains were almost larger than the sky. In the parish rectory there, the cook had taught him how to make a sweet, caramely substance called *dulce de leche*, by stirring milk and sugar on the stove until it blended and crystallized. Theresa had said the place sounded wonderful, but he'd insisted that it was all different now, after the military coup, so there wasn't much point talking about it. *Sometimes the world falls apart*, he'd told her. *Or parts of it.*

She had still been full of questions. *Will God forgive anything?* Whenever she spoke to Lawrence, things had always seemed important. They had never said very much, always saving their energy for what mattered most.

If you ask it with a pure heart.

And what if your heart isn't pure?

He had smiled. *Then you're human.* On the stove, Lawrence's pot of *dulce de leche* was beginning to simmer: that slow, inward march crawling in from the edges of the pot that would emerge, some minutes later, in a rolling boil.

Theresa had remained quiet. She was not perfect, and she knew it. There had been times when she fought with her mother; there were times that she made her cry.

Don't worry, he'd assured her. *God forgives most things before you even ask.*

Theresa had never heard that idea, but she'd decided to believe it. Then she had taken a spoonful of the *dulce de leche* and spread in onto a piece of bread: a thick-hot carpet of sweetness. *Lawrence*, she had asked. *Is there really a Hell?*

What do you think?

She had shaken her head, licking the gooey liquid from her fingers. *I don't think so.*

And why is that?

Because God wouldn't be that mean.

He had stopped stirring the pot then. *Hell isn't just the opposite of goodness. It's this life we're living now,* he'd said. *Hell is having something good and knowing that it still isn't enough to make you happy.*

Those thoughts had left her wordless and staring. There were still so many questions: who he was, what all he'd lost, and whatever goodness it was that he thought he still had in life. Most of these questions he had never really answered. Sometimes, he had talked to himself. Theresa had wondered if he was still trying to talk to God; she had wondered if he really might be a little bit crazy.

But she could not remember enough; that was the problem. The pieces of things approached each other and sat stubbornly along the side lines. And she was tired of memory, tired of the indelible weight of the past. Another cry choked her. She let go of the gates, pressing her hand once again into her pocket and yanking the rosary beads out into the dim lamplight. She considered them briefly, then raised her hand and flung them over the top of the low gate. Then, turning back toward the car, she climbed inside, started the engine, and stared through the narrow windshield. The night blanched along the sidewalks under the narrow streetlights that lit the seminary gates. So much of the highway was dark, dark. She trembled, and shook the feeling away. *Is this what you wanted? Is it?* She sobbed again—oafish, loud—her knuckles pressed white around the steering wheel. Her foot slipped and the clutched popped. The engine died. She cried harder—convulsed and shivered as her face ran with tears and snot and all the grief that she had never seen Lawrence admit to. All that grit and sadness. She felt exhausted when she was through. Exhausted and half lost, she pulled wearily back onto the highway, aware of her situation, but nearly too tired to care: no money, no map. She followed the signs slowly and steadily toward Sacramento, leaning on stale memory and intuition for the rest. She gazed down at the waning gas gauge. The reckless energy was leaving her. She felt tired; she wanted to sleep. She wanted to be some place safe—some place that wasn't Galt or Medford or even her home in Fairfield—that place where all of those confused memories crowded around her like a second skin.

She knew, of course, that she was heading for Nathan's house. She didn't know street names, but there were things she recognized:

a certain freeway exit, a gas station or diner, a line of homes. It felt adult, what she was doing, maneuvering the dark streets, navigating her way to her brother's home. Once in town, she turned the corner onto L Street and followed the thin lines of houses. One block, and two. Her body was, by then, too fatigued even to feel the nervousness that was crowding again under her skin like a rolling boil. *What was she doing? What would her mother think? What would Nathan?* In the yard, a small lavender-colored bicycle lay on its side. A corner of that lawn had been interrupted by a shovel and scattered dirt. Already, she missed Tomás—missed his bready odor, warm and alive—missed his hands moving delicately along her skin. She had liked the way that felt: to be the object of attention. To feel like a piece of artwork: something appreciated, something in the process of being created.

A faint light was on upstairs. Nathan, she thought, must be reading some magazine quietly to himself. Julia, of course, would likely be in bed by then. She knocked softly on the front door. Waited. After another moment, she knocked more loudly. And again. A small chill passed through her—cold. It was cold for a summer night. She glanced nervously behind her at the Z car. No money for fuel, no map, no plan. If Nathan didn't answer, she wouldn't have enough gas to make it back to Fairfield. She didn't have the money for a hotel. She knocked again. A light came on in the hallway. She heard a rustling and a small, mewing voice. After several moments more, the door shuddered and clicked slowly open. Widened. The porch light came on, flooding her in light, like a movie star or a criminal. She stood there shivering, squinting at the backlit figures standing there. The little girl, Julia, clasped her father's hand, pulling closer to him, and Theresa thought suddenly of acrobats: pairs of performers flying through the air, their hands coming clasped and unclasped. Arms spread, wings coming open. Gasps stuck in the open air.

"Julia," her breath came out in a rush so that she had to catch herself against the door frame. "Don't you remember me?" The little girl's fingers wrapped more snuggly into Nathan's, while Nathan himself stood firmly in the doorway.

"Theresa," he breathed, clutching the little girl's hand. "God, I thought that might be you."

Maxine, 1951

It took Buddy well over a month to find her. For some time, she imagined, he must have waited for her to come back. But Fernando's was a big, established club; the ownership had several other venues throughout the city. Maxine was a successful camera girl. One of the best. When she told them that she would quit if they didn't move her, they listened; she had a new job the following week.

In the end, she didn't know who had told him: darkroom Joe, or one of the gossipy women, or the management. But it didn't matter. Buddy was a persuasive man; he got the things he wanted. So when she saw him standing at the bar of The Glass Mile, sipping a shot of scotch and grinning, she just knew. It was no use resisting. He had found her, and he would have her. And she would have him, too.

It was easy. The Glass Mile was further south than Fernando's; often enough, she stayed the night over at one of the girls' apartments who lived there in town. After work that night, she called Gerald to tell him that she wouldn't be coming home, then she took Buddy's hand and followed him to the curb. They hired a car to Half Moon Bay, where Buddy had a weekend home. The steps were steep, careening upward from the sea. By the time they arrived, it was well after midnight, and the moon was moving back down the sky, the light lifting off the water like something coming unglued.

Everything that Buddy had said was true. All the things he'd promised to do to her, he did. He was a worldly man; he knew things. And all that night, he made love to Maxine in ways that she didn't even have words for: leading her body into charged surprise, and leaving her off just before climax, so he could pick her up again later. Buddy Maxwell played her like an instrument; he knew her body better than she did. Her husband, on the other hand, was entirely different. He had had some experiences before they were married. She knew that; it was what one expected from a man. And it was just enough that he could teach her things about what they could do for each other. But there was plenty, too, that he didn't know about—things that they had had to learn together. He would lay her body down and hold onto it, trying to get things from it which he was sure were there. He wasn't efficient, but he was hard-working; he wouldn't give up until she had had her pleasure. And when he came inside her, it was delicious each time: how grateful he was to her, personally, for what had happened to him.

* * *

By the middle of the next day, they were still in Buddy's bed. The salt smell was unmistakable, and the ocean was rolling below them. That's when she told Buddy that she was pregnant. She had thought that he would be furious, but he didn't even seem surprised. He nodded. Then he got up from the bed and went to his armoire, pulling out a cigar and lighting it: "Direct from Cuba." He held it up, and she could see the shape of the leaves, glowing.

"Didn't you hear me, Buddy?"

"Maxine, I heard you. I heard the voice of a woman who is at a particular place in her life and can't make up her mind which way to go. And now she's looking for someone else to decide things for her."

She dug her fingers into the sheets. The shapes of the cigar leaves glowed. "That's a horrible thing to say!"

"True things often are." He laid back down on the bed, pulling the damp smoke into his lungs and sloughing it out away from her, toward the open window. "I'll give you something else to chew on. I'll marry you. Tomorrow, if you like. Or the next day. Just as soon as you get yourself free from that husband of yours, I'd be happy to pick you up and marry you and raise your little baby like my own son. I'll take you both around the world—show you things you never thought you'd see. Now, what do you have to say to that?"

The air in her lungs felt light and heavy at the same time. "You're a heel!" she snapped. "That's what I have to say."

Buddy nodded smoothly. He enjoyed his cigar carefully, like it was yet another part of a woman's body. "Well, now, that's one way of looking at it."

"Did you know I was pregnant?"

Buddy pressed a line of smoke efficiently from the side of his mouth. "Maxine, a man doesn't know—he suspects. To know for certain, he has to wait until a woman tells him—or her waistline doubles."

"Mr. Maxwell, you're shameful!"

"On the contrary, Maxine. You've shamed yourself, and I'm setting up an alternative."

"But you knew—and you made love to me anyway."

"Would it have been better if I hadn't been willing to touch you—or to save you from the mess you've made for yourself? Really, Mac—isn't this all a bit rash?"

Maxine fell quiet; there was plenty of truth to what he was suggesting. But Buddy was so sure of himself, so calmly sexy and pleasurable, that it made her angry. Her husband was a different sort entirely: he was a man who would cry after lovemaking, and try to hide it from her. His love was so covered over and inexact, it was almost painful, but she knew that it was there. With Buddy, she never had to wonder. There wasn't anything to worry about. You could see everything with him, she thought: it was all there, right on the surface.

"I love my husband," she snapped back. It was the wickedest thing she could think of to say.

Buddy's chest rose evenly: square and smooth and lovely. But Buddy kept his cool, as he always did. "As well you should," he answered. "He's a good man. Too good, most likely. You probably don't deserve him."

"You're evil!" she shrieked.

"That's right, Maxine, and a lot better matched to you. Now just calm down, doll. I'm trying to give you options, and you don't want any. Is that it? You just want to go on being the tragic figure, tied down in life? You've got a good mind, Maxine, but if you want to do something grand with yourself, you've got to make decisions. Firm ones. Ones you believe in."

She stared back fiercely. The dark edges of the cigar flickered and fumed. "And do what?" she demanded. "Follow you?"

"It's a start, Mac. You never know what it might lead to."

She had never known a man like Buddy before—someone who had access to so much—but she did know men. And she knew that they liked to keep women, especially ones with big spirits, like her.

So she told Buddy that he was wrong: if you've got a big mind and a big heart, you can live anywhere, doing anything. "It's people like you," she told him, "who don't know enough of yourself, that you need all this adventure. I've had mine already. So you can go off to India or Hollywood or Australia for all I care. I'll stay right here with my husband and my baby and my whole big mind."

* * *

When she got home, that boy Lawrence was there. He stood there staring dumbly at her, and if Maxine looked at him hard enough, she could imagine that this was his fault. All of it. He made her feel guilty, just looking at him. And furious. He was so helpless; he needed a mother. But it was too late, she thought. It was just too goddamned late for that.

"Where's Ringling?" she demanded. "I need to talk to him."

The boy looked scared; he pointed toward the kitchen. "Ringling!" she yelled, running into him, where he stood pouring a glass of milk from the cool glass container. He looked pleased with the milk, and the glass, and its coolness on a sultry morning like that one. Ringling, her precious boy, always looked so satisfied with everything in his life. It was the one thing that still made her glad.

"What is it, Mac?"

But she just stood there staring at him. He was beautiful, this first man that she had raised. Maxine hoped her sons would be like him: lean and rippling. He was athletic now, almost fully a man, and had a small, compact power—not nearly as large or imposing as Gerald, but his arms were sharp with muscles, and his back narrowed down straight and clean. He looked like the kind of man that a woman could rely on. "Oh, Ringling!" she cried again, knocking herself into his chest, between his arms, still balancing that creamy glass of milk. His body was so in control of itself; his future was unquestionable. Whatever she had given up, it had really been for him. And that was all right, she thought. He was there. The fact of his beautiful existence was enough.

Ringling set his glass against the counter and passed his arms loosely across his sister's back, in the same half-gesture that her father used to make: half holding her, half letting her go. These men, she had never quite understood why, always seemed so aware of how little she really needed from them. "It's all right, Sis."

He was trusting, and loyal, too. Maxine knew that he wouldn't leave her, no matter what. She could have told him everything—the whole story. But Ringling was too precious for that, she decided. Too perfect. She hoped he would remain like that forever.

"I'm pregnant," she finally cried, collapsing into his chest. "I'm going to have a baby."

"But Mac, that's great." He pulled his sister out away from him, holding onto her shoulders and peering down so that he could better see her face. "That's terrific news. Gerald—he'll be so happy."

Lawrence, 1977

That morning at the window, first frost. A cold October morning, mid-month. The leaves hadn't even finished falling, but already there was snow. It was early; dreams still echoed through his skull like the last fading air around a loud, ringing bell. Slowly, he began to dress—visiting the whiskey bottle by his bedside between shirt, socks, and shoes. Outside, the light was loud and merciless, no matter how frigid the weather. Again, winter was settling in: the trees shaking off color like an unwieldy coat, baring themselves for the bleakness ahead. Naked and strong, like splinters against the sky. Lawrence could write home about this: what Gerald could never imagine, with his California and his tropical war. It had been nearly three years, and he had had barely a word from the Williams. Not since the brief trip home for Ringling's funeral two years ago. No letters, no phone calls. No one missed him; that was the terrible truth of it.

Outside the apartment building, there was a feeling of gel in the air: a kind of cold bounded up by warmth. A buoyancy. Lawrence's boots crunched down the walk to the bus stop. It was a good, reassuring sound; he kept walking. The earth was still warm—the currents of rivers and lakes still moving—but the air held a heaviness, stiff and palpable. It made moving difficult. In some ways, he had found, October was the worst month: the new cold, the profound loss of color. This was when he knew that it was coming: six more months of winter. No more green-purple-gold-orange-emerald-pink. Just white, then brown, then more white on top. The endless piling of snow on snow. And if not that, then bare brown. And cold. The lakes moving into hibernation. The snow and silence and ice. A dull mood settling in. A delicate vein of depression. That low throb. Like the first grain of a hangover, coming on now.

Lawrence made his way down Summit Avenue, past the centuries-old homes, wide front lawns, and views of the city below. He moved past them—four, five, six city blocks—not waiting for the bus to take him to his uninspiring job at the bank, not thinking about the cold. At the end of the neighborhood, he came to the cathedral, sitting there at the close of the avenue, its huge weight crowded up over downtown, the street diving down at an angle— driving downward toward the center of town, with all of its commerce and purpose. He stopped. He considered the cathedral, its round, weighty insistence: gilt-edged, ribbed, and majestic. The huge cupola like a woman's pointed breast, round and bronze and standing at attention. Like the prostitute Eau Claire's melon-colored skin beneath her blouse. The evening before, he had asked to kiss it, and she had refused. "You love me," she'd answered, accusing. It was the seventh time that Lawrence had hired her.

"No," he had promised. "I don't." But she was right. This was why he had finally succumbed to it: because there was no other comfort that he could dream of. That first evening, when they had arrived in the motel room and Lawrence had lain half naked across the sturdy, uncomplicated bed, he had come while she was still putting on the condom. The fury of his eyes shuddered and folded. But the woman had laughed it off. "Ain't the first time," she told him. "Men get nervous. You'd be surprised." Then she pointed toward the adjoining toilet and told him to go clean himself up.

Her name was Eau Claire, for the rural Wisconsin town of her birth, two hours east. "There's usually two or three a month who don't even want sex," she had told him over the stream of running water. When Lawrence came back, she was lounging across the bed, still clothed, except that the front of her blouse was partly unbuttoned. His hands were pink from the concentrated effort of the soap. He looked at her, the suggestion of her breasts leaving him partially aroused. "People get confused," she had concluded. "We all have needs, and folks usually think it's physical."

What Lawrence wanted now was a sign—something to tell him what he should do. But when he entered the vestibule, no one was there. No one else's faith had called them out so early on a weekday morning. There was no mass until eleven. No stray woman tidying hymnals or snuffing candles. The church breathed in its own, slow shape. Four broad chambers, like a heart: an entry, two low walls of pews facing each other, and the canopy above the raised pulpit like an enormous throne. High up against the ceiling, twin stained glass windows threw a purplish glow about the church. He took a seat in one of the pews and mashed his fingers together. Above him, Christ sagged against the cross. "I don't love you," he had promised her. *I don't—I won't.* But it didn't matter; he knew she wouldn't be back.

Goddamnit, Lawrence gulped the pungent cathedral air. His breath caught. *Fuckingdamn.*

A man in priest's vestments emerged from a side chamber and bowed slowly as he passed the altar. He shifted through the aisles. Yawned. There was a slight squeak to his walk, suggesting loafers: rubber-soled and soft like aged skin. But the old priest wasn't paying attention; he hadn't noticed the tired young man sitting below the statue of St. John: weary and faithless, with a faint odor of liquor. Lawrence's eyes followed him around the periphery of the church, past more and more pews, until he reached the door of the confessional and stepped inside. *A sign.*

Fuck. Fuckingdamn.

The priest shut the door with a small bark that likewise echoed, and stopped. Lawrence got up; he moved toward the confessional. *Goddamnit. Goddamn. Stop it!* he told himself. But he could not. His brain spun ahead without him: *Goddamn. Fucking damn.*

Once he was inside the stall adjoining the priest's, he could hear the man's breathing; he could smell the nicotine on his breath. He was old and slow: an aging priest from the old guard. "Bless me Father, for I have sinned."

There was silence, and a fluttering of vestments, as though the man hadn't expected an audience that early. He cleared his throat: "Tell me, son, how long has it been since your last confession?"

How long? Years. Lifetimes. At least as long as it had been, Lawrence thought, since he had sat there where the priest himself was, speaking mildly through that thin, brass-lace screen. Confessional boxes, he thought briefly, are nearly always the same: the three joined booths, low-lit and smelling of left-over incense. A small, metal screen linking your words to someone else's anonymous life. But it didn't work that way. Lawrence knew; he had taken confession. Instead, it was like peering through a person's life: gazing right into their mind and out the other side again. People revealed themselves. There was a lot of fear; that was what he remembered most: people's fears about what would happen to them, or to someone they loved, because of what they had done. People believe so much in reciprocity, Lawrence thought. They prayed for forgiveness and for the fortitude to endure the things they must.

The man coughed: a wet, chesty cough. "Well, son? What is it that you wish to confess?"

There again: it was impossible to know. Nothing. Everything. Was Lawrence really responsible, he wondered, for all the small disasters of his life? "I don't love anything," he said aloud.

"What? Young man, I don't understand you."

Lawrence's chest and shoulders began to shiver. *Goddamn.* "I love the wrong things."

The priest was quiet for a moment; his mind was moving slow. "Put your trust in God," the man coughed. "He can help you."

Fuck. Damn. God-fucking-damn. Lawrence's mind was poisoned; the words wouldn't stop. "No," he whispered, shaking his head.

"What, my boy?"

Lawrence looked up. "I need forgiveness!" he cried.

"Yes, my son? God is listening. What have you done?"

Fucking-goddamn. They wouldn't stop: the words formed of their own accord. "I've had impure thoughts."

"Against whom?"

"Our Heavenly Father."

The man's bench creaked as he rolled back on his weight. "What," he asked carefully, "is the nature of these thoughts?"

Shitfuckdamn. Lawrence's mind was moving more slowly with the liquor. He had now that familiar sensation of his *self* rising above him, stepping faintly out of his skin and pushing itself up beyond the realm of his own skull, so that it sat there above him, quietly, watching his conversation with the priest. From that other place, Lawrence told the man: "I don't know how to love God anymore."

"But you must. We all had to find a way."

"No." *Fuck. Damn.* "I can't. He's gone. He left."

"God forsakes no one. He loves you. Accept that. You must accept His love."

Oh, Jesus. His breath caught more sharply. *Oh, damn.*

"You can be forgiven." The old man's breath smelled of nicotine and something acidic. Lawrence felt him moving closer to the little brass mesh window between them. He was getting excited. "All you have to do is ask. Are you asking?"

Lawrence didn't answer. His limbs were getting heavier now; he felt his chest restrict.

"The Lord provides for us all."

But Lawrence didn't figure the Lord had provided for him in a very long time. His heart banged: he was alone—still so alone.

"Our Father never leaves us," the old man insisted. "Tell me, son. What have you done?"

Lawrence rose without responding and bolted from the confessional, running loud and lurching through the church: *Tell me, tell me! What have you done?* The heart-like church throbbed around him, his long body loud and weeping. At the door, Lawrence collided with a man who was just coming in. "Excuse me," he said, his eyes fixed at the level of Lawrence's chest. He was wearing a camel-colored coat, fringed with a soft pelt around the lapels. Lawrence's pulse banged at his ears—the whole huge cathedral behind him, aching in its emptiness. "Excuse me," the man said again. He had an accent. *An immigrant*, Lawrence thought. And one with money. Then the little man moved past him, his polished shoes clicking at a higher register against the marbled floor. Lawrence nodded, watching him for a moment: the way he walked quickly and confidently into the church. How much had this man noticed? Had he smelled the liquor, the shame? Had he heard Lawrence running from the old priest? Did he know? Did he understand any of what had just happened?

Outside, finally, there was his sign: the man's car, pressed up against the curb directly below the cathedral steps, still warm. Steam pulsing off it like halo after halo into the frigid air. No one else was in the parking lot. Lawrence didn't think about it; he got in. It was cold outside—so cold! The man had left the engine running, the heat on. Lawrence moved his hand toward the keys, let their weight collapse gently into his palm. His mind moved at odd angles. Clearly, the man planned to be gone for no more than a moment. Lawrence's breath plugged at the windows in a fine, moist film. He looked through it toward the sky: loops of light and dark, the clouds full of snow. A terrible place. But somehow the Lord provides; He always does. Sin or salvation, it was so simple. Lawrence clicked the keys into gear, the way Ringling had taught him when they were still driving for the show. And no one said anything—not God and not the priest. Ignition on, the wheels pressing gently forward in the building snow. A crime so clean, it didn't even feel like a crime. How easy it was in the end, Lawrence thought, to find providence. The wealthy man's slick black car easing out into the world with him: headed south, then west, toward California. Toward home. *Thank god, thank god.* How good and clear it was, he breathed. So effortless, really, in the end: the inescapable answers to things.

Theresa, July 1979

He didn't ask her exactly what had happened at the house; he didn't have to. Nathan did not need to hear the details of things in order to believe that Theresa had reached her limit. He told her that he was glad she had come. Glad that Tomás had fixed the Z car, and that it had miraculously delivered her there to Sacramento. Across the living room, Julia sat quietly, folding her five-year-old thoughts into the pulp-textured pages of a coloring book. Having woken up that late at night, she refused to go back to bed alone. But while her aunt and father talked, she made no comment; she did not so much as lift her head. Theresa had learned that her niece was a child of singular concentration; she knew how to find one small place in the world and to claim it as her own.

"You made it here alone," Nathan said, thrumming his fingers against the sofa arm in a way that made her unsure whether he was pleased or nervous at the thought.

"I'll be sixteen next week."

He nodded: "We'll go down to the DMV—make it official." He watched Julia trace slow circles with a red crayon, playing carelessly through the lines. After another moment, he added, "It's probably good for you to be getting a break from Mom."

Nathan's living room was intimate and comforting: a sofa and a pair of sitting chairs filling the end of the room that angled out to face the front yard. Theresa fingered the deep plush of the sofa where she sat. "She's tired of Tomás."

Her brother looked up. "She doesn't want him working there?"

"She thinks he's dangerous—to me."

Nathan considered her. "Should she?"

Her fingers traced the mottled lines of the fabric that lined the sofa. "No."

Nathan sat quietly for a slow minute. The night still echoed darkly through the window behind him. "You know you can stay with us for as long as you want to."

She looked up. "I will—I want to stay here for a while."

"Good," he answered, and he promised to call the next day to find out how much more work needed to be done on the house. "I'm hoping he can finish it all before he leaves."

"Leaves?" Betrayal rose like acid in her belly.

"They're going to Missouri."

"Missouri? He didn't say anything about that." People disappoint you. She was learning this: they don't always intend to, but they do.

"His mother is from there. They have relatives, people to help them out."

"Missouri," she repeated, raising her hand to her head.

Nathan shifted in his chair. "You'll have to sleep down here tonight," he told apologized. "But tomorrow we'll get a room upstairs set up for you. You can stay as long as you want."

She nodded, watching her niece work dutifully through her coloring pad.

"I'm sure Mom will miss you," he said, getting up off the couch to go get her some bedding, "but it's good to get a break." A moment later, he came back with arms full of linens and set them gently on the couch cushion beside her. "I'll bet you'll sleep hard," he grinned softly, and she nodded, still watching Julia fill in the careful lines of her coloring book. Relief, she thought, or safety or comfort—or whatever it was that she had finally reached—had never felt so exhausting.

* * *

Several months earlier, when Lawrence had gotten back from Minnesota, Theresa had understood that he was dangerous. People in her family did all kinds of things—shot elephants and got

282

stabbed and went off to fight wars—but nobody had been to jail. It wasn't something that happened to them. If it had happened to Lawrence, it meant that he wasn't one of them. She remembered this detail more clearly than all the rest: the simple fact of his difference.

Her mother hadn't been happy about it, either: "I thought we were done with this."

But Gerald had held firm. "Just give the boy time."

"He's not a boy anymore, Gerald!" Maxine had snapped. "Look what he's done already."

Stealing a car, Theresa knew, was not the worst thing that a person could do—but doing it for no apparent reason was frightening because it didn't make sense.

"He had money; he was taken care of," her mother went on. "It should have been enough."

Not much about Lawrence had made sense; Theresa could understand this better now that she was older. He wasn't a man like her father and brothers, who had each made something of themselves. There had never been a woman, or a job that lasted. The danger, Theresa decided, must come from some place inside him.

"He needs us, Maxine." Theresa remembered her father sounding tired.

But her mother hadn't wanted to listen: "You're wrong about him, Gerald. You always have been."

What was even worse, it was irresponsible: "Your father shouldn't let him stay here with us," Theresa's mother had told her. "It isn't right. Just think of the danger he's putting you in."

By the time she was fifteen, Theresa's breasts were soft, immobile lumps resting in the stiff white cups beneath her blouse. The rest of her had filled out, too: her hips and thighs and the soft little cushion around her middle. Her mother said that she was something to look at now, and that was a problem.

"You be careful, Theresa." Her expression was severe.

All around her, the girls at school were becoming beautiful: filling out in some places, lengthening in other. Their slender necks, their fingers and cheeks and jaw lines taking on importance. They were good Catholic girls, and they knew how to mature between the lines: lip gloss instead of colored lip sticks, neatly rolled socks, a certain kind of shoe. Real cosmetics were not allowed. But there were things—a tiny bit of powder, a strong-smelling soap—that couldn't be faulted. They were becoming lovely in spite of themselves. In health class, the nuns warned them about it: what men want, what they can do. It seemed that everything about womanhood was dangerous and masked. It made Theresa tired.

"Give me a break, Mom."

"No breaks, Theresa. You're young. You don't understand what all can happen."

Maybe not, but what she had understood was that there was finally a threat that was outside of her. Not something that she herself was responsible for—failed trapezes and botched eye liners—but something external that might get her no matter what she did: *It wasn't my fault.* Sometimes, things just happened. That kind of worry made Theresa bolder. She understood now the kind of power that belongs to women: beauty, meanness, secrecy. Always something invisible, always something difficult to trace.

* * *

"What was it like?" she had asked Lawrence one day. "Being in jail?"

He'd looked alarmed, like she had just accused him of something.

"What? Don't you want to talk about it?" Theresa was wearing her best dress, the yellow one with loose sleeves and a tight bust that her mother had bought for her down in San Francisco. After enough practice, she had finally learned how to make use of her elegant presents: lip liners and eye shadows and hunks of cream rouge. They were lovely and impractical gifts—things that Theresa could never wear to school or church. Most of the time, she wore them at home, wandering around the house feeling mildly beautiful. Like something important that no one would ever get to see.

Lawrence had shaken his head. But there was a longing in him; Theresa could tell. He wanted to answer the questions that she asked him; he wanted to get them right. There was something in her that he couldn't say no to. "It's very quiet," he'd said finally.

"But what about the other people? Criminals?" she'd pushed. "Wasn't it full of them?"

His head had tilted: *yes, yes.* The spaces of his eyes were filled in black, with just a faint blue jelly around them.

"Wasn't it terrible?" Theresa had demanded.

He'd nodded.

"But everybody says that; you must have known it would be."

His head had bobbed woefully; he couldn't meet her gaze.

"So why did you do it? Why did you steal that car?"

He had grimaced then. Theresa knew that he would keep going, if she insisted. But she had stopped. His face was a net of pain: an expression full of grief and powerlessness. It made Theresa tired, too. So she'd turned away and started back upstairs. Suddenly, she didn't want to know anymore.

* * *

When you live with craziness, you find ways around it. After her initial outburst, Maxine had given up. She didn't talk about Lawrence anymore; for her, it was like he wasn't even there. Theresa had begun to feel the same: he simply wasn't worth it. There was nothing in him anymore that inspired respect. Nothing interesting.

And in those days, there had been more immediate concerns. Theresa's father, for instance, was about to retire, and her parents had gotten busy loving each other again. The little pink packages of womanhood had stopped appearing; whatever was left to know, Theresa would have to figure out on her own.

"When your father came back from the war," her mother had told her, "all I wanted was to be alone with him, someplace far away from everyone else. Just us." She'd said it with a kind of satisfaction, like it was finally going to be hers. No one would ever have said they wanted Theresa gone, but still, she worried, now that her father was coming home. She felt expendable. And stuck—too young to leave home and too old to want to stay.

In the privacy of her bedroom mirror, Theresa inspected her new shape, which didn't look anything like her: breasts that stared back large and round, with thick, pink nipples. And her hips, bending and fleshing out. Her body curved and in and out, textured and soft. She moved, and the glass image moved with her: sexy, sultry, new. Theresa didn't know if she liked these changes—all that womanliness that she still didn't know quite what to do with. But it barely mattered. In those days, her family was so busy moving away from each other. No one was paying much attention; all those tangled secrets were still her own.

Except with Lawrence. "God is watching." He would whisper his edicts suddenly from the corners of dim rooms that Theresa had just entered. He sat ghost-like on couches or kitchen chairs, with the lights turned off, doing nothing. It was startling; most of the time, she hadn't seen him waiting there.

"God is listening," he insisted.

But Theresa was getting tired of him, and scared. She didn't have any more patience for his kind of misery. "*What?*" she had finally screamed. "What the hell do you think he's listening for?"

And he'd just stood there, waiting for the words to figure themselves out: "God is listening." His head had bobbed up and down, loose against his neck. The pupils of his eyes were large and dark—like it was a cartoon character staring at her. Whatever was inside him, she decided, had gotten lost. The humanness, the organization.

"What are you talking about?"

He'd looked stunned. His eyes rounded like a small child who is discovering something terrible about the world. Her mother had been right: dangerous. Theresa had turned around to leave.

"He loves you," he'd whimpered, collapsing down into one of the sticky, vinyl kitchen chairs. "You're a lamb. He loves you." And she'd left him like that, shaking his head in his hands, exhausted by the slow realization that God or fate or whatever it was seemed to favor other people over him.

* * *

But Theresa wasn't so sure about God and his big, inexhaustible love. The next month, her father was diagnosed with colon cancer. None of them had had any reasonable answer to that. Theresa remembered sitting quietly on her hands in the living room, where her mother had stomped in circles: "They say he's gonna die!"

Maxine's only defense against the world was getting noticed. She'd stamped her feet and screamed into the empty air, like something you should do at a distance, out of doors. But she had stood right there in the living room, clenching her fists and steaming. And Theresa had understood that their lives were really broken now. This time, there wasn't any doubt.

After the funeral, she and her mother hadn't had much to say to each other for a while: her mother got crazy and Theresa got quiet. Sleep had been difficult; there'd been nightmares and restless nights. In the medicine cabinet, she'd found her mother's sleeping pills, and she had taken them; she hadn't bothered asking. When Theresa cried, she did it quietly, and downstairs, where her mother couldn't hear her. They got to be like strangers, all of them living there together there in one house.

And she supposed that Lawrence had done what he could. There had been certain kindnesses. Theresa might walk into the kitchen for a glass of milk, and it had already been poured. Dishes got washed. Laundry was folded and put away. He knew their home intimately—its turns and textures and needs. It was like he was seeing inside of their minds.

The bravest he ever got was once when he had found Theresa crying in the little alcove behind the kitchen. He'd come upon her wordlessly, like he always did. But that day, he had done something he'd never done before: he touched her. Gently, wrapping his arms around her and holding on. He'd smelled clean, like the soap from the upstairs shower. Her father's brand. It had been startling and natural all at once: a strange ease of intimacy. Her father was the only other man who had ever held her like this: sweet, comforting, willing himself to be enough to quiet her. She had leaned into him slightly, imagining for a moment that he really could help.

"God is still there," he'd whispered.

Theresa's body had stiffened. That was not what she had wanted to hear; not at all. She'd pushed away then, shouting: "No! No he's not! He's not there. Thinking that only makes you disappointed."

Lawrence's hand had fluttered to his chest and rested there

loosely, where the heart would be. "You're a lamb," he'd said once again. "God will take care of you."

But Theresa was already leaving him; she was already gone.

* * *

When she woke up again, her hands were knotted into fists, the nails dug deep into the pads of her hands as the moonlight from the front window flooded over her. Her breathing was quick—much too quick for sleep. Closing her eyes, she could see it again: that other moon, from months before, dripping its way into her bedroom. It was difficult to see clearly, waking in the night like that. Difficult to make out what was actually happening. Theresa's eyes flipped open again. She put a hand to her chest to steady her breathing. Upstairs, she knew, Nathan and Julia were still sleeping soundly. She tried to be quiet, tried to still the tugging at her chest, reminding herself that it was just a memory. Just a bitter dream.

But it was so convincing: some strained, unsettled tension that Theresa had nearly forgotten. A startling familiarity: a strange man, looming about their house, some kind of imagined threat. There were no lights on; she remembered that, too. Just the moon and their porch light below. Theresa had moved her head, her nightgown shoved up against her neck, like it had gotten thrown wildly in sleep. The blanket, too, was kicked away. She was cold. Her eyes had tried to focus. She couldn't see anything, but there was a sound. A slow movement in the room. Her heart pinched: *I might not be safe.* Her mind, still drugged from the sleeping pills, had moved slowly. So she had thought about her body instead, trying to wrap her mind around each piece of it, to make sure that she was still there: legs, arms, stomach, toes. The sharp, cold air had echoed against all of it. No pain, no strangeness. She was still there.

But she wasn't alone. There had been a form. A darkness in the room that was thicker than the other darkness: a shape, large and sitting quietly over her. Not moving, either. "Daddy?" she whispered, but she'd known that wasn't right; he was gone. That strange shape wasn't her father, and it wasn't God. There was a man in her bedroom in the middle of the night, breathing slowly; her mother had been right. He watched her wordlessly, and Theresa remembered that he wasn't one of them; she remembered that he did inappropriate things. She gasped: *This was something that was happening to her right then; it was not something that she was doing.* And she knew that it was dangerous, just like her mother had warned. But Theresa's heart stayed calm. She had a big, brave heart, even if her mother wouldn't believe it. Theresa knew what was out there, but she didn't let it defeat her. Because that is what her mother had taught her. She put her mind again to all the pieces of herself: heart, lungs, elbows, ears, thighs, fingers, throat. She felt the cool air on her skin, the fabric wadded up against her neck. But she knew that she was all there—safe and untouched. And there, right in that moment, that had been enough.

Part V: God's Language

Lawrence, 1979

In the days and weeks after Gerald's funeral, Lawrence found the girl changed. She moved about the house like a hollowed-out fire. She might stop suddenly in the middle of a room, forgetting herself. She might sink into a chair in the dark and sit like that for hours. Her quiet devastation worried him, so he watched her—more closely, even, than he had watched her before. She was wistful and restless. At first she didn't sleep. Then she slept too much. It was impossible not to notice. Lawrence saw the pills she took—her mother's. He knew how many were left. Each evening, the pattern was the same.

After Gerald left them, there was no one to keep things in order. Even early on during his illness, lying prostrate in the study downstairs, his presence had had the effect of holding the house in a kind of stasis. People behaved well around him; he was that kind of a man. And his remaining family had understood what he wanted: stillness, calm. He didn't have to tell them. But afterwards, there was nothing but grief to give shape to their lives. When they happened upon each other, Mrs. Williams looked at him with eyes that boiled. Lawrence thought she must not know him. She was listless and angry; she barely ate. Sometimes, for no particular reason, she screamed things that didn't make sense. *Useless!* she would cry. *Horrible!* When Lawrence overheard these outbursts, he tried to absorb them; he tried not to let them touch the girl. But he couldn't know how useful his efforts were. Theresa said nothing. She didn't speak to him anymore, or to anyone. He thought of Latin stuck in the throat—of changes that are too strong to recover from.

Because there was nothing else left to do, he prayed. Each night at Theresa's bedside, he watched over her, reciting all the careful words that were left to him: *Salve Regina, Gloria Patri, et Spiritu Sancto.* Sometimes, she cried out in her sleep. Sometimes she turned and twisted around and around and would not settle. He watched her, and he wanted to put his arms to her—to comfort her—but he didn't dare. He could only stay with her, mumbling benedictions under his breath. One hour, and two. Until he was satisfied, and he could bear to leave her again.

At first there was just the watching and the praying. Then, after several weeks of this diligence, Lawrence let a hand trail lightly along the girl's cheek, to give her his blessing. It was nothing sinful. He loved her—the incredible softness of her. It was like touching something holy.

Each time, there was a little bit more. This is how holiness happens, he thought: not in a flash, but quietly. Slowly. It is a practice; it requires attention and concentration. Because of how he loved her, he was coming closer to her. Blessing her, watching her. Slowly, he peeled away the layers of things: one night a bedspread, so that he could see better the shape of her. Another night, he raised the sheet itself, until she was lying there in just her night clothes. That blue nylon gown with the eyelets along the front, short at the hem and handed down from her mother. He did it, he promised himself, just for the focus. This was something that he needed: to see her. So that he could pray more clearly and deeply. So that he could save her.

In the day time, he understood that it was working. Weeks passed, and the mother stayed in her room, still spiteful and broken. But the girl began doing things: writing checks and cooking meals. She rode her bicycle to the store and kept the pantry full. She got things done. And she was steadier, less tired. Lawrence could see it. And he knew that she needed him: she needed someone to hold her up invisibly, so that she could do all those things to keep their lives going.

For a time, Lawrence had been happy then. He had a purpose, and so did the girl. But happiness exaggerates; happiness can be dangerous, too. He still wanted to touch her. He tried not to allow himself, but it became too much. One night, he fingered just the delicate nylon of her nightgown. He leaned in to smell her: sweet and bitter, like vanilla. He pressed his cheek against the flesh of her wrist, her hand. And she didn't move. God, he decided, was giving this to him—to keep him in this world for a little longer.

In so many ways, he felt that he was already going away. It had been happening for a long time. Each day, he felt himself more removed from things, until finally there was nothing left to stop him: one evening, he lifted the nightgown. Just a little, to see more clearly her ankles, her round, white calves. It was just for the focus, he told himself. It had become so difficult to think clearly about anything. And then another night, he pushed it higher, over the knees. It was like a practice: something that kept him steady. Each night, there was another piece. Just a little bit more. *Oh God, oh God.* His breath caught. *She was so lovely.* Her body firm and round and salty smelling. There was something deep and pungent coming out of her. Her stomach, the soft, slight curve of her breasts. Lawrence reached toward her. He needed her. Each night, he wanted a little more, until he was gazing down, finally, at the whole of her. Not touching, but gazing: the soft, full wonder of her. And he understood that it was wrong. Not evil, exactly, but not right, either.

Throughout it all, her breathing remained the same. She did not flinch; she did nothing at all. Lawrence was crying by then. Because, looking at her, he wanted her. He wanted her so much. But he would never hurt her—he would *not.* Sometimes, he kissed her. Just a little bit. The soft flesh of her belly, her wrist, her palm.

But then one night she woke up. Or not quite. Lawrence wasn't sure. Theresa's eyes flew open, but she didn't say anything. They flickered and moved. She stared at him blankly, and some unintelligible language fell out: the language of sleep. Lawrence sat bolted to the little wooden rocker at her bedside; he didn't move. He watched her, and she stared back: the pupils large and round and blank enough for night vision. There was another little gasp: sleep speak. Her head was turned toward him, but she was looking past Lawrence—looking *through* him. They stayed like that for a long moment. *Oh God*, Lawrence's heart galloped through him. What would she say? What would she do? Never, he thought, are we prepared enough to understand each other. But eventually, the girl's lids sank back down, and her body fell back into the sheets. He waited a moment and tucked the clothing and the covers back over her again. Then he left her as he always did: tilting the door carefully open, tilting it carefully shut. He breathed heavily in the hallway and thanked God in a small voice.

"Lawrence!" The woman's voice filled out the corners of a loud whisper. For a moment, he waited: How long had she been standing there, considering? "Lawrence!" She stood there darkly, her arms crossed in front of that tiny body of hers. His mind spun out: How much did she know? How many evenings had she hidden herself in the room across from Theresa's, watching him work?

She pushed out into the dim hallway, where they could see each other.

"Mrs. Williams, it's not what you think."

"I don't care what it is," she hissed. "What you are doing is terrible, Lawrence."

He didn't speak; nothing in his life had told him any different.

"You don't even know how bad your sin is."

Lawrence's heart clambered and whined. He felt the old shock settling through him. In those days, the attacks came on stronger and stronger. Gerald's liquor was almost gone. He stared back at her with whatever energy he had left.

"You don't even know who she is to you." The crystal shape of her voice kept his mind, vacillating farther and farther away.

Who?

"It's evil," she pushed on. "What you're doing. It's shameful."

"Who?!" Lawrence's body bolted, sick to the core.

"Shhh!" she whined. "Do you want to wake her? Do you want her to *know*?"

He shook his head. Once it started shaking, it wouldn't stop: *no no no!*

Mrs. Williams straightened her body in the dark hallway. "She's not yours. She's mine, and I won't let you hurt her. I *won't*."

Lawrence's hand found its way to his chest. He tried to steady himself. "I love her."

"Of course you do," Mrs. Williams spat. "She's the only one in this house worth loving. She's the only thing that's pure. You and me, we're not pure."

He stared at her in amazement. "God can forgive anything."

"But he doesn't," she said. She shook her head, a sadness coming into her eyes that he had never seen before. "No, Lawrence. Everything has its limits."

Standing there in the hallway, Lawrence felt a terrible recollection passing through him; but he didn't know quite what it was. He couldn't understand what she meant.

Mrs. Williams shook her head, her voice lowering. "You don't even know who she is."

Against his chest, his fingers burned, as though he were on fire. All of him: a man on fire. He held himself there, shuddering in the hallway, falling against the wall, the quick trumpet of his lungs opening and shuddering. "Tell me," he whispered. "Tell me what to do."

"You've got to get away from here. You can't keep living with us."

His head nodded against his chest. "But it's all gone," he whispered. "I don't have anyone else."

"We're not yours. Lawrence. It was a mistake. All of this. It's not healthy." Her expression waxed smoother now, into something more like sadness. "You want too much from us. We just don't have it."

What is too much for a man to want? Lawrence didn't belong to the world. Or to this house. Or to anyone.

"Who?" he asked again. "Who is she?"

But Mrs. Williams just shook her head. Her voice was sad. "She's going to find out, you know."

He nodded, terrified. "Please don't tell her," he whispered hoarsely. "I'm sorry. I'm so sorry."

"Oh, Lawrence, don't say that," she breathed. "Just look what's happened to us. I've been sorry my whole life. But it's not enough. It never is."

Maxine, 1946

He wasn't at all what they had expected: a shy kid, soft-spoken and polite. With such a menagerie of people raising him, Maxine had assumed that Lawrence would have turned out differently: a bit more brazen and wild. But he didn't misbehave, and he didn't ask many questions. Gerald laughed about it; he said the boy would make a good soldier. "The first thing you learn in the Army," he had told his wife, "is how to keep your mouth shut."

"Gerald!" she had scolded. "Don't ever say that. The war is over."

"Oh, Maxine," he had joked lightly. "Don't be so sensitive."

So they quarreled. It was normal; a lot of couples were bickering back then. Life after the war wasn't what anyone had expected.

"I'm not," she had insisted. "I'm just being practical. That boy needs more of a sense of himself. He's too serious."

But Gerald liked him. The boy was a challenge—a project that kept his mind occupied. And for several years, until the Williams had children of their own, it had almost seemed like the right decision, bringing him there to live with them. Gerald talked to Lawrence more than he did to anyone else: about the war, about all those terrible things that had happened over there. It felt like a betrayal; he hadn't told Maxine nearly so much.

For months, she had tried to invite conversation, telling Gerald about her own life during the war and all the exciting advancements that she had seen. The country was doing so much better. They laughed loud and worked hard and made all kinds of innovations.

Didn't he think it was wonderful? But her husband didn't respond. Even before the boy had arrived, Gerald was clammy and private.

"You don't tell me hardly anything," Maxine complained.

"I tell you the important parts."

"No you don't," she scolded. "How am I supposed to be with you? I don't hardly know you."

Coming back, the men were so different from what anyone had imagined—even themselves. The pace of things at home was too much for them. When they'd left, the country had been different: slower, more pensive and careful. There hadn't been enough work, but there had been plenty of time to sit back and think about it. Now, the world moved more quickly. And the men were surprised by this life—by what it expected of them. People had jobs. There was work or school programs that you could go to. There were all kinds of things to be done.

But the soldiers weren't ready yet to be men again. They had gotten used to being something less than men. *Caged rats*, Gerald called it. Sitting out there on those islands, trying hard not to go crazy. They had gotten used to smaller spaces; they were accustomed to time dragging on and on. For a while, Maxine had liked listening to her husband talk this way: how the men used to sit on the beach smoking Bull Durham pinched off the black market, or guzzling Pabst, if there was any to be had, and staring out at all that ocean, feeling like they weren't going anywhere. But later on, she got impatient; she was ready for their lives to begin again.

"We've lost three years already," she reminded him. "Almost four."

"We don't need to hurry into things," he answered. "There's no harm waiting a little longer."

But Maxine knew what people said about couples like them; all around them, other people were starting families. "Oh, Gerald, don't you want us to have children, too? Don't you love me anymore?"

"Of course I do, Maxine."

"But you won't hardly talk to me."

"I'm trying, Maxine."

But there were still those nightmares: still so many hidden things that he wouldn't tell her about. Maxine tried to be patient; she tried to be the best wife she could. But the months went on, and they weren't going back to Texas, and Gerald wasn't getting any better, and Maxine wasn't supposed to complain about anything.

"I waited three years for you, Gerald." She looked at him, hard.

"The war just isn't something to talk about, baby."

But Maxine couldn't wait any longer; she just could not stand it. "Don't you think I had other offers?" she snapped. "I had a lot of other offers."

Gerald's eyes flashed; he raised a hand to strike her.

"Oh, why don't you just do it, Gerald!" she belted. "Why don't you just make yourself into the monster that you are?"

"I'd do a damn lot worse than that, Maxine."

"You're wicked," she breathed.

"The world's wicked."

"But you don't have to act like it," she stamped. "Not here in this house!"

When they had finally come back together, it had hurt, how much they had been apart. And it just kept on hurting, even though they were together again. It took a long time to get over feeling like that. Everybody was going through it: the whole country was turned on its head. Women were giving up their jobs so their husbands could go back to work. There were some men who'd come back to find their women gone; and many women who'd never had husbands slowly realized that the GIs weren't really the kind of men that girls dream about.

Gerald pulled his hand away.

"Don't you think I have nightmares, too," she hissed. "You made me give up our *child*, Gerald."

Gerald inhaled sharply, his great barrel chest heaving and falling. "I was trying to protect you, Maxine."

But it still hurt: Maryann and the secret clinic and the whiskey and the stale hotel room next door. She wasn't ready to forgive him—not yet. "I don't need that kind of protection," she spat. "You don't give me credit for enough."

They both got quiet then—and whose fault it is, really, when love dies out of a marriage? Or when it goes dormant for a while? Life goes on so much longer than anyone imagines, Maxine thought. Years and years go by after you've already learned the central things you have to learn.

"Maxine," her husband's voice was much softer now. "We'll have children. Plenty of them. As many as you want."

But she didn't care what he said just then. She was sobbing; she wouldn't be comforted. "You think you're the only one who hurts, don't you, Gerald?" she blurted. "Well, I hurt, too. Every day."

And that's when she had gotten foolish: that's when she told him about the little boy in Selma. The one who would be seven years old by then, staying with a strange spiritual couple who couldn't have any children of their own.

Gerald balked. "You have a *son?*"

"It was rape," she shuddered. She was shivering by then: heaving and crying and gesturing widely. "But I didn't understand it back then, because we were still technically married, Freddy and me."

Gerald's jaw snapped shut. He stared back without speaking. Maxine remained nervous and loose-edged. She went on and on. "But John knew. She understood. She was the one who shot him." So she had told him about that, too: how John had found them there in the bar, struggling around afterward. Freddy was done already—it had happened so quickly—but he was still trying to have more of her. And Maxine was screaming at him to get off. All she could think about was that damn vinegar; she didn't want babies—live ones or dead ones. And John heard them screaming, and she stood there quietly and picked the pistol up off the counter. "Hey, Freddy," she had said, to get him off her friend. He jumped up and whipped around, and she had shot him, just like that. Right in front of him, into the chest: that one little hole, killing him.

"So don't you think I hurt, too, Gerald? Don't you think I got wicked memories, too?"

But Gerald just stared at her quietly and didn't say anything for a long while. It was terrible for her when he went inside himself like that. Maxine couldn't guess what he was thinking: If he would still love her, or if he would leave, or if he would tell someone about what all had happened.

Finally, he said: "You left him, Maxine? Your son?"

"With the nuns, Gerald. We took him down to St. Ann's afterward, where Ringling stayed. We didn't know what else to do."

"Your *son*, Maxine?"

"And then I brought him to California, after you left. I got a place worked out for him to stay. You see? I can take care of things, Gerald. I *can*."

But Gerald Williams was a huge, aching man. He had too much feeling about things, his wife had realized; that was the main problem. All those dying boys over in the Pacific. He hadn't even been the one to lead them out into battle. He wasn't responsible for them, but he *felt* responsible. He couldn't get over the fact that the world just didn't belong to him.

"We've got to go get him, Maxine."

"No, Gerald." She slapped her hands down across the edge of the bed where she sat. "He's better off with them. I promise."

Her husband rose to his feet. "He's your son, Maxine. *Our* son."

Maxine shook her head; it was just too much. And she wanted her husband to understand. But that's the thing she had come to learn about men: they don't deal so well with pain. Especially from the past, when there's nothing left that they can do about it. "It's over."

"Where is he, Maxine?"

"They want to keep him," she insisted. "They love him. They told me."

Years later, after they had so many children of their own, Gerald would apologize for this. Quietly. And just once: "Where *is* he?!" He had taken Maxine's wrists together in one of his hands and held her there, half-suspended in air. If he had wanted to, she knew, he could have snapped her in half. That knowledge left her limp with dread and arousal, both. She was in love with her husband, whether or not she wanted to be. And their love had gotten a little bit violent, though it wouldn't always be that way.

But she wouldn't tell him, so he tossed her down onto the bed and turned instead to the bureau, tearing through her drawers until he found them: a banded bundle of letters from Nancy Wells. Most of them were unopened. He ripped the top off of one and pulled it out, reading: *Lawrence is doing well, you'll be glad to know. He likes books so much, my husband has begun to teach him to read, even though he is only four years old.* Gerald looked up at her quickly, then opened another. *Dear Mrs. Williams,* he read. *Thank you for your kind installment from the last month. With this money, I bought Lawrence two new sweaters for the winter months. One blue and one red. He looks darling in both. Next week, we are going to make holiday shortbread for our Bible group. Lawrence is such a help in the kitchen. I am sure you miss him terribly. Please let us know whenever you would like to come up for a visit.* In the envelope, there was a picture of tiny Lawrence, dressed in the red holiday sweater. Gerald sunk down next to his wife on their bed, staring at it: that smug-faced little boy. Thin and doll-like. He looked a lot like Maxine.

"Mac," he breathed. "How could you?"

But she didn't want to look at those pictures; she didn't want to have anything to do with them. "You want to control so much!" she shrieked. "But you can't, Gerald! You can't! Life's not like that. You think I ever got to decide anything in my life? That I ever controlled anything? And you think that makes me a wicked person? Well, fine. If you want to leave, leave. I can get another job. I've got my brother. I don't need to be married, you know."

"But you are married, Maxine."

She turned on him, enraged. "People get out of marriages all the time."

She knew she shouldn't have said that; of course she shouldn't have. But there were so many things back then that shouldn't have gotten said, and did.

Gerald looked coolly at her for a moment. Then he flipped the envelope over and studied the address.

"Gerald," she begged, "he doesn't belong to me anymore. He doesn't love me. Please. You've got to understand. I can't be his mother. I just can't."

But that's what her husband wanted: to see her compromised

like that. They were both so angry about the way that things had turned out, and it made them angry with each other. It didn't make a lot of sense, but it was so easy to do.

Years later, it was still difficult to understand. "I'm sorry, Maxine," Gerald breathed in her ear, close to sleep. They were middle-aged by then; they had had many good years between them, and many children of their own. And still, he couldn't say exactly why he'd done it. Who had he been trying to punish: himself, or his wife? "I was just scared," he whispered. "You were always so big and brave all the time. I worried I wasn't man enough. I had to find a way of keeping you. To bring you back down to me. To make sure that you would be mine forever."

Theresa, August 1979

Her mother looked nervous. She never looked nervous, Theresa thought, but there it was: the distinct twitching and fretting of fingertips and cotton fabric; a hand straying to her temples. Maxine flickered her gaze briefly out toward the trees in Nathan's front yard, going autumnal. "Your brother told me," her voice sounded thready and unused. "He told me about what you'd remembered." She cleared her throat, turning her attention back to her daughter, sitting across the coffee table in one of Nathan's wingback chairs. Two days earlier, the weather had snapped warm again—sticky and insufferable—in one last blast of summer heat, so that now the fans in Nathan's living room breezed lazily around them: a generative hum, an intermittent rush of air.

"He was in my room, Mom—in my *room*." Theresa felt the thread of hairs at her nape rustle and lift, rustle and lift. She tugged loosely at the rubber band that held the lank mass together.

Maxine shook her head. "It's not what you think."

"Mom," she projected carefully over the clatter and hum of the moving air. "I saw him. He was *there*."

The lines along Maxine's face bowed slightly. She looked disappointed, Theresa thought—as though she regretted coming. Nathan, recognizing the need for this private conference, had taken his daughter to an afternoon movie; so now they were alone, finally, for the first time in two weeks. "You're tired," her mother concluded. "You've gotten worn down."

Theresa pressed her palm against the face of a plastic table fan that sat whirling beside her. "That's not what I'm talking about."

"Baby, I don't want you to think that it was so terrible, what happened."

She knew that what her mother said was true, but the memory of that near danger was still so fresh. "Mom, he was in my room. Anything could have happened." That understanding left her feeling old. Adult. "And you *knew* about it?" she pressed. "You *knew*?"

"It's not what you think." A hand fluttered to her throat. "He didn't hurt you."

"How would you know, Mom?" Theresa's voice pitched upward. "You weren't watching—you hardly came out of your room!"

Her mother's brow creased more deeply: "Theresa, don't yell." The fans blared loudly, gyrating on their plastic axles, trembling and bleating into the hot, filmy air. Maxine raised her own voice above them: "A mother just knows."

Theresa shook her head. "You weren't even paying attention."

"Maybe you don't know as much as you think you do."

Theresa sat back in her chair. Anger was such a funny thing, she thought: The moment you become really aware of it, it has already reached its peak. She looked at her mother: a tiny woman sitting on the sofa across from her. Her hair slightly off center, her hands worrying themselves into the fabric at the hem of her blouse. *She regrets this*, Theresa thought to herself. *She wishes it had never happened.*

"How's school?" Maxine asked briskly, smoothing out the creased fabric along her thigh. "You found a new one? You picked out something nice?" She was dressed in a pair of slacks and a thin blouse. Her belt looped around her a time and a half, a bit too snugly. Outside, the leaves on Nathan's alders had gone golden. *She looks old*, Theresa thought. Two weeks—that was all it had been. They hadn't seen each other in two weeks, but already her mother had aged.

"We don't start for another week," she clarified.

"But you like the place?" her mother looked eager, almost child-like.

Theresa told her she did. A fresh start: that's what she wanted just then. At the public high school a quarter mile from Nathan's house, no one knew her or her family's complicated history.

Maxine's head bobbed. "There's a carnival up here next week." Her voice had gone breathy, distracted. "I thought maybe we could go. For your birthday," she suggested. "I'll bet Julia would like that, too."

"Mom," Theresa started again, trying to keep her voice calm. "He was crazy. He really could have done something terrible."

"Theresa, it's not what you think." Maxine plucked again at the hem of her blouse. She looked up. "You used to like him. You did—for years."

"I shouldn't have," Theresa decided. "I shouldn't have talked to him like that."

Maxine leaned forward. Her blouse caught in the breeze of the fan so that the pale, flat surface of her breast came briefly into view. "He wasn't an animal."

"But he was dangerous. You said so."

Maxine fell back into the sofa, throwing her head toward the breeze behind her so that the hairs at her temple flared upward. "You're not *listening*, Theresa."

"So tell me, Mom. What is it?"

Maxine rolled her head along the back of the sofa. She pinched at her throat. "Lord, it's so hot in here. Don't you have something cold to drink?"

Theresa watched her mother wiggling along the sofa cushions, the skin at her forehead prickled slightly. She was fretting. Theresa got to her feet. "I'll get you some water."

"Oh," Maxine's voice wavered. "Haven't you got something else? Nathan used to buy that nice lemonade. From the place downtown?"

Theresa breathed deeply, moving toward the kitchen. The freezer air was smooth and strong as she fished around for the ice. From the living room, she could hear her mother shifting restlessly in her seat. She was dabbing her brow when Theresa came back with the cold lemon drink. Her expression brightened. "Oh, yes," she breathed. "That's it." Her mouth slurped along the glass. Theresa watched the thin cord of her mother's throat shifting up and back down as she moved busily though the work of sipping the liquid in long, audible gulps. *Two weeks*, she thought again, and her mother had become almost comic. Some kind of edge to her was gone now.

"When did you forgive him?" Theresa asked as the sucking got louder, the bottom of the glass coming clean.

"What?"

"Lawrence. You always hated him."

Her mother shook her head, swallowing one last mouthful of juice. "I never hated him."

"What then? You told him Dad's death was a mistake. You said it should have been him."

Maxine moved her tongue slowly around her mouth, ferreting out all that sweetness, and set the glass down along the taut fabric of the sofa cushion beside her. "I don't want my children to think I'm a villain."

Theresa paused. "That's not what I meant. I didn't say that—nobody ever said that."

Her mother turned toward her. "I don't want you to think badly of *him*, either. You don't understand all of what happened."

And that, of course, was just the point. "Mom, who *was* he?"

Her mother sighed, leaning back into the sofa. "Good lord, baby. It's so hard being a mother. You have no idea."

Theresa flinched. "Mom," she urged, "I'm ready for this now. You've got to tell us—you owe it to us."

Her mother's hand fluttered upward through the air. "And what? The world doesn't owe me a thing or two?"

Theresa met her mother's gaze head-on. The calm to her own voice surprised her: "It's not a competition."

Maxine's head swiveled; she slapped the sweat from her brow. "You don't want to know, Theresa."

"Yes," she felt sure of this, "I want to know what happened."

Her mother's face fell. "Why? Why do you want to drag all of this back out? It's over and done with."

But the answer was so obvious: "Because it affected me—*Lawrence* affected me." She drew a careful breath. Steadied herself. "He might have tried to rape me."

"No he didn't!" Maxine's hand came down against the sofa

cushion and the fluted lemonade glass tipped over, sugary ice cubes sliding out onto the fabric. Theresa leapt upward. "And you just sat there!" she reminded her mother, leaning over to sweep up the spilled ice. "What am I supposed to think?"

"You're being judgmental." Maxine squirmed against her seat. "Just like your father. You want the whole world to make so much goddamned sense. Well, it doesn't, Theresa. People don't always do what they're supposed to do. Life just doesn't work out that way."

Theresa palmed the ice back into the glass and set it down squarely on the coffee table in the middle of the room. "Why didn't you try to stop him?" She was standing over her mother now: her whole nearly sixteen-year-old stature steady and strong and still so impossibly young.

"He wasn't going to hurt you, Theresa."

"Mom—a man in my bedroom?" She swallowed again; the heat pressed in around them. "You don't know *what* he could have done."

And suddenly, her mother burst: "Don't you think I was afraid of him, too?! Don't you think I knew what he was capable of?" Her voice was shrill and screaming. "Drinking all the time like that? And I knew about him—I did. I knew how he shot those lions and stole a car and gave up God and counted sleeping pills that a fifteen-year-old girl stole from her mother. I knew him, Theresa, from when he was a boy. He had a sadness in him so bad it drove me crazy. That kind of thing builds up in a person. So don't you think I was worried? Living alone in the house with a man like that?"

She looked up, breathless. And she had startled Theresa, too, who stood there wide-eyed, afraid: "Like what, Mom? A man like what?"

She sucked the air violently into her lungs. "Broken-hearted," she answered. "From the beginning."

Theresa watched her for a moment, her hand pressed over her chest as she steadied herself back into a gentler rhythm. Theresa sank cautiously back down onto the chair across from her mother. That was it, she thought. However history had gotten stuck, it could just stay there. She didn't care. Her mother was right; she didn't want to know anymore. It was just too goddamned much. "Forget it, Mom," her tone flattened. "It doesn't matter."

But her mother's head kept nodding. A hand was at her chest, the air was still coming constricted through her lungs. "It matters," she said, "because you still don't believe me about the things I did for you." She paused again and drew a good breath. "You were always so literal minded. You wanted to know things absolutely. You wanted proof. And I tried, baby. I tried to give you that. Because I wanted you to love me. God, I wanted that. You have no idea."

"Mom," Theresa's voice lowered. She shook her head. "This is crazy."

Her mother looked up, her forehead creased. "Do you, Theresa? Do you love me?"

"Mom, will you stop it?" She swallowed. Hard. But Maxine would not stop—not until Theresa had told her again that she loved her. That she always had.

"Then you'll believe me?"

"About what?"

"That I watched out for you. That I made sure it wasn't worse."

"Mom," her tone flattened. "Things could have been a lot better."

"But it was all right. They only got so bad, and we survived." Her head bobbed, like someone coming back to something they've known for a long time.

"Not Lawrence," Theresa reminded her. "He didn't survive."

Maxine looked up stiffly. "He wouldn't have, Theresa. He wasn't that kind of person."

Theresa's grip on the armrests loosened. "Why? Because he was quiet? Because he couldn't figure things out on his own?"

"He wasn't wanted—not from the beginning." Her mother's hands had worked themselves into tight fists, sitting tensely at either side of her thighs. "It was your dad and me—we were to blame. We shouldn't have brought him to stay with us."

"Oh Jesus, Mom," Theresa picked up her hand and pressed to the side of her temple. "Forget it—just forget about it. Something terrible happened to him before he ever came here."

"I know," she said, shutting her eyes again. "It was me—it was my fault."

Lawrence, 1979

The boots he chose were Gerald's boots: the same heavy, steel-tipped work boots that the man had worn all his life, buying a new pair each year, when the soles had rubbed down to slick black plains against the leather. They fit Lawrence because he had always been tall, though Gerald's weight had stretched the bindings so that the boots clung loosely at Lawrence's ankles. He tightened them as much as he could. Yanking and pulling and winding. He did it without thinking, like an act of meditation: his hands, folding themselves over the threads of the boots.

He had been watching himself for days now: the movements of his body, the slow process of his mind. Sometimes he stopped in the middle of some activity and could feel his own gaze. He was, quite simply, coming apart: his mind and body barely sharing the same space any longer. But still God did not speak. That much Lawrence had learned by then: God makes no direct comment. Not in lost languages or the quiet channels of a church. And all the noises of our lives—loves sought after, loves that came at us unexpectedly—they are just our own slow music, reflected back to us.

He paused on the landing outside of Mrs. Williams's bathroom door. She had begun sleeping again, finally. And in her sleep, she was delicate. Each evening before bed, she wrapped her hands carefully into a pair of felted gloves, scented lotion rubbed into her palms and between her fingers. Lawrence pulled a pair of these gloves from the drawer beside the sink. They were tiny and kitten-like. He held them briefly to his nose to drink in their feminine scent before slipping them gently into the front pocket of his shirt.

Turning to leave, he caught sight of himself in the mirror. People who have lived a long time together, he knew, begin to take on each other's form. This happens even between married people, who have no blood in common. So he looked in the mirror, and he saw a man as tall as Gerald, though much thinner. The muscles of his arms were tight, smooth knots of flesh. Lawrence was long-limbed and silky. Thirty-nine years old. And he wondered if he had ever really looked at himself in that way before. Like a body: like an object that exists in the world for other people to admire. It was an experience that he knew he could not repeat, the way one sees something as it is just leaving: the burning tail lights of a neighbor's car, or a disintegrating flower. Noticing the scratched out letter on the license plate, the way those inner petals fold together like fingers.

The calm that precedes a suicide is like a gift: the decision has been made. There is no room for reflection now; there is only action left. Lawrence had already gathered the rope. He had practiced with the noose, discovering a way to twist it around his neck—slim and veined as the rope itself—tightly enough to make sure there would be no slippage. And the tree, he had already chosen that, too: those curved branches, thick and ungiving. He had noticed them for years, coming clean each winter: bowed and naked and strong. As a boy, Lawrence had followed Ringling up their twisted path. He knew their shape: which branch was thickest, which ridge would hold a man's heel or palm. So he moved easily now, pulling himself from limb to limb, the noose draped casually along his shoulders, swinging easily between branches until he reached the place: that one thick spot in the foliage where the branch was heaviest. He sunk down into that place where two branches met, straddling one between his legs, leaned slightly against the other as he unwound the rope and tied one end around the tree, draping the other end over his own throat. Then he was climbing downward, shifting himself toward the edge of the branch, and falling. Weightless. He was gone now: disappeared entirely. Watching his own body slip out of the tree and catching against the rope like an anchored ship.

Maxine, 1940

She knew she could go crazy: she knew that's what happened to people like her. So Maxine was scared, going into labor. Who knew what might come out of her? Dead babies and screaming histories? And what's worse, nobody had told her how bad it would be: like a fire. Giving birth was like an honest to god fire. It tore through her and kept on tearing, even after the thing had been taken out of her. She laid there weeping after it was done. And a wail went up like a siren: her son. She turned her face away; she couldn't look. So they took him away and she stayed on there in the delivery room, so frightened and exhausted that her breathing took on a rush. She couldn't control it. She was crying, flopping her arms around so wildly that the nurses had to hold her down. The doctor yelled at her. He told her not to breathe so fast. He administered a sedative and left her there, feeling numb and icy-palmed and still terrified. Because the fire hadn't stopped—not even after the physical pain was over. That fire kept licking her. Licking and licking, eating away her strength like lace.

When she woke up again, there was no clock in the room. No windows, either. Maxine was in one bed out of six. The only light coming in was from the quiet hallway to her left. She could hear the careful movements of a hospital outside, people filling out charts and making careful recommendations in low voices. Two women in the beds across from her were sleeping. Another woman was speaking softly with a man, their fingers moving slowly over each other.

She watched them bleary-eyed. Her body was still more tired than she had ever imagined it could be.

But mercifully, the heat and the stinging were gone. She didn't feel well, but at least that part was over. She also didn't remember coming into this room; she didn't know how long she had been there. Maxine thought of little Ringling, and her stomach lurched. She wanted desperately to know the time.

"Excuse me," she whispered. "'Scuse me, please. What time is it?"

"Nine-thirty, ma'am," the man said.

Maxine nodded, thanking him. So, it had been nearly a full day since she had left Bella Vista, taking a hitched ride down the hill once she figured out that she was going into an early labor. Not even eight months, and the little baby just couldn't wait any longer; he didn't hardly want to be a part of her long enough to get himself made first.

Nine-thirty, Maxine thought. John would have opened the bar by now. She was reliable, and Maxine was grateful for that. Even the pregnancy, John had kept in utter secrecy. So Maxine had carried that baby to seven months without anybody knowing. Her body was so small, and she had taken to wearing John's big men's button-down shirts while they worked at the bar.

But there were things that still troubled John. "What you gonna do with that baby?" she had been asking Maxine for months. Once the birth started getting closer, she said it more and more. John was sad—though Maxine didn't know what made her feel worse: shooting Freddy or not doing it fast enough. Because there she was now all big and bloated and not much use to John or to herself. "What you gonna do with that baby?" Maxine told her she didn't know. Things were rough, and most folks didn't want to raise a baby that wasn't their own. People knew that abandoned babies came from bad mothers: women who got themselves into trouble. They figured it must get into the child, too: all that badness. Maxine remembered stories from girls on the circus. People that Della had known: how they had stopped working the show for a few months and came back alone. She had heard other stories of those babies dying—or worse. They would get left with baby farmeries, where people looked for homes for them, but often didn't find any.

But Maxine's friend Doris out at Bella Vista had said she shouldn't try to have an abortion, either. She'd had one, and it had turned out badly. Now she couldn't have children at all. So she told Maxine that she'd better just go ahead with it.

"I don't care," Maxine swore. "I don't want children—I don't want any more men in my life. Not ever."

"Oh, Mac, you say that, but it won't stick," Doris had told her. "This here's just a real bad experience. But you'll have better ones, I swear."

Doris was just glad that they were both alive. The day afternoon of the shooting, she had hurried up to Bella Vista, demanding to see every square inch of the girls. A few weeks later, when they found out that Maxine was pregnant, John just about went dumb. Her eyes boggled, and she got the shakes. "It's all right," Maxine had told her. "It happens to women all the time." John never had many words, but right then she didn't have any at all. Her eyes became glassy and strained, and Maxine thought she was going to retch. So she knew she couldn't tell Doris, or anybody else, what had really happened. She would just stick to the story that she and John had made up for the authorities. Nobody had paid much attention to it, anyway. They saw Maxine all bruised up, and nobody said a word. "Don't you worry, John," she'd said. "You don't need to worry, now. There's nothing else left that can hurt us."

She was wrong, though, because there were complications afterwards. The baby was fine, but Maxine was ill. The doctor couldn't say what it was, so she decided herself that it was a broken heart—the kind new mothers get. Maxine knew a little something about that, from seeing her mother after Ringling was born: that big terrible sense of how much your life isn't so important anymore. All that newness can just astound you.

* * *

When they finally brought the boy into the room so Maxine could see him, she was filled with a deep, weighty dread. Seeing him meant knowing him, and knowing him meant that he belonged to her.

She struggled to sit up. The bed sheets were damp and twisted; Maxine was sweating. Ever since the labor, she hadn't stopped. She didn't hardly know her own body anymore.

Once she was upright, Claire, the nurse, laid the baby down into her arms. Maxine sat there for a moment considering the wrapped infant, holding him flat and far away from her, like a burning log. Of course she knew how to hold a baby; she had raised Ringling almost from infancy. But she couldn't manage closeness with this baby. The nurse nudged him gently toward her; the baby sniffed.

"This is your first?" The nurse's mouth was little and pink. It was difficult to guess her age. She was a large woman with a fat face and tiny features, so she looked sweet and mild and unspecific. She reached down to lift the baby. "Like this," she said, rocking him. "Make a cradle with your arms." The layers of her chin wobbled slightly with the rhythm of it. Her face curled into a sweet expression, and she lowered the bundle to demonstrate. "Look," she said. "It's your son."

Maxine looked, but the baby's eyes were closed. His face was red and round. He didn't look like anybody, really. Except maybe Freddy, when he was mad and about ready to explode. Maxine glanced back at the nurse. How could she tell her that this little baby scared her? Claire was rocking him fondly, laying a finger along the side of his face, and his little eyes fluttered open. They were a strong, watery blue, like Maxine's father's. Beautiful.

The nurse pressed the baby back into her arms. "Hold him close," she instructed. "Against your bosom." Maxine's heart began to pound. She was sure that the baby could feel her pulse winding wildly through her. He whimpered slightly and moaned, working his mouth into a wail. She kept holding him, and he continued wailing. She looked again up at the nurse, who was motioning her to jostle him softly, bounce him like womb movements. Kiss him. Whisper his name. A thousand little intimacies that mothers use to calm their children. Maxine glanced at her fingers: no ring. And she wondered over this woman's supreme understanding of things as Lawrence continued to wail. "Shhh," she whispered, rocking him. But it was useless, and Maxine knew it. Her own body, too, was shaking, convulsing with hiccups that startled the child. She couldn't stop sobbing, or that horrible weight in her limbs that felt like a disease.

"I can't," she cried. "I can't do it."

The nurse watched her for a moment, her eyebrows raised up like a cricket's hind legs, concerned. Then she took the baby and told Maxine not to worry. "You're tired now. We'll try again later."

She clucked fondly at the infant and jostled him against her big, sturdy breasts until he stopped crying. Maxine saw the way they comforted each other, and she felt envious of something that she couldn't even name. Then Claire turned to leave. "It will get better," she promised.

Maxine nodded, even though she knew that nothing would change. That baby didn't want her. They didn't belong to each other, Maxine knew. And they never would.

"Are there more women like me?" she asked when the nurse came back. The baby was gone, and Claire was worrying her way around the bed, pulling up the corners of the bed sheets and shifting Maxine toward the edge of the bed so that she could take her down the hall for a bath. "Sure dear," she said, pressing Maxine up into a sitting position. "The first one's always an adjustment."

But that's not what Maxine had meant. She was talking about women who didn't want their babies. Women like her who were all full of shame and didn't know how to talk about it.

"Your little boy is a sweet baby. Very good natured. You'll find your way with him."

Then she slid her hands underneath Maxine and picked her up in those big, heavy arms of hers. Plucked her out of the bed like she was nothing but a child herself. "But what if I don't?"

"Shhh," Claire whispered. "You don't worry about that now. You need to rest."

She held her patient to her, and Maxine could feel the thickness of her pulse. She could smell the loam of her. Claire was a big woman. Big-boned and big-breasted. And unembarrassed. She was a nurse; bodies were her business. And she held Maxine's easily, gentle but confident. Her hands and arms were warm. The odor coming off of her mixed with the smell of a nurse's day: baby powder and antiseptic and sweat. As she carried Maxine from the bed and moved them toward the little wheeled chair, she let Maxine stay there for just a moment: suspended, feeling that clean, solid heft beneath her. The woman's arms. Her good, heavy strength. And underneath that, only air.

Theresa, August 1979

"Can you forgive her?"

The earth lurched upward, and they were tossed back into the air, shifting in the cradled metal of the Ferris wheel. It moved forward and stopped, to load another couple below.

"What is there to forgive?" Theresa pressed her toes against the steel-lined edge of the cart. "She didn't want him to be born, and she didn't want him to die."

Nathan turned his big, bullish head. "But you're angry about it."

"I never said I was angry."

"Theresa," his expression softened. "It's all right."

Then they were moving again. The basket tilted backward under their weight. Ahead of them in the next gondola, Julia shivered beside her grandmother, quietly delighted. Even at four years old, Julia was gorgeous: olive skin and almond eyes and luxuriant black hair. Maxine's gaze flickered over those restless fingertips, that smooth crown of hair; she gave the girl a squeeze.

"You really didn't know, either?"

Nathan shook his head.

"How did she do that?" Theresa watched her mother and Julia rising upward in front of them. "How did she manage to keep a secret like that from all of us?"

Nathan tipped his head backward, his eyes slipping shut for a moment in the sunlight. "She did a lot of things that should have been impossible."

Above them, Julia's body wiggled excitedly; this was her first experience at a carnival. She shifted around in her seat to flash them a bright-eyed expression. "Look!" she cried, pointing out the view.

Nathan glanced up and nodded as his daughter slipped back around, fingers settled on the paint-chipped safety bar. She leaned affectionately toward her grandmother: immune to history, unaware of whatever crimes or betrayals Maxine might have been responsible for.

"Do you really think she blames herself?" Theresa's voice lowered.

"Who knows?" Nathan shook his head. "It matters more what she feels about you—about us. That's what's left now." Nathan pressed a hand thoughtfully across his chin and rubbed the skin, a little too rough. For a moment, the cranking Ferris wheel shifted them into the topmost position. To the south, they could see Sacramento unfolding in its web of concrete and glass and snaking, southbound highways, the river running along its edges, and the neat, commercial district pushing up from the center, just large enough to be called a city. Finally, there was Old Sac, down by the river, its wooden sidewalks littered with tourists. Downtown, the buildings sparkled, clean and confident.

"She misses you," he told her. "She wants you to come back."

Theresa nodded: "I know." Then she pressed her head onto his shoulder and shut her eyes. Underneath them, the Ferris wheel continued to wind around its axis, shifting cyclically through the skies of Sacramento. In another two years, she knew, she might be anywhere: San Francisco, San Diego, Phoenix. Any place she wanted to go. The house had sold well. There was money, Nathan had assured her, to send her to college. To support whatever it is that she decided to do.

Afterwards, Julia stepped carefully out of her basket, lifting first one foot and then the other. She handled her body like a miniature athlete: gracious, moving pieces of herself slowly and patiently, waiting for the rest to catch up. Theresa watched from above: those tiny feet planted carefully, that narrow torso traveling upward. Julia stood for a moment in that self-same spot before following the carnival worker's gestures to move forward so that he could bring the next basket down with a squeaking halt. Julia gazed back at her father and aunt—calm, flushed—as they approached. Her fingers wound innocently into her grandmother's. Maxine glanced downward, her own expression waxing childlike, exposing her sudden delight: *Julia, beautiful Julia.* "Wasn't that fabulous?" she breathed, and the little girl beamed upward, nodding sharply.

They moved away from the crowd exiting the Ferris wheel, and Nathan leaned forward to tidy the bow in Julia's hair, the slick yellow fibers crossing efficiently beneath his fingers. The gesture surprised Theresa. "So, Julia," he asked, bending down and slapping his palms brightly against his thighs. "What next?"

Already, they had eaten caramel apples and cotton candy and corndogs on sticks. They had been to funny houses full of mirrors that had stretched them into long, gaping shapes or laughable short ones. At the 4H barn, Maxine had led them into a stall to watch a pig give birth. *Julia, look!* she'd lifted the child, her eyes widening as she watched the crowning sow. But Julia had not cried; she had not looked away. Maxine's enthusiasm had carried her with those girlhood stories about their old Texas ranch or the magical characters on her father's show: Dinky, the fat lady, balancing a parasol behind her as she followed a tightrope wire carefully over two feet of air, the man who spoke in tongues, and Tattoo man, who had colored the gaps on his skin with indelible ink once he'd started drinking too much and ran out of money for more tattoos. This was their legacy: the pulsing history that carried them all.

"Let's go win something!" Maxine's hands rubbed together ferociously, and the little girl beamed. "Do you want to go to the midway, Julia?" The girl clapped, delighted, and Maxine looked up to Nathan and Theresa for approval. Her eyes stuck and unstuck briefly across her daughter's gaze before she wrapped Julia's fingers together and drew them all forward through the crowds. Theresa followed them through the midway with its barrage of colors and smells: the odor of sweat and buttered popcorn and trampled grass and dust; the carnies with their uniforms stuffed into their pants, grease along the edges of their fingers; and the huge stuffed bears and lions and cartoon characters strung by the neck and lined up along a wire so they tilted downward, grinning maniacally, row upon row upon row. As her mother chattered on to Julia, the girl's eyes glowing in the unbelievable whir of Maxine's history, Theresa caught sight briefly of a man's head: curling black hair, narrow frame. *Tomás.* She turned, but of course it wasn't him. It couldn't be. Tomás was in Missouri, beginning his new life: taking care of his mother, finding work. Her stomach soured in a quick moment of grief, and then it was gone.

When they finally stopped at a booth, the space was narrow—no more than a dozen feet wide—and covered at the edges with a faded emerald-covered flocked curtain. The sides of the two facing walls were covered with stiff toy animals: the kind stuffed with cardboard so they are never much good to anyone once they get them home. Dogs with brightly-colored ears and spots. Tigers with goofy, bared teeth. A laughing turtle with an enormous shell. They climbed in weight and complexity as they crawled up the wall: the more times you won, the larger the prize. In the middle, balloons were tacked against the back wall, poorly sorted and many of them already popped, their rubbery remains still push-pinned to the wall. Julia clutched the wood at the edge of the booth, plastic-feathered darts in her hands, carefully considering. She lifted one, holding it delicately, and lofted it into the air, where it bounced harmlessly off the gluey back wall amidst the balloons. The attendant didn't say anything. He stared lazily beyond the walls of the game. His dress was carnival issue, a button-down shirt with thin pink and white stripes along the half-length sleeves and collar and front seam. The name "Ace" was stitched above the pocket. The uniform was dirty. Clearly, Ace didn't care much for appearances: hair stringy, nails yellowed from tobacco, two or three days of shadowy stubble. Julia threw another dart. And another. Nothing took. Ace's eyes flickered over her concentrated face. He leaned forward, his pants hung low at the hips, and picked up the darts, handing them back to her for another dollar: "Everybody's a winner."

A few paces to one side, Theresa stood quietly watching her mother and niece pay out their dollars and work over the angles of the dart toss. Nathan moved closer to her, throwing an arm around her again and giving her a quick squeeze. She smiled up at him, and they stood quietly for another moment, watching the darts bounce in and around the sticky, insistent balloons. Ace grunted again: *Everybody. A winner.*

"She likes Julia."

Nathan pressed his weight onto a hip. "They haven't had much time together before."

"I guess it's easier with her."

Nathan tipped his head, watching her curiously. "Theresa, she cares—don't you think she cares for you?"

Theresa shoved her fists into her pockets. "She's afraid of me."

"She doesn't want to lose you; there's a difference."

They watched Julia and Maxine hovering together, tossing darts haphazardly against the sticky backdrop. At her side, Maxine's hands flexed, the tips of her fingers coming together, rubbing slightly at the memory of some lost desire.

Theresa shook her head, tired; her fingers relaxed in the pockets of her jeans. "How do you do it, Nate? How do you forgive something like that?"

Nathan considered. He cleared his throat and padded the trodden grass with a shoe. "Before Julia was born, I knew that Michelle and I weren't going to last. I knew that. It was terrible; I just didn't know how long it would take. But when I saw her, when I saw Julia, I didn't care. I learned to forgive a lot."

"Because it's not easy, being a parent?"

"Because life's just too goddamned precious." His expression folded: the quiet passion of a man who is not accustomed to bringing his emotions to the surface. And Theresa understood that the parameters of pain in her brother's life were sustained—they were buoyed—by perimeters of joy. "Mom tried," he assured her. "Probably more than we knew." Then he was moving away from her, and Theresa knew that her brother was finished worrying about the past. "Julia," he called, sidling up beside his daughter. "Here," he said, lifting a plastic dart to show her how it was done. "You've got to go for the full ones—they're easier to pop."

When Julia finally won, the prize was one of those small, stuffed dogs: five inches tall and stiff as wood. Its purple ears matched the small felt ring around one eye and a large spot on its back. Its expression was sad but comforting, like a basset hound. "Here," she handed the pup to her grandmother, beaming; and Maxine took it—a bit surprised, but flattered. Then she hugged her aunt and grandmother once each—quick and exuberant—and dashed off behind her father. They watched her go: already so lovely, already so much to be missed.

"Why didn't you tell us?" Theresa wanted to know.

Maxine looked up startled, the pup dangling from her fingers by its bright, felted ears. She stood there quietly, suddenly so uncertain of herself, like a little girl who has just been caught at something.

"He was our brother." The words felt strange in her mouth. "Why didn't you tell us sooner?"

Her mother turned, her eyes following Julia, Nathan's hand padded along the girl's back. "It hurt," she said. "When he died—when he killed himself. In case you want to know, it did hurt me."

Theresa's eyes flitted across Julia's prize. "But you could have told us about it earlier. Maybe things would have turned out differently."

"People have their limits, Theresa." Her mother's shoulders seized slightly. "I couldn't risk it," she looked at her daughter meaningfully. "What that might have done to our family when you were all still so young."

Theresa watched the sky unfold in quick-moving clouds. The clink and banter of carnival games clamored around them. "We could have handled it, Mom."

"Oh Theresa," she lifted her face toward the sky, radiant and half-horrified. The little felted dog swung nervously from her fingers. "What must you think of me?"

"He was our brother."

Maxine nodded. She shut her eyes briefly and opened them again, tugging the little dog to her chest and holding it tight. "It's good," she said. "It's good that you loved him."

Theresa breathed. This was as close, she understood, as her mother would come to putting the truth out into the open: *Mothers are not perfect. They do not love perfectly. Even nature sometimes beats confused against itself.*

"I still wish you'd told us, Mom. I wish we'd known."

"You're right," her breath came out heavy, like a sigh. "But I was scared for you. I didn't know how strong you'd turn out to be."

Nathan and Julia pressed slowly through the midway ahead of them. They should follow, Theresa knew; they should catch up. But she stood watching her mother for another moment. It really was too much. They should have been having that conversation ten, twenty years into the future, when they could, as adults, compare notes on motherhood and chuckle together over all those near failures—all those heartaches. But her mother would never be predictable or appropriate. She was fierce; she was imperfect. Selfish, even—perhaps that most of all. Even so, there was heart to her: a ferocious will to love. "I wish you would come back to live with me," the stuffed animal swung again at her side, "in Fairfield, or Sacramento—anywhere you want."

Theresa considered carefully. "That's what you want?"

"Oh, Theresa," her mother's eyes widened; the little dog froze between her fingers. "Oh *yes.*"

"Here in Sacramento?"

She nodded. "We'll get a house—a smaller one—anywhere you want. There's so little time left," she swallowed. "Before you'll be grown."

Theresa stood there for a moment, the liquid lining of her arms running down into her fingertips. She was wanted; she mattered. Of course she knew this—but how different, finally, to hear those things out loud.

"I'll think about it," she promised. "I will."

"Oh, Theresa," her mother's eyes widened hopeful—almost giddy. "Thank you."

They stood awkwardly for another moment, not quite sure how to accept the careful pool of acceptance that was filling the spaces between them, seeping out of them, after all that had happened, like relief. Golden and tired and warm. Then her mother shifted the moment again, blurting suddenly: "You were the hardest one for me to mother." She hugged the dog more closely, an expression of genuine surprise crossing her face. "You taught me the most."

Theresa stared. Swallowed. Her eyes flickered into the distance, catching the shapes of Nathan and Julia ahead, their fingers tied up together in the sweetness of whatever imperfect connection sustained them. Then she felt a hand come across her shoulder: her mother's thick-strong fingers rising to rub softly along the spaces at her back and neck. "Thank you," she said again. The hand dropped from her shoulder, and Theresa accepted it gently into her own as she turned back toward the place where Nathan and Julia were standing, and finally they began to make their way back toward the emptying parking lot—past the work, the stench, the utter madness of a carnival.